A Maryland Equestrian Novel

Horse Gods

The Dressage Rider's Betrayal

L. R. TROVILLION

Oct 2021

First Edition

Hippolyta Books

HIPPOLYTA BOOKS

Printed in the United States of America

ISBN: 9780990899563

Cover: Bublish, Inc.
Interior Formatting: Champagne Book Design
Editors: The Write Helper, Amy Harke-Moore;
Traci Finlay, Editor

You may be deceived if you trust too much, but you will live in torment unless you trust enough.

—Frank Crane

Chapter One

WE'RE GOING TO PRISON. I EXPECT IT TO LOOK AWFUL, BUT when we turn the corner and the brick building comes into view, a little furry thing with scrabbling claws starts doing laps inside my stomach. Maybe the breakfast burrito I scarfed down a few hours ago was not a good choice.

Brenda, the social worker assigned to my case, has been talking to me all morning about good choices in life. She drives and steals glances at me. I think she's checking to see if I'm listening. I'm not.

We turn in a long driveway. My God. The fence is about a hundred feet tall with rolls of razor wire coiled all through and over it. It looks like it could keep an army of stampeding elephants in there. On second thought, considering who's inside, that's not a bad thing.

Brenda pulls in the parking lot not far from a squat building in front with the name Maryland Correctional Facility for Women on a big sign over the doorway like it's some kind of college or something. She undoes her seatbelt and reaches into the backseat. I get out. I'm tired of smelling the strawberry air freshener fighting with the lingering scent of menthol cigarettes. Rather smell the cigs.

It's warm for late October. The sun is just coming over the guard tower, but for some reason my hands are really cold. Brenda calls out something like "Wait for me," from the other side of the car. Sure, like I'd go in there alone.

"Regina." She walks around to my side of the car, breathless from digging that huge tote bag out from the backseat. "I want you to know that you do not have to go in. If you decide not to see her, I can meet with her alone." She squeezes my arm above the elbow and smiles. I hate that.

"Nah, I'm okay," I tell her and smile back. She's only doing her social worker job. Give her a break, I figure. I step toward the entrance.

Inside, a blast of refrigerated air hits my face. A guard right by the door stops us. The black butt end of a pistol is sticking out of its holster. I've never seen a gun, a real one, up close before. Brenda fishes around in that Mary Poppins bag of hers and pulls out her ID and some letter. The guard waves her over to the metal detectors.

"Put your items on the belt," he says in a way that tells me he's repeated that line a million times this week already. "All items on the belt, empty your pockets of any change and loose items, and step through, please."

I pull my phone out of a back pocket and drop it in the plastic tray. Brenda's purse vomits its contents all over the bottom of its bin. On the other side of the metal detector, a lady in the same guard uniform waves us over to the desk. Her face sags like a bulldog. No one here smiles, that's for sure.

We get visitor badges. Good, because I sure wouldn't want them mistaking me for someone who needs to stay here. Then another lady guard walks us to the back door. She holds it open for us to walk through first and announces, "This way to the visitation block," like she's giving a tour. I was really hoping something would be wrong—improper ID or not a visitors' day after all—and they'd turn us back and I could go home. Instead, this lady is taking us to the big building. The real prison.

Where she is.

I look up at the sun like maybe I'll never see it again.

We walk through another set of doors and inside. Man, there are a lot of doors in this place. The visitor area is pretty much like I imagined—cinderblocks painted in baby poo green and furniture that makes the stuff at school look chic and modern. More guards. The lady guard keys in some numbers, and a heavy door opens with just a *click* and a *whoosh*. No clanging bars or jangling locks. The door closes with a whisper behind us, and we're led down a long corridor.

"In here." She holds the door. "Have a seat. The matron will bring the prisoner."

The prisoner. That's what she's called now. Funny, most of my life I felt like her prisoner.

The room has some inspirational posters with glowing sunrises and smiling family members holding hands in a meadow or some stupid crap. There's a water cooler against the far wall behind two rows of chairs. I think they're bolted to the ground. No one else is here. The weird thing is there is another room, much smaller, on the other side of a Plexiglas wall. Inside the little room there's a table with a few chairs. A door in the back opens and she walks into the little room.

I haven't seen her for more than a year now. Under the fluorescent lights she looks even more fake-tan orange than before. Maybe it's the jumpsuit that's just about the color of mud. There's an inch of dark roots where her hair has grown out. Must not be able to get a hairdresser appointment in prison as often as she's used to. She turns to a uniformed woman behind her, waves her hand like a queen, and the other woman sits in a chair in the far corner. I pull my eyes away to see our escort push some button and open a door to a portal that connects the waiting area with the fishbowl room. She leads us in and announces, "Your visitors are here."

She turns her orangey face to me. Smiles. But only for a second before she pulls her lips down into a clowny frown. "Regina, your hair!"

My hand floats up to run fingers through my shorn-off curls, but I stop it in mid-air.

"I don't like short hair on girls." She has no problem expressing her opinion. "It makes you look like a thug or…"

She struggles to find more insults to hurl at me. Maybe *prisoner*, I think, but keep the thought to myself.

"Hi, Angela," are the only words I allow past my lips. I know that will piss her off even more.

"Angela! What happened to Mom?"

She comes at me, arms spread wide, but the lady guard steps between us. "I'm sorry. No physical contact."

"That's absurd. She's my daughter." Angela tries to step around, but Lady Guard is a linebacker. "We haven't seen each other for a year."

Angela uses her imperious queen voice around here, too, but Lady Guard doesn't back down. Instead, she pulls out a chair from the table. Even though I think she meant it for me, Angela takes the seat and pulls out the one beside her for me. I choose the one across the table. Brenda stands by the door.

"I'm so glad to see you, dear." She places her hands on the table and leans in. Her nails are short, unpainted. I don't think I've ever seen them that way. "I want to hear all about how my sister is treating you down at that dust bowl she calls a horse farm. I've always hated Texas."

Angela takes a deep breath, ready to continue. No doubt she has no interest in hearing about how I'm doing, but that's when Brenda steps over to us, clutching a folder to her chest.

"Who are you?" Angela asks.

"Nice to meet you, Ms. Hamilton. I'm Regina's caseworker, Brenda Schwartz." Brenda holds out a chubby hand.

Angela shakes with only the tips of her fingers, turns her chair away from Brenda, and crosses her arms and legs. "My daughter is not a case, Miss Schwartz."

"Of course not!" Brenda blushes to the roots of her hair. Her face is already shiny. Brenda dumps the folder on the table and takes a seat next to me. I smell that fake strawberry smell from her car oozing off her clothes now. "I've been appointed by the State of Maryland to ease the transition, you know, answer any questions and go over the rules governing the resumption of custody."

I don't usually listen to Brenda much, but now I've heard a word that makes that furry rodent in my gut start scurrying around again. Did she say custody? "What's going on?" My voice is loud in the little fishbowl. "You said we were visiting."

"Now you've ruined my surprise, Miss Schwartz." A little vein in Angela's neck throbs. I know that sign. She turns to me. "Regina, I've got good news."

The back of the chair is pressing on my spine as I lean as far away as possible. Angela's eyes bore into mine until I drop them to the folder on the table between us. Brenda must have known about this.

"I'm getting out in ninety days. Isn't that great? The State has come to its senses finally, it seems. And you'll be back with me. You won't have to live with Sophia in Texas anymore. Isn't that wonderful?"

She keeps asking me if this or that is wonderful and all I want to do is throw this damn table through the Plexiglas window and escape. Why didn't anyone tell me? Aunt Sophia flew up with me and never said anything. I thought we were visiting for the long weekend.

"Why?" My voice cracks.

"Why?" A small laugh bursts from Angela. "Because they realized they made a mistake. The sentencing was ridiculous for"—she flaps her hand in the air as if waving away a stink—"insurance fraud. Really."

Angela assumed I was asking a different question, a question about her, of course. What she didn't say about the insurance fraud was the fact that it involved killing several show horses. Brenda says nothing. She's shuffling papers in that stupid folder.

"Five minutes," Lady Guard says.

"Tell me, Miss Caseworker, have you arranged it so my daughter will be ready to come home with me when I'm released?" Angela slaps the table. "And Regina"—my eyes snap up to meet hers. "Call me Mom, not Angela. What kind of a way is that for a daughter to talk?" She looks around the room for agreement. The matron nods.

Brenda pushes papers at Angela with brightly colored sticky arrows printed with *Sign here!* all over them. Based on the legal talk, she ..knows her job all right. She probably imagines she's helping to reunite a family or some other social worker crap.

We stand. Lady Guard goes to the door, and that's when Angela takes two steps over and wraps her arms around me like a boa constrictor. She whispers, "And we will pick up where we left off. You understand?"

Chapter Two

I GET IN THE CAR AND SLAM THE DOOR. BRENDA TAKES HER TIME TOSSING that suitcase bag of hers in the back before she gets in. I glare at it, slouched against the backseat. It's full of signed papers that say I'm going to be turned over to Angela when she gets out. In three months. Like I'm her property or something. Like I'm a horse she just bought. God help me. If I were just a year and a few months older, I'd be legal. If they would just keep her in prison another year and half…

Brenda pushes the ignition button, cranks the air up a notch, and slings an arm over the back of my seat to look behind her before backing out.

That's when I turn on her. Her face is close to mine. I can see where makeup has slid into the lines around her mouth. "Did you know about this?"

She steps on the brake and slides the gear into park.

"You must have known. Why didn't you warn me?"

A gust of air escapes her lips, and she sits bent over like a deflated balloon.

There's a little twinge in the bottom of my gut, and it's telling me not to be so mean—she has my life in her hands, so to speak. I ignore it. "You're not even going to explain to me what happened in there? You didn't tell me she was getting out. You didn't even ask me if I wanted to go live with her, which I don't. Aren't you supposed to ask what I want?" The thump of blood pounds in my ears.

"Yes." She squirms in her seat. Her thighs make a squeegee noise against the fake leather. "I thought it was better to discuss it with you first." She fingers her Ravens key fob. "But your mother asked that I keep it a surprise, so I—"

"My mother is a criminal." The words blurt out. "She doesn't get to ask anything. And I'm not going to live with her." Words get choked off as a band around my throat tightens. I'm not going to cry, not in front of this zombie social worker who just wants to get my case off her desk. I look out the passenger window.

"I thought you'd want to be back with your mother."

"You thought wrong." My breath steams the glass.

"Regina." I hear her sigh and it pisses me off more. She's probably going through her mental checklist entitled *dealing with a troubled teen*. Well, I'm not going to help her.

"I'm here to help you."

A burst of laughter explodes out of my chest, and I turn to tell her what I think of that idea… Her face is serious, earnest. My mouth clamps shut.

She keeps talking. "I was appointed to smooth the transition when your mother is released. It was facilitated through the State of Maryland. I'm not sure you realize it, but she never lost custody, not really. Your aunt is just standing in during your mother's, well, being unable to care for you." She puts a hand on my arm. It's moist and warm. "I'm here to facilitate your visits prior to her release and to get you settled in school. Basically, to make sure everything goes okay. That's my job."

"Screw your job." The hand is snatched away. "And it won't be okay." I could say why, I could explain, I could do something to make her feel better, but I don't. What I really want to do is open the door and start running. Run, and get as far away from the place where Angela sits waiting and planning.

Brenda is better at this sitting without talking thing than I am. I ask, "And what if I don't?"

Her fish lips open, but she says nothing. She keeps giving me the earnest look.

"What if I refuse? What if I don't go live with her? What if I get a job and, I don't know, live somewhere?" It's clear even to my ears this plan is half-baked.

Then she surprises me. Her face doesn't melt into an indulgent *isn't that a silly idea* sort of expression. She doesn't even ask the usual adult question: What about school? Instead, she scribbles a number on the back of her business card and hands it to me.

"It's called being an emancipated minor. We can talk about that option, Regina, if you want to."

A little anger and frustration leak out of me through a tiny crack. A crack of hope.

"But there are a lot of other issues to discuss before pursuing that decision."

"Like what? I'll do whatever, I don't care." The car is getting cold with the engine off, but that fake strawberry scent is as strong as ever.

"School, supporting yourself… According to the courts, your mother made a mistake and now she's ready to start over. A petition for emancipation would require you to make an appeal to the courts claiming Mrs. Hamilton is an unfit mother. It requires proof."

The little gap letting the light of hope in gets sealed up. I'd have to go to court against Angela? A last sigh deflates my chest and I slump in the seat.

"Is it worth going through that? Think about it. Is living with your mother that bad?"

No one knows. Mostly because I never told anyone. I stretch the seatbelt away from where it's rubbing against my neck. "It's that bad." I turn to Brenda. "How long have you known my mother?" I know the answer. Probably talked to her twice at most. With an armed guard present. I never had the benefit of an armed guard.

"Not long." She nods toward the backseat. "And there's nothing in the files, no red flags on her other than the conviction to indicate—"

"Take me home. Okay?" I spin around to face front. Brenda doesn't answer but starts the car.

Home. Funny name for where me and Aunt Sophia are living. To save money, she agreed we could stay in the farm manager's trailer on Wade's farm. Wade—Angela's boyfriend. Not a nice guy. Now it looks like we'll be staying a lot longer than just the weekend. When Aunt Sophia came with me back to Maryland, I figured it was so she could visit her sister, and, well, I suspected she was going to ask for more money for taking care of me. Now I know it was to dump me here. Wonder how long she knew about Angela's release, too.

"Aunt Sophia doesn't want me, either," I tell the cold air in the car.

"Sophia yields legal guardianship when your mother is released. It's not a matter of wanting or not." Brenda puts the car in reverse.

"Sure." I cross my arms over my chest and resume staring out the window.

"I want to help you, if you'll let me." Brenda pulls out of the parking lot and I watch the guard tower and concertina wire disappear in the side view mirror.

No one can help me.

Chapter Three

AUNT SOPHIA DROPS ME OFF AT CORY'S BARN BEFORE HER JOB interview. Says she hopes to earn a little extra while she's stuck in Maryland babysitting me until Angela's release date. She didn't call it *stuck*, but I knew what she meant. For me, the only good thing about being back is seeing my best friend again.

"Oh, my God, I haven't seen you in forever!" Cory lopes down the barn aisle and tackles me in a hug. Horses spin in their stalls. "I've missed you so much."

The smell of horse sweat mixed with liniment drifts off her coat when I wrap my arms around her and squeeze back. We start to tip. She lets go, just in time before we both crash to the floor.

"And your hair!" Cory rubs the flat of her hand over the top of my shorn head, like she's petting a dog. "So, how long have you been back?"

"Got here yesterday."

"What's with your hair?" Her face scrunches. "I like it," she lies.

"Right." I run my hand over the spiky short curls.

Cory cocks her head. It's a familiar habit. Last year, when we rode on the jumper circuit together—well, not together, against each other—I figured out she does the head-tilting thing when the course is especially hard. Seems like a million years ago when we were riding together, but in reality it's only been a year and a half. Something tightens in the back of my throat. In the end, she went on to the big shows, and I got packed off to East Texas. Everything here looks so familiar and at the same time different. Stuff went on while I was gone. Cory had good stuff happen, I had…

I slump onto a tack box and lean against the wall. Cory shoves me over and sits down beside me. The warmth of her thigh seeps into mine. I look down the barn aisle and see faded ribbons strung along the horses' stalls. The scene blurs and I reach up quickly to blot my eyes. Sitting up straighter, I put on what Angela calls my smart-mouth voice.

"Hey, so what's new with that geeky boyfriend of yours? Did you find anyone better yet?"

Cory's eyes pop open wide, but then she laughs. "No, no one new, but thanks for asking. Kevyn's still at Harvard. He's coming back for Thanksgiving."

Her voice is all chirpy, happy, making a little dark snake in my stomach wake up and pay attention. I stick my chin up and wave my hand around like the Queen. "Hah-vahd, la-dee-dah."

She pinches my arm. The corner of her mouth turns up. "So, not to change subjects or anything, but how hot were the cowboys in Texas? You must have had some working at your aunt's ranch? C'mon, details."

Another bad topic. The mention of cowboys, and I smell the hot beer breath on my face and feel the rough hand groping up under my shirt. He had me by my ponytail. It never paid to be caught in the tack room alone after dark when Aunt Sophia's workers were hanging out drinking. That night, I took the shears to my hair. To change the subject, I do the I'm-going-to-vomit sign. "Nah. Only if you like toothless, smelly fat guys. No hot ones like on the covers of those romance books you read."

"I do not." Cory leans away. Her pale eyebrows inch together.

Score. "Gotcha." Why do I enjoy getting Cory to react? Maybe it's her perfectness. A little too much of it.

"Okay, so what do *you* want to do?" She nudges my knee with hers.

"We could go to a diner and pick a fight in the parking lot."

Cory gasps. "Not funny, Regina. I was scared for a whole year the cops would come arrest us for that."

"Just kidding. C'mon." I nudge her.

Cory sits hunched, her arms wrapped around her sides.

"C'mon!" I shove her. "I never *told* anyone. I thought you'd get a laugh over it by now."

A hint of a smile. "Yeah, you should have seen that jerk run." She jumps off the tack box. "I have a better idea." She disappears down the aisle and returns a few minutes later, leading a horse. "It's Prophet," she announces.

She didn't need to tell me.

Prophet was my horse. Or, I should say, my mother's horse that I was riding on the show circuit. We were supposed to sell him for big bucks, but like most of my mother's plans, things didn't go the way she wanted. And when horses don't live up to her expectations, they tend to die of sudden and mysterious causes. Luckily for Prophet, when he started his downturn, someone was there to save him.

The big gelding is so dark and shiny he's almost black. I'm on my feet moving toward him like I'm caught in a Star Trek tractor beam. "My boy, Prophet. How you been?" His ear cocks my way and a low nicker rumbles in his throat.

"He remembers me." My voice is husky. God, I feel like such a girly sap.

"Of course he does." Cory hands me the bridle. "The rest of his stuff's over there." She nods to a saddle resting on a stand and a brush box. "I'll get Pressman. Can't ride Epiphany yet because her colt will go crazy. We can do a quick trail ride before evening feeding."

"I'm not really dressed..." I rotate my feet outward, showing off old running shoes.

"I'll lend you boots and a helmet. No excuses."

I didn't want to make excuses. I didn't want anything to change her mind before I got back on Prophet again. The brush glides over the familiar territory of his body as if I had ridden him yesterday, not over a year ago. I know every bump, scar, and whorl of hair. As if in a trance, I'm tacked up and on his back, my feet swimming in the oversized jodhpur boots. We head out the back of the barn, along the broad path between the paddocks, and into the woods. A little bubble of something light sparkles in my chest as I lean forward to run my hand down Prophet's muscular neck. *You were my horse.*

Cory points at a dark gray mare on the other side of a huge field.

"That's Epiphany and her foal. He's huge and gorgeous."

On cue, a dark colt trots toward us as if his hooves never touch the ground. He has a heart-shaped star on his forehead and three white stockings.

"Flashy," I say.

"You know it. Eye candy. Vee can't wait to see what he'll become."

The foal spins and runs back to his mother. "Epi okay? I mean, she didn't have any problems because of that disease she got?"

"No, but we haven't really done much with her. When the foal's weaned and we start working her again, we'll know for sure."

Cory uses *we* like now she's a partner with Vee, the head trainer. That little jealousy serpent sticks out its tongue at me. I mentally tell it to shut up. Cory's my friend. I'm happy she's got a great place to train and ride.

It's about ten degrees cooler when we enter the woods. The sun filters through the bare trees and dapples the ground. The horses' feet brush through a carpet of crunchy, fallen leaves. Cory rides ahead, single file, along the narrow path.

"I guess I missed a lot. Epi had her foal, you got to ride Prophet at the big shows, and now it's like you're a real partner with Vee or something." Hiss, hiss.

Cory spins around in the saddle. "I hope you're not mad I rode Prophet. I really wanted to see you ride him at Washington, but—"

Her words are cut off. What she couldn't say was, *but your mother was arrested and you got sent away to Texas to live with the only relative who would take you.* I run my hand along Prophet's neck again. "Yeah, it's okay. He was better off with you guys, than, you know, what Angela would have done with him."

Cory faces forward, and we ride to the sound of shuffling leaves and birds calling from the trees. A deer crashes through the woods to the right, pauses, and darts in the other direction. Prophet's head goes up, sniffing for danger.

"It's okay," I tell him. "I got you covered."

We come out into a broad field, the plowed ground littered with discarded cornstalks. I ride up alongside Cory, and the horses' footsteps fall into rhythm with each other.

"When do you go back?" she asks.

I pretend I didn't hear her.

"Regina?" Cory nudges Pressman so he's right beside Prophet. "What's up?"

"I'm not."

"Not what?"

"Going back. My aunt brought me up here to dump me back on Angela. She's getting out."

"What?" Cory's eyes go huge. She's had her run-ins with Angela, too. "They can't do that. I thought she was supposed to be in for another couple years."

"Me, too. Guess not. She appealed and got her sentence commuted or something. Whatever that means. Supposedly for good behavior. More likely, she threatened or bribed someone. I wouldn't put it past her."

"So, what are you supposed to do? Go back and live with her? Act like nothing happened? You helped put her in prison—"

"I know! Don't remind me." Prophet jigs a little and I realize I'm clenching my legs. "Sorry," I say to him but maybe to Cory, too.

"What are you going to do?" she asks again. Pressman slows to a stop. "Wait. I have an idea." She sits up taller in the saddle. "You can live with us. Jessica's gone a lot, so maybe—"

"Thanks, Cor, but I doubt the courts or whatever will hand me over to your mom. Or anyone else. Not without a big fight from Angela. And Angela always wins her fights."

Cory nudges her horse, and we head out walking along the edge of the field. We ride side by side, but I can see her eyebrows scrunched under the brim of her helmet. "How about Vee?" she asks. "Maybe she could help you? Give you a job—"

"Yeah, right. Angela would love that." Sarcasm drips over the words as they leave my mouth. Angela and Vee are mortal enemies. Cory's just trying to help, but it isn't like I haven't already thought of every single idea to keep me from going back with Angela. Even some crazy ones. I feel a little bad I bit her head off, so I add, "Plus, I'm still a minor. I don't have a lot of say in any of this."

The sun begins to sink below the treetops.

"We better get back." Cory turns Pressman's nose back toward the opening into the woods and the path that returns to the farm. Just as we step through the gap, Prophet drops a shoulder and spins. I lose a stirrup and struggle to grab up the slack in my reins. Not fast enough. He bolts past Pressman on the narrow trail, causing my knee to hook with Cory's as he passes. She grabs the rein on her side and pulls Prophet's head around. His hooves dance as he scans the woods around him, eyes wild.

"What's your problem?" I ask the gelding while my heart thumps against my ribs. "There's nothing here."

That's when a guy materializes, seriously, out of nowhere. He's wearing a camo jacket and a dark woolen cap. Cory's seen him now, too. Even Pressman is jigging, antsy to leave.

"Hey," Cory yells across the wooded expanse. "No hunting here. It's private property."

So now I'm wondering if it's not such a great idea to piss off some guy in the woods, wearing camo and probably doing something illegal already. Yeah, we're on horses, but if he has a gun…

"I'm not hunting." His voice is low but carries across the distance. I can't tell how old he is or much about what he looks like. He blends with the light and dark of the leaves.

Cory calls again, "This is private property. No hunting."

He starts toward us. He has something with him, on his arm. It's not a rifle, but I'm not sure I want to stick around to find out what.

"I told you I'm not hunting. Not yet."

I don't like the sound of that. "C'mon, Cory, let's just go. It's late." The sun is setting, leaving the stretch of path ahead of us in semi-darkness. The man dodges around a tree, working his way to the path where we've stopped. In a shaft of light, I finally make out what's on his arm and gasp.

A huge bird—a hawk or a falcon of some kind—is perched on his forearm. The bird lifts its wings, riding the waves of his arm movement, struggling to keep its balance. A leather thong of sorts is tied around its claws, which are huge. Prophet eyes it and scuttles backward. He's rigid and tense under my seat—a sign he's going to bolt.

"Stop!" I call, struggling to squash the waver in my voice. "Please, stop. My horse is terrified of that thing."

He stops on the spot. "Sorry. Guess I didn't think of that." He twists his body to hide the bird behind him.

Up closer he looks our age, a high school kid. He's wearing thick leather gloves. His cheeks are flaming red and his eyes, I see now, are very blue.

"What are you doing with that bird?" I ask.

"Training her. She's a new one. Just caught her a week or so ago and this is our first time out. I didn't think anyone would be around this late."

"Training her for what?" Cory asks.

"Hunting." The guy smirks when he tells Cory that, and a thin, invisible thread connects me to him. He likes to tease her, too. The bird guy takes a step back, off the trail and into the brush. "Gotta go."

In no time, the woods swallow him again.

"Weird." I let out a breath, and the thin connection snaps. Prophet stops pacing.

"Yeah, that's for sure." Cory frowns and urges Pressman forward.

"You know that guy?" I call to Cory's back. She doesn't answer.

The sun is dropping behind the trees so we turn the horses for home.

When we get to the paddocks surrounding the farm, the horses stretch their necks and snort with relief. Just outside the barn, I slip down, loosen Prophet's girth, and lead him inside. "So, do you know who that guy was?" I ask again.

Cory pulls off her helmet and tosses it on a hay bale. "I think so. His name's Declan something. He goes to my school, when he goes, that is. He's really strange."

"How? Besides creeping around the woods with wild birds, that is."

Cory's laugh rings around the empty walls of the barn. "Yeah, that's a new one to add to the weird list. He and his dad live around here, in the woods. I hear he hunts things and eats them." She grimaces, shivers, then rakes her fingers through her long hair. "And, he wears camo all the time and smells like wood smoke. I don't really know him, but kids say he and his dad live like totally off the grid. No TV, phones, anything. My friend works at the Food Lion and she says Declan comes in there a lot to do, like, the whole family shopping thing."

"So they don't just eat what he kills." I don't know why I'm defending this strange guy I don't even know.

"What?" Cory isn't listening. She takes the saddle from me and hikes it up on her hip. "So, if you're not going back to your aunt's in Texas, where are you staying?"

I turn to Prophet, sling an arm over his back, and bury my face in his neck. The smell of horse—sweat mixed with leather—slows my breathing. Deeper. Without turning, I murmur into the unyielding muscles of his shoulder, "I'm staying with my aunt in a trailer on Wade's farm. It has mice, and the carpet smells like stale beer and dog piss."

"Wade?" A sharp gasp.

Cory's heard the stories about him. I hear her set the saddle down. Arms slide around me from behind.

She presses her cheek against my back and whispers, "Oh, Regina, you got to get out of there."

Chapter Four

Since I'm going to be staying in Maryland, Aunt Sophia has to enroll me in the high school near Wade's house. At least I'll know one person here. Maybe two, if bird boy shows up. The secretary frowns at her computer screen. Her desk is covered with frog statues. The wall calendar has pictures of exotic frogs. She kind of looks like a frog with a wide mouth and eyes that bug out. She hands my aunt about a zillion forms to fill out, and Aunt Sophia asks about a zillion questions. A bell rings and kids pour into the hallway. I check each face, hoping to spot Cory. Most walk head-down like zombies, staring at phones. A few glance up at the large glass wall surrounding the office. One guy in a neon green-and-white rugby shirt forms his lips into kissing motions, so I give him the middle finger salute.

"Mrs. Zaccarro, you say that Regina is not your daughter, correct?" the Frog Queen asks Sophia. "You'll have to present legal guardian documentation and…" Her voice drones on as poor Aunt Sophia flushes and digs through her purse for all the papers she has on me. My papers, like a dog at the pound.

I go back to staring out the window. That's when I think I see him. A flash of camo behind a big girl in a dark blue hoodie. The bird guy. He's not wearing a hat, and I see now he has red hair, like mine. No. His hair is even redder.

I'm out in the hall before I know what I'm doing. Miss Froggy calls after me, something about not leaving the office without an escort, but I just keep walking.

"Hey!" I call to the back of the camo jacket, disappearing down the hall. What's with this guy? What was his name? "Declan!"

He stops and turns. It gives me a chance to catch up. When I do, I realize I have no idea why I'm doing this.

"Hey. Remember me?" His face tells me the answer. A definite no. "We met you in the woods the other day. Me and my friend were riding and you had your bird."

"Hawk."

"Right, hawk. Anyway." I stop, because really, I don't have anything to say to this guy. He's a familiar face—maybe that's it. He scratches the end of his nose using precisely one finger and stares at me with the ice eyes.

I blurt out, "Hey, do any hawks have blue eyes?"

What kind of a dumb question is that, he must wonder. But he doesn't let on I'm being an idiot.

"I don't know. But that's an interesting question. I never thought about it." He looks lost.

"Hey, maybe I'll research it and find out for you." Why am I talking to this guy? Another bell rings. Miss Froggy sticks her head out the office door and waves her arm.

"Gotta go," I tell him.

He doesn't answer, just melts into the crowd.

By now Froggy is red in the face and calling my name. She kind of shoves me back into the office with a not-too-gentle push from behind.

"Your schedule." She holds some papers out for me. When I take them, she ducks behind her desk. More papers slide across the expanse of her desktop in my direction. "Sign this. A statement of our school policies, dress code, absentee rules…"

I ignore the papers and look around the office.

"Where's my aunt?" I think maybe she's gone to the restroom.

"Said she had to leave."

"Leave? Why did she leave?"

Froggy types and squints at her monitor. "You're late. Second period. You'd better get going." I grab the wad of papers, shove the schedule in my pocket, and dump the rest in the trashcan on the way out.

Second period was World History, so I was totally lost. In Texas, we were doing Ancient History, so I was only off by a couple hundred centuries. After that was gym class, and since I didn't have a uniform or sneakers, I spent the whole period sitting on the sidelines like a conspicuous loser.

For the hundredth time today I look at the room number on my schedule and double check the one on the door—the last class of the day. English. I walk in and Declan is in the back of the row along the windows. He's looking outside, and I half expect to see his bird out there waiting for him. As soon as I sit in the desk next to him, he turns to me like he knew I was there all along.

"Can't find any raptors with blue eyes." He shakes his phone as if to indicate the answers were not in there. "Their eye color changes, though, as they age. Usually starts out as yellow, then a darker orange or brown, depending on the species. Have you *seen* a blue-eyed one?"

"I've never even seen one, up close that is, until yesterday."

He smiles and a dimple appears on the left side, high up on his cheek. A sheen of russet stubble covers his face, but you can only see it in the strong sunlight from the window. I'm wondering if he's hot in that camo jacket he always has on.

"You can meet her if you want. But, I guess I should know your name in order to make a proper introduction."

"Thanks. Oh, name's Regina." He seems to have gotten the idea that I'm interested in his scary birds.

"I just trapped the red-tailed hawk you saw. She was hurt, so I might have to keep her."

"You don't keep them?" A few students filter in and take seats. The teacher's back is turned, writing what looks like a reading assignment on the board. "I don't get it. You train them and do all that work, and then you just let them go? Don't they try to come back or anything?"

He scrunches up his face like I said something stupid.

My eyes narrow as I plow on. "Seems ungrateful, after all, you take care of them, spend time training them, and they just fly away. What if they get lost or attacked or hungry, or something?"

"They know the way home if they need to come back." He flashes the dimple smile. "They're not pets."

My cheeks burn. I feel like Bird Boy is laughing at me. "So, what are they? Hunting weapons? Do you have a license for that bird?" I can't stop my head from cocking in a *gotcha* gesture.

He rubs the back of his neck and looks up at me under some ridiculously long pale eyelashes. He nods. "Yup, I'm licensed to carry." His teeth are square, white, perfectly straight.

I lean in for my brilliant retort, but the English teacher, Mr. Curtis, walks down the aisle, dropping copies of a paperback book on each desk. I pick mine up. There's a close-up image of a wolf staring back at me. With blue eyes. *The Call of the Wild.* I glance over at Declan. Same eyes?

Returning up the aisle, the teacher asks me to stay a minute after class. "Will that be a problem?" he asks. "With your transportation or anything?"

"Sure. No problem," I tell him. "I have no idea how I'm getting home, anyway."

Mr. Curtis has a big forehead, with wisps of yellow hair sticking up from his head. "What do you mean?"

"My aunt dropped me off this morning." I don't want to sound like a helpless little kid. "We just moved here," I add, "and I don't know what bus I'm supposed to take."

"I'll take you," Declan says. "I have my truck."

The teacher nods at him, satisfied. He returns to the front of the room and asks a question about the major themes in Jack London's works.

"You don't have to," I whisper to Declan. When I lean close, I realize Cory was right. He does smell like wood smoke.

"I never do anything I don't want to," he whispers back.

And I believe him.

Chapter Five

AUNT SOPHIA IS BENT OVER THE OVEN WHEN I WALK IN THE kitchen. She shuts the door, tosses a dishcloth on the counter, and takes a big swallow from a plastic cup by the sink. Then she spots me in the doorway.

"How was your first day?" Her voice is talk-show-host bright.

"Great," I tell her and dump the pile of books on the counter so I can open the refrigerator.

"Any teachers you like?"

I take a swallow from the liter bottle and catch Aunt Sophia's eye. She makes a face and pulls a glass out of the cabinet and hands it to me.

"They're okay." We're not talking about what I want to talk about. Whether she knew Angela was getting out and why she didn't tell me.

Sophia brushes by me to get something from the drawer under the stove. Pans crash together, filling the void with noise. She examines a skillet with rust around the edges, then bends to put it back. I toe the drawer shut.

"Did you know Angela was getting out?"

Sophia snatches up her plastic cup.

"Well, did you?"

She takes a small sip. "Angela might have mentioned something when I talked to her."

"Uh, huh. Like, maybe, she said she was being released from prison a couple years early. Did she mention that?" I can't keep the sarcasm from rising up and spewing out of my mouth. I know it won't help my cause.

I'm right. She sets the cup down and a hand goes to her hip. Just like Angela. "Does it really matter when she gets out? Does it change anything? I don't think so."

I close my eyes and remind myself, she's not my mother. "Aunt Sophia," I start, take a deep breath, and make my voice even and flat. "The difference is if she got out a few years from now, I'd be older, and I wouldn't have to go live with her."

Sophia looks at me and drops her gaze. A flash of worry crosses her face. Worry, but maybe not for me. Her brown speckled hand gropes for the cup without looking.

The kitchen clock is loud, ticking. We stand, leaning on the counter, not looking at each other.

"You know what she did," I say.

Of course she does. She drains her glass and sets it down crooked. It almost tips, but she catches it in time. "Angela did some bad things," she says, "but she's different now."

"Some bad things?" Sarcasm roars back. She makes that monster sound like a naughty kid. "She killed horses for money. She threatened to hurt my friend and poison her horse." Now I have to look away. "And worse stuff."

Sophia pushes off the counter and stands up straight. "She's different now." Her voice is determined, hopeful. "They're letting her out early. Why else would they do that?"

"She's fooled them, that's why."

Her breath is laced with liquor. She doesn't believe her own words.

I grab the book on top of the stack and head to the other end of the house, to my room, and shut the door.

The bed is hard and narrow, but the pillow smells like a cedar chest, reminding me of fresh shavings. I bury my face in it.

When my phone pings, I roll over and see it's Cory.

How was the first day? Wish I could have met you for lunch.

I text her: *Horrible. Got ride home with Declan. Lunch tomorrow?*

Wait. What? The weird kid? Details tomorrow! We can ride again, ok?

I flip the thin bedspread over me and close my eyes. What feels like only two seconds later, Aunt Sophia taps lightly on the door and calls dinner. I rub my hand over the ridges on my face where it pressed against the chenille pattern spread and wipe away the trail of drool. My phone pings and a finger of dread tells me it's Cory texting to cancel. I'm wrong, it's Declan.

Drive you home again tomorrow?

Declan. The weird kid, Cory called him. I'm not so sure she's right. Or, maybe he is weird, but in a way I kinda like.

Chapter Six

THE CAFETERIA SMELLS LIKE WET MEATLOAF. THE VOCAL BUZZ IS interrupted by an occasional scream like some jungle bird. It comes from a table of girls in the back corner. They're all dressed alike. I get up to toss my lunch that's too gross to eat into the overflowing trashcans near the girl gang. Carefully balancing my tray on top of the trash mountain, I hear it. The word. *Prison*.

Without turning, I catch one of them out of the corner of my eye—a girl with her hair tied up in a bun, her shiny forehead framed in a blue headband. She clamps a hand over her mouth and tracks me with her eyes, while her shoulders shake with laughter. I push the double doors open and escape to my locker for an algebra book I need before class.

My favorite seat in any classroom is the one farthest back in the corner, but today some other girl is sitting there, so I drop my backpack on a desk closer to the front. As soon as I sit, the girl with the blue headband comes in and sits behind me. When I lean down to pull the algebra book out of my backpack, the girl leans forward and whispers.

"What did your mom do?"

I'm not sure I heard her right. Or, I can't believe I heard her right. Gripping the book, my hand shakes. "What?"

"Your mom. What did she do to end up in prison?"

My cheeks flame hot. I slam the book down and sit facing the front.

The girl next to Headband urges her on. She whispers, "Did you ask?"

A finger drills into my shoulder blade. I sit straighter and don't turn around.

"Hey, no offense, okay?" the poker says. "I was just curious."

I scoot my desk forward as much as possible before it jams into the back of the one in front of me. The teacher writes hieroglyphics on the whiteboard, and I know this is not going to be a good class for me. Whispers I can't make out swirl around me.

"Pass your homework forward," the teacher says, and the edge of a paper taps against my arm. I take it without looking back and pass it on.

More whispers. A snort. The teacher's voice is just background rumble as my ears strain to make out what the girls are saying. When the bell rings, everyone jumps out of their seats at once like a choreographed move and heads to the door. Sliding the book and papers into my backpack in slow motion, I take my time standing up, heading for the door. I don't want to run into Headband and her friend. My strategy backfires. As I approach, I see both are just outside the door, talking. The tall girl has her phone out and is showing the other something on the screen.

"Regina? Hold up a minute." The teacher calls, just as I'm ready to bolt down the hall. Mrs. Navarro stands behind her desk, her hand summoning. She's younger than most of the other teachers. Her long dark hair is pulled back on the sides and she's wearing a straight-cut herringbone dress that makes her look more like a CEO than a teacher.

"Since you just moved into the area," she begins and clears her throat, "you may experience some trouble until you catch up to where we are in the curriculum. I want you to know I have after-school study sessions. Students come and tutor and I'm always available for extra help." She smiles.

Wow, so the crack about needing extra help means she must have looked at my homework already.

"Okay," I tell her, stepping toward the exit.

Something slams against the classroom door, rattling it in its frame. Another bang, like a locker door. Yelling. Words like punches jump out from the general roar of noise in the hall.

"Give it back. Now! I'll f-ing kill you." A girl's voice.

"Cat fight. C'mon!" A guy's voice.

Mrs. Navarro is through the door like a sprinter. I follow in time to see a blond-haired girl struggle up from the floor and launch herself like a running tackle at Headband. Figures she was involved. Books, papers, pens, and other stuff are strewn along the corridor. An open locker stands empty. A three-ring binder is at my feet, its rings sprung open, papers loose and escaping down the hall.

Mrs. Navarro calls for everyone to stop, but no one pays attention. Two guys stand in front of Headband and catch the girl charging at her. They have her by both arms. Her head is down and she shakes it like a mad bull. Her fine hair sails around her head in a shimmering halo. There's a single purple streak in it that disappears and reappears among the almost white strands. When she raises her head, her eyes are rimmed in black. Was she crying?

"Don't touch my stuff." She shoots hate beams at Headband.

The boys laugh and swing her back and forth by the arms. She struggles when they lift her off her feet, causing her to run in place like a cartoon character. Her black-smeared eyes catch mine. She looks like a helpless animal in a trap.

"Stop this. Put her down!" Mrs. Navarro orders.

"She started it," Headband's friend says. "Willow is crazy!"

"I don't care who started it. It ends now." Mrs. Navarro steps up to the boys and gives them a hard look. They unhand the girl, who shrugs them off.

Teachers always say that—that they don't care who started it, but they really do. Mrs. Navarro goes over to talk to the boys.

I bend to pick up the notebook at my feet, gathering a few loose pages covered in green ink. The handwriting is neat, precise.

"That's mine." The blond girl, Willow, snatches them from my hands. She holds them against her chest as she bends to pick up the loose papers. I squat beside her to help, handing her a mish-mash of pages.

"Thanks." A suspicious eye watches me. Pale hair falls over the other. Her hands scrabble to pick up more papers. Blue veins show through the pale skin.

"She's a total jerk." I nod in Headband's direction. "She was picking a fight with me in class just now. You know, before…"

I hand her another wad of papers. We both look up at the source of our misery. Headband is talking fast, waving her hands around. She's explaining to Mrs. Navarro that she didn't do anything. Her voice is loud, so she's heard over everyone else.

"I just asked her what she was writing. That's all. Then for no reason she went berserk."

Willow stands. "You didn't ask. You took my notebook!" She shakes a fistful of papers. "You had no right."

Mrs. Navarro's back is to us as Headband goes on with her story. Willow bends to gather up pens—all green—scattered down the hall.

"Freak." A guy in ripped jeans nudges Willow from behind with his knee. She falls forward, catching herself on her hands, narrowly avoiding a face plant. The pens drop and scuttle along the floor. No one saw. The small guy looks around and kicks her.

Kicks her. Kicks her like I saw a creep do to a dog once. A dog that was lame and trying its best. I leap up, a fury rising in me for all the injustice I've just about had enough of, and before I give it any thought, I slam the binder across the back of his head. Hard. "Leave her alone, you jackass."

He spins and comes at me. He's a lot bigger now that I'm standing next to him. His face is red and his nostrils are huge. A meaty hand grabs the front of my jacket and shoves me backward. The locker ridges dig into the back of my head. I kick up and out. My ankle wrenches with the blow, and he bellows.

Kids pour out from everywhere. Mrs. Navarro, in her pretty dress and black pumps, is standing in the middle with her arms spread like a traffic cop. Willow is on the floor, grabbing at that stupid notebook that started this whole thing. Three men run down the corridor at us.

This is probably going to be another bad day for me.

Chapter Seven

THE BIG GUY WITH A BALD, POINTY HEAD IS THE ASSISTANT PRINCIPAL. He's the enforcer. The two other guys with him look like Secret Service in their white shirts, black pants, and ties. Except they're too flabby to be real Secret Service. They grab the boys but not the girls. They tell us to follow them to the office. We march along the corridor, kids all staring at us. I want to disappear.

The office is the same fishbowl I was in yesterday when Aunt Sophia dropped me off like a dog at the shelter. The two girls—Amy, Miss Headband, and her friend Evelyn—tried to get out of coming, but Bullet Head—Mr. DiGiorno—tells them to stop arguing and fall in. Yup, he says *fall in* like we're in the army. Inside the office, Amy steps up and starts again with the "We weren't doing anything," but DiGiorno holds up a beefy hand. She shuts up. Thank God.

"Sit down, all of you," he says.

Inside the office there's a couch and two single chairs. Willow drops into the end of the couch nearest the door. The jackwagon who kicked her takes one of the chairs and Amy grabs the other. Evelyn looks at the couch where Willow is and leans against the wall. I sink down on the opposite end of the couch. Willow is looking down, clutching that stupid notebook to her chest. She looks like some delicate origami creature all folded up on herself.

"Okay," the principal says, perching on the front edge of the secretary's desk. He folds his arms. "Amy Predergast, you start. Tell me what happened."

And she's off. To hear her tell it, she was "just asking Willow what she was always writing in that notebook" and then Willow went crazy and attacked her. I can tell even DiGiorno doesn't buy it. Willow doesn't look up. She's picking at a hangnail.

"Miss Morozov? Willow?" He says her name again, but she still doesn't look up. She sits very still, like those fake mannequin people at the mall. Like he's going to forget she's there or something. He doesn't forget. "How did your locker get emptied onto the floor?"

Willow tucks her feet up under her. She doesn't look at Mr. DiGiorno when she talks but keeps her head bent, her voice low. "I don't know. It happened when I wasn't looking."

Mrs. Navarro's voice comes from behind me. "When I came out into the hall, the contents of the locker were on the floor. Along with all the papers from her notebook. Amy and Evelyn were involved. There was name-calling."

"I don't care so much about that," DiGiorno says. "I want to know which students struck another student." He looks at all of us in turn.

I know the answer to that question. Willow might have hit Amy before I got there and certainly would have again if she hadn't been stopped. The big guy and his weasel friend hit Willow, but I don't think anyone saw. Then I did my thing with the notebook. I'm afraid of how this is going to go down.

Amy pipes up. "Willow hit Evelyn. And she was going to attack me, but Mrs. Navarro showed up."

Willow finally looks up. "After you trashed my locker and stole my notebook."

Evelyn leans forward. "She did not."

DiGiorno holds up the stop sign hand again. He's frowning. "Mrs. Navarro, when you came into the hallway, who was fighting?"

She steps into the center of the office. "Well"—she looks at Willow—"the girls were fighting. Books and papers were all over the corridor."

"When you say fighting, did you observe anyone hitting or shoving anyone else?"

I feel like we're in Judge Judy's court or something. Poor Mrs. Navarro wrinkles her forehead like it hurts her to think.

"No." It's a long, drawn-out *no* as if to say, *not exactly, but I might have more to say on the subject given a chance.*

DiGiorno turns to the weasel sitting to his right. "Mr. Preston, what did you see?"

The weasel hitches one side of his mouth and cuts his eye over to Amy. "I saw Willow slug Amy. She said she was going to kill her."

"Is that true?" DiGiorno has Willow in his sights.

"Miss, I asked you a question. Is that true?"

She's folding up even smaller. I can't stand it. Why doesn't she defend herself? "He hit her." I turn and stare at the Preston kid.

DiGiorno's bullet head swings in my direction, and it's like he sees me for the first time.

I point at the other guy. "Then he kicked her. When no one was looking."

Weasel Preston shoots me daggers. I lift the middle finger of my hand resting on the arm of the couch nearest him. He catches it. No one else does. I hope.

"That one hit me." He points at me. "Look, my head's bleeding." His hand rubs along the back of his head but comes away clean.

"All right." DiGiorno slaps the top of his desk with two flat palms. "Zero tolerance means just that. No threats, no physical assaults. Mr. Preston, Miss Morozov, and...." He looks at me again. He has no idea who I am. "All three of you—detention. Four days."

Willow's head shoots up. "But I have a job after school."

"Should have thought of that earlier. Four days. And I'm calling your parents." He jots something down, then looks at me under heavy brows. "What's your name?"

I tell him. He figures out I'm new. With the pen poised over a sheet of notepaper, he asks me for my parents' names and phone numbers. Amy snickers. Evelyn elbows her. DiGiorno looks up, waiting for an answer.

"Angela Hamilton," I tell him.

"Right. Angela. Mrs. Hamilton. Your mother?"

I nod.

"Phone?"

"Not sure."

"I'm not playing, Miss Hamilton." His eyes are fierce. "How do I get in touch with your parents?"

The room goes quiet and every set of eyes beads in on me. They're waiting for me to be ashamed. To be embarrassed, humiliated. A smug smile blossoms across Amy's face. I lift my chin and make my voice as steady as I can.

"I don't have a father. If you want to talk to my mother, you have to call the Maryland Correctional Institute for Women. I don't know the number cuz I never call her."

A sharp intake of breath. Mrs. Navarro turns her big brown Bambi eyes on me. Just what I didn't want to happen. Willow's looking at me, too, but it isn't pity—or disgust like Amy and friends. It's something I'm not sure I can describe. Curiosity?

Chapter Eight

DETENTION IS HELD IN A TRAILER MADE INTO A CLASSROOM JUST outside the main building. It's called a learning cottage to make it sound better, but, seriously, I've been in nicer horse trailers.

Willow sits at a desk next to me, still clutching that ratty notebook of hers. She leans over and talks out the side of her mouth all Humphry Bogart-like. "Your mom's really in prison?"

I shrug. I don't want to talk about it. Besides, the teacher's got his eye on us. The rule is no talking in detention. Fine with me.

The bad part is it's for four days. No meeting Cory after school to ride Prophet. No more rides home with Declan. I slump down in the hard seat and stare out the window. I don't want to admit it, even to myself, but I've started looking forward to him driving me home. He asks me questions and not ones about my mother in prison. Stuff about me.

The other kids in the fight yesterday got off because no one saw them hit anyone else. Except for Weasel. He's sitting on the other side of the room, his legs spread wide, fingering his thin facial hair. I can tell his ears perked up when he heard *prison*. Jerk.

Willow goes back to writing in her notebook when I don't answer. She doesn't seem insulted or anything. I go back to staring out the window.

Willow clicks her green pen and clips it to the notebook. She slips a tiny scrap of paper between my thigh and the desk seat. I open it. It's written in green ink.

What for? She looks over at me.

Wow. Her, too. What do they want me to say? Let me tell you about my mother—she's a monster. She kills horses for money and maybe anyone else who might be in her way. And I know I'm in her way big time. All I know is Angela doesn't forget, much less forgive, people who do stuff to her.

Why should I tell Willow anything? I look up at her. She's waiting. Her eyes are so pale blue, almost fake looking. And her white hair is fine and wispy around her face, it's like frost.

I flip the scrap of paper over and scrawl two words: *horse killing.* When the teacher's head is bent over some papers, I toss it on Willow's desk.

Her question starts a film running through my head of all the things Angela's done. Oh, I guess the *charges* were fraud. She swindled an insurance company out of a whole lot of money by killing a horse insured for thousands. But she didn't stop at just one. And second-degree assault. But there was so much more. I finger the scar on the inside of my arm, above the elbow.

Willow reads the words and nods. She seems satisfied. No more notes in green ink get passed to me. Weasel, unable to catch any juicy details from across the room, goes back to drawing on his forearm with a Sharpie.

There's nothing to do in here. We're allowed to do homework but no phones or music or anything. The teacher sits up front, and judging by the sour look on his face, he's probably grading papers. Some other kid, a guy with hair that's shaved in a lightning bolt, is in here with us. Wonder what he did.

"What is that?" I whisper to Willow, pointing to the notebook.

She draws it closer. "Writing and stuff."

No more details. She shoots me a look, like a dog that's used to being called over to someone only to get a beating. Before she slams the cover closed, I see a drawing of a horse's head on the bottom of a page. It's pretty good.

I check up front. The teacher isn't looking. "You ride?"

She nods. Her hair floats around her head. "Dressage."

I'm having a hard time picturing Willow on a horse. I'm having trouble picturing Willow outdoors for that matter. "Dressage?" I know my face is making that crinkled up I'm-smelling-cat-piss look. Dressage. Not for me.

The teacher's head shoots up. "Girls, no talking allowed."

After an eternity, the bell rings.

"Same time tomorrow," the teacher calls and gives a cheery little wave as we rush to the door.

"Crap," I mumble to Willow's back as we file out. "Stupid detention is messing up everything."

She agrees. "Eddie's going to be ticked off if I don't get the horses in on time."

"Wait, who's Eddie?"

"Farm manager."

"You work at a barn?"

She nods. "Twin Elms."

We slump along the empty corridor, and I tell her that I used to ride, too. That I had a jumper qualified for Washington but never got to show him. When we come to the front doors, I push one open and scan the empty parking lot with a silly bubble of hope that Declan's truck will be there. It isn't. I pull my coat front together and zip it against the cold breeze. "Gotta walk home now, too."

Willow spins around. "Then come to my barn. I'll drive you home after."

I must have a doubtful look because she insists. "No, really, c'mon."

"Right now?"

She grabs my sleeve and tugs me across the parking lot to a little car that looks like it's held together with rust and dirt. We head out along the roads, and after a while, things start to look familiar. I know we're near Vee's farm where Cory works. For a split second, I consider asking Willow to drop me off there instead. But I guess that wouldn't be very nice. She turns down a long tree-lined drive. This is some farm. Not exactly what I was picturing.

"The owners have three Grand Prix stallions here. We mostly take care of the mares and help with starting the babies." She has a tour-guide sound to her voice. I'm wondering who's *we*.

"The cool part is, we get to ride the ones who aren't showing, just to keep them exercised and stuff, on the off season. It's really great. I learned to ride piaffe this summer."

This is the most I've ever heard her talk.

We pull up in front of a complex of buildings. For sure, the biggest must be the indoor arena, but there is a maze of other smaller ones that look like they connect to various barns. The whole place is shimmering gray with burgundy shutters and doors. The grounds are perfectly trimmed and mulched.

When we get out, I notice the gravel parking area has ridges from recently being dragged and raked of debris. People are coming and going out of the barn—women in boots, workers wearing hoodies, a man in a suit… Definitely no kids. It's not a kids' kind of place.

Willow opens the trunk. She hooks her arm through the chinstrap of a helmet and grabs a duffle. "Can you get the blanket?"

I pick up the blanket, cleaned and wrapped in plastic, and follow Willow into the barn. It is just as beautiful on the inside. The aisle is paved in some squishy dark bricks that give when you walk on them. Each stall has a brass number and name plate. The honey-colored wood doors are framed in wrought iron, and there's not a scuff or a chip missing from any of them.

"Wow. Is this place brand new?" I ask.

"Nah. The owners have been here for at least twenty years, I heard."

I follow Willow past at least thirty empty stalls, and this is only one wing of the place. We come out in a central area, like the spoke of a wagon wheel. I gasp.

She turns and smiles. "Yeah, right? I had the same reaction the first time."

At the main entrance there's a double door you could drive a carriage through. It has two glass lanterns on either side. On the opposite end is a stairway that leads to what looks like a second-floor gallery.

"This way. I'll show you where the working students keep our stuff."

That's the *we*. Working students. I follow her past the entrance of the indoor riding arena and stop to look. The area is bathed in light from windows that cover the entire far end wall from a few feet above the wooden kickboards to a two-story pitched roof ceiling. Near the windows a man is longeing an enormous bay horse tied down with what looks like enough rigging to steer a tall ship. Its neck is arched and muscled, and his hooves never touched the footing, but fly through the air.

Willow peers over my shoulder. "That's one of the stallions. He's a bastard."

I search her face to see if she's kidding. She's not.

"Saw him stomp on a kitten and kill it. He's mean, just plain mean."

"Who owns him?"

"The trainer, Galen Ekerd. Heard of him?"

I shake my head.

"No one else gets near that horse."

"He's the head trainer?"

Willow tilts her head at the pair. "They're a good match."

Before I have a chance to ask why, she walks off down the aisle. At the end, we come to a small room that's set up like an apartment with a kitchen. A few people sit at a table in the middle. It's covered with fast food wrappers, show programs, and empty plastic water bottles. No one pays any attention when we come in. A bank of lockers stands along the wall opposite. Willow spins the dial on one, opens it, and tosses in the blanket and helmet. She stops at the refrigerator, extracts two Cokes.

"Want one?" she asks.

A guy at the table turns around to face us. "As a matter of fact, I would." He flashes a smile, showing a row of amazingly white teeth against a face the color of coffee with just a splash of milk. High cheekbones give his face an exotic look, but even though he's pretty darn gorgeous, he still seems friendly.

"I wasn't talking to you, Trey." Willow holds the can out to me.

Trey's black eyes settle on me. "New recruit?"

"Nah." Willow pops open the can. "A friend from school."

"Too bad. We could use more help around here." He stands. He's tall and lean, towering over me. His dark blue britches, piped in white, hug his hips and muscular thighs. He thrusts out a hand. "Trey Morales. Nice to meet you, ah…" The eyebrows shoot up.

"Regina Hamilton." I switch the can to my other hand and grasp his.

He lets go and gestures to two women at the table. "And this is Rachael." The one with dark hair pulled into a ponytail smiles. "And Janie." Janie gives a little wave, and I notice the ring of tattoos around her wrist, disappearing up under long sleeves. They go back to their conversation, but Trey remains standing.

"Did Willow take you on the tour?" he asks.

"No time. Eddie will kill me if I don't get the brood mares in, and I'm already late."

"I'll help you." Trey gathers the wrappers on the table and balls them up. Lifting on tiptoes, he arches the paper ball toward the trashcan, but it misses and bounces off the rim. "Not my sport." The blinding smile again beams in my direction.

A woman with black straight hair comes through the door, spots the wrapper on the floor, and bends to pick it up. The conversation at the table stops. Willow takes a step back.

"Does anyone work here anymore?" She slams the paper ball into the trash.

"We're just leaving to get the mares." Willow grabs a fistful of the back of my down vest and tugs me to the door. Trey pulls a jacket off the back of his chair and follows us out.

"Eddie?" I ask.

"None other," Trey answers, fiddling with the zipper. "*The* boss lady."

We head down yet another barn aisle, but it's not quite as fancy and perfect as the others. A few stalls have mismatched tack trunks in front of them, and others have been chewed or worn in places.

"These are the young horses' stalls, the ones not ready for sale yet." Willow pokes Trey square in the back. "And the working students' horses for the special ones who get to keep a horse here."

Trey, as if on cue, takes two huge strides ahead, stops in front of a stall, and slides open the door. He does a game show host gesture for us to step up to the threshold. "Speaking of special, here he is."

A chestnut face comes to the open doorway. It's a long face, made to look even longer by the thin blaze running from almost between his ears and disappearing over the top lip. I step closer and realize the horse is enormous. He probably has to duck to get through the doorway.

Trey drapes an arm over his neck. "This is Delta Dawn Doggie. Horrible racetrack name. He's Tucker now."

"Huge," I say.

Trey flips his mane so it lies all to one side. "Dressage horse in the making. He's going to show the world Thoroughbreds can do it, too." He cups the horse's chin, swings his head around, and plants a sloppy kiss on the end of his nose. "Okay, work to do, guy," he tells the horse, pushing him back and closing the door. He looks at us. "What? I love this horse." He's not apologizing.

"Spoiled," Willow mumbles and walks toward the outer doors.

While Trey adjusts the cooler hanging on a rack by the stall, I jog to catch up to Willow. "Who's spoiled, the horse or the owner?" I'm smiling.

She looks over her shoulder. "Both." She's not smiling, and I wonder what's up. Before I can ask, Trey falls into step with us.

"So, you're a working student and you get to keep your horse here?" I ask.

Willow snatches a halter off a rack by the door. "Not a working *student*. He trains with Galen, and he doesn't live here like the rest of us."

Trey holds up his hands, palms out. "Whoa. I started same as you. And only you ladies are allowed in the working student living quarters. What can I say? I still *work* here."

Willow looks like she's going to say something but instead turns and slides open the big outer doors.

A gust of wind blows in, sending wisps of hay down the aisle. The sky is battleship gray and getting darker as Trey's words start to register.

"You *live* here?" I ask her.

The silent nod. "All the working students live here." A pointed look at Trey. "Most all. That way Eddie can make us work anytime day and night." She marches off down a small hill into the creeping darkness. Trey and I run to catch up.

"Your parents don't mind?" My thoughts are racing. I could work here. Trey said they needed help.

Willow runs her fingers through her hair. The nails are dyed to match the purple streak. "There's only my dad. And he was glad to see me go."

Ouch.

Trey catches Willow in a big hug. "But we're glad to have you. Even if you're mean to me."

I look back at the cluster of buildings lit up and cheerful against the darkness closing around us, and a tiny, timid bubble of hope springs to life.

Chapter Nine

I CAN'T GET TWIN ELMS OUT OF MY MIND...AND THE IDEA THAT THE working students live there. It could be my ticket to escape. Escaping the farm manager's trailer where Aunt Sophia and I are living under Wade's watchful eye. The living room walls here are covered with fake paneling, and I think the carpet is held together by mud and dog hair.

Brenda is here again today. Checking on me. She's sitting on the couch I won't ever sit on. I drag a wooden kitchen chair into the living room.

Aunt Sophia is in the kitchen fixing coffee, she says, but what she's really doing is leaving me alone with Brenda. To talk. So far, Brenda's doing all the talking.

"Your mother's release date has been set."

I nod.

"In three months. A little over. February eleventh." Brenda flips some pages in a folder.

I nod again. What does she want me to say?

"She wants to see you for Thanksgiving. The correctional facility is hosting a dinner for the families."

"Prison."

"What?" Brenda looks up from her papers. A cross between annoyed and confused flashes across her face.

I shrug. "She lives in a prison. Can't you just call it that?"

So now she just looks annoyed. "You're expected around four that afternoon. Your aunt is invited as well, of course."

"Why are we talking about Thanksgiving? It's not even November yet."

Brenda puts the folder on the coffee table and tosses her reading glasses on top. She looks like she's going to say something, but Aunt Sophia walks into the room with Girl Scout cookies. Sophia pushes the folder aside and sets the plate of cookies down. "How do you take your coffee?" she asks.

"Black."

Not sure why but this surprises me. I figured Brenda for a four-sugars-and-heavy-cream type. While Aunt Sophia fusses around with the coffee cups, she mentions having to make arrangements at her farm in order to be away so long.

Brenda slides her folder closer and sets the cup on it. Her eyebrows scrunch together. "The state can help with expenses, if that's a problem. I had it on authority that you'd be guardian until—"

Sophia waves her hand. "No, no. It's okay. I will. I mean, I'm all set to stay here until…"

She trails off. Until she hands me back to her sister. Like an abandoned dog nobody wants.

They talk about me like I'm not in the room.

"Regina's expenses, of course, are fully covered up to the release date." She picks up her glasses and starts counting weeks. "The Thanksgiving event is in about six weeks."

Aunt Sophia nods. "Okay."

No one asked if I wanted to go.

"What if I don't go?" I say.

Brenda stops looking at her calendar. "Don't go?"

"Yeah. What if I don't want to?"

"Regina." Sophia sighs and collapses in the armchair.

"No one asked. Why should I?" My arms cross over my chest. If I stick my lip out I know I'll complete the picture of a kid having a tantrum. I uncross my arms and try to sound reasonable. "Look. I don't want to go see her, I don't want to have Thanksgiving at a prison, and most of all I don't want to live with her when she gets out."

Brenda stares. Sophia looks away.

"She's a psycho. Doesn't anyone get that?"

Aunt Sophia opens her mouth to protest, but I guess changes her mind. Brenda reaches for a cookie. It's quiet. The refrigerator dumps a load of ice into the bin. Brenda's breathing though her nose makes a little whistling noise.

She chews her lip. "There are very few alternatives in your situation."

I smell the strawberries again. She must be sweating. I swear that car freshener has leeched into her skin.

"So what are they, because I can't—" The words are bitten off by a stupid ring that tightens around my throat.

Brenda puts her cookie down on the very edge of the plate, like she's studying how to balance it there. She sucks in a deep breath. "A minor can become a ward of the state and enter the foster care system until reaching the age of majority. That's eighteen in Maryland. But I don't recommend this route." A quick shake of her head. She ticks off the options from the social worker's playbook. "A minor has to have someone assigned as her legal guardian in the absence of a parent or in a situation involving an unfit parent." She slides her eyes away. "Your mother has not been declared an unfit parent."

"Not yet."

A million thoughts crowd my mind—like what I could tell Brenda to convince her Angela is the definition of an unfit parent. About the times she'd lock me in the feedroom in the barn all night if I argued with her, or dump a horse's water bucket over my head if I rode badly. My eyes slide over to see Aunt Sophia still looking at the cup in her hands. If only she'd agree to keep me for just another year, I'd be old enough to be on my own. But she won't. She won't go against Angela. Getting Angela declared unfit probably means paying a lawyer a ton of money. And there's no time. She's getting out.

Brenda ignores my comment and bends down two more fingers. "Joining the armed forces or marriage of the minor, wherein the spouse becomes guardian…"

I wouldn't last two seconds in the military taking orders, and I'm sure there would be some rule that Angela would have to give me permission. Getting married? That would require I actually had a boyfriend. Dead ends.

The last finger bends. "Or, as I mentioned before, declaring yourself an emancipated minor. Again, requires an appeal to the courts that the parent is unfit."

Aunt Sophia stands. "But none of that is necessary." She grabs the cookie plate even though it isn't empty and sweeps off to the kitchen with it.

There's a pause.

"That's what she thinks," I say.

Brenda frowns. "Regina, I'm concerned now."

About time. My mouth falls open to say something sarcastic, but at the last minute I shut it and wait. Maybe I'm learning after all. A rattle of china and the dishwasher turning on tells me Aunt Sophia isn't planning on rejoining us any time soon.

Brenda taps the folder. "All I've had to go on is your records. Nothing there is of particular concern, but obviously there's more. Something, well, maybe you haven't shared with anyone."

Ugh. Sharing. Social worker talk. "Well, yeah, like the fact that no one in all of this planning has ever asked me what I want."

"How can that be?" Brenda looks genuinely surprised. "The wishes of the minor are taken very seriously when these cases are decided."

"Well, no one asked. If they had, I would have told them I'd rather live on the streets than with Angela."

Now she clams up. She's doing that psych thing where they don't talk and hope you do. Well, I'm great at this game. We sit and stare at each other.

"I cannot live with Angela." The same words spill out.

"Why?"

"She's a psycho."

"You said that. How so? Tell me."

I twist in the hard chair. "Well, for one thing, she won't let me have any friends. She monitors everything I do online. She doesn't allow anyone to come to our house. When I was a kid, I was never allowed to do sleepovers or hang out after school with other kids."

"A lot of parents monitor online contacts. There can be real dangers on the Internet. But why do you say she didn't allow you to have friends?"

"Because she didn't. She wanted to control everything I did. I wasn't allowed to do sports or join any clubs in school. If I was late coming home, she'd freak out and throw out my dinner..."

"She'd punish you by not feeding you?"

I wish that were the worst punishment.

"After a while I figured it out. She was supposed to be my only *friend*." I do the air quotes. "So, I stopped asking kids over. I stopped talking to kids at school. I started playing it safe." My eyes skitter to the window just over Brenda's shoulder. I'll never be safe. Not with Angela. Especially now, with Angela and Wade together.

"What else did you do to feel safe?"

Brenda's voice is low, calm, floating over the hum of the dishwasher.

"I never felt safe." A film loop of memories swims across my vision. I'm standing on the scales, and Angela grabs me by the arm, twists it. "She'd yell at me if I ate certain things. She told me I'd be fat and ugly and she wasn't going to have any fat and ugly kid. She made me weigh myself in front of her every week, naked, even when I was in seventh grade. If I went over the special number—that's what she called it—she'd lock me in my room for the weekend." I check Brenda's face. She urges me to continue. "She also was freaky about my hair. Said it had to be long." A side of my mouth creeps up. "Showed her, I guess."

"Regina, there may be a control issue here."

No kidding. "I'm not going back to living with her no matter—"

Aunt Sophia rushes in and thrusts her cell phone at me. "It's your mother."

I take it. I know what she did in the kitchen; she called and rat-
ted on me. I put it to my ear like it's a venomous snake and hear
Angela's voice, disembodied but sharp, down the hollow-sounding
line. "Regina, this is your mother. I'm only allowed five minutes, so
listen carefully…"

She tells me I'm coming to live with her and it's not open to discussion. She threatens me, but in such a way that no one listening
would think anything of it. But I know. I know the secret threats.

"Wade is hoping we'll all live together at his place, dear. Wade
would be terribly disappointed to hear otherwise. And we don't want
to disappoint Wade, do we?"

Disappointing Wade is dangerous. For everyone.

Chapter Ten

DETENTION FINALLY ENDS, BUT SO DOES THE NICE WEATHER. ON MY very first day of after school freedom, Cory invites me to ride. Afterwards, I slide the jumping saddle off Prophet's back and drape a cooler on him right away. Wind rattles the barn doors in their tracks. One big gust blows the door out like a sail. Prophet dances on the crossties while I struggle with the door.

Cory rushes over. "We'd better shut all of them." A polo wrap drops on the floor and unrolls down the aisle. As soon as she latches the door, quiet settles over the barn.

"I hate wind." She brushes a loose strand of hair away from her eyes. "And cold." She falls into step beside me. "Basically, I hate winter."

I try to stomp on her boots, but she jumps away. "Waah, waah." I rub my eyes. "What a cry baby! Remember when we used to show on the winter circuit? Now that was cold."

"Butt ugly cold." She does a comical shiver. "But I'd do it again in a heartbeat."

"Liar."

She goes quiet for a minute and I wonder what's up.

"It wasn't as fun without you. You know. Afterwards." Her eyes search out mine and I glance away.

She doesn't say it, but afterwards means a whole bunch of things. Afterwards was when Angela threatened to kill Prophet but Cory's aunt bought him and saved his life. Afterwards was when I couldn't ride him in the Washington International, even though I'm the one who qualified him. Because now he belonged to someone else. Afterwards Angela went to prison, I went to Texas, and a whole bunch of other stuff I'm not even sure Cory knows about.

"After I got exiled to Texas, you mean?" I feel the tight smile and wonder if it's fooling her. "Hey, I'm sure all those fancy jumper shows you went to didn't compare to what I was doing." I hook my thumbs into my belt loops and do a bow-legged swagger up the aisle. "I learned me some reining horse riding. 'Sides, I really rocked them cowboy boots."

Cory has a great smile. Her eyes kind of crinkle up and disappear when she laughs. I like to make people laugh. It hits me I haven't been doing a lot of that lately.

"You didn't ever wear cowboy boots," she calls over her shoulder as she leads Prophet back to his stall. "Can't see it."

"Did too."

She wrinkles her nose. "Nope. Don't believe you. Next you'll tell me you also have a silver belt buckle with your initials on it." She shudders. I can guess why. She's probably remembering that creep her mom used to date, Bucky. Always wore a silver buckle, unless he was undoing it.

My turn to wrinkle my nose. "No, but the boots, sure did. Didn't bring them, well, because I didn't think I was staying."

A cloud passes over and darkens the barn. I want to say something funny again, but I can't think of anything.

"Hey!" Cory slides the stall door shut. "I know a really cool place where we can try on cowboy boots. Let's go. It'll be fun."

We park in the lot off Main Street and cut through an alley. The air carries the smell of French fries, and I remember that I'm supposed to be home starting dinner. Oh, well.

"Here it is." A display of cowboy boots, hats, and silver jewelry decorates the store window.

Cory pulls me inside. The smell of leather is a drug hitting my system. My shoulders relax as I breathe it in. Leather equals happiness, comfort. Horses. I follow Cory up a small flight of stairs into a front room packed with boots. They're lined up on shelves against the wall, on stands and tables. A pair with long fringe catches my eye.

"Can I help you ladies find anything?"

I turn around. A lady with really black hair holds a big shoe box. I'm afraid she's going to tell us to leave because it's obvious, at least to me, that we can't afford any of this stuff. But she's smiling.

"Ah," Cory starts. "My friend left her boots in Texas and she misses them."

Cory is such a dope.

The lady sets the box down. "Well I don't blame her." She's wearing boots, of course, but they're really wild ones in shiny black with white inlay. They match her black minidress, cinched at her waist with a belt of silver medallions. A turquoise necklace dangles and sparkles at her throat.

"You want to try those on, sweetie?" she asks. That's when I realize I have the fringy ones in my hand.

"Go on," Cory urges. She sits on a low bench and pulls me down next to her.

"Sure, ah, but I have no idea what size."

The lady measures me and disappears into a back room.

"I can't buy these," I whisper, tilting the price tag so Cory can read it.

She shrugs. "So what? Try them on. Have some fun."

Fun. That's been missing for a while. I lean back and see myself in the mirror placed on the floor across the room. I look different, and it's not just the short hair. My eyes are black holes and my mouth is turned down. I give the reflection a sneer and the finger. Yeah, maybe I do need to have some fun.

"Here they are," the lady says. She tells us her name is Lori. She lifts a boot out of its nest of tissue and hands it to me. I pull it on and, of course, it fits.

"Look in the mirror!" Lori walks me over to the enemy mirror, but now all I'm seeing is me from the knees down. The fringe sways when I walk, making a gentle slap against the leather boot. They're soft brown like a fawn with stacked heels that make a solid click when I cross the floor. I don't ever want to take them off.

"Try on these." Cory holds up a dark mahogany pair with leather-tooled swirls.

"You try them. I'm not taking these off."

Lori steps to the rack and pulls a bunch down for Cory to consider. They have their heads together, talking. The soothing brush of the fringe whispers to me. *Remember the card?*

I pull out my wallet and slide the credit card out from the zippered lining where it has sat, untouched, for more than a year.

I walk over to the bench and pull the boots off and shove them in the box before I change my mind. "I'll take these." Cory's mouth forms a surprised little round shape, but she doesn't say anything.

"You sure, honey?" Lori asks. "You don't want to try on some others?"

I shake my head no.

"I'll just put them by the register." Lori tucks the box under her arm and heads to the front of the store.

Cory struggles back into her shoes. "You're buying those after all?"

"My mother is." I wave the credit card.

Cory grimaces and makes a little sucking noise through her teeth.

At the register, my hand trembles when I hold out the card. What if it doesn't work? Angela might have cancelled it a long time ago. When she gave it to me we were traveling on the horse show circuit a lot. She said it was for emergencies. For emergencies *only!* I hear her voice in my head. Well, I'd call this an emergency. Her getting released from prison is one big, major emergency to me.

Lori slides it in the machine. I hold my breath.

Cory gives me a sideways look that asks the obvious question: *What the hell are you thinking, Regina?*

"That will be two sixty-five." Lori hands me a pen to sign and turns to put the box in a bag.

Cory kicks me. "What are you doing?"

I scribble my name on the receipt. "I don't know."

But it doesn't matter. Nothing does.

Chapter Eleven

THE NEXT DAY IS WARM FOR A CHANGE. A LITTLE TINGLE SHOOTS through me when I see Declan's truck idling in his usual pick-up spot outside school. I'm pulling the passenger door shut when his fingers circle my wrist. He pulls, stretching my arm out, exposing the inside. Should have kept my jacket on.

"What happened to you?" He points to the purplish streaks just above my wrist.

"Cowboy boots." I snatch my arm back and hug it to my side.

"What did they do? Walk across your arm?" His brows come together, wrinkling his forehead.

When I look down at the marks, I see Wade's hairy fingers, twisting. Last weekend he came storming into our kitchen, waving a credit card bill. His face was red, and something pulsed on his jaw when he yelled.

I pull down my shirt over the marks. I act like it's nothing when I explain. "Wade, my mom's boyfriend. He's handling all the bills, and he was mad I bought them, that's all."

"Yeah? So mad he tried to break your wrist?" He pushes that stupid hat he wears back on his head. It's clear he's not going to let it drop.

"No." I let out a little laugh, like I'm saying *of course not*. "I started to leave. Go to my room, so he grabbed my arm. He said I couldn't just walk away."

Declan makes a little harrumph noise like a dog does when it circles and finally lies down. I could tell he wasn't buying it, my explanation. It was more than a grab. I rub my wrist. I don't want to talk about it. I don't want to tell Declan what he really did.

"Then he said I have to pay it back."

"How much?"

"A lot." And I don't have any idea how. "So, it will probably be like a hundred years from now when he gets the money."

Declan's finger zooms across the space between us and lightly touches the bruise. A beam of sunlight hits his blue eyes, lighting them up as they catch mine. "What else did he do, Reggie?" His voice is flat. No-kidding kind of flat.

"Nothing."

Declan's head cocks ever so slightly. Do his eyes narrow a bit? He doesn't believe me.

"Really. I swear. Can we go now?"

He puts the truck in reverse, eases out of the parking spot, and pulls onto the road. It feels familiar, comfortable to be with him in the truck driving home. But today he isn't talking. Maybe I made him mad because I didn't answer his questions. When people get quiet, it usually means they're mad. And that's never good.

After a few strange turns, I sit up taller to read the street signs and look around. "Where are we going?"

He doesn't answer.

"Are you kidnapping me?" I smile. Sort of like I'm kidding but not really.

"Yeah, I'm kidnapping you." One side of his mouth inches up in a half smile, half smirk. A smilerk. "To whom shall I address the ransom note?"

"La-dee-dah. To whom." I give a limp wrist wave. But then I'm thinking that's not too funny, seeing as I'm pretty sure there's no one who would pay to release me. In fact, I start to think his joke about ransom notes is pretty snarky. "You can just take me home, okay?" I don't want to sound too bitchy, but I do. I cross my arms and stare out the side window.

"C'mon." He nudges me in the shoulder.

I figure he'll say he's sorry, but I'm *so* wrong. He keeps going. "Think about it. Who would pay to get you home safe? Really."

"I don't want to play this game."

"No one? Not your mom?"

I give him a hard look. Incredibly, he doesn't get it and just keeps it up.

"You believe that your mom wouldn't pay to get you back? To save you? Your own mom?"

I spin to face him. I haven't said much about Angela to him, but I'm going to set him straight right now. "My mother is crazy, okay? Yeah, maybe she'd pay to get me back just so she could torture me some more." The truck bumps and dips as we turn onto a dirt road. "And where *are* we?"

He slows, but the dirt track sends us both bouncing around on the seat. My shoulder slams against the window. The tires spit gravel chunks against the undercarriage.

He ignores my question. "What did she do?"

He just doesn't know when to quit. The air gets stuffy all of a sudden, and I have this urge to scream. A big bulge of high-pitch screaming air rises up from my chest into my throat, but when I open my mouth, a stream of word vomit spews out instead.

"Why doesn't anyone understand she's a psycho? Huh? I don't *get it*. She does horrible things, all the time, and everybody just wants to forgive her. You know what she used to do? She used to interrogate me on what I had to eat every day when I got home because she didn't want me to get fat. If I ate something she didn't approve of, I wouldn't get supper for a few nights, or she'd make my favorite food and eat it in front of me. She picked out all my clothes and made me wear what she set out. If I got less than a B in class or if I screwed up at a horse show, she would yell at me all night and forbid me from talking to friends or watching anything. When that stopped working she upped her game. She broke my things or locked me in my room."

"How old were you?"

My heart's thumping against my chest. I'm shocked that Declan doesn't have that poor-girl-sympathy look on his face. I take a breath and get my voice under control. I slow the words. "She's always been that way. When I got older, she just got worse." I turn away to look out the window.

"What did you do?"

"What did I *do*?" I turn to him. "What could I do? If I got mad, she'd do something worse. If I acted sad or anything, she'd say, 'I'll give you something to be sad about.'" She took my dog and dumped him at the animal shelter. Told me she got rid of him because I didn't appreciate what she'd given me, and I'd have to earn things from now on. Once she…never mind." My throat closes up with that sad blob that keeps trying to escape. I push it back down. "So, okay, can we stop talking about her now?" I smile. A smile I've practiced and I know works pretty good when I need it.

"Sure." He pulls up in front of a log house and stops. "We're here."

The house has an open front porch with two steps leading up to it. There's a woodpile on one side and two rocking chairs. Smoke streams out of the chimney. Wood smoke. Now it makes sense why Declan always smells like a campfire.

"This is your house?"

Declan puts the truck in park. "Yup. Home sweet home."

I give him the what-the-hell look, but he's already opening the door and getting out. So I pull on my jacket and get out, too. Declan comes around the front of the truck and grabs me by my coat sleeve while I'm still zipping it up.

"I want to show you something."

One thing I realize—Declan walks fast. He drags me a few steps behind him before he gives up and lets go. Two big Labradors, one yellow and the other chocolate, come out of nowhere and join us.

"Meet Buck and Thornton," he says, giving the yellow one a thumping pat.

Behind the house, down a path, there's this pen. I'd call it a pen because it has a square wire area with wire covering even the top. It's attached to a wooden shed with a door to the outside. My face must be telling him I have no clue what we're looking at.

"It's a mew." Declan leans over to scratch the chocolate lab.

"Yeah, still don't know what it is."

He goes in the door, so I follow. It's dark, so my eyes struggle to adjust.

"Holy crap, what is it?" Some hulking, feathered thing with glowing eyes moves in the corner. I lurch backward, bumping into a dog.

Declan steps around me to shoo the dog and shuts the door. "Don't worry. She's tied." He pulls the cord for an overhead light and takes off his hat. Standing directly under the bare bulb, I'm shocked at how really red his hair is. "This is Rosie. You met her in the woods that day."

Now that I can see clearly, and up close, the thing is even more frightening. A huge bird with a hooked beak sits in the corner. Her golden eyes never blink. Wrinkled claws grip a log perch about as big around as my arm. I don't want to think what those claws could do to a bare arm.

Declan roots through a box on the shelf and hands the creature a tidbit. "She's a red-tailed hawk."

"Her tail's not red."

He laughs, and over his hand he pulls a thick leather glove that reaches right up to his elbow.

"You're not going to let it loose, are you?" I want to slap that smile off his face.

"Nah, she's not ready for that yet. She's just learning to take food from me. See?"

He pulls another piece of some raw, disgusting-looking meat from a lidded pail and walks close to the bird. She eyes him and cocks her head. In slow motion he moves his hand toward her and strokes the side of her beak with the meat. In a blink, she snatches it.

"Holy crap," I whisper. "You still got all your fingers?"

He pulls the glove off and wiggles them in front of my face. "She just learned that. Next, I teach her to fly to me for the food."

"You're crazy. You're going to let that thing fly at you? Then what?"

"She has to learn to come to me. When she's able to do that, we can start the real training. Learning to hunt together."

Rosie turns her head and peers at us with one eye. She looks sneaky, like she's planning to do something really bad. I don't trust her. Declan rummages around in that smelly pail of meat but comes up empty-handed.

"Darn. Got to go in the house and get some more out of the freezer. You can wait here—"

"No way. No way I'm staying here alone with that thing."

I push him out the door and shut it behind us. He tries to tell me again that she's tied and all, but I don't trust her. We walk along a flagstone path that winds toward the back door of the house, past the driveway on the left. On the right, a three-board oak fence runs along open pasture, past the house, down a hill, and disappears in the woods. Over the lip of the hill, there's another wooden structure. One with a big door.

I jog to catch up with Declan. "Hey, is that a barn?" The words are barely out of my mouth when a chestnut horse breaks from the woods, runs up the hill, and skids to a halt in front of us. I take a step toward her, but Declan grabs the back of my coat and pulls me back.

"Be careful. She's not too friendly sometimes."

"Is she yours?"

The horse's nostrils flare. She paces the fence.

"My mom's.

"She's gorgeous. What's her name?"

"Red Mare."

"Yeah, I can see that, but what's she called?"

"Just that, Red Mare. I only heard Mom call her Sweetie or Panda Bear, never her real name. Dad knows what it is, but he won't tell anyone. He just calls her Red Mare."

I feel my face scrunch up. "He won't tell anyone what the horse's name is?" I step over to the fence and lift my hand slowly. The mare stands, eyeing me, as I run my hand along her neck. Her coat is crusted with mud, and her mane is long and tangled. "How come he won't tell you her name?"

Declan looks toward the house and sighs. "It's a long story."

"Okay. Maybe you can tell me sometime." I work some of the tangles out of the horse's mane. She stomps but doesn't run off.

"Horses like you, I guess."

As soon as I look away, the pinch of horse teeth penetrates through my jacket at the shoulder.

"Ouch, you little…" I spin around and she runs off down the hill.

"Told you. Can't trust her."

I watch her head toward the barn. She moves over the ground fast, sure-footed and smooth. Already I'm wondering if she can jump. "What does your mom do with her?"

"Nothing now." Declan shields his eyes to look at the mare. "My mom's dead."

Chapter Twelve

WILLOW SAID THE COSTUME PARTY WOULD BE ALL PEOPLE FROM the barn—the working students, owners, other trainers, and people the owners hang around with. I wasn't going to go, but she said it would be a good chance for me to meet everyone and that would help a lot when I ask for a job. And at this point, a job is what I really need—not just to pay Wade back for the boots, but if I could get a job at the barn, I'd have a place to live, too.

When Aunt Sophia pulls up to the address to drop me off, she makes a low whistle.

"Rich neighborhood. I imagine you'll meet some nice people tonight."

I'm not so sure rich equals nice the same way Aunt Sophia puts them together. I open the door. "Don't worry about picking me up. Willow said she'd drive me home afterwards."

Aunt Sophia is still eyeballing the sprawling mansion, all lit up with floodlights. Cars pull up behind us and people get out.

"I'll get out here," I tell her, and jump out, careful not to catch my black scarf in the door when I shut it.

She eases the car around the circle driveway and disappears. As I walk up the stone path, I notice no one really answers the door, it just opens. A blast of overheated air and a sweet, weird smell hit me—a mix of pumpkin spice and pot. Inside, I head to the kitchen, looking for Willow. I don't recognize anyone.

The kitchen is huge. Every countertop is covered with bottles. A long table holds all kinds of little hors d'oeuvre things. My stomach reacts with a loud gurgle, so I saunter over there, still searching for Willow. I shove a thing covered with puff dough in my mouth, take a napkin, and stuff a few more in my pocket.

"Doesn't your mother feed you?" A masked guy in a pirate outfit laughs at me. Not sure if he's Jack Sparrow, maybe with a touch of Zorro. He's tall with long legs stuffed into tall black boots. A sash around his waist holds a fake sword.

My face goes hot. "I didn't eat dinner." The image of the fish sticks in the toaster oven makes me wrinkle my nose.

"Have some of these, then." The pirate lifts a plate of crackers covered in fancy doo-dads with toothpick spears and shrimp nestled against each other like a row of commas. I notice he has some kind of accent as he smiles and pushes the plate at me.

"So, you're armed as well, I see." He points to the plastic sword I've got strapped to my belt. "That means you're a swashbuckler, too?" He has a small gap between his front teeth.

"No, a ninja." I know my costume's kind of lame, but it was all I could come up with on short notice. It was easy to find black tights and a black turtleneck and to wrap a black scarf around my head, although it's getting too hot for it now. The Dollar Store sword tucked through my wide sash looks like something for chopping off heads.

The swashbuckler takes off his plumed hat and holds it against his chest. "Of course! I should have guessed. Let me get you a drink. Wine?"

I nod dumbly, and before I can say anything, he sweeps across the kitchen through the crowd. I lift one foot, then the other. The floor is so sticky, I feel like a fly caught on it. A girl with pink hair spiked on one side comes in and pulls open the refrigerator, then slams it shut. She looks familiar, and I think she may be one of the working students I met at the barn. She scans the room, her eyes rimmed in black about an inch thick. I wonder if she's cold dressed in a lace camisole and fingerless gloves up to her elbow. Her bare arms are muscular. A tattoo in gothic lettering snakes along one bicep: *The lake of fire is the second death.* God, whatever that means.

Her eyes land on me. "You watch you don't get recruited tonight, little ninja girl." Half her mouth tilts up in a smirk.

Before I open my mouth to ask what she means, the pirate shoves her aside and slams a bottle on the counter. "Watch it, Janie."

It was the same girl at the barn. Janie. She had dark hair then. She tugs at the top of one of her gloves, pours a full glass from the bottle, and holds it up like she's toasting. "Right, Galen, here's to making money the old-fashioned way."

Galen. With the mask and the hat, I didn't recognize him. And he was nice to me. Janie brushes past him and leaves, just as he pours me a full glass of the amber-colored wine. I tip a tiny bit into my mouth. It's cool and buttery. He smiles and nods.

"A decent Chard. Our hostess knows her wine." His *w's* come out more like *v's*—*vine*. He lifts his glass and rattles the ice in it. "But I prefer bourbon."

What does this guy want? He sets his glass down on the counter very carefully. I stand up straighter, figuring *here it comes.* And I'm right.

"So, I hear you're a friend of Willow." *Villow.* "I also hear that you're a rider. But I know who you are, and I haven't introduced myself." He removes the Zorro mask and thrusts out a hand. "I'm Galen Ekerd."

I shake. His hand is dry and callused. All I can think about is that this is the head trainer, the one Willow called a bastard. He doesn't seem so bad.

"Willow invited me to see where she works. It's an incredible place."

"We're very lucky, yes. But a place is only as good as its horses. We also have some fine animals." The kitchen fills with more people, loud laughter. He moves closer and a whiff of bourbon precedes his words. "But it is a big place to run. Lots of horses to care for. We are always looking for good helpers. People like you, who know horses. Willow tells me you know how to ride."

"But not dressage," I blurt out.

He laughs. "You young girls always with the jumping. You are a rider already. We can teach you the fine points." His long fingers wrap around my forearm and squeeze. "Please, think about it."

I see Wade's face, angry, shaking the bill for the cowboy boots. "What would I have to do?"

Galen turns to the hors d'oeuvres platter and shrugs. "Same as the other girls. No stall cleaning, we have workers to do that. You would start with the mares. Take care of them, feeding, exercising those who need it. Simple. Then we see." He pops a cheese cube in his mouth. "About other jobs." He looks over my shoulder. "Ah, here she is. Late as usual." He pulls a card out of his pirate coat pocket and circles a number on it. "Call me. We can talk more." He slips into the crowd, but I hear his voice calling to someone in the next room.

Willow is wearing a floor-length pale blue dress with puffy short sleeves. A dark blue ribbon circles the dress just under her boobs and is tied in a huge bow at the back. Another ribbon holds a few strands of her hair at the back of her head.

"What are you supposed to be?" I ask.

She looks down at her dress like she's trying to figure it out, too. "Wendy. You know, Peter Pan."

"I guess. Hey, where were you?"

"Why? When did you get here?" She looks worried. "Galen gave me extra work tonight, so it took longer." She doesn't wait for my answer but threads her way out of the kitchen through a hallway of zombies, witches, and vampires. As we get closer to the huge, sunken living room, I feel the bass line of the music thumping in my chest. I'm sweating under my ninja costume and the plastic sword has whacked more than a few people already, causing angry scowls to turn in my direction.

"Hey, Willow." I have to yell to be heard. She stops. "Who are these people?"

She looks around. "People from the barn, but I don't recognize a lot of them." She nods at the pink-haired girl. "That's Janie. You met her at the barn."

Great.

Willow is supposed to drive me home, and I'm ready to go now. Since she just arrived, I figure I'm stuck for a while. "Hey," I poke her in the back. "That Galen guy offered me a job just now."

Willow turns to me. Her face is not happy. "You talked to Galen?"

I step back but bump into a bare-chested guy dressed like a Roman Centurion who shoves me away. "Yeah. Just a job feeding horses, maybe riding some. Are you upset? If you don't want me to work here—"

"It's not that."

I wait. I hope the silence will prompt her to answer the question that's burning a hole in my brain: Then what's the problem? "I thought that's why you invited me to come here tonight?" Maybe she thinks I'm competition. Maybe she doesn't really want me around...

Her shoulders drop. "It is. I thought that we'd talk to Eddie or the owners. He's...just be careful around him, okay?"

I picture his smiling white teeth and his sophisticated way of talking, and so I think I get it. Maybe Willow has something for him. "Okay. Yeah. I definitely will, and, besides, I don't see having much to do with the head trainer, anyway."

Willow nods. She flashes a smile. "Right, Eddie's the one who gives the orders."

A shriek of laughter pulls my attention over Willow's shoulder to a girl on the couch. She's sitting facing a guy, her legs folded under her. A glass of something dark red bobbles in her right hand, held high and out of the way as the guy licks her neck. The glass tips...and that's when I see him. Beyond the living room, in the entrance foyer, Wade is leaning against the banister at the bottom of the stairs. He's not wearing much of a disguise—just surgical scrubs covered in what I hope is fake blood.

"Oh, God." I duck behind Willow. Even though Aunt Sophia said I could come, he'll probably find some reason to punish me for being here.

Willow follows my stare. "What's the matter?"

"That guy." I jerk my head in his direction. "The one dressed like a doctor."

Willow scrunches her face. "The vet?"

I step farther away from the entrance of the foyer. "You know him?"

"Sure. He seems nice."

"So does Galen."

Her face registers my meaning. "Point taken. How do you know him?"

A girl in a skimpy nurse's uniform approaches Wade and wraps her arm around his waist. He pulls her to him.

"He's my mother's *boyfriend*." We both take a second look around the corner. "But doesn't look like it now, does it? C'mon." I pull Willow along after me, heading back to the kitchen, maybe out the back door. All I want is to get out of there, but I file away this little tidbit of information about Wade if I need it later.

The kitchen is still a sea of people, but much drunker people now. I make a beeline to the back door when it opens and a familiar person appears and rushes past me.

"Hey, that's Trey," I tell Willow, trailing behind.

She raises her hand and calls to him, but he lowers his head and plows through the crowd.

"Hey, what's up, Trey?" Someone tries to hand him a drink, but he pushes it away.

We turn and watch as people part like the Red Sea. Trey enters the crowded living room, looking left and right. When he turns his gaze to the foyer, his eyes narrow. The crowd closes around me, and I can't see much. Through the gaps, I watch as Trey approaches Wade. They stand toe-to-toe, although Trey is a much slighter build. Not wanting to get too close, I stand on the other side of a wall and listen. Scraps of words float over the music and noise: Rachael. Missing. Code. Police.

Wade's face darkens, and he steps forward into Trey's space. Galen materializes out of the crowd and stands behind Trey. He leans forward, talking in Trey's ear. Trey shifts his head aside like avoiding a fly, then his body jerks. Wade opens the front door, and they disappear outside. The door slams shut. No one looks up. No one notices.

I run to the back door, slip out alone, and skirt along the bushes to the front of the house, wrapping the black scarf over my face. Why do rich people have so much outdoor lighting?

Wade, gripping Trey by the arm, walks along the far side of the line of cars parked along the circle driveway. Before the darkness of the wood-lined drive swallows them up, I see something glint in Wade's hand. The rhythmic thump of the party music seeps out the walls and mixes with the call of a cricket. The juniper bush scratches my face, and my knees cramp up from crouching. A distant sound of a car engine, tires on the drive, gets closer, but I don't see anything. I shift my position and strain to hear. Maybe I should go back inside? Find Willow and get out of here. My muscles scream as I move to stand, but just then Wade appears under the light. Alone. Does he have more blood on the front of his scrubs or did I not notice before? I lean back and flatten against the brick wall of the house. He tugs at the bottom of his scrub's shirt, frowns at it, but opens the door and disappears inside.

I pull out my phone and call Willow. Voicemail. I text her and wait. No answer. I text her again: *I'm outside. Take me home. Now!* The damp mulch seeps through my thin leggings. I stare at my phone as it goes dark. Where is she? I scroll through my contacts and see the battery is low. I have to reach someone for a ride soon. Cory. I push the green button and pray, *please answer, please answer.*

"Regina?"

Her voice hits my ear, and I feel a prick behind my eyes. My nose is running. I sniff, wipe it with my sleeve. My voice is raspy. "I need your help."

Chapter Thirteen

AT SCHOOL ON MONDAY I'M SO TIRED. THE CAFETERIA SMELLS LIKE dirty dish soap, and all the noise is hurting my head. Cory pulls a sandwich out of her lunch bag. I watch her unwrap it and lick the oozing marshmallow off her fingers.

"I don't know how you can eat those things."

She takes a big bite. "What?" she asks around the brown blob in her mouth, releasing a waft of peanut butter in my face.

"Those peanut butter and marshmallow sandwiches. What do you call them?"

"Fluff-a-nutters."

"Yeah, they're gross. I don't know how you can eat them, and, besides, that's a stupid name. It's a little kid sandwich."

Cory drops the sandwich on her plastic tray. "Wow, Regina, what's your problem?"

"No problem." I look away.

Thing is, she's right, I do have a problem. A big one. I feel jumpy like my skin is conducting electricity all along my body and my insides are getting jolts every few minutes. Jolts when I think about Trey. And the knife. Or whatever it was I saw and thought was a knife. I want to tell Cory I'm sorry, but I don't. I look out the window. I haven't slept much since Saturday night, since the party. I keep replaying in my head what I saw. What I think I saw—Wade dragging Trey off and blood on his shirt afterwards. The insides of my eyelids feel like sandpaper scraping over my eyeball every time I blink, and a spidery-legged creature feels like it's crawling around in my stomach. A swig from Aunt Sophia's vodka bottle this morning didn't help my nerves like I thought it would. Actually, it was close to a couple of swigs I poured in my orange juice. I feel Cory staring at me and drag my eyes back to the table. She must have said something I didn't catch. "What?"

"I asked, did you tell your aunt yet?"

I strain to get my eyes to focus on her face. It's like there's Cory and a second ghost of Cory. "No."

"You gotta tell someone."

"Tell them what?" My voice is loud. I don't have control over it. I swallow down the rest of the words crawling up my throat. "I didn't really see him *do* anything. And besides, who am I gonna tell?"

Cory's head cocks. "Um, the police for a start. Maybe that social worker lady."

"Brenda?" I snort.

"Well someone." Her eyes bug out and she leans across the table. She lowers her voice, soft against the clatter of dishes and loud conversations around us. "What if he hurt that guy? Or killed him? You're the only one who saw anything."

I look away. "I know." That's why I can't sleep.

Cory lifts a slice of bread on the sandwich and inserts a few potato chips. Something burning crawls up my throat and I swallow. My stomach is so empty it feels like it's on fire, but one bite into the pizza slice on my plate and I know I won't be able to get it down. I'm too afraid to say anything. What if no one believes me. Like last time. Then Wade would know I know...

Cory won't let it drop. "Do you know anything about what happened to the guy? Did he show up for work the next day?"

"He's off on Sunday. Willow said he should be back today."

"Willow." Cory's nose twitches.

"What?" I bury the pizza under a pile of napkins.

"I don't know why you went to a party with her in the first place." She stuffs the wrappings in her paper lunch bag and balls it up. She waves to some girls passing behind me, and when I turn, I see it's those perfect ones she hangs around with now. The yearbook staff and tennis team types.

"I went to the party because Willow was going to help me get a job. She at least is helping me, okay?"

Cory drops the sandwich. "Like I'm not?"

"I didn't say that."

I'm the first to look away. Again.

"And what happened to Willow, anyway? She was supposed to drive you home, right?"

"I don't know."

"Did she call? Say she was sorry? Ask if you were okay?"

"No. Okay? She didn't. But I texted her I got a ride, so maybe…" Maybe what?

Cory's eyebrows shoot up and almost disappear under her hair. "Maybe…? Maybe she met someone and forgot about you?"

My lips press together. My brain is struggling with words rolling around my skull like marbles. I get a hold of one, and another pings it away before I can say anything. I look at Cory's eyes. She's boring into my head. I look away and try to focus. I shake the slushy ice in my cup and suck on the straw.

"So why you busting on Willow so much?" I ask in as casual a voice as I can pull off.

Cory takes a big breath and lets it out. It makes me think of my mother before a lecture, so I'm already getting pissed at her before she even says one word.

Cory squirms in her seat. Whatever she's got to say is going to be hard for her, and I'm not going to give her one break.

I give her a hard look. "Go on."

"For one thing, she carries that notebook around with her all day and doesn't let anyone touch it. That's weird."

"I've read it." I still don't look at her. It's a lie, I've only glanced at a page with a horse drawn on it, but I want to shut her up. She's acting so superior.

It works.

"Yeah, she let me. She's told me she's working on the script for a computer game. It's really good." I push my congealed pizza slice farther away.

"Okay. So she also is a lot older than most of us in her class. Like she's stayed back or something. And she doesn't have any friends. You know." Her words trail off.

I look at my friend, and I wonder if I really know her. What does she really think about me if she judges Willow like that? I don't have to explain, but I do.

"Willow's dad is in the military. They moved a lot and she missed some school, that's why. When her mom died, he threw her out of the house. So, Cory, maybe Willow and me have more in common than me and you. And she's a really good dressage rider. You probably didn't know that, either." I check for a reaction.

Cory's eyes shift left. "That's a surprise."

"Yeah, well, maybe you shouldn't judge before you know anything."

She starts twirling a piece of hair. I know she's upset now. She twirls her hair when she's nervous. We're friends, we know these things about each other. I know that she likes to buy fancy underwear, usually purple, at Victoria's Secret, and she knows I would sell my soul for a Five Guys chocolate shake with peanut butter mixed in and whipped cream. We also know the scary things about each other, too. The dark stuff. The things we could use as weapons. If we weren't friends.

Something is still eating at her. She takes another breath and lets it out. She won't look at me, so I know I'm not going to like it.

"Regina, it's just that she has kind of a reputation." She lifts her hand to stop my reply. "I'm not saying I believe everything kids say, but…" A shrug. "She's weird, you have to admit it, and—"

"Weird?" I lean in and place my palms flat on the table. "Just like what you said about Declan, remember? But you know what?"

Cory sits back and folds her arms. "What?"

"Maybe they haven't had everything go their way, like your perfect friends." I wave at a table of girls. "Maybe they've got stuff you don't know about. Did you know Declan's mom is dead?"

Her face flushes. "Regina, I didn't mean—"

"And Willow lives at the farm where she works cuz her dad threw her out. Maybe that's why I don't judge them when everyone else says they're weird." My words roll out like a runaway train. My face flames, and my tongue is too big for my mouth. I suck on the straw, but nothing comes up. I don't know why I'm so mad. I don't know why I'm taking it out on my best friend. But I don't stop. "And"—I shake the cup at Cory—"she rides really tough horses there so she can show once in a while. She doesn't have anyone to just buy her a horse and hand it to her."

That does it. Cory's eyes narrow, and I know she's rolling my words around in her head. I can almost see them written in rotten black letters, floating in the air between us. She looks like she's been punched in the gut. I suck in air, sharp, wishing I could roll those words back into my mouth and swallow them.

Her voice is dark, icy. "Are you talking about Prophet?"

My head twitches, more to shake the thought out than to say no.

"Because I never asked my uncle to buy him. I didn't know anything about it."

I can fix this. I can save our friendship and make this go away, if I apologize. I can tell her I know, I'm sorry, I didn't mean it the way it came out. But the mean dark snake coiled in my gut won't let it go. Prophet was *my* horse. I did all the work, and she got all the glory. Some horrible child version of me takes over, and I lean back and cross my arms. "He was my horse."

"You mean, he was your mother's horse." Cory stabs a finger in my face. "And you *know* what she was going to do to him."

I know Cory's right. Angela was going to kill him for the insurance if she couldn't attract the big money buyers for him. I loved that horse. I got him through all the bad stuff, and I took care of him. A ring tightens around my throat. I feel the prick behind my eyes, and I can't cry. I can't. I sniff in air that smells like dirty dishes, and I just want to put my head down and cry. No one understands. I thought Cory did.

"I wanted to get him to Washington. Epiphany wasn't going to make it, so you took mine." The evil words spew out of my mouth, and the whole room shrinks down to Cory's face. Everything around her is a blur. I'm not sure, but she looks sad. She should be mad. She should be really mad at me and tell me I'm wrong and I'm selfish.

"I don't think I know you anymore." She stands up and snatches the balled-up paper bag.

I stand up and the room tilts. I haven't eaten. I grab the edge of the table. A flash of concern crosses her face.

"What's wrong with you?"

The bad kid, the evil black snake is still in control. I hate the bad me but I can't shut her up. She has to have the last word. "Well, maybe you never did."

I watch my best friend turn her back and walk away.

Chapter Fourteen

FOR SOME REASON, I EXPECT THE PRISON TO LOOK DIFFERENT THIS time. I don't know why it should, maybe because I'm different. But it's the same. I'm in the same strawberry-stinking car of Brenda's, and we're pulling into almost the same parking spot. We go through the same routine with the same security guard taking my cell phone and purse and doing a metal scan. We walk through the same doors and wait in the same hard, plastic chairs.

But one thing is different. We're three weeks closer to her release date.

Brenda pats my knee. "I'm glad you decided to come."

Like I had a choice. I smile and keep my mouth shut. This time I have a plan.

The door opens with a clang, and a jailer lady—a different one—steps in the room, followed by Angela. More changes: Today Angela's hair is freshly colored, so it has that metallic shine under the florescent lights. She tosses a sneer at the guard standing by the door before she sits down across from us.

"Regina, dear, it looks like my sister's a better cook than I remember. You've gained a little weight? Hmmm?" One eyebrow shoots up.

To a normal person, this sounds okay. But to my mother, gaining weight is a sign of weakness. She hates weakness almost as much as she hates overweight people. And overweight is anyone who doesn't look like a skeleton with some skin stretched over it.

"Don't worry. Aunt Sophia's doing a great job taking care of me."

I scramble to add something that will hit her hot buttons. "I especially like our dinners out at Burger Express. I usually order a double."

She gives a little shudder but keeps her cool. She's on her best behavior, but my plan is to make her explode. Let people see what she's really like.

Her voice is light, playful. "You tell my sister she had better make sure you get a nutritious dinner and not too much of the junk food." She looks at Brenda for the first time. "Isn't that right, Mrs.—"

She's forgotten Brenda's name.

"Brenda Schwartz. But you can call me Brenda. I assure you, Mrs. Hamilton, the agency is keeping Regina's best interests in mind at all times. Her home situation is closely monitored by myself or another caseworker."

Angela makes a noise like a cross between a harrumph and a sigh. Brenda has no doubt been dismissed from Angela's thoughts. Her eyes bore into mine instead. "I'm looking forward to having you home again, dear. I've got lots of ideas for the business, and I really need your help."

My first thought, only thought, is that I'm not going home with her. I won't live with her and Wade at the farm and I'm not helping with *the business*, even if it's legitimate this time. "What kind of help?" I say instead, cocking my head. Her eyebrows raise a fraction. Is that a hopeful look on her face? Then I whip out the dagger. "You know I don't have your skills for murdering horses."

A sharp intake of breath. From Brenda? Angela rears back in her chair as if slapped.

"That's in the past." Angela's words are flat, rehearsed.

"And what about Wade?"

"What about Wade?" Her voice is edgy, dark. She shifts a quick glance at Brenda.

I want Angela to suffer. I lean in and whisper. "You know."

Her face darkens.

Brenda's voice breaks into the dark cocoon of our stares. "Mrs. Hamilton, I think it would be advantageous for you to discuss your expectations for Regina with me, her caseworker, so that we can sort everything out. I'll continue to monitor her progress after your release, to make sure she is settling in to her new situation."

"My daughter's not a case. I've told you that." Her words drip acid.

"Of course not." Brenda sits back. "She is, however, my responsibility—"

"No." The word is loud in the tiny room.

Brenda blinks. She shakes her head in a nearly imperceptible motion as if she's trying to wake up. It's interesting to watch other people deal with Angela. They expect her to be rational. To follow certain rules. Fat chance.

"No, Mrs.—" Angela waves her hand when again she can't remember Brenda's name. "She's not your responsibility now or ever. She's mine. She is my daughter. She will come home with me. She will resume riding for our business, and she will follow my directions. Not yours."

The room is still.

I hear the guard shift her feet behind me. I wonder if she's got her hand on her gun.

"And you…" She leans forward and gets in my face. I force myself not to look down. "You will not mention the past to me again. I've paid for that mistake with my time here."

Brenda takes in a breath as if preparing to say something, but I beat her to it. I don't want Angela to calm down, to regain control. I want her to explode.

"Which mistake, Angela?" I'm treading on really thin ice. If this doesn't work, and they still send me to live with her… "You call dead horses *mistakes*? Do you mean the jumper we had that accidentally"— air quotes—"severed his tendon in the field just after we found out he had navicular changes? He was insured for a ton of money. Or was it another *mistake*? Like Norton, maybe."

Brenda doesn't know anything about the other horses Angela had killed. She probably doesn't have any idea what I'm talking about, but Angela does. Red blotches explode up her neck, racing across her orangey tan face. I'm not supposed to know the story of how she swapped horses and killed a stand-in for the insurance money. How she betrayed Vee, her best friend, stole her farm, and crushed all her dreams. Angela grips the edge of the table. Her mouth opens and shuts. Now she knows I know, and there's no turning back. Her chest rises and falls. Still, she doesn't say anything. I wait.

Brenda's voice is steady. Her counselor voice. "Let's get back on track with what concerns us now—the future. The past is the past and we have to move on."

Damn. She had to pick now to find her backbone and take charge.

Angela releases a breath. She sits back in her chair. "Yes, I agree, Mrs. Schwartz."

Now she remembers her name. She's not taking the bait.

"Regina will likely have a lot of emotions to work through. That's what I'm here for. To help both of you navigate through them." Brenda's soft hand covers mine. I shoot her a cross look. She's ruining everything.

"It will be fine. Once she's home with me again, everything will fall into place." Angela has that scary smug look on her face again. She's back in control, and she's counting on controlling me. "Won't it, dear?"

I can't open my mouth to answer. There's a concrete brick on my chest, and no air is getting in. Angela probably knows what I was doing, and it didn't work. She'll make me pay for it as soon as she can.

Angela turns to Brenda. "I'm not worried about Regina. She's just like me, impulsive. Perhaps a bit too emotional as well. But we'll work on that."

I'm not just like you. I could never be like you.

The guard calls time. We all stand. It's over. We're leaving. They're going to send me home with her in a few months. A scream forms in the back of my throat that I have to swallow.

"I see your hair is growing out some finally," she says, eyeing my head. "Thank goodness, Regina, we can't have you looking like a man!" A little laugh. "Whatever got into you to cut off all your beautiful hair?" Angela's hand, wrinkled and heavily veined, betrays her age. It reaches out, then stops and drops to her side.

My head droops. I stare at the floor, watching my feet as we retrace our steps out of the prison. Outside the air has turned cooler. Brenda's passenger door creaks open and I get in. The plastic seat is cold and I have to pee.

"I'm not living with her."

Brenda turns the key and backs out of the parking lot without a word. She must think I'm a broken record.

I study Brenda's profile. "You don't know her."

"Then tell me."

Brenda drives down the road until she spots a donut shop and pulls in. It's late. The sun is sinking behind the strip mall, so inside the shop is empty, but the warm haze of sugar and grease coats the air. I head to the restroom, and when I get back, Brenda's seated in the last booth with two Styrofoam cups of coffee. She pushes one across the table to me.

"Tell me what's going on. Now. So I can help you."

I don't know where to begin. I have a million thoughts, flashes of memory, running in front of my eyes like a film projector on fast-forward. Brenda cups her hands around the coffee but doesn't take a sip.

"Okay, here's an example," I start. "When I was a kid, I always asked her where my dad was, you know, what happened to him. She told me different stories depending on how old I was. In middle school, I really started bugging her about this and wanted to know his name. I had some idea I might find him and see if I could go live with him. To escape. My birth certificate said his name was Cedric Glasgow. I imagined he was from Scotland. Maybe he was a Grand Prix rider that my mom met at the shows. I built up this whole person who never existed." I sip the coffee. It's scalding hot and burnt tasting.

"What do you mean?" Brenda shifts in her seat.

"She made him up. She tells me later that it was a fake name. She picked two names of famous horses on the jumper circuit and said that was his name. It was a joke. I have a fake-name joke for a father. Then she told me she did it because he had no right to me. Whoever the real he was. She said I was all hers, and she never even told him I existed, and never would."

Brenda presses her temples. "I'm sorry, Regina. Legally, there isn't much we can do." Her mouth becomes a flat line.

"That's not the point. Yeah, it would be great if I could find him, but I've given up on that fantasy. The point is, she thinks she owns me. I'm like property to her. She controls everything I do, any friends I have, what classes I take in school—"

"Some parents, especially single parents, can be more controlling because they feel as if all the responsibility is on them alone. You—"

"No, you don't get it." I push my coffee aside before I spill it. "I'm her *project*. When I don't measure up, there are consequences. That's what she calls them." I'm biting down on my bottom lip. It gives me a second. Long enough to get the words right. I can't look at Brenda's face when I say it. "She broke my collarbone once. When I was eleven. She was giving me a jumping lesson on my pony, and she thought I wasn't listening. I wasn't riding up to her expectations. When I stopped, she walked up to me, pulled me out of the saddle, and threw me on the ground. I heard it pop. Everything got sparkly and I threw up. When I couldn't move my arm or get up, she dialed the hospital, but before anyone answered she looked down at me and said that's what I get for disobeying. For not trying hard enough. 'I made you all by myself,' she said. 'And I can put an end to you just as easily. Remember that.' It was her right, she said. Her *right*."

Brenda swallows hard. "She said that?"

I nod. I feel a little weight shift off my chest. "That was the *first* time."

Chapter Fifteen

TEN DAYS OF WORKING AT TWIN ELMS WITH WILLOW AND I'VE YET to sit on a horse. Eddie has me working in the mare barn, bringing them in, feeding, and cleaning tack. I've hinted around that I can ride, too, but she usually just laughs and hands me a new chore to do, like scrubbing out the water troughs. I miss riding. I miss Cory. But after what I said to her, there's no chance I'll be going over to her barn ever again. And I can't blame her for unfriending me. I essentially told her she wasn't as good a rider as me and the only reason she got to show on the indoor circuit was because someone bought her a really cool horse. My horse.

Nice job, Regina.

That's not my only problem. Now I'm tanking English because I haven't read the stupid book—*Call of the Wild*—so here I am after school with Willow again. Extra help, Mr. Curtis calls it. We're supposed to be writing an essay on the themes in the story, but Willow is scribbling in her notebook. Her nose is almost on the page. I look down at the book and read a paragraph. Right away, I don't remember what I just read and close the cover.

"Hey." I scoot closer to Willow while keeping my eye on the teacher. Willow glances up. "Did Trey come back yet?"

She shakes her head and bends over her notebook again. Since she lives there, and I'm only working a few days a week, I figured she would know more.

"Did anyone hear from him?"

She pulls out a blank piece of paper and her pen scratches across the paper.

I flip open *Call of the Wild*, resolved to read it, and bend over to fish a pen out of my backpack. A slip of paper appears between the pages that I swear wasn't there two seconds ago. I pull it out slowly. The words on the top say: DESTROY AFTER READING. There are about a million exclamation points afterward. It's written in fat, rounded letters. Willow's handwriting. I hold it in my lap under the desk and scan the message:

T never showed up, but his horse is still there. Mr. Sympathetic says he's sending him to the auction next week if T doesn't show. We were told not to talk about it.

I look at Willow, and she dips her head in a small nod. Her hair falls over her face, and she doesn't brush it away. I rip the note into a gazillion pieces and stuff them in a pocket. I wish Willow had seen what I did that night. I wish someone, anyone else saw Wade with Trey and would tell. Someone besides me. Someone who Wade couldn't get to. And if Trey *is* okay somewhere, why doesn't he come back? It doesn't make sense. Trey loved Tucker. He would never abandon him. Someone at Twin Elms must have checked the hospital or police station by now. So how come no one knows anything? The chicken wrap I had for lunch starts climbing up my throat.

I swallow and suck in air. The classroom is hot. The clock is ticking too loud, and I hate the smell of the dry erase marker the teacher is using to write the class assignments on the board. I shrug out of my jacket and drape it over the back of the chair. When I spin around again, there's another note stuck in the pages of my book.

E needs you to work tomorrow. Heard she's going to teach you to ride Eleganz. You're taking Trey's place.

Chapter Sixteen

THE SUN IS GOING DOWN BEHIND THE TREES WHEN WILLOW AND I finally get out of after-school English help. A gust of wind sends leaves and a Styrofoam cup through the empty parking lot. Willow turns long enough to wave and say, "Don't forget tomorrow," before she gets in her car and drives off. My phone pings. It's Aunt Sophie.

Called in to work. Hope you can catch a ride home. Left a frozen mac and cheese for you. Sorry!

I'm getting ready to text back that I don't have a ride home and it will be dark soon, when I spot someone leaning against the wall by the Dumpsters. He's wearing a woolen hat and camo jacket. Declan. A flood of relief is accompanied by little birdwing flutters against my ribcage. I send mental signals telling it to stop.

His face is red from the cold. "Hey, Reggie. Need a ride?" He pushes off the wall.

How does he know? Was he waiting for me? I heft my backpack onto a shoulder and walk over. "Sure, but you don't have to."

"I don't have to do anything." He flashes a smile and starts walking across the lot.

"It's just that I don't want you to think I'm just using you for rides."

His thick-soled boots clomp in the still air. I struggle to keep up, hiking the backpack up onto my shoulder.

"I don't care if you are." He stops and looks me right in the eyes. A spray of faded freckles run across the bridge of his nose. There's a soft, reddish sheen of a beard along his chin and up under his jawline, like he didn't shave it quite evenly.

He doesn't move.

Am I supposed to say something? My nose starts to run from the cold. "It's just that I'm not a user, you know. I like you—you're a friend, and not just because you give me rides…"

God, I sound like an idiot. Crinkles around his blue eyes deepen when he smiles. A crooked canine gives him a wolfish look, and I get this flash that if I could take that stupid hat off his head and dress him in some normal clothes, he'd be really hot looking in a Prince Harry sort of way.

"Where's your truck?"

"Over there." He points to the far side of the lot. "And on the way you can tell me what else you like about me besides the rides. I'd like to know."

My face flames. I touch it with a cold hand and walk ahead. I can never tell if he's kidding. He opens the passenger door for me, then gets in. The truck smells like disinfectant and mint. I kick my backpack away from my feet, and a little leather cup with a tassel on it rolls against my foot.

"Oh, good, you found it." Declan leans over me to retrieve the leather thingie. For a brief second, his body is heavy and warm against my thighs. "I've been looking for that." He strokes the tassel between two fingers and surveys it for damage.

"What is it?"

"Rosie's hood. It's her favorite one. I lost it last time we were out."

"Rosie? The bird? She has more than one little hat?"

"It's not a hat." His mouth turns down a bit as he tosses the hood in the glove box. "I can explain, but only if you're really interested. My dad says not to bore people with falconry stuff."

"Sure. I'm interested." Not sure I sound convincing.

One eyebrow scrunches. A side of his mouth lifts and makes a little dimple on his cheek. "You are not. But that's okay."

He puts the truck in gear, and we roll away from the school in silence. I tug my phone out of my jacket pocket. "I'm just letting my aunt know I got a ride after all. She got called in to work. Can't wait to heat up that delicious frozen dinner she left me."

"Come home with me. It's Wednesday, so we're having spaghetti and meatballs."

"I really shouldn't," I tell him.

"Why not?"

No one's home at my house. I shrug. "Right. Why not? Thanks."

As soon as Declan opens the door, the two labs bound out, beating thick tails against our legs. Inside, he shrugs out of his camo jacket, hangs it on a coat tree, and bends over to pet the dogs.

"Hey, Thornton. What have you and Buck been up to?"

My mouth drops when I realize where I've heard those names before. "Like *Call of the Wild*?" That book is haunting me.

He pulls off his hat, leaving spikes of hair floating around his head in a static-charged red halo. "Yeah, I read it the year we got them as puppies. I got to pick their names, so..." A shrug.

He holds his hand out, waiting to take my coat. I drop my backpack at my feet and struggle out of it. The house is warm and smells of wood smoke and garlic. The interior is almost exactly how I pictured it would be—one big room all made of rough wood panels. A dark leather sofa and armchair are grouped around a stone fireplace in the center of the back wall. Every surface is covered with papers, books, and notebooks. A laptop is partially visible between the cushions at the end of the couch.

Declan grabs my hand. "C'mon in." The hand, dry and warm, holds mine for an instant, then gone, leaving a tingling feeling on my fingers. A clatter of dishes comes from an adjoining room, and something drops on the floor.

"Dad, I'm home. I brought Regina with me."

A man wearing a cardigan sweater with leather buttons, some of them missing, appears in the doorway. He's holding a big spoon, dripping something red onto the floor. His hair is sticking up on one side, like he just got out of bed. "Who's Regina?"

Declan hooks a thumb at me. "She is." He doesn't offer any more of an explanation. I stand behind Declan, hoping to go invisible if this is a problem.

Declan fishes around for something in his coat pocket. "I said she can have dinner with us."

Declan's dad walks over, switches the drippy spoon to his left hand and holds out the other. "Of course. Welcome." Before I can say anything, he spins on his heels and disappears in the kitchen. A minute later, he rushes back with an extra place setting, fumbling with the silverware, setting it down wrong.

"Regina? Right, your name's Regina?" His eyes are bright blue like Declan's. "That means queen. Did you know that?" His eyebrows rise. They're dark and thick with sprouts of hair going in all directions. He's still looking at me, with the eyebrows up, crinkling his forehead. He wants me to answer him?

"Names mean a lot to Dad." Declan saves me. "He says people's names are important because they shape their lives. That names say something about them. Animals, too."

Declan's dad is nodding. "Yes. Names have power."

What the hell does that mean? I think about my name and frown. Angela picked it, not me. "Yeah, but it's not like we pick our own names." I clamp my mouth shut. Maybe I've insulted him, arguing about his name thing already. But instead he smiles at me like I've said something brilliant.

"That's right. You may not have selected the name, but the cosmos did. Your name was already picked out for you, no matter who signed the birth certificate. According to legend, the namer possesses authority over the one named."

Again, I think of Angela, and I don't like anything he's saying.

"But I haven't given you my name." He thrusts out his hand again. Mine disappears inside his large, dry grasp. He holds on and lays his other hand over both. "Aldwin Kendrick, Professor of Mythology, specialist in ancient Celtic Studies. By the way, in Old English, Aldwin means old friend or some such translation. But I prefer Al." He lets my hand free. "One must consider carefully when giving a living creature its name. In the Old Testament, God gave Adam that task. It's not to be taken lightly."

"Declan means 'full of goodness' in Gaelic." Declan smirks.

His dad looks at the place setting and switches the positions of the knife and spoon. "His mom gave him that name. Insisted on it."

The fire pops and a log shifts, sending up a spray of sparks.

"I got to check on Rosie," Declan says. "And feed the horse. You want to come?"

Even though I'm scared to death of his stupid hawk, getting to see the horse again is worth it. "Sure."

"Take the dogs!" his dad orders. The labs run to the door.

We grab coats, and I'm almost knocked over by Buck rushing through the door. It's getting dark. The dogs take off after something in the yard and I follow on Declan's heels down a flagstone path across the yard to a pasture gate. A few yards away, a weak light leaks from under the open barn door. I hurry to catch up with Declan, who has disappeared inside. When I step through the doors, I'm hit with the familiar smells of hay and horses.

"Thanks for waiting," I say.

Declan misses the sarcasm. He's scooping grain from an aluminum trashcan and pouring it into a bucket. The barn is small but clean. Everything is tucked neatly into corners or hung up. There are three stalls, only one with bedding. Each has a door to the outside and another that opens up to the center aisle. The feed room is just inside the door.

"You want me to get her for you?" I ask, picking up a halter and lead rope.

"Nah, she just comes in." He dumps the grain in the stall's feed bucket and opens the outside door to the pasture and calls, "Red! C'mon, dinner!"

His breath sends a cloud of white, sparkling mist into the darkness. At the sound of galloping hoof beats, Declan runs back through the stall to the aisle and slides shut the inside door. The latch slams closed just as the red mare materializes, her nostrils flaring. She gives us one stern look, then dives into her feed bucket.

"You think she's okay to eat?" I ask. "She seems a little jazzed up."

Declan picks up the empty bucket. "She's always like that." He walks back to the feed room and measures out a ration for the morning. "She's a monster."

The mare has her nose in the bucket, but one eye follows every move I make. "Don't worry, girl, I'm not going to take your dinner." I wait until she's finished and is pulling at a rack of hay before I reach my hand in to stroke her neck. Her long coat is still crusted with mud. In the light it looks like she's a bright red chestnut when she isn't filthy. She may also have a small white sock in front—it's hard to tell—but definitely has two stockings on each rear leg. Her mane is twisted in dreadlocks, studded with debris.

I reach to scratch a place near her shoulder, and she leans into my hand, hard. She stops pulling at the hay, but keeps one eye on me. I pull back my arm and lift the latch on her door.

"What are you doing?" Declan appears with an armful of hay.

"I want to pet her, but I can't reach—"

"You can't do that." He steps in front of her door. "You can't go in. With her."

My hand drops from the latch. "What are you talking about?" I feel my head tilt, my face scrunched.

"You can't trust her. Really." He tosses the hay over the wall into her hayrack.

"You mean no one ever handles her?"

He leans against the wall and watches the mare. His Adam's apple bobs as he swallows one, two times. His voice is low.

"When we have to, we do. Like for the vet and stuff. Generally, I just let her in and feed her. When she goes back out, I close the outer door and clean her stall."

"It's clear no one brushes her." I hand him the halter, but he doesn't look at me. "That's horrible." I lift the latch and slide the stall door open a few inches. His eyes lift to take in what I'm doing. I expect him to tell me to stop, but he doesn't.

"Just be careful, okay?" His eyes catch mine. "I don't trust her."

I wait for the mare to move so she's facing me before I take a step closer. She shifts, and standing next to her, I realize she's tall. A lot taller than I thought. Maybe sixteen three hands or more. The scent of wet earth hangs on her body. Her eye is dark, wary. Furry ears flip back, forward. I hold my hand palm up and she sniffs it. Her mouth moves against my empty palm, and her thick tongue swipes it once. "Do you have a treat to give her?"

Declan pulls his gloves off and searches a pocket. "These?" he asks, holding up a roll of foil-wrapped candy.

"Perfect." I break two free and hold them out for her. "Give me a brush."

"Reggie—"

"It's okay. Trust me."

"It's not you I have a problem with." Declan hands me a soft brush and leans against the doorframe.

"If you don't want her, why don't you just sell her? She's a nice horse."

He shrugs.

"What're her blood lines? She's Oldenburg, right?" I note the brand on her flank as I run the brush along her shoulder. The mare stands still, but her eye stays on me.

"Yeah, something like that."

"We can look it up. What's her registered name?"

Declan steps away from the door. I turn and ask again, expecting he didn't hear me. "I know some sites where we can look up her breeding. If you want—"

"I don't know her name."

"It'll be on her papers."

"Yeah, well, maybe Dad has them."

"So, ask your dad what her real name is."

"I told you, he won't tell me."

The mare head butts me. When I don't offer her any more treats, she goes back to her hayrack. "What do you mean Professor Names-Are-Important won't tell you the mare's name? What's with that?"

Declan frowns.

I slip out of the stall and slide the door shut. "I mean, that's kind of strange." A shrug. "Considering…"

"I know." He moves the box of brushes and settles on a pile of hay bales. "It's cuz of my mom." He sighs and picks at the hay. "Dad hasn't been right since she died."

I wonder what *right* means, but keep quiet for a change. Instead, I make him scoot over on the hay so I can sit down.

"She was sick a long time, but in the end, it was still a big shock for him, like he didn't believe it was really going to happen." He lifts his head. The end of his nose is red. He pulls out strands of hay and tosses them on the floor. "Dad was a professor. He taught at a university in Dublin, where he met Mom. She taught in the Biology Department."

"So your mother wasn't a mythology professor, too?"

He laughs and shakes his head. "God, no. Ma was a scientist. Black and white, evidence and proof. She's the one who introduced me to falconry, though."

He stops plucking at the hay and his hands rest on his thighs.

"But when she died a few years ago, Dad stopped teaching a lot of his classes. Then, after a year or so, he didn't go back at all. He had a bunch of jobs in colleges here in Maryland, but one he said was too far to be worth the pay and another he said the head of the department was a moron. By last year he didn't have a teaching job anywhere. He did some online stuff, then that…well, I'm not sure if he got fired or what. Dad's kind of a perfectionist about things, like, he has to dou-ble-check everything. Very OCD. Maybe he drove people crazy, I don't know." He looks off into a dark corner of the barn. "Now he spends most of his time writing articles for what he calls scholarly journals. I guess they pay him for it. Means he doesn't have to leave the farm anymore."

"Why doesn't he want to leave?"

He hops off the hay and brushes off his pants. "Not sure. Just makes him nervous to go places, he says. Crowds, open spaces, a lot of stuff makes him nervous. Once he was at the supermarket when he started shaking and couldn't find the exit. He called me to come get him. Never went back. Didn't go out again. Ever."

My hand barely touches his jacket between his shoulders. He turns away. I press and feel his breath. "Because of your mom, you think?"

His shoulders hunch. Shaking me off? My hand drops. My face heats up against the cold and it's my turn to look away. Did I go too far? The warmth of his hands grasping both of mine shoots through my fingers, my hands, up my arms. He pulls me off the hay and his arms go around my waist, pressing against me. His breath is hot against my neck, contrasting with the frigid air of the barn. His voice is deep, thick. Words rumble, vibrating against my chest.

"I don't know what's wrong, Reg. He won't leave the house, and he won't tell anyone the name Mom gave the red mare. He says it's a test. A very weird test."

His voice breaks and he won't look at me. Instead, his hand slides up my back and cups my head. Fingers tug at a curl. I don't dare move. I don't even shift my weight. He takes a deep breath, and I feel his lips near the top of my ear.

"When Mom was dying, she asked him to sell her horse. She gave him the name of trainers who would help sell Red, but Dad didn't listen. He said he'd know when the right person turned up."

"How?" The word is barely a whisper.

Declan huffs and pulls away. "He said because they'd know her name. It's stupid, I know." He picks up the mare's halter and places it on a hook.

A million questions run through my head, but I'm learning to keep my mouth shut.

Declan's mouth twitches. "The power of names, remember?" He bows his head and shakes it slowly back and forth. "He says the mare is a *Fiolair*—a seventh filly born to a mare who was also a seventh mare. She's magic. She'll protect her rider, her true owner, he says. Irish legend. I think he actually believes all that mythology stuff he's studied." He scoffs. "When Ma knew she wasn't getting better, she told him to cut the crap and just find the poor mare a good home."

"Your dad must have loved her a lot."

Declan sighs. "Yeah. A lot. So much, he couldn't sell her mare. And now he's waiting for a sign."

"A sign? Like, from the grave?" I shove my hands deep in my pockets. My feet are numb from the cold. "What kind of sign?"

He looks up at the red mare. "From the horse gods."

Chapter Seventeen

ECLAN WIPES HIS PLATE WITH A PIECE OF CRUSTY BREAD. HIS EARS, red from the overheated room, stick out like autumn leaves against his pale face. A tiny dot of spaghetti sauce marks the very center of his chin. I don't tell him it's there but make some exaggerated swipes across my mouth with the napkin.

"I think Queen Regina is trying to tell you you've got something on your face, son." Declan's dad spears a mini tomato out of the wooden salad bowl. He pops it in his mouth and chews one-sided, like a horse. "Another thing. Do we have to endure that vulture staring over at us every meal?" He points his fork at Rosie, perched in the corner of the room.

After feeding the hawk, Declan had carried her into the house.

"It's part of her training," he explains. "She has to get used to all kinds of situations."

"Like dinner parties?" His dad winces like he's stepped on a Lego with bare feet.

"We could put her hat on her," I say. "Then she wouldn't be able to watch us."

"Hood." Declan's ears flame redder. He's told me already about a million times it's a hood. Hoods are used to cover the hawk's eyes and keep them calm, especially when transporting them to new surroundings. I still think they look like little hats or helmets.

"I like the hood with the sticking-up feather," I say, hoping for a laugh. "It's appropriate for formal dinners."

Mr. Kendrick guffaws. "You're a sharp one." He wags a finger at me.

Declan smirks a crookedy smile. "I'll get Rosie's formal wear out of storage for our next dinner." He pushes his plate away and leans back, a hand resting on his stomach. "That was great, Dad."

"There's more in the kitchen. Regina?" Mr. Kendrick half rises from his chair. "Would you like some more?"

"No." I signal stop with my hand, and he freezes in midair. "Thank you, but I'm really stuffed." My plate is wiped clean.

Dinner is over. I wonder if Declan will drive me straight home. Rosie rustles her feathers. I'm warm and sleepy and I don't want to go. Not yet. I want to know more about the red mare.

I raise my eyes to find Declan's staring at me from across the table.

"Regina brushed Red Mare tonight." Declan turns to his father, seated at the head of the table.

Mr. Kendrick places his coffee cup down in slow motion. They both look at me like I'm about to turn into the Blue Fairy or something.

"Yeah, no problem. She was fine." I back up the casual tone with a one-shoulder shrug. "She was really dirty. Besides, I wanted to see how many white socks she had." I figure I've got to explain the white socks thing to two guys who don't know horses. "There's this old saying about the number of socks on a horse. It goes, one white leg buy him, two white legs try him, three—"

"White legs sell him to your foes," Mr. Kendrick chimes in. "Four white legs, feed him to the crows. My wife taught me that one. Always made her laugh. Red Mare has two whites." Suddenly the smile melts and his face droops.

I figure it's the memories—Red Mare and his wife. Maybe I shouldn't have brought it up. My eyes search Declan's face for a sign that everything is okay. He rolls his lips in and looks off into the corner of the room, at Rosie. Great. I'm feeling really awkward, but then Declan's dad seems to shake off whatever he was thinking and smiles.

He takes a big gulp of coffee. "There are lots of myths and superstitions about horses," he says and leans back in his chair.

Declan slumps. "Dad, I have to take Regina home soon."

"What kind of superstitions?" I cut him off.

Mr. Kendrick scoots forward and plants his elbows on the table, his hands clasped in front of him. "All the horse cultures admired the animal's strength, valued its contributions to warfare and commerce, but the Celts more so than any other people. Celtic horses of legend could move over land or water. The fierce water horses, the Kelpies, could lure men to their death in the sea. Some horses were magic, able to traverse both the world of the living and the dead. Others could change form from horse to human and back again. The ancients of that island worshipped the horse. They were gods."

"The horse gods." The words leave my lips before I know it.

Declan shoots me a glance. A warning?

Mr. Kendrick unclasps his hands and grips the edge of the table. "Gods indeed."

I hold my breath, hoping he continues.

He pushes back in his seat. His eyes, intense under the crazy dark eyebrows, make me think of Rosie's. It's like he can see all the stories and all the people he's talking about.

The fire snaps.

His voice rumbles on. "The ancient people were protected by the horse gods, according to legend, but eventually they all turned their backs on them in the end. All except one man."

"Who?" I want to hear the story. "Why didn't he give up, too?"

"Where do I start?" He opens his hands, palms up. "Such a long story and such a short night we have."

I don't want the spell to be broken. It is a spell, coasting along on a wisp of smoke, circling the room before it's sucked out under the door into the cold. Mr. Kendrick's face glows pink across the cheeks and the tip of his nose. I wonder if he's got something extra in his coffee mug—that would be the case in my family—or if he's just excited talking about this stuff.

"Start with the part where the horse saves Nuallan." Declan stands and clears the plates off the table. "That's the good part, anyway, and I have to take Regina home before midnight."

When he disappears in the kitchen, Mr. Kendrick leans toward me. His eyes are shining, red rimmed. A whiff of garlic reaches my nose.

"Are you a Celt?" A quick nod to my hair. "You're a true red, like my Declan."

I touch my hair. It's getting longer now. I scrunch up my shoulders and let them drop in a dramatic gesture. "I have no idea."

"That's a shame. You should know. It's said people with red hair have a higher tolerance for pain than any other people. It was a survival skill for the ancient Celts, the warriors." One eyebrow arches. Just one. "No idea, huh?"

He doesn't ask why I don't know. I like that about him. He perks up. "No matter, I'm sure you are. So, I'll tell you the story of your people."

My people. That's a weird thought, that I have people. That I'm part of a larger group beyond my insane mom, mysterious father, and alcoholic aunt. Declan returns from the kitchen and goes over to check on Rosie, who looks like she's sleeping. The fire has burned down to just a glow, and I glance longingly at the couch. I wish I could lie down, have someone tuck an afghan around me and sit at my feet, telling stories. I want to hear all about my people and their horses until I fall asleep.

"We have about half an hour before we got to go, Dad, okay?" Declan's voice from across the room scatters my thoughts.

"Where was I?" Mr. Kendrick looks up, confused.

I don't think he ever started, but I tell him he was at the part with the guy and the horse.

"Right! As you know, at the time the country had been at war for decades. The people had lost their way and had stopped worshipping the horse gods. They had turned to the gods of their enemies. As a result, the king of all the gods sent a mighty flood to wipe out the cities and villages of the ungrateful people—the very people the gods had vowed always to protect."

"Sounds like the Noah's Ark story." I clap a hand over my mouth, afraid he'll be mad I interrupted him. Instead he winks.

"There was one man, however, who had remained faithful, who continued to trust the horse gods even though their cities were being overrun by the enemy and they had suffered starvation for years. This man refused to bow to the enemy's gods. His name was Nuallan." He taps his index finger against his cheek. "As I recall, that's ancient Irish for noble or famous. Anyway, the water rose and swept over the seawalls. It washed away the people, their homes, their animals, even the horses. And yet, the water kept rising. Nuallan ran through the town, calling to people to follow him to the highest hill and to appeal to the horse gods to save them, but they didn't listen. They cowered in their homes, clutching the statues of the false gods and praying to the very ones who were bringing their destruction. By the afternoon of the flood the skies had turned dark. The cold seawater breathed a thick mist into the air, which blurred all the earth as far as the eye could see. Nuallan, with the last shred of his strength, made it to the top of the mount and cried out to the leader of the horse gods, 'Airdri! High King! Have mercy on your servant!'"

Declan appears beside me like a shadow and quietly pulls out the chair to sit down. Under the table, a finger hooks mine. He gives me a sideways glance. I open my hand, and it's enveloped in the warmth of his. Declan's dad stares into the dying fire.

"Does Nuallan die?" I ask. "Does Airdri save him?"

"Huh?" He shakes himself, maybe shaking off whatever he was thinking. "No! No. This is the best part." His eyes go wide. "As the frigid waters rise higher, above his knees, to his chest, freezing his blood, Nuallan fights to stay conscious. He shouts to Airdri, King of the horse gods, until his voice is nothing but a whisper. He prays on, trusting in the promise of the King's protection. A promise made to his people centuries ago. The water reaches his neck, and in the cold he senses his mind failing. The whole world is swirling white and silver—the sea foam, the mist, the gray sky. All he can hear is a roar from the waves and the roar of blood in his ears as all sense leaves his body. His head dips and slips under. The cold, like needles, shoots stabbing pain through his eyes, and he thrashes to the surface, struggling, praying. It is then through the mist he sees something move. Or did he? Everything is gray. The waves splash against his cheek, slapping him with pain. The figure comes closer. The mist parts around it, and Nuallan sees it is a horse—a silver horse—swimming toward him. The horse comes close and turns its back to Nuallan. With stiff fingers, red from the cold, he grasps the ropey long mane and clambers onto its back. The horse swings its head around and nudges his leg before he starts swimming—no!—somehow galloping over the water. Nuallan entwines both hands in its mane to hold on as they ride to safety."

Mr. Kendrick sits back. A satisfied smile spreads across his face.

"That's it?" I ask. "How do they get out of the flood? And what happens to Nuallan if, like, all his people are dead and everything?"

"Oh that's far from the end." He lays a hand on my arm. "But it's getting late and Declan tells me he has to see you home." He glances at Declan, who nods. "Come back again, and I'll tell you more of the story. You might like the part where Nuallan learns to see the future by peering through the horse's ears."

Declan stands and lifts Rosie from her perch. "That would be a handy trick. Reggie, hand me Rosie's *hat* so I can put her back."

Hat. I catch his eye and have to smile back.

Then the smile melts. Would it be great to see the future? I'm not so sure.

Chapter Eighteen

I HAVE TO MEET WITH BRENDA ONCE A WEEK, SHE SAYS, ACCORDING TO state law as part of Angela's early release program. I've decided, since the donut shop talk, that she's not as useless as I first thought. Aunt Sophia drops me off at the office building in downtown Columbia—where everything looks alike—and promises to be back in an hour. I walk in and it hits me. Brenda's office is not what I expected. I mean, it doesn't look like her at all. Color-splashed modern art covers the walls, and the furniture is space-age trendy, all black vinyl and sharp edges. But there's one thing in here that is definitely Brenda—the blast of over-heated air has a distinct strawberry scent.

I sit in the chair facing her desk. She holds up one finger to wait and turns back to her computer. It gives me time to check out the diploma on the wall behind her—Johns Hopkins University. Brenda's wearing a rumpled oxford shirt with a tiny whale on it and her hair's messed up like she just rolled out of bed. When she finishes typing, she whips off a pair of sparkly purple reading glasses and lets them drop on the end of a chain. If she gives me any touchy-feely advice about forgiving Angela, I'm ready for it. I've even got a smart answer ready.

"Regina, what you said last time was of great concern. I've contacted the Child Protective Services and looked into options—hypothetically, you understand—for your care until you reach the age of majority."

I sit bolt upright.

She holds up her hand in a stop sign. "I'm having your files reviewed, and I mean all of your files, including medical records dating back several years in order to prepare a case if need be before family court. But I'm not promising anything. The records *may* show a suspicious enough pattern to cause concern. But, I must emphasize, I'm not promising anything."

"I get it. The records won't mean anything when Angela explains that I grew up on a horse farm and of course I'd have broken bones and injuries." I mock Angela's tone, "It's to be expected, Your Honor, it's a rough sport."

Brenda shuffles some papers on her desk. "There'd be additional testimony."

"Whose testimony? Do I have to say something? In front of her?" I despise the tiny quiver in my voice.

"Don't worry about that now. Let me ask you this: at any time were the police called to your home?"

A hangnail on my thumb demands my attention. My stomach clenches like someone put a cold clothespin on it. When the cops came. That night. I don't look at Brenda. "Yeah," I tell her. "But not sure there's any record of it." I check her face.

"Why's that?" Her pen hovers over a piece of notepaper.

"No one was arrested in the end."

She brushes away a strand of hair. "Might still be a record if the police were called. Why don't you tell me what happened." Her eyes catch mine. I look away.

"You can't take notes. You can't write any of this down."

She drops the pen. "Okay, no notes."

"And you can't tell anyone. You have to promise." My whole body leans toward her on the word *promise*, begging her to understand.

She hesitates, then whispers one word. "Promise."

I sink back into my seat. I don't know where to start. I curl a leg up under me and slide sideways in the chair—that way I can rest my head against the back and not have to look at anything but the wall. I've never told anyone this. Even Angela doesn't know the whole story. I can't find the opening, the words that will start it. My mouth opens and shuts like a landed fish. When I shift, the chair squeaks.

"Take your time, Regina. To start out, tell me how old you were."

"Eleven. I remember because it was almost my birthday."

Brenda's voice is calm, like she's talking to a spooky Thoroughbred. She is, I guess, because that's exactly how I'm thinking. Bolting for the door is a good option. She asks if the incident was in our home.

"At the farm, yeah. Wade, Angela's boyfriend, was there to treat a client's horse that had colic. It's bad when horses get it," I explain to her. "They can twist a gut and die."

"Horrible."

"Yeah, well, there's some worse things." I suck in a ragged breath. "The client, a guy who boarded his horse with us, was always complaining about stuff. Plus he was late with his board payment, so even though his horse was sick, he had Angela really pissed off. The two of them were having a big fight when Wade showed up. The boarder, his name was James, was threatening to call animal control on Angela. He accused her of not feeding his horse any hay. Said she caused the colic. When Wade walked in, James had Angela backed up against the stall and was screaming in her face. Angela screamed back pretty good, too. The poor horse. A girl who worked at our farm back then, Penny, was holding the horse in his stall, keeping him on his feet."

I look over and Brenda nods. The heat kicks on. I shift my eyes back to the windows and watch the dust float in the sunbeams for a while. My heart's beating in the base of my throat. I will my voice to stay steady for the next part.

"Penny was great. She was so nice. When Angela yelled at me for doing something wrong or riding bad, Penny would pull me aside later and tell me I did okay. She gave me stuff, like earrings she said she didn't want anymore. Besides, she was a great farm manager and really knew the horses. Knew all their habits, food, allergies, things they liked, didn't like."

A burning ring clamps around my throat, and my vision blurs. "Anyway, when Wade showed up, James backed off from Angela real quick, and she disappeared into her office. The horse was looking bad. His head was hanging low, and he was all sweated up from the pain. When Wade went in the stall, I heard Penny filling him in on the horse's vitals—temperature and respiration. That's when I went down to the other end of the barn to the feed room to set up for the evening. I wasn't there long when I heard banging on wood, solid, like a horse kicking the hell out of his stall. I figured James's horse had gone down and was thrashing around. I ran out to see if there was anything I could do to help.

"That's when I saw James take a swing at Wade. They were in the aisle. Penny was in the stall, crying. Angela came running from the office, from the opposite direction. Wade blocked the punch, twisted James around by his arm, and slammed his face up against the wall. Wade leaned in and said something to James I couldn't hear, then let him go. Wade was smiling. A weird smile, like he was happy. That's when James lunged at Wade, knocking him to the ground. James threw himself on top of him, fists swinging. Angela grabbed a pitchfork off the wall and swung it at the back of James' head. He rolled off Wade, and I think she would have speared him like a tuna, but Wade jumped up and pulled him up by the jacket, held him against the wall, and started beating him. There was so much blood. But the worst thing was the expression on Wade's face. Not expression, really, because it was blank, like he was filling out a report or some other boring task instead of beating a guy to death. Angela screamed to stop. He didn't. When she grabbed his arm, he shoved her away. James slid down the wall and Wade kicked him. That's when two cops showed up and pulled them apart. I think Angela called them but I never found out for sure.

"Wade had blood all over his face and down the front of his shirt, and James was on the floor curled up and not moving. His head was bleeding and his face was pulp. Everyone stopped. Wade's raspy breathing and the static from the cops' radios were the only sounds. No one talked. Then Penny, standing in the open doorway of the stall, said, 'He's dead.' Well, the police went nuts thinking she was talking about a person.

Brenda blinks and rubs her eyes. "Penny meant the horse was

dead." I nod. "So what happened with the police?"

"Wade fixed things. Told them James hit him first. He did. We were all witnesses. At least for the part we actually saw. 'Isn't that right, James?' Wade asked. By now, one of the cops had James sitting with his back against the wall. The cop asked if he wanted to press charges. James looked at Wade and shook his head. Of course, Wade didn't mention the fact that he had just killed James' horse. An ambulance came and took him to the emergency room. After a bunch of reports were taken, the cops left."

"Killed?"

I'm surprised Brenda caught that part of the story.

"Yeah, but I didn't know that until later."

"How did you find out?"

"About an hour later, after things had calmed down, I was outside dumping a wheelbarrow in a place around the side of the barn that's hard to see. Wade came out to put stuff away in his truck. While he was standing there, Penny walked up to him. Her face was red, and her eyes were puffy from crying. I was headed back to the barn, but something told me to wait. She said something to his back that made him spin around. I couldn't hear much, except when she got a little mad and said, 'I told you the horse was allergic to Banamine. When you walked in the stall, I told you that first thing.'"

"Banamine?" Brenda's eyebrows lift.

"It's used to treat colic. Relaxes the muscles, relieves pain. Usual stuff vets use in an emergency like colic. One injection and the horse is usually feeling a lot better right away. Except if the horse is allergic. They can break out in hives or have trouble breathing. The really bad ones go into shock and die. Like that horse."

"And Penny told Wade the horse was allergic?"

"Yup. He knew."

Brenda folds her hands on the desk. This is the hard part to tell. The pressure ring around my throat tightens, and I look at the door. If I tell her, what will she do? What good will it do? But I want her to know why I can't live with Angela...with Wade. But if he knows I know, if any of this gets out…

"Do you want some water?"

Her voice snaps me back. "No. I'm okay." I straighten in the chair, both feet planted on the floor. My fingers entwine, pressing together. "I kept listening, hidden behind a half wall of the manure bin, looking through the cracks in the boards. Wade didn't act surprised. He didn't say he misunderstood or he was sorry. He didn't make up any excuse. His face was swollen now and one eye was turning dark. Penny asked why he did it. Wade sneered. 'Someone's got to pay,' was all he said. He turned his back on her, rummaging around in his truck, pulling out the drawers that hold all the meds and stuff. Penny moved around to get next to him. She looked up into his face, and I saw she was really angry. 'You don't care that you killed an innocent animal?' I heard her ask him. Some other stuff, too, then she said she was going to report it. She started to walk off, and he grabbed her arm and spun her around. He had something in his hand. Penny yelled, 'Hey, get off me,' but he pushed her up against the truck. I couldn't see around him, but when he moved out of the way, he had a needle in his hand. Penny started to slide down to the ground. He grabbed her, pulled open the passenger door, and shoved her in. He had to swing her legs around before he closed the door. He took a look around, probably to check if anyone saw him, then calmly closed up the back of the truck, walked around to the driver's side, and got in. Penny was slumped with her face pressed against the glass, her eyes closed."

"He drugged her? Because she threatened him?"

I nod. My face is wet and my nose is running.

Brenda pushes a box of Kleenex to the edge of her desk. I tear out a wad and press them against my nose, eyes. She gets up and leaves, but comes right back with a little plastic cup of water. The sip feels like a cold bullet burning down my throat and hitting the bottom of my empty stomach.

Her hand lands on my shoulder. "Are you okay, dear?" The hand is quickly removed, and for once I wish she'd put it back. I look over my shoulder at her and try a smile. Pretty weak effort, but she smiles back.

She lowers herself into the chair behind her desk again. A dark expression passes over her face before she asks, "What happened to Penny?"

A sound like air escaping from a balloon echoes around the room, and I realize it's me. Another squealing sob escapes before I cover my mouth with the wad of Kleenex. I can't stop shaking my head no, no, no, no. I feel rather than see Brenda move to get up as the words burst out. "She disappeared. No one saw her again!"

The Kleenex is a pulpy gray mess. Brenda takes it, tosses it away, and sits down in the chair next to me. A rock has been lifted off my chest, but at the same time I have a shaky feeling of regret, second-guessing. Should I have told? Can I trust her? It's like when you buy an expensive dress—or cowboy boots—and as soon as you walk out of the store it hits you. You can't afford what you've just done. Problem is, I can't return the words to my mouth. I see the words *Penny never came back* floating like a poison mist through the air and back down my throat.

"You told your mother?"

I nod. My throat is raw. "I told Angela what I saw—that Wade took Penny away. Maybe she told Wade because the next day she said I was seeing things, and it was just a matter of time before Penny took off because she was a druggie. I shouldn't have told her," I whisper to Brenda. "That's when she took my dog to the pound. Said liars didn't deserve to have pets."

Brenda heaves a sigh as she lifts herself out of the chair. She stands beside me. A quick double pat on my shoulder again. Tap, tap. Then a squeeze. "The police may have a record of the call. I'll check that, too."

"It was a long time ago."

"This agency has good relations with the records department. I can check missing persons as well. What was Penny's last name?"

Brenda puts on a warrior look, and it gives me courage. She's ready for action. "Her last name was MacCorkle. Not even sure if Penny was her real name. Could have been Penelope or anything, I don't know."

She jots it down. "There are also records of people, uh, who haven't been identified. The records are cross indexed to help find matches."

"Thanks." My voice is flat. "But don't let anyone, especially my mother, know you're searching for Penny." She didn't believe me then. Would anyone believe me now—would Brenda? If I told her about Trey? I struggle to sit up. "Hey, if you're talking to the police and stuff, can you ask about someone else?"

An eyebrow goes up. "There's more to the story?"

"Different story." I wave my hands like I'm clearing the air. "Can you ask the police if anyone has reported a guy named Trey Morales missing? Just, well, he hasn't shown up for work, and his roommates don't know where he is, either." I shrug. I don't want to say more about it until I know for sure. "It's just that he's a really nice guy, and we're all worried about him. If you're calling anyway…"

Brenda writes down his name.

"Can you call now?" I lift myself out of the chair and stand over her desk.

"Right now?" She glances at the clock. Then me. Something in my face must convince her to pick up the phone. I jot down a description of Trey as she exchanges small talk with someone at the department she must be pretty friendly with. She waits for someone else to come on the line. I check out that hangnail again, but my ears are like giant funnels, hoping to scoop up any information I can catch.

"Yes, Officer, a man by the name of Trey Morales. Age? Uh"—she looks at my notes—"approximately twenty-two." She reads the description I hand her. "About five foot ten, dark curly hair, brown eyes, medium build but athletic…what?" Her hand goes over the mouthpiece. "He says something just came in this morning. He's checking the computer."

Finally someone reported him missing.

The officer must be talking again because Brenda is nodding. She scribbles some notes, and I try to read them upside down.

Roommates reported missing since Saturday. Nothing missing from his room.

Her hand stops writing. "What's that? They found his car?"

"Where?" I ask.

She waves at me to be quiet.

"Abandoned at the reservoir? Near the Linden area of Patapsco State Park. Okay, thank you, Officer. No, I don't know the man. A fellow employee was concerned he hadn't shown up for work. I was checking for her." Brenda looks at me.

I mouth *thanks*. She's keeping me out of it.

She puts the phone down slowly and continues to stare at it. "They found his car in a parking area near the woods. Looks like it had been broken into. The driver's window was smashed, so they don't know what they'll be able to determine by going over it, but it was hauled away for forensics guys to go over it, anyway. I don't think they wanted to tell me any more than that."

Brenda has a strange look on her face.

"What's the matter?" I ask.

Her voice is flat. "I'm worried about you."

Chapter Nineteen

EDDIE SCREAMS AT ME FROM THE MIDDLE OF THE ARENA. "FOR GOD'S sake, will you stop perching on that horse's back and sit your butt down in the saddle?" Her breath sends a plume of condensation swirling around her head. She's given me a few lessons on Eleganz, a "schoolmaster" she calls him, but I don't think I'm dressage rider material. At least in her opinion.

"I *am* sitting," I eek out through clenched teeth. My butt bones are raw. The horse is so broad it feels like my legs are being ripped off at the hip joint. His head is up in my face, and I'm sure he wants to pull me out of the saddle by the reins.

"If you don't sit down and engage your core, he'll pull you out of the saddle." Now she's reading my mind. Eddie takes a tentative sip from the thermos cup grafted to her hand before she yells out more instructions.

Dressage. Not loving this.

Eleganz pulls against my shoulders like a Clydesdale bearing down to pull a wagon out of the mud. We trot around on the same stupid circle, and I don't know about him, but I'm ready to nudge him up into a gallop, escape through the open arena doors, and take off across country—maybe over a couple jumps.

"You're gripping." Her voice mirrors the exasperation on her face. "And you're pinching with your knees. He can't go forward if you're pinching."

She talks like I don't know how to ride or something. "I'm not!"

I open my knees so wide there's an inch gap between them and the saddle, and the stupid horse shoots forward. I get thrown backward. When I recover and grab up the slack in the reins, Eddie has a smug I-told-you-so look on her face.

"You can bring him back to a walk," she says. I'm being dismissed. "After you untack, come by the office." She walks out.

I *can* ride. But Eddie makes me feel like a beginner—like I'm ruining her horse. I walk Eleganz to cool him out. He stretches his neck and hangs his enormous head with his nose almost trailing in the dirt. What does Eddie want to see me in her office for? Not to give me a raise, I'll bet. I tick off all the work I've done, especially since Trey has been gone, preparing what I'll tell her so she'll see I'm worth taking on as a working student. I *can* do the riding, I just have to convince her.

The big horse wasn't even warm, so I put him away and stand in front of the office door. I hear Eddie in there—a desk drawer slams shut, the end of a phone conversation. I don't want to knock. I don't want to go in and hear what she's going to say. It's like some force field is holding my arm down by my side.

The door swings open. "Oh!" Eddie takes a step backward. "I was just going to find you." She spins around, leaving the door wide open. I walk in, close it, and stand in the middle of the room. Eddie perches on the edge of her desk. "I'll make this quick. You asked me when we hired you whether you could become a resident student. Well, I've evaluated your work and you're doing fine, more than fine on stable chores, but resident students have to be able to contribute more. They have to be able to work the training horses, do some warm-ups at shows and—"

"I can ride." My words bite off hers. She eyes me and I shift my weight. "Really, I've ridden for professionals."

"Jumpers."

"I qualified for Washington—"

"Again, not on horses training for dressage competition. I don't doubt you have a lot of experience, but it's the wrong kind." Her words are the kiss-off. End of story. You're not our kind.

"I can learn."

Her face scrunches like she's got a gas pain. "We really need riders in our program who can pull their weight. Especially now."

I know why especially now. Now that Trey is gone. I take one step toward her desk. "Please. I really want to learn." This job is my one hope right now.

Her shoulders slump, and she lets out a big sigh. "Okay. We can keep working on some lessons when I have the time and re-evaluate your application down the road."

Down the road won't help me. Down the road, I'll be living with Angela. And Wade.

She pushes off the desk and stands to leave.

"How about Trey's horse?" I ask, desperate.

She stops. "What about his horse?"

"Well…" I'm not really sure where I'm going with this.

Her brows scrunch together. "What about Trey's horse?" she repeats.

"I—I just thought, since he's a Thoroughbred and trained as an eventer, maybe I could ride him over fences, cross-country and stuff until Trey, uh…" My words dribble to a halt. What? Shows up again? Not likely.

"Trey isn't paying us to work his horse. Besides, if he doesn't turn up again soon and pay his board, or work it off, the horse will have to go."

"Go where?" I remember Willow's note. Ripped into tiny pieces.

"Auction. Sold. Donated to a riding school. I don't know." She digs in her pockets, then sweeps the room with a panicked look. "Where's my damn phone?"

I spot it under some papers on the desk and hand it to her. My mind works furiously to come up with some advantage to me riding Trey's horse that Eddie will see. I seize on one idea. "Until Trey comes back, the horse'll have to be worked. He's a Thoroughbred. If you sell him—even if you give him away—he'll need to be in shape, to not act insane. I could ride him, keep him going."

Her thumb stops scrolling across the screen of her phone, and her head snaps up.

"Until Trey comes back." My face burns from what I learned in Brenda's office. *If he comes back.*

"Right." She draws in her bottom lip, making a sucking noise, and jams the phone in a back pocket. "Right. Until Trey comes back. Okay."

I bolt out of the office before she changes her mind and go straight to Tucker's stall. Trey's horse is walking circles, wearing a path in the bedding. I look in on him, and he rushes to meet me on the other side of the bars. I never thought of it before, but this horse looks like he's in jail.

"Hang in there, boy," I tell him. "Trey'll come back."

"I'm not so sure." A voice behind me, or my own thoughts?

I turn, my heart pounding in my ears, to find Willow standing behind me. Her wispy hair is flattened from wearing a riding helmet.

"What do you mean?" A step closer and I detect the sharp smell of liniment wafting off her clothes. "Did you hear from him?"

She wraps her small hands around the bars of the horse's stall and stares in at Tucker. A barely detectable shake of her head to say no. "I just have a bad feeling."

I stand beside her, watching the horse walk his stall. "He's not happy," I say.

"He misses Trey." Slowly she turns to face me. Her eyes are glassy and a little red around the edge. "No one's heard from him, not Eddie or the owners, but his stuff is still here." She turns back to Tucker. "And he'd never leave his horse."

I think about telling her what I learned at Brenda's, but for the second time today I keep my mouth shut instead. I'm not sure who to trust.

She shakes her head. "He drove his car to the party. It was there most of the night, but then was gone. And payday was Monday," she says with emphasis. "Would he take off without getting his paycheck?" She leans closer, her breath like licorice. "I think something bad happened to him."

No, he wouldn't just disappear without his pay or abandon his horse, especially knowing these people would sell it to the meat men in a heartbeat for the board.

I lower my voice. "Has anyone gone to his house? Looked for him?"

Willow turns, her back to the wall, and she slides down to sit on the floor. I squat next to her. She pulls at a loose thread on her sleeve.

"He had a room in a house with some other guys. When he didn't turn up that first day, Eddie called looking for him, but none of his roommates had seen him. They just figured he was here at the farm, that maybe he had to stay for an emergency or something."

"So no one reported him missing right away?"

Willow's eyes are dull, unfocused, when she looks at me. "No one."

The quiet is shattered by a clattering, like a bucket rolling down the aisle. Then a shout. "Oh, my God! Help! What's wrong with him?"

I scramble to get up and reach down to pull Willow to her feet.

"What's going on?" I yell.

We run to the next aisle, the one the boarders use. At the end there's an open stall door. A horse is thrashing, bumping into and kicking the walls.

"Help me! Goddamnit, someone help!" A woman pokes her head out of the opening. We run down the aisle. The horse inside is a huge, dark bay—one of the high-level dressage stars that Galen's been training. No doubt the screaming woman is the owner.

The horse's sides are heaving. Green snot drips out of his nose and he's sweated up around the neck and chest. His sides move in and out like a bellows. He coughs. The woman waves her hands, startling the horse. "What's wrong? What's going on?"

"Choke." I grab the horse's halter off the stall door. "Get him out of there before he tries to eat or drink anything else."

The lady steps back when I enter the stall, so I slip the halter on the horse. His head lowers and a stream of spit, mixed with hay bits, drips across the floor. He snorts.

"He just started this. I was giving him a treat, and he started heaving and coughing," the owner says.

I lead the horse into the aisle. Panicking, he dances from one foot to another. The owner, a small woman, stands close by, fussing with his mane and murmuring pet names to him. The horse raises his head and skitters away. I need to calm him down.

"Do you have any Banamine?" I ask her. Blank stare. "No? Run to the tack room and ask Eddie. She keeps some in there for emergencies. And call your vet."

She looks at me like I've smacked her. I wish I could.

"I'll help you find it." Willow grabs her by the elbow.

The clack of her boots on the cement fades as they disappear to the other end of the barn. I ease the horse's head down and talk to him in soothing tones.

"Did you bolt down your dinner, big guy?" I stroke his neck and keep a little pressure on the halter.

He stops dancing around, coughs, and another blob of mucus runs out of his nose. I wipe it with my sleeve. Rubbing his neck, I feel a lump. The chunk of whatever is lodged in his esophagus. He gulps, swallows, and coughs. The lump doesn't move. Gently, I explore the edges with just my fingertips. It's hard and round, bulging from his muscular neck. It must be huge. His flanks darken with sweat and wave in and out with the effort to breathe. He rolls his eyes, showing the white edges, as his mouth opens wide with another enormous cough, but the lump is still there. Saliva drips from his tongue. I probe the lump again, pushing a little harder, nudging the edge forward. Maybe if I could just dislodge it—

He makes a noise like a dog's bark. Spittle and snot fly out, along with an almost whole apple. He shudders like a dog, his metal shoes skittering along the cement aisle. Then stillness. Calm.

As I bend to pick up the apple, the owner jogs back toward us. She has two tubes of Banamine in her fist and Eddie right behind her. Willow has disappeared.

"He's okay now," I call, rolling the slimy apple in my palm.

"What did you do?" the lady asks. She sounds more suspicious than pleased as I pass her the lead rope.

I hold out my hand. "I got this out. Was stuck in his throat."

Her brows knit together. "I always put an apple in his bucket after a ride, for a treat. He's never choked before."

The horse is trying to snatch the apple out of my hand again, so I take a few steps away to dump it in a trash bin. Eddie walks over to me and checks over her shoulder to make sure the owner is out of earshot.

"You did a good job. Mrs. Dubois is an important client, but a little..." She looks back to check on the owner scolding the horse in baby talk.

"Clueless?"

Eddie struggles not to smile. It's a quick smirk, then she's back to business. "Thank you, Regina. Quick thinking handling the situation." She starts to walk away, but pauses. "I've thought about what we just talked about—riding Tucker. If you take that on, worse comes to worse, the barn will pay you a percentage for your time if and when he's sold. If not, we'll work out some sort of compensation in lessons. Deal?" She doesn't wait for an answer. She walks back to Mrs. Clueless again, telling her she needs to cut up the treats.

Worse comes to worse? Can it get much worse?

I follow her. "Did you hear anything about Trey?"

Eddie doesn't turn around. She doesn't answer, but Mrs. Dubois perks up.

"Trey? That nice kid who takes care of the horses?" She cocks her head like a little dog. "What's happened to him?"

Eddie shoots me a cross look. "Nothing's happened to him." She lets out a long breath. "We're pretty sure. He just hasn't come in to work the past few days."

"Or shown up at home," I add.

Eddie's dark eyes narrow at me. "I'm sure there's a reason."

"Yeah, like someone killed him," I say under my breath. No one hears me. At least, I hope not.

Mrs. Dubois stops futzing with the horse's mane. "Has anyone checked with the police? They must know something."

"Call the police about what?" A man's voice behind me asks. Eddie and Mrs. Dubois look over my shoulder. My spine goes stiff. I know who it is without turning around.

"Dr. Wade," Mrs. Dubois' face lights up. He has that effect on middle-aged women with lots of money and nice horses. "We're talking about that nice boy who's missing."

I don't want to turn around, to see Wade's face while we're talking about Trey. To see him act like he doesn't know anything about it. I set my face because I have to act like I don't know anything about it, either.

"This girl thinks something happened to him." Mrs. Dubois tilts her head at me.

Slowly, I turn to see Wade only a few feet away. He sets his medical bag down and runs a hand along the horse's shoulder. When he looks at me, a smile is frozen on his face. His eyes narrow.

"She does, does she?"

Chapter Twenty

I'M SITTING ON THE FRONT STEPS OF THE SCHOOL, WAITING FOR DECLAN, when Cory runs past me. I can tell she just realized it was me because she stops at the bottom and turns enough to look over her shoulder. Real quick, and turns back. I haven't seen her since that day in the cafeteria. When I said those things. She drops her backpack and stoops to tie a sneaker. I could stand up and go say something to her. What? I'm sorry I said you're a crummy rider and your family stole my horse out from under me? I could ask her how Prophet was doing, but she'll take it the wrong way, like I still blame her for losing him. My leg muscles twitch, like they're going to make the decision for me to stand up and go talk to her, but then it's too late. She calls to a friend—probably a real friend—picks up her backpack, and jogs off. A gust of wind whips hair across my face. I let it. Holding my coat closed with one hand, I struggle to pull the hood up. Cold seeps through the brick step right through my jeans, so I stand up.

"Hey." Willow runs down the steps. "Need a ride?"

She's wearing a lined jean jacket and fleece boots. No hat or gloves.

"Nah, got one." I think of Declan's dinner invitation. Monday night is always meatloaf and mashed potatoes, he told me. My stomach growls.

"Just checking." She kicks the step with her heel. "I know you need a ride sometimes."

She hunches against a breeze that whips a few of her words away. "I heard they found the car." Her voice cracks.

"What?" I ask, but I know what car she's talking about. "I heard that, too. Near the park. You hear anything else?" There's always barn gossip. Maybe she learned something new about Trey's disappearance.

Willow sniffs and runs a hand under her nose. "The cops came by to ask Galen and Eddie some more questions. Before they went in the office, I heard them ask stuff like when was the last time they saw Trey and if his things were still there. I didn't hear the rest. I didn't want to ask Eddie what was going on, she can be such a—you know." She gives a lip curl like she smells a stinky cat box. "I talked to Galen when he was getting ready to get on his psycho stallion—Revanche— so he was paying more attention to not getting kicked than he was to why I was asking questions about Trey. So, I told him that Trey's stuff was still in his locker." She balls her fists in the pockets and hugs her coat tighter. "I asked what the cops found out. 'Nothing,' he told me. They didn't even search the woods. He was kind of laughing and said it figured. Cops probably thought Trey was just some illegal stable kid. Probably was mixed up with drugs or some other trouble and that's why he disappeared."

A flash of heat toasts me inside my coat. "Did they say that? They don't even know him." I picture Trey, his head bent and eyes closed praying over a hamburger at lunch. He smiled at everyone. The few times I saw him, he was calm with the witchiest mares. I never heard him raise his voice. Ever.

Willow shrugs bony shoulders.

"So no one even searched for him?" I ask.

"They checked the hospitals and stuff. Not the woods. Oh, and they took his stuff," she adds as an afterthought. "Well, not every-thing." She pulls one hand out of a pocket and opens her fist. A balled-up leather riding glove slowly uncurls. An expensive one.

Before I can ask her why she took it, Declan pulls up in the truck. "Gotta go. See you at the barn."

She holds the glove out to me. "For Trey. Until he's found, we'll remember him."

"You keep it," I tell her. I know I won't forget.

Willow pulls me into a hug. She's so bony and light, the wind could lift her off the step and carry her away. She whispers, "I'll help you with Eleganz. Don't worry what Eddie says."

I squeeze her back. Time is running out, and I need that job as a resident student. I pull back but the strap of my backpack catches on one of the rivets on Willow's jacket.

"Hold on," she says, lifting the pack and unhooking the strap. "Got it."

"Thanks." The pack settles on my shoulder. "And for the help with Eleganz, too."

Running down the steps to jump into the passenger seat, I don't look back. The heat is cranked up to full blast and I rub my hands in front of the blowers. As we pull away, I wave to Willow still standing on the steps, but she doesn't see me. The low sun cuts a slice of light across her face, illuminating the bottom half, but leaving her eyes in darkness.

As we drive along the road, Declan leans forward, craning his neck to look through the dirty windshield at the sky. "We won't have a lot of time."

"How much time does Rosie need to kill something and eat it?"

The question only earns me a pained expression. "She may not find anything. She may fly to the top of a tree and sit there."

"And not come back?" I can't believe he would take a chance of losing her after all the work he's put in to her training.

"Happens. But I brought some insurance." He pats a leather pouch clipped to his belt. I don't want to ask what's in it.

Rosie is loaded in a big box in the back. It's called a large hood, Declan tells me. We have had fun comparing the names for falconry equipment with the comparable stuff used for horses. It's not exact, but her hood is like blinkers, the jesses like hobbles, this long line he flies her on I like to call her longe line. It's a crease, he corrects me. She even wears bells like a horse pulling a sleigh. "So we can find her, if we lose sight of where she's at," he says.

The place we're going has a lot of perfect hunting areas, Declan explains, which means it has lots of scrub bushes where rabbits hide surrounded by tall trees for Rosie to sit in until she spots one. Even though it's late, at least the wind died down and the sun is out. For now.

Declan pulls into a gravel drive that leads to a parking area. "The owner gave me permission to hunt here anytime I want." He tells me like he has to explain. We get out, and he puts on heavy leggings like chaps and gets his special glove. I look around. The land is rolling, grassy hills ringed by trees. There's a gray wooden building in the distance that looks like an old barn. Otherwise nothing. I'm thinking what a great place to ride. Declan takes Rosie out of her box. She rides on his gloved hand like a boat on a wave. Her tail hangs down or flips up like a rudder, balancing on Declan's arm. Orange eyes take everything in. She lifts her wings and flaps, only to be caught by the leather leash attached to her feet. I jump back as she flutters and swings under his arm and back on top to perch.

"Don't worry." Declan holds up his other hand. "She's okay. She's just anxious to get started."

"What do we do now?" I ask while Declan unties her. Before he can answer, she spreads her wings and soars to the top of a tree ahead of us.

"Keep an eye on her," he says as he draws a long stick out of his pack. He wades into the thicket and thwacks at the underbrush.

I tilt my head, sheltering my eyes from the low sun. "What if she doesn't come back? I can't believe you just let her go."

Declan is bent over beating the shrubs. He twists to look upward at Rosie, then moves forward. Whack, crunch, the noise would shake the dead out of their hiding holes. When we move down the trail, Rosie flies to the top of a nearby tree. Declan straightens and shelters his eyes under a hand to look for her. "She's doing exactly what she's supposed to." He cups his mouth and calls, "Come on, sweetie, I'll find you a rabbit!"

Sweetie? How he can call that feathered killer sweetie is beyond me. Just as I'm about to tease him about it, the sound of bells rings out, and a red and white blur streaks past.

"She's got one!" Declan high-steps through the brush to where Rosie disappeared in the thicket. A piercing squeal. I imagine what's going on under the bush and keep back. Declan cautiously parts the branches and leans down to look. "Oh. That's okay," he consoles and reaches in to retrieve the bird. She's covered with broken twigs and dead leaves. "It got away."

Everyone is disappointed but me.

"I know another place," he murmurs to her, brushing off the leaves. He walks ahead down a slope and crosses a dry creek bed. In one fluid movement, he lifts his arm and Rosie flies off it like an extension of his own body. She flies to a treetop and calls. Declan walks along, taking a whack at any bush close enough to reach without stepping into the brush. Rosie glides from treetop to treetop, following us.

I catch up with Declan and fall into step. "It's amazing she does that. Follow us, I mean. Why doesn't she just fly off?"

"We have a deal. Like a contract. I give her food, or help her find food, like today, and in exchange she hunts with me."

"She must love you."

When he turns to me, his blue eyes look brighter against the cloudless sky. "She doesn't love anyone. It's a business arrangement." He checks her location and whistles for her to catch up. "I'm not kidding myself into thinking anything else. In a year or so, I'll release her back to the wild."

"You're kidding!" I grab his sleeve to slow him down. "You're going to let her go? Forever?"

He stops. "That's the deal. She's a young bird. Most of them die their first winter. Hunger, traffic, tangled in wires... I teach her to hunt, she survives, so I let her go in a year or two so she can breed more red tails."

"A regular circle of life." There's a sarcastic edge to my voice I didn't want to come out.

"They're not horses, Reggie." He starts walking.

I jog to keep up. "I didn't mean...I mean, I know how much this means to you." My nose is running with the cold and I reach out to grab his coat sleeve. "I just have trouble *getting* it."

He checks Rosie's position at the top of a nearby tree, then sinks down on a fallen tree trunk and pats the spot next to him. I sit. For a while, he just pokes his stick in the ground, swirling the leaves around. "I think she's tired." He juts his chin at the bird. "Or she's not hungry enough."

"What do we do now?" The sun is slipping behind the tree line.

"Wait."

I'm not good at waiting, but I resolve to sit still and give it a try. The low sun warms the side of my face. A bird calls and I glance up. It's some little dark bird. She hops off a nearby limb and joins a group that swoops and flutters away. Rosie's head turns, watching them.

"Do hawks eat other birds?"

"Sometimes."

"Seems like cannibalism." I think he's going to give me another lecture about hawks but instead laughs. He's not wearing his hat today so his red hair glows in the slanting sunlight like it's on fire. I wonder if mine looks as red as his and rub my hand over the longer strands growing out. "Hey, you know, we're all reds."

"Huh?" One eyebrow dips.

"Me, you, Rosie. Even Red Mare. We're all reds. Redheads. According to your dad, we're different."

"My dad." He leans his elbows on his knees. "He's got a lot of interesting ideas."

We sit and watch Rosie, who watches us.

Declan's voice is low. "My dad thinks we have a special destiny—reds, that is."

A smirk comes over my face. "Yeah, mine's real special."

Declan inches closer, removes his glove and hooks one finger around my pinkie, pulling me closer. Warmth spreads along my leg where it presses alongside his.

"I'm trying to escape my destiny." I'm surprised how hard the words sound in the quiet woods.

"Your mom?"

I nod, but he knows. I told him everything. He takes my hand in both of his.

"I can't go back." I choke out the words before my eyes start filling up with water. We've already gone over all the options, the dead-end options, and I'm grateful that he doesn't feel like he has to say something stupid like other people do—stuff like, "it will all work out" or "it may not be as bad as you think." He lets go of my hand and drapes his arm over my shoulder. The weight of it feels good. My head drops to his shoulder, the stiff canvas of his jacket scratches my cheek. His voice rumbles in my ear when he speaks.

"I hope you'll take me with you," he says. The corner of his mouth curls up. "Where ever you end up."

I look up into his face. A rush of heat and sparks tingles through my body. "No way I'm leaving you behind, Bird Boy." I'm smiling so hard my cheeks hurt.

He stands, grabs both my hands, and pulls me up so quickly I lose my balance and fall against his chest. In an instant, his arms wrap around me. Warm, soft lips press mine. I suck in a breath, quick, and he presses me closer. His tongue lightly touches my bottom lip as he pulls away, holding me at arm's length. So close, his eyes are not pure blue, but have flecks of gray and green, surrounded by pale lashes. A hand sweeps over my hair, urges my head forward, closer. He plants a kiss on my forehead. It feels like a blessing, something sacred. A promise.

Rosie calls from above us.

He breaks away. "We'd better get her home. She may not be hungry, but I'm starving."

My stomach unclenches from the flip it performed, and I realize I'm hungry, too. I don't know what to say about what just happened, so I act like nothing happened and look up at Rosie. "How do you get her back?"

"All the girls fly to me, Reggie. My secret is"—he rummages in the little bag attached to his waist—"bribing them with food." He holds up a morsel of something raw.

"It's not meatloaf, is it?" I ask behind his back.

He looks over his shoulder and smirks. A heavily gloved hand goes up high in the air, holding out the treat. A shrill whistle sounds in the empty air. "Step back and don't move." He waves his other hand in a signal to get back farther behind him. He doesn't have to ask twice.

Rosie cries and soars down from the tree at a hundred miles an hour. The words *bat out of hell* spring to mind, and until now, I had no appreciation for their meaning. With a wave of enormous wings, her talons grip his glove, and she teeters to a perfect balance, snatching up the tidbit.

"Right! Good girl." Declan runs his bare hand lightly over the bird's back. He cocks his head. "Ready to go?"

I fall into step, keeping my distance.

"I can't believe a wild bird would come to you. Just like that."

"She knows the deal. When I call, I'll feed her. I've never let her down, and I've never taken food away from her. That builds trust."

His face is only a foot from the razor beak that tore a piece of flesh to bits minutes ago. Talk about trust.

"Too bad you can't train people that way," I mumble. "Even when you hold up your end of the bargain, they'll still rip your heart out given the chance."

Declan frowns at me. "Not everyone, Reg."

Back at the truck, Declan returns Rosie to her giant hood. It still looks like he's locking her in a dark closet. When we climb into the cab, he holds up a thin leather glove.

"This yours?"

I take it from him and stroke the soft leather with my thumb. "Not mine."

He searches the floor, lifting one foot and then the other, searching for a mate. He runs a hand down the crack in the seat cushions. "Only one. I don't see the other."

But now I see what it is. I picture it in Willow's hand earlier, when I met her on the steps. I hold the glove up, pinched between my fingers. "How the hell did it get here?" Then I remember Willow hugging me, getting her jacket caught on my backpack. Did she slip it in a pocket? Why?

Declan starts the truck and dials up the heat. Cold air blows through the vents.

"The glove belongs to Trey."

"The guy who disappeared?" I'd told Declan about the party.

I nod. "Willow said she found it in his locker before the police took the rest of his stuff."

The scrunched brows tell me he's as confused as I am. "Then how did it get here? Why only one?"

"Willow took it. She wanted a reminder of him, I guess. Then she tried to give it to me for some reason. There's just one, so it's not like anyone can use it." I stroke the leather, replaying the weird conversation with Willow in my head. "She also said the police didn't do a search of the area. Maybe she's got some idea the glove can be used in a search, with dogs and stuff." It's dumb, I know. I shrug. "I have no idea."

"No good now, for the dogs I mean." Declan takes the glove and tosses it on the dashboard. "It's covered with her scent, yours, who knows what else by now."

Declan would know that kind of stuff. He hunts with his dogs as well as with the hawks. He backs out of the parking area, and we rumble down a gravel lane for a mile before hitting the pavement, but instead of going the way we came, he turns in the opposite direction.

He catches my confused expression and says, "Short cut home." His arm slides along the seat behind me. Out the side window I watch the bare trees glide by. A brown road sign sends me bolt upright in my seat.

"Linden Area? Here?"

"You'd think the sign said 'Dinosaur infested tar pits.'" Declan laughs. "Yeah, so? The farm backs to the state park."

We glide by the entrance to the park. My head swivels to follow the sign as we pass. "That's where they found Trey's car."

Chapter Twenty-One

DECLAN PUTS ROSIE AWAY IN HER BIRDHOUSE. HE'S TOLD ME A million times what it's really called—a mew—but I still think of it as her shed and yard. It's inky dark as we make our way down the path to the barn to feed Red Mare. I hate calling her that, so I've been thinking up names for her. Also tried to find out her real name, but since Declan doesn't know her breeding or the name of her sire or dam, there's no place to start. It's a dead end.

Inside the barn, Declan goes through the same routine of dumping her grain, calling the mare, and running back through the stall, slamming the door shut.

"Stop." He half turns but his hand doesn't drop from the stall door's latch. I sigh. "I can't stand watching you treat her like a man-eating tiger. She's a *horse*."

He stands straighter. "She's unpredictable, Reg. I don't want anyone to get hurt."

"She hasn't hurt me, has she?" I've been brushing her, picking up her feet, getting her more comfortable with humans again. I remember his words and throw them back at him. "How do you build trust?"

Red splotches bloom over his cheeks and he looks down into the empty grain scoop in his hand.

We look out into the dark night. Red Mare hasn't appeared.

I shut the outside door, take the empty scoop from him, and slide some grain out of her feed bucket. "You earn trust by building it step by step. Right? That's what you said you do with Rosie. I'll make the same deal with Red Mare. I'll feed her and keep her safe. She won't feel like she has to defend herself."

He nibbles on a thumbnail but doesn't say anything. I heave an especially loud sigh and retrieve her halter and lead from the hook outside her stall and reach for the latch. "I'm going to *walk* her in."

"Reg, she hasn't been handled in a while."

"Look, I've trained all kinds of horses. My whole life I've had to work with whatever crazy horses my mom dragged home. Ones jazzed up from the racetrack, rescues, hurt ones that were..." Declan's eyes lift, look over my shoulder. He's not listening.

"Dad?"

Mr. Kendrick is standing near Red Mare's stall. He juts his chin in my direction. "Let her."

I'm not sure how long he's been there or what he heard.

I turn to him. "We have to try. We have to give her a chance—a chance to be good."

Declan gestures to the outside door. "It's pitch dark out there. Maybe we should do this tomorrow, earlier, when it's light out." He raises his brows, seeking agreement. He looks from his dad to me. When no one agrees, he throws up his hands. "C'mon. Red could kill her out there. That crazy mare's plowed me over, and I'm twice Regina's size."

"Says the guy who lets a winged razor blade fly at him at about a hundred miles an hour and carries the feathered death machine around on his arm, calling her sweetie."

Declan laughs. Finally.

"I'd rather take my chances with a horse"—hands on hips, I nod toward Rosie's pen—"than with that thing you trust your life to."

A high whinny seeps through the walls, followed by an impatient hoof striking against the door. Declan shoots me a see-I-told-you look. He runs a hand down my coat sleeve as his blue eyes bore into mine. "She's dangerous. Please don't do this."

I don't know what to tell him. I only whisper, "Trust me." Before shooting the bolt open to the back door, I check to see that Declan has joined his dad outside the stall. There is nothing between me and the mare's supper other than a wall and my ability to gain her trust. I open the rear door enough to slip through.

Red snorts when I appear in her pasture. The outdoor lighting, combined with the sliver of light from the crack in the door, is enough to see her outline and watch her movement. She spins and trots off a few steps, tail held high. I draw in a breath, let it out slowly, and watch the cloud vapor under the light. My fingers grip the grain scoop. God, I pray I know what I'm doing. I cock my head, straining to catch any sound, but it's silent, except for the whispering swish of the mare's tail and the blood pounding in my ears.

Could she really be a dangerous, crazy horse? The times I've groomed her, petted her, she didn't seem so bad. I take a step closer to the light so Red can see me better while I shake the grain. She faces me, her head sky high. Her nostrils open wide, sucking in the scent, assessing my strange presence in her yard. Not good.

It's freezing. But I have to remain still, waiting for her to make the first move. Gloves do nothing to keep my fingers from going stiff. I swish the grain, making a noise like beads against the bottom of the plastic bucket. Her ears flick once, back and forth. I take a quick glance at the door behind me. No. I have to be positive, strong.

"It's okay, Red." I keep my voice light, soft. "It's okay, girl. C'mon, Red." The name Red sticks on my tongue. It's wrong. Its harsh sound brushes my ears and makes me wince. She needs a real name. I shift my weight from one foot to the other. Come on, horse, don't be so stubborn. As I shake the grain back and forth in a steady rhythm, I go over the names I've always liked for horses, but none of them are any good for this red mare. I feel she needs a name that at least starts with R, like Red. I test out a few, speaking them into the dark. Rhiannon, like the song. Nah. The mare snorts. She doesn't like it, either. Rubicon. Too warlike. An impatient stamp.

"Then come on and get some food," I tell her.

The mare lowers her head. Her eye is on me. A good sign. I want to call her to me. A name! I hear Mr. Kendrick's voice in my head.

There's power in a name. Authority to the one who bestows it. The mare looks behind her, watching something in the dark, beyond the reach of the light. She stands stock still, her breath in the cold air shooting from her nostrils like a dragon. Oh, God, I think there's something out there. She may run off. Or worse.

I squint into the darkness beyond, expecting to spot a pair of shining eyes or the movement of deer. Something normal that would explain her frozen stance. The wind picks up and the cloud cover shifts. The mare's back goes stiff, her tail up. Her neck strains ever higher to see into the dark. The edge of her eye glints white in the dim light.

Then it happens.

The moon breaks from behind clouds, shining so brightly that the frost on the grass sparkles like it's been dusted with diamonds. Just above the ground, a glowing mist hovers. It swirls like cotton candy, twisting in the breeze, spinning in drifts. It rolls toward us from the edge of darkness like a wave coming ashore. The mare and I stand, watching. It makes me feel closer to her, that just the two of us can see this weird thing moving. Coming. The edge, tumbling over the ground, reaches the mare's hooves. It swirls up her legs, almost to her belly, making it look like she's swimming in whitecaps. Like Nuallan's horse in the flood waters. She takes a step toward me and brings it with her. How is this possible? The air turns damp and smells like snow as the horse calmly stands inches away. The breath I've been holding escapes in one huff. Her eye is dark and calm. She lowers her head and blows on me, like a sigh.

A name pops in my head like someone murmured it in my ear.

"Roheryn." I speak it out loud. It's soft. A whisper. Its breathy sounds swirl in the frosted air. I lean toward her and lower my voice.

"Roheryn."

I say it louder. It's round in my mouth. "Roheryn. C'mere, girl. That's it."

Head lowered, she stretches her neck to the handful of grain in the scoop. Her lips flap and press against it, sweeping up each grain. I let her finish, then slowly raise my hand to stroke her neck, along her shoulder. She stays beside me. Stuffing the scoop in a coat pocket, I slide her halter off my shoulder and show it to her before slipping it on her nose and up over her ears. She keeps her head low. I step back, watching what she'll do.

"You want more grain, Roheryn, you've got to come with me." I snap the lead on the halter and open the stall door with a nudge from my hip. On a loose lead, she steps in beside me. I take her to where Declan and his dad are standing outside her stall before I slip the halter off and let her bury her head in the feed bucket. "Good girl, Roheryn," I tell her. I repeat the name so she gets used to it.

I close the back door and secure the latch.

"What did you call her?" Mr. Kendrick chokes out the question.

I glance up at his flushed face. From the cold? His eyes are wide, round, staring like Declan's hawk. My hand trembles as I hang up the halter on the door.

"Where did you hear that name?"

"I'm sorry." I don't even know what I'm apologizing for.

"Dad, what's wrong?" Declan grabs his father's coat sleeve. He shakes him off.

"Where?" Mr. Kendrick's voice rasps.

I can't tell him someone whispered it to my brain just now when the sparkling fog rolled in. Because that's crazy.

I shrug. I don't look at him. "It's the name of a horse I heard of in a movie." I remember it now. Lord of the Rings. I didn't even like the movie much. "There were cool horses in it. A red one was called Roheryn."

"Yes!" His eyes stretch wide. "Horse of the Lady!" He grabs both my hands in his. "Regina, my queen." He smiles at me. "But you heard her name, didn't you?" He cocks his head, eyes narrowed.

A tingle runs up my arm. How does he know? A tiny nod. "Yes, I heard it. When the frost rolled in."

What's going on?

Chapter Twenty-Two

I INSERT THE KEY IN THE FRONT DOOR AND TURN IT QUIETLY IN CASE AUNT Sophia has gone to bed already. I'm sort of hoping she has. Instead, when the door cracks open, a blast of voices from the TV hits me. Aunt Sophia's sitting on the couch, wrapped in a crocheted blanket, watching football. When I drop my backpack on the floor, she looks over, smiles, asks me how my dinner was, then turns back to the game before I can answer. The sound is on so loud, I'm surprised I didn't hear it through the front door.

"Hey," I raise a hand to wave on my way to the kitchen, still wearing my coat. It's freezing in here.

She calls over the commentator's blaring voice, "I got some ice cream."

The freezer is empty and frosted over like an ice cave except for a single pint of Ben and Jerry's. My favorite, New York Super Fudge Chunk. Bless her. With a spoon and the half-eaten pint, I wander back into the living room to get my backpack. I've got a ton of homework, but it's late already. I should have come home earlier...

I collapse into one of the ratty armchairs. The TV images flicker across my eyes, but nothing registers in my brain.

How *did* I come up with that name? The mist whispered it in my ear? Right. Or, like Declan's dad hinted, his dead wife chose me and murmured the name. Like a secret password. A hint that I'm to be trusted with Roheryn.

After we got Roheryn settled and went back to the house for

dinner, Mr. Kendrick told us about his wife and said the weirdest thing. "Horses can fly between the worlds—between the living and the dead." I sat in front of a plate of meatloaf with mashed potatoes lifted half way to my mouth.

"My wife, Siobhan, was Irish, did you know that?" he asked. "I was in Ireland on a teaching sabbatical when I met her. Declan was born there."

Like that explained anything. I shook my head no, so he went on.

"After a few years, when Declan was still a baby, we moved back to the States. We both taught at Loyola for several years, until…" He stared at his plate, swimming in congealed gravy. "She died of cancer. She suffered."

The clock ticked so loudly in that room.

"Before she died, I made her promise me something." Blue eyes, like Declan's bored into mine. "I made her promise she'd give me a sign. Something to let me know she was all right…afterwards." He shook his head and smiled. "She was a joker. She laughed at my 'myths, gods, and nonsense,' she called it. Always the scientist—a biologist, after all—she knew there was no such thing as the afterlife or spirits or anything of the sort. No proof, you know. So, just to appease me she made a deal. Siobhan had a pet name for the mare. No one knew it but me. She called her Roheryn, the lady's horse. It was to poke fun at me, giving her a name in Elfish, a made-up language from a made-up mythology—*Lord of the Rings*. It was her way of laughing at me."

Declan pushed the potatoes around with at his fork, never lifting his head.

"In the end, she told me she'd try to reach me. She wanted to believe…then. I held her hand and had to lean close to hear her. She said, 'I'll send Roheryn.'"

His fingers wrapped around a thick mug of tea, but he didn't drink.

"After she died, I never spoke the horse's name. I couldn't sell the mare, you see, because I wanted to believe. But I was starting to lose hope." He looked down at his hands, spread apart. "But you have to leave that door open, you have to look for miracles for them to happen." He glanced up at me. "I left the door open, and you stepped through it."

Even over the blare of Aunt Sophia's football game, I can hear the wind rattling the loose gutter outside. Aunt Sophia turns to me. Her eyes are puffy with dark circles under them. She reaches for the remote and turns down the volume. "I spoke with your mom today."

I scrape the spoon around the sides of the ice cream carton and wait. No doubt she got some new orders from Angela.

"She said she's looking forward to seeing you at the Thanksgiving dinner."

There's a touchdown, lots of screaming, and Sophia's eyes flick back to the TV.

"Yeah, well, I guess Angela will be disappointed when I don't show up."

She doesn't hear me.

I figure I'll go in my room, curl up under a blanket, and do my English reading assignment. *Call of the Wild*'s Alaskan setting matches the freezing temps in this house. I pick up the empty carton, stand, and take a final glance at the game—Cowboys versus the Giants. No wonder Aunt Soph's glued to the game. She's a huge football fan like everyone in Texas. I remember sitting around the living room in her house with about a dozen people each week, watching football, eating chili, and hollering at the bad plays.

"You miss Texas, Aunt Soph?"

Her head swivels in my direction. "Huh?"

"I never asked if you miss being in Texas. Are you worried about your horses and stuff?" Until now, it's never occurred to me that Angela was screwing up her life, too.

She tosses the remote on the coffee table. "They'll be okay. It's only for a while, and I'm happy to help out." A flash of a smile.

"I never told you thanks for taking me. For all last year and everything."

She pats the seat next to her. "Oh, Regina dear. That's the least I could do. Your mom is my sister, after all."

I place the empty ice cream pint on the coffee table and perch on the couch's armrest. I try to picture Angela and Sophia as kids. "Was she normal then?"

Her face scrunches.

"Mom? Was she a normal kid, or was she messed up then, too?"

Her shoulders droop. "Oh, Regina."

"No really." I drop onto the grungy couch beside her, and our hips sag together. "You know there's something wrong with her."

One eye is bloodshot, like she was rubbing it hard. Her face is fleshy, swollen, but hints of the resemblance to Angela are there. But her skin's not orangey, it's gray. I check on the end table, and, yeah, there's the red Solo Cup.

Her chest rises and lowers once with a deep breath. "I'm sorry." She rubs her thumb over the buttons on the remote. One push to turn the volume up again will end the conversation.

She shuts the game off and tosses the remote on the coffee table. "My sister was always different." A grimace, like she's struggling with a memory...or a decision. "She learned early on how to manipulate people, to make sure she got what she wanted. No matter what."

I bite my bottom lip, waiting. I want her to go on. For someone, finally, to admit there's something wrong with Angela. I let out the breath slowly and ask, "Was she always like that?"

"She's worse now, but yes. When we were kids, she broke things, usually my things, if she didn't get what she wanted. So she learned that threats worked really good on people. For her, it was an added benefit if it hurt them besides. She started with breaking, destroying property, prized possessions, then she stepped it up a bit when she was a teen."

"She got worse?"

"Smarter. She realized *things* could be replaced. Then she went after what couldn't be fixed or replaced."

"Like?"

Aunt Sophia picks up the remote but doesn't click it on. "She ruined reputations. Got me fired from the best job I ever had, to control me. When that didn't work, she went after my marriage."

The electric heater ticks, struggling to keep up with the cold in the room.

"She's bad, Aunt Soph."

Tears hover on the edges of her eyes. "I've found the best approach is to get as far away from her as I can and stay away."

My voice comes out pleading. "That's what *I'm* trying to do. But no one's helping me."

Sophia's face closes up, and she clicks the TV on. "I'm sorry. She's your mother. Legally, I can't do *anything*."

My breath comes out with a ragged sigh. I'm so mad no one has had the guts to stand up to Angela. I stand like the couch is on fire, lift my backpack and grab the empty carton. On the way through the kitchen, I slam it in the trash. The TV's volume swells as the announcer screams about a penalty. A shove to my bedroom door makes it slam shut, shaking in its frame.

The bed creaks when I crawl onto it, fishing through my backpack for the stupid copy of *Call of the Wild*. I dump it on the bed. Pens, notebooks, loose papers, and a lip balm spill out, but I don't see the book. Swiping everything aside, I spot a pink paper about the same size as notepaper. But I don't have pink paper. I hold it under the dim light on the nightstand. Across the top is printed *Pfederpass*. Horse registration papers? Underneath, a bunch of words, probably in German, are printed alongside an embossed Oldenburg breed logo. I don't recognize the horse's name, but the owner is listed as Kendrick. Roheryn's? Another paper, thin and printed with fading ink, is clipped to it. The handwriting looks like a woman's with lots of loops and curves.

The spirit of horses can fly between the worlds of the living and the dead.

Underneath the faded ink there's another line written in bold, capital letters.

I'm giving you these papers as a token of trust. You've given me back my belief in bigger things.—Al Kendrick

Chapter Twenty-Three

TREY'S HORSE IS TALL. REALLY TALL. AND ALL OF IT LEGS. TYPICAL Thoroughbred. He looks especially weedy and thin surrounded by the blocky warmbloods in the boarder's barn. Rooting around in the working students' tack room, I locate his saddle and bridle. Trey had marked his saddle peg with the horse's name, Tucker, next to the outline of a fish. I run my finger over his handwriting, neatly penned with a Sharpie, and wonder for about the millionth time where he could be. It's been almost three weeks, and no one has heard anything. At first it seemed like the police took his disappearance seriously and came by the barn for follow-up questions, but now everyone is just waiting. For what? For him to waltz in again and tell us he was in a hospital suffering from amnesia or was kidnapped and narrowly escaped? A feeling, like electricity shooting right through me, hits as I look at his handwriting. The feeling whispers, *Trey is dead.*

I shake it off and slide the saddle down from its peg, sling the bridle over my arm, and head back to Tucker's stall. I already finished setting up for evening feeding, brushed all the horses in for training, cleaned the tack, and hung the bridles exactly how Eddie likes them. There's exactly one hour free before I have to help get the horses in, change blankets, sweep, and start all over setting up for the morning. Rushing to get on, I whip off Tucker's blanket, causing static sparks to crackle—sorry, fella!—then run a stiff brush over his legs and neck to knock the big chunks of mud off and saddle him. As we walk down the aisle toward the outdoor arena—the dressage boarders never seem to ride outdoors all winter—Eddie spots me. My heart sinks when she picks up speed to intercept us.

"Feeding early tonight. Vet's coming to do inoculations for the horses leaving for Florida."

"So, that means…"

"Means you have a half hour." She pointedly checks the time on her phone. Slipping it in a vest pocket, she looks Tucker up and down. "How's he doing?"

"Great." I mean it and try to make my voice sound light, upbeat. "He likes going outdoors. Does better out there." I nod in the direction of the outdoor arena. Good thing because Galen is always training his psycho stallion, Revanche, or giving lessons in the indoor. Like now.

Eddie grunts and pulls down on her woolen hat. Her face is chapped from the cold. She lingers. Strange, because I never see Eddie standing still. She's either running to a lesson or a meeting she's late for, or she's barking orders at the working students while handling some other task herself. She pulls her hand out of her pocket and holds a sugar cube under Tucker's nose. "I know, I tell you not to feed with the bit in. But not my problem, right? You're the one who's got to clean it." She smiles. Another first.

The horse snatches the treat. You can hear the crunching over the sound of Galen sitting in a corner of the arena, yelling instructions to a rider. A small woman wearing shiny tall boots and a designer vest rides by the opening. She's on a horse built like a tank, her legs reaching only half way down his sides. Eddie turns to watch as well. Galen's voice, high and lighter than usual, coos encouraging remarks about her riding.

"That's it, Magda, dear. Push him forward into the bridle. Steady hands. You're doing wonderfully."

Magda's face is a teeth-clenching grimace, trying to hold the horse together and push him forward at the same time. The horse's expression mirrors hers. His neck is over bent and sweating.

"He's really coming round now, dear. That's terrific!" Galen shouts from his seat, a horse's cooler draped over his lap.

"Doesn't look terrific to me," I murmur.

Eddie catches my eye but doesn't say anything.

"You tell me I'm not a good enough rider, but I'm much better than her. Why's he telling her she's doing great when she isn't?"

Glaring at Galen, Eddie scowls. "Those clients just want a big horse, a trainer who can get on and fix them, and lots of compliments about how great a rider they are. They're not interested in learning how to ride. Certainly not what dressage demands."

I search her face for a clue as to how far I can push before she gets mad at me. I take one more step over the line. "So he's just lying to them. To make them feel good."

She nods. "Basic math. They've got money."

Magda saws on the reins to bring the big horse's head down into a tight frame and grinds into his back at the sitting trot.

Eddie turns her back. "And the only one losing out is the horse."

For the second time today, I see a glimmer of something human in Eddie.

"If she were a jumper rider, that Magda lady would be dead by now," I say. "You can't fake ride a jumper at Grand Prix level." I don't wait for a reply and move toward the door but don't get farther than a few steps.

"Hey, Reggie," a familiar voice calls.

Declan stands at the entrance, backlit by the waning light. I have a sinking feeling I'm not going to be riding tonight.

He comes over, sizes up the situation with me holding a tacked-up horse, and apologizes. "I guess I'm a little early. Sorry."

I introduce Declan to Eddie and explain that he's my ride home. After I say it, Declan gets a funny look on his face. Maybe because I made him sound like a chauffeur instead of a friend. Boyfriend. Whatever. Besides, Eddie's not even listening.

"Oh, and I brought this." Declan wrestles to pull something out of a large coat pocket. A man's leather riding glove. "Figured you might want it back."

Eddie steps closer. "Whose is that?" She takes the glove and stares at it and I get the feeling she knows exactly whose it is. I stand behind Tucker and think. I don't want to get Willow in trouble.

"I found it," I sort of lie. "I stuck it in my backpack and figured I'd ask around, find out whose it was. I guess it must have fallen out in Declan's truck." The majority of this story is true.

Declan's brow scrunches. Again. He's not liking anything I say today. I'll explain it to him later. Eddie folds the glove into her pocket without a word.

The sound of tires on loose gravel crunches near the entrance and a burgundy truck with a white cap pulls up. Every muscle in my body goes on high alert. The vet is here early, and now I'll have to help hold horses. Worse yet, I know which vet it is. Wade.

Without a word, I turn Tucker around to bring him back to his stall and untack. Declan walks beside me. I don't want to look at his face, so I keep the horse between us.

"I'm sorry about what I said, you just being a ride," I say. "Eddie doesn't like it when the workers have their friends hanging around." *Or worse, boyfriends.* "That's why I said you were here to give me a ride."

"That is what I'm here for." His words are short, clipped. He's acting overpolite, but, really, what it means is he's pissed at me. Or worse, hurt.

"Mad at me?" I duck under Tucker's neck and smile up at him. He flashes a smile back, and my breathing comes easier. "And I didn't want to say anything about Willow *taking* the glove. Eddie is really strict, and with Trey disappearing and the police asking all kinds of questions, I don't want her to get fired. She lives here." I run a hand down his sleeve. "Okay?"

"I get that."

I slide Tucker's saddle off and hand it to him. "Put it on the rack over there, please."

Declan walks across the aisle, struggling to hold on to the saddle and pad with the girth trailing and bumping his knees. He wrestles it onto the stand and steps back, reading the brass nameplate attached to the cantle. Even old and scratched, you can still read the stylized script: *T. Morales*.

"It was his?" Declan turns and peers into his stall. "Is this his horse?"

My rhythmic strokes over Tucker's tall back falter. "Yeah." I run a hand down the horse's neck. "Trey loves this horse. Got him off the track when they were going to dump him at a sale."

Declan leans against the stall doorframe. "What's going to happen to him? You know, if…"

That's the question no one can ever finish. If, if, if, like there's a chance Trey really is still alive all this time. I make my hand start moving again, doing something useful, something that feels normal and familiar. Declan asks again.

"I don't know." It comes out sharp, snapping back at him, without meaning to. Tucker head-butts me, his way of begging for a treat. I run my hand down the horse's long face, between the soft curving nostrils, and let it drop at my side. "Eddie says he'll go to auction. To pay the back-board money."

"Can they do that if the horse belongs to someone else? Like, don't you have to have, I don't know, a registration or something to sell him?"

"After a certain number of days of unpaid board, the horse reverts to the farm's ownership. It's usually in the boarding contract." I step closer to Tucker and lean in, soaking up his warmth. "If a horse is abandoned…" I turn and rest my cheek against the horse's solid shoulder and breathe in the familiar scent. "Tucker will be shipped off to a local auction, run through for whatever they can get for back board. He'll be scared, maybe act up some. No one will want him—a big ex-racehorse at a cheap auction, they'll all figure he's hurt or crazy." I rub my face against his side, wiping away tears. "I have to save him." My voice is strangled. "It's my fault." Both arms go around the horse's neck as I cry into his hair.

Declan's body presses into mine. His arms wrap around my waist, sealing me in a cocoon of warmth and darkness. His face, scratchy, brushes against my cheek as he whispers in my ear. "Why is it your fault, Reg?"

His voice is warm tea, running down inside me. He doesn't tell me I'm wrong or I shouldn't feel the way I do. He asks me why. He wants to understand. I shift and breathe in the cold air. The horse stomps once but stands still.

"I didn't say anything. I didn't *do* anything."

Declan squeezes me tighter. His answer. I've asked myself over and over what I should have done that night. Should I have gone to the police? "What could you do? You didn't really see anything," he reasons. "One man walked away, the other returned to the party." His lips brush my hair.

"But I saw *something*." The same argument playing over and over in my head. "I saw Wade take him outside, disappear, and come back alone with blood on his clothes. Maybe a knife. Then Trey never came back. Maybe if I had said something right away, the police could have found him, saved him. He's probably dead, and it's my fault. And now his horse will be dumped, too." My voice is muffled by the horse's side and Declan's fleece jacket. "And I'm still too scared to go to the police."

Declan spins me around to face him. Two strong hands grip my upper arms, his face peers into mine. "Listen. Maybe you saw nothing. Besides, it's not your fault, Reg. None of it is. If they find Trey, he can tell them what happened. If not—" His words are cut off by the sound of footsteps on the aisle outside.

Eddie slides Tucker's door open and makes an impatient hand gesture. "You ready." It's not a question. "Vet's starting with the boarders' horses. Let's go."

Wade stands behind her holding a bag and a fistful of syringes. We both step out of the stall. Eddie frowns at Declan but doesn't say anything.

Wade raises his hand holding the syringes and indicates Tucker with a sideways tilt of his head. "Bring him out. We'll start right here."

"He's not going to Florida," I say, looking at Eddie with raised eyebrows. "I thought we were just doing the horses who were leaving."

Then it hits me. Tucker may not be going to the show circuit in Florida, but he's probably leaving soon. Somewhere not so good.

"Not your call," Eddie tells me before heading off to the office.

I grab a lead and clip it onto Tucker's halter. He's in the aisle only a moment before Wade swabs his neck and inserts the first needle. He works in smooth motions, efficient, mechanical. Deadly.

"He's done." Wade tosses the empty syringes into a compartment in the open box. He turns, almost colliding with Declan. "Here." He holds out the box. "If you're hanging around, make yourself useful." Wade flashes a smile full of perfect bleached white teeth. The smile is practiced, and it somehow manages to charm people.

Declan grabs the box with one hand and holds out the other one. "Declan Kendrick, sir."

Wade grasps it, one shake. An eyebrow lifts a fraction of an inch.

"And you're Tucker's owner?" he asks.

"No, I'm just here to help. This horse belongs to a guy named Trey Morales."

I check Declan's face for signs...of what? Testing Wade? Seeing how he'll react to that name? No reaction. Wade's face remains neutral.

Wade shifts his eyes away, pats his pocket, and pulls out a pen. "I'll note that down for billing. Thanks." He heads to the far end of the aisle, checking stall numbers against a list in his hand. I fall into step a few feet behind.

Wade looks up at the number over a stall and slides the door open, handing me the horse's halter without looking at me. I pull out a young Oldenburg who is shipping out in a few weeks for his first big show.

"You do any hunting?" Wade lifts a chin in Declan's direction, indicating his woodland camo jacket.

"Some. Was out this weekend."

"Humph." Wade digs around in the box, filling another set of syringes for the chestnut horse. "Thought deer season didn't start till after Thanksgiving."

"Not deer."

Wade holds the syringe aloft, squeezing out a fine spurt of liquid, and taps the side. "Not deer, what then?" Smile.

I lift my eyelids open wide behind Wade's back to send a message to Declan. My brain screams at him, *Don't tell him anything!*

"I hunt with birds, not guns. We go after rabbit, squirrel. Whatever the hawk catches. Mostly around the Patapsco."

The tips of Declan's ears turn red. Wade nods, encouraging him.

"Falconry, really? I didn't know anyone did that anymore. Thought it died out with kings in the Middle Ages." Wade swabs the chestnut's neck and stabs the two needles in quick succession. "Done." He nods for me to put him away. "So, Declan was it?" He crooks a finger for him to follow as he consults the list. "Where are you allowed to hunt falcons around here?"

"Hawks."

Declan is sucked into Wade's wake, following in the sticky trap of his faked interest in falconry. That, and the fact that Declan is so damn polite he wouldn't be rude to anyone, even Wade. I try to catch his eye again, to warn him to keep quiet, but they walk ahead, shutting me out.

Declan names the farm we were at the other day and describes some other hunting areas. He blathers on, and I want to chuck something at the back of his head. "But I like Linden Hill Farm the best because the brush hides a lot of game, and it's surrounded by tall trees for the hawk." Wade nods, encouraging Declan to describe Rosie, where she lives, what she eats, all the while smiling and asking lots of intelligent questions. He doesn't call her hood a hat.

We work down the list, all the while me holding the horses in silence. Maybe it's okay. After all, Declan's not telling him anything important really, and it means I don't have to talk to him. After about an hour, we're finished. Wade leaves to pack up his supplies in the truck.

"Well you were certainly chatty." I can't keep the sarcasm out of my voice.

"What did you want me to do, Reg, just not answer his questions? Because that would be normal." His turn for sarcasm.

He's right, of course. I close the last horse's stall door a little too hard just the same.

"And, besides, we don't know for sure—" He looks down the aisle and bites off his words. Wade strolls back to us, empty-handed.

Declan flushes pink and draws a set of keys out of his pocket. "Right. So, I can take you home now if you're done?"

"No need of that, son," Wade says. "Regina and her aunt are living next to my place. I'll take her."

Son? Really? He's laying it on today.

"That's okay," I jump in. "You probably have other calls to make and Declan doesn't mind…"

"Nope. I'm done for today. Hop in the truck." There's no room for argument the way he says it. His truck is parked by the entrance, now dark with the early sunset.

"I'll get my stuff." I want to ride with Declan, talk over what happened. I want to be in his truck, warm, sitting right next to him with the heater blasting and all his weird bird junk rolling around on the floor. Instead, I look in his eyes and try to communicate how much I don't want to be trapped in a vehicle with Wade, with only a foot of space between us. All I say is, "See you in school tomorrow."

Wade makes an impatient *let's go* gesture.

"See you," Declan turns. "Oh, and Dad said you're invited for Thanksgiving dinner. Thursdays are usually roast chicken night, but for this he'll make an exception and fix turkey." A corner of his mouth turns up in a half-smile.

A warmth spreads through me even down to my frozen feet.

"Regina has Thanksgiving plans with her mother," Wade says. "But be sure to thank your father, anyway." His eyes lock on mine as he cocks his head in the direction of the truck.

I grab my helmet and backpack on the way out and walk to the parking lot without a word. Declan gets in his truck, raises a hand to wave, and pulls out. Wade fiddles with the heat, then spends another ten minutes or more writing down notes and checking something. Finally, he shifts into reverse and backs away from the light of the barn. The truck's cabin is plunged into darkness. The country roads have no streetlights, and the sky is starless.

"Seems like a nice kid."

I nod. "Yeah."

"Friend from school?"

He already knows this. We said we would see each other at school tomorrow. "Uh-huh."

Wade's head nods rhythmically like he's figuring something out with every question. We drive in silence while I look out the window.

"I guess you'll miss seeing him at school?"

I pivot to scan his face. Is he joking? "What are you talking about?"

"Oh!" He steals a glance at me, then focuses back on the road. "I guess your mother hasn't told you yet."

My stomach does a flip and clench.

"She's decided to move you to the private school, Glenwood Academy. I thought she told you." His voice is flat, expressionless.

The hell you did, you manipulative bastard. A hint of amusement shines from his eyes. My heart is a lumbering beast in my chest, pounding to get out, but I keep my voice just as flat as his. "No, she didn't." Short sentences, so I don't scream or worse, sob. "When did she decide?" I don't care when she decided, really. What I want to know is when she made it a point to punish me by cutting me off from friends. It's her way of making me more dependent on her. Always her.

"I'll let her tell you about it," he says. He's lost interest. Since I didn't go completely nuts, his fun is over.

I go back to staring out the window into darkness.

"You're also expected for the dinner."

I know what dinner he's talking about. They can expect all they want. I'm not going.

"I'll be picking you up that morning to go over around eleven. Your aunt should be ready, too, so tell her."

"You can tell her because I'm not going."

I brace for the shout, maybe even him grabbing my arm. What I'm not prepared for is laughter. More like a burst of air through his nose and a chuckle deep in his throat. It gives me chills more than a slap across the face.

"Your mother wants you there, so you're going." He says it easily, like we're talking about a normal family, a normal Thanksgiving invitation, a mother who's worked all week to put together a lovely dinner... He peers through the windshield into the dark, looking for something. The truck veers onto the shoulder, tossing me against the door. The transmission grinds when he throws it into park. My hand zooms to the door handle, but the automatic locks click shut. I look around, feel my eyes stretched wide. I don't know where we are, even if I could get out and run. The hard metal of the door presses against my back as he turns to me. Only the bare outline of his profile and the dark bulk of his body is visible in the dim moonlight.

"Maybe I should make a few things clear for you." His voice is low, controlled, like a teacher introducing a lecture topic. He raises a hand in front of my face, and I flinch. He laughs and bends down the first finger with his other hand, ticking off his points. "One, you do not pay rent. You and your aunt live on my property, free, no expense. Two, you still owe me a couple hundred for those fancy boots you had to have. Somebody's got to pay for them. Three, you're a minor. You have no say in what you do, where you go to school, places you live, or anything else. Do you have that?"

He takes his hand away and shifts in his seat, struggling to get something out of a jacket pocket. I can't make out what.

"Do you have that?" he repeats, waiting for me to answer.

"Yes," leaks out past my lips in barely a whisper.

"So, let's talk about what you *can* do. You can keep your job until you pay back the boots. Got that? Then, you come back to work for your mother when she's released. You ride who she tells you to ride, and you don't make any trouble."

I don't answer, waiting for the other shoe to drop—the *or else*.

The truck engine purrs and despite the heater huffing out warm air, it's still cold. My hands ball into fists inside my pockets.

Wade leans toward me, and the moonlight cuts a slice across his eyes. "You working with that kid's horse?"

He means Tucker. He knows I am. He saw me tonight with him. I don't turn, but answer "yeah" to the black glass window. My breath leaves a blurred smudge. "He's Trey's horse."

Curiosity makes me turn and check his face, what I can see of it. To get a hint of what he's got in mind.

"You like him? A good horse?"

My brows crush together. Where's he going with this? "Yeah, he's good." I don't tell him Tucker is amazing. He has a ground-covering stride and is a natural over the jumps.

"Be careful." The words are light, easy. He says them like other people say *see you later*.

"Why?" The question bursts out before I know it. He smiles. I wonder what he knows about Tucker. Maybe he had to treat him for something I don't know about—a past injury that crops up.

"Why?" he repeats and laughs. "Because if you're not careful, there's consequences. Understand? Follow instructions. Don't pick fights."

Then he puts what he's been holding on the console between us. A syringe, loaded with cloudy liquid, rolls back and forth in the shallow tray. He's not talking about being careful with Tucker—he's telling me to be careful, to do as I'm told, and not pick fights with Angela. With him.

"Are we clear?" he asks. One finger reaches out and moves the syringe so it points to me.

The other shoe drops. I behave, or else whatever is in that syringe will find its way into Tucker's neck if I don't.

Chapter Twenty-Four

As soon as I get home, I shrug out of my coat and throw it on the couch. Aunt Sophia isn't around because the TV is off and the heat—if you can call it that—is turned way down. In the kitchen, I find the Tupperware container of leftover taco meat, pour a bunch of rice and hot sauce on it, and heat it in the microwave. The cracked vinyl on the kitchen chair scrapes my leg when I sit. I debate getting my coat while punching the contact number for Brenda. I'm going to get the story straight with her about being transferred to another school. Hitting the number a second time, I still get dead air. The microwave beeps, so I grab my taco glop and push Declan's number. He answers right away.

"I'm home," I tell him. What I really mean is, I'm okay. "But get this. Wade said Angela is having me transferred to a new school."

Declan exhales. A habit he has, stalling when he doesn't know what to say.

"And," I continue, "Wade threatened me. Kind of. Not me, exactly, but the horse. If I don't stop making trouble."

"What did he say?"

The scene in the truck plays out before my eyes like a movie trailer. The syringe, rolling on the console. Him telling me to be careful. I paint the exchange as best as I can remember it for Declan. "So he didn't really come out and threaten me. He's too smart for that."

Dead air.

"You don't believe me." My fingers tighten on the phone.

"No, I do. It sounds pretty sketch."

Now I start to wonder. Maybe the syringe was one left in his pocket from the inoculations he was giving all afternoon. Maybe it was just sticking into him or he found it in his pocket and didn't want to leave it there. But what was the warning about? Be careful of what?

"Or, could he just be warning you to be careful with a strange horse? Did he say anything about what was in the shot—"

"No. I told you. He asked if I liked Tucker, then he warned me and took the needle out of his pocket and slapped it down in front of me." Ugh. It sounds flimsy even to me now. "But never mind. I'm trying to call the social worker and fix the school transfer thing, but her number's not connecting for some reason."

"Huh. Weird. Maybe try another phone. A landline if you have one."

"What difference does that make?"

He's quiet for a while so I wonder if my phone has dropped out. When he answers, his voice is flat. "A lot. If someone's blocked that number."

"What?" But it dawns on me what he's talking about. Parental spyware. "How do I find out? Never mind. I'll talk to you tomorrow. In person, okay? Don't text."

I push end and toss the phone on the table like it's radioactive. The old landline phone with its long cord hanging to the floor looks like something from *Leave It to Beaver* days. I never checked whether it worked. Glancing at the clock, I figure Brenda might still be in the office at quarter to six. I pick up the receiver, hear the familiar buzz of a connected line, and dial Brenda. She answers after only one ring with her name and title.

"Hi, Brenda, it's Regina Hamilton."

"Regina?" Her voice sounds odd. A mixture of surprise and something else.

"Yeah, I'm calling because I need your help. Wade just told me—"

"I didn't recognize the caller ID so I picked up. Listen, Regina, I'd like to help you, but I've been taken off your case. You've been referred to…"

I don't even hear the rest. Taken off my case. Another person I'm separated from. A person who might have helped me. My hand sweats holding the plastic receiver to my ear when I think about what might have happened to cause Angela to do this. If Brenda raised the suspicion of abuse, if she mentioned the broken collarbone, searched medical records… I push the bowl away. The smell of the taco meat turns my stomach.

"Why? What am I going to do now?" The whine in my voice echoes back in my ear.

"I'm so sorry, Regina. I really am. There's nothing I can do." Brenda sounds distant, like she's stepped away from the phone.

Nothing anyone can do. How many times have I heard that?

"Call Mrs. Gentry. She'll help you."

I imagine her finger hovering over the red disconnect button.

"Wait! What did you say? What does Angela know?"

The phone clicks, and the dial tone sounds in my ear.

Chapter Twenty-Five

I T'S POURING OUT, WHICH SEEMS IMPOSSIBLE SINCE IT'S SO COLD. THE rain on the metal roof of the indoor arena sounds like a million hammers pounding on it at once. Most of the boarders won't ride when it's making noise like this because it scares the horses, so I pretty much have the place to myself. Even though it's dark and blowing wind outside, the arena is welcoming with its bright lights and the few colorful jumps I dug out of storage.

Tucker has really taken to jumping. I figure it was a mistake for Trey to try to make him into a dressage horse. When he comes down to a challenging fence, his ears flip forward and he leans against the reins. Too much sometimes.

At the base of the small vertical jump, he lifts and flies over it with room to spare. On landing, he tosses in a little buck for good measure. I laugh.

"What a clown." Willow appears in the entrance with a client's mare. In no time, she's got this big horse taking light steps, moving in half pass, and almost cantering in place for a ten-meter circle. I give Tucker a loose rein to watch the pair, moving like they're performing a ballet. She makes it look easy. Meanwhile, Tuck and me are more like a downhill skier racing through a slalom.

I give his sweaty neck a pat. "He's a hell of a jumper," I shout over the rain. "I'd love to show him."

Willow checks her position in the mirrors lining the long side of the arena. I see a frown on her face in the reflection. "Maybe Trey will let you."

We both know that's not likely. Not likely that we're ever going to hear from Trey again. But we keep up pretending.

I dismount and flip the reins over Tucker's head to lead him out. Willow rides over and leans down to say something. The rain is pounding harder, so I can't hear. She might have said *locker* or maybe it was *Tucker*.

"What?" Tucker noses at the other horse. Willow's horse squeals and pins her ears, so I pull him away. "I can't hear anything."

Willow circles the mare to get closer. "I have to tell you about the glove."

"Yeah, you do. What's the idea of stuffing it in my pocket? That's a weird thing to do without telling me." What did she expect me to do with it?

"Do you still have it?"

"No, Eddie does."

Her face pales, and she leans over more in the saddle. "Because I didn't really find it in his locker. It was in—"

I hold a hand to my ear and shake my head.

She straightens, turns the horse, and calls over her shoulder, "Tell you later."

Eddie appears beside me. She points a finger upward. "Is this ever going to stop?"

I hunch my shoulders and watch Willow put the mare into a working trot along the far side. I wonder what she was going to tell me.

Tuesdays I don't have to work at Twin Elms, so that's when I go over to Declan's early to work with Roheryn. I've started calling her Roh for short. She head-butts me as I clip the longe line onto her cavesson and send her out on a circle. At first when I started working her on the line, she played up so hard, bucking and running, that she almost pulled me off my feet. But the work is paying off now. She's learned—or, more likely, acknowledges that she knows—the commands for walk, trot, and canter and does it without trying to kill me. Her dark eye always has a questioning look, even now, when I ask her to do anything a little different. She's a mare who has to be convinced. First, convinced it's a good idea, and second, that it was actually her idea, as well. I get that.

"I can't believe that's the same horse."

I look over a shoulder to see Declan on the other side of the fence. There's really no good place to work a horse on their farm—it's so hilly. This spot outside the barn is the only relatively level ground, and I've worn a track in it already.

"I'd like to get on her soon," I tell him. I can't really see his face under the hat, but I bet he's frowning.

"You think she's ready?"

I purr the word *walk*, and the mare drops from a forward, ground-eating trot to a swinging walk. Her head tilts and an ear cocks toward me.

"Yeah, I think she is," I say, signaling for the mare to approach me. Last week I discovered she would sell her soul to anyone who would scratch her floppy ears, so I give one a brisk rub. Walking to the barn, I tell Declan my plan.

"I can't really train her here. The footing is bad, and there's no ground person to help out."

He points to himself.

"You know what I mean. Someone who actually likes horses," I tease. "I don't know how hard she'll be to start back under saddle. It's been, what? Three years since…" I don't want to say *since your mom died.* "Since she's had anyone on her." And I know this mare can be tricky. I unconsciously rub my upper arm where she sunk her teeth into me, before I learned the ear rub bribe.

Declan nods. One side of his mouth lifts, and he gives a quick nod. "Tell my dad. He'll let you take her."

That's another thing. My mind's on fire with everything going on. I have to say something about the registration papers. What did that mean? Why did Mr. Kendrick slip them in my bag and not say anything?

The mare walks into her stall and pulls some hay from the rack. As I'm hanging up the longe line, Declan digs in his coat pocket and pulls out a torn slip of paper. He stares at it like it's written in hieroglyphics. "Meant to ask, did you lose this?" He holds it out to me.

The scrap looks like the corner of an envelope. The writing is in black ink, all caps with a backward slant. A little spark of recognition fires but dies in a flash, and I can't recapture it. It looks familiar. Besides that, there's nothing much to the note—just a four-digit number and the word Camelia.

"Camelia? Like flowers?" I ask.

Declan shrugs. "I guess. I found it on the dashboard of the truck. I think it fell out of that glove."

"You sure? Trey's glove?" I look at it again. The writing. The same as in the tack room, labeling Trey's saddle peg. I stare down at the scrap again, hoping maybe this time some miraculous meaning will appear. "Can I keep this?"

"Sure." He nibbles the end of his thumb. "Maybe you should give it to the police, though. If it was his."

He's right, but I don't say anything. The slip of paper feels like a message from Trey, like it holds some secret I can't figure out. Will the police? Will they even try? We're not sure it was in Trey's glove. I'm nodding my head, yes, I'll turn it in to the police, but at the same time I'm trying to imagine telling them where it came from. You see, Officer, this girl took the glove and gave it to me, and then I lost it in my boyfriend's truck, and he later found this little piece of paper that may have been in it. This paper that doesn't say anything other than the name of a flower and a number. It may be a florist's phone number. Oh, and while I'm here, Officer, maybe I should tell you that I saw Trey get in a fight with a guy who took him outside, returned with blood on his shirt, and Trey disappeared. I never mentioned that before. Why? Oh, I thought it wasn't important.

I shove the paper in the back pocket of my jeans and decide to ask

Willow if she knows anything about it tomorrow. The carrot tossed into Roh's bucket makes a hollow thunk.

Declan strokes the face of his phone with his thumb and frowns. "Give me your phone, Reg. I want to check something out."

I fish it out of my pocket and hand it to him.

"The data icon's on. Have you checked your battery usage?"

"Blah, blah, bars and battery usage. I don't pay attention to that tech stuff."

"If your phone's got spyware on it, you might want to." Declan holds the phone closer, scrolling through some settings.

I look over his shoulder. It has been acting weird, and I could never get through to Brenda. "I have had to charge it more lately. I just figured it was getting old."

"Maybe. Or something's running in the background. I can probably clear it."

"But no one's had my phone. Wait. Just when I go to the prison, they take it."

"They don't need access to the phone to put it on. They only have to notify the network provider." He holds out his. The screen is cracked, and it's encased in something that looks like it would protect it in a nuclear blast. "Take mine while I check yours out. Okay?"

I take his, and he shows me the unlock sequence. "I never lock mine."

He gives me an eye roll and drops my gold sparkling phone into the pocket of his camo jacket.

When I turn to toss another flake of hay into Roh's rack, Declan pulls the back of my coat. "C'mon, I still have to feed Rosie and I'm starved. Tuesdays are my favorite—Indian food night."

I grimace. I've never had Indian food.

Declan enters the house with Rosie riding on his arm and me a safe distance behind. The hawk glides to her perch in the corner of the room. As soon as I step inside, I'm hit with a cloud of warm, moist cooking smells. Spicy. Exotic. Like perfume you can eat. My mouth knows more than my head and starts watering, sensing something delicious is moments away. The squeal of the hinges on the oven and a slam announce the entrance of a steaming platter of puffy little triangles of pastry.

"Samosa," Mr. Kendrick says as he places the platter on the table. He jogs back to the kitchen.

"What are they?" I ask, trying not to sound rude.

Declan snatches one, tossing it from one hand to the other. "Hot!" He devours half in one bite.

"You're eating before our guest?" Declan's dad stands in the entrance, holding a covered dish with two oven mitts. He shakes his head and looks at me. "His mother did teach him manners. He's apparently forgotten all of them."

Declan speaks out of the side of his mouth, struggling to swallow. "Sorry. Couldn't wait." He hands one to me, wrapped in a paper napkin turning translucent with a butter stain.

I nibble a corner. Flaky pastry like a croissant. I bite off a big piece, and the inside sends a vapor up my sinuses of intense spice mixed with buttery goodness. A smile breaks out when the warmth spreads to my chest.

"Right?" Declan is nodding at me like he made some statement. "Wait until you try the vindaloo."

Sounds like a Caribbean voodoo dish, not Indian, but I'll try it if it's as good as these pastry pillows. I take my usual seat at the table next to Declan, with Mr. Kendrick at the head and closest to the kitchen. The fact that this has become my seat means that I've been here for dinner a lot lately, and it worries me that maybe I'm wearing out my welcome.

The stuff called vindaloo should be illegal. It's so hot my eyelids are sweating, but poured over jasmine rice it's like wrapping my stomach in a warm blanket. I pull at the sleeves of my sweatshirt, trying to get it off over my head. Declan pulls the other sleeve and almost topples me out of the chair. After dinner, we sit around like we're all in a food coma, and Mr. Kendrick launches into a story.

"Our hero, Nuallan, made a fine riding horse out of the silver horse that saved him from the flood waters. Do you remember that?"

"He was saved from drowning by a horse swimming by."

Declan's dad nods, and his smile makes me feel like a school kid who got a hard answer right.

"The land was divided by two kings. One ruled in the north from the ocean cliffs to the mountains. This king had five sons whom he sent out across the seas to conquer new lands and bring back riches for the kingdom. Of the five, only one returned. He married a foreign wife and brought her back with him. She had black hair, the color of the Dark Sea that beat against the cliffs. The other king ruled the south from beyond the mountains to the flat lands that opened to the Sapphire Sea on the other side. This king was not as cruel and had no sons. Nuallan preferred this king's land simply because it suited his horse to graze on the open pasture and grasses. He didn't have any use for kings or kingdoms or riches. Every day he sought enough to eat and a place to rest for the night. His horse was enough riches for him because Nuallan had learned something that no one else knew."

"The horse was magic," I blurt out. I cross my arms. It's easy to be brave when you're riding a magic horse.

Mr. Kendrick raises a glass with a tiny bit of amber liquor in it. "He was, indeed." He takes a sip and continues. "Although Nuallan lived simply, his reputation spread. You see, Nuallan had never been defeated in battle and was never taken prisoner or subjected to any lord or king. One day while traveling along the road he was stopped by a grand carriage. A woman with raven black hair stuck her head out and admired his mount."

"The wife of north king's son, right?"

A quick nod. "She offered to buy the silver horse because it would look impressive pulling her carriage. Nuallan told the woman his horse was not for sale. He did not know that he had spoken with the wife of the king's son, a woman who had never been told she could not have something she wanted. The carriage drove on, but a courier came galloping back to summon Nuallan to the court."

"Oh, no. So she gets his horse?" My face is hot. "That's not fair."

Declan laughs. "That's what I always say. These stories are never fair."

Mr. Kendrick leans back in his chair. "True. But they aren't about being fair. They're about how a hero acts in the face of injustice. Or deceit, betrayal…"

"I hate that."

Mr. Kendrick raises bushy eyebrows. Declan looks at me.

Twisting in my chair, I start over. "I mean, I know life's not *fair*." I put the air quotes around the word. "But would it be so awful if once in a while the bad guy gets destroyed in some horrible way? At least *some* of the time?"

A warm hand covers mine. "Regina, I like to think that life *is* fair. Good always wins. The problem is, sometimes it takes a lot longer than we'd like." He pushes his empty glass away. "Besides, we don't know if the evil queen gets the horse or not…" One eyebrow arches.

I open my mouth to reply, but the phone rings. He slaps the table and stands. "Saved by the bell! We'd sit here all night debating philosophy otherwise."

He walks to an old phone on an end table by the couch behind us. I guess he doesn't have a cell phone.

I turn to Declan. "I have to give him back the papers. How can I ask—"

That's when I hear the word *police*. Declan and I turn to see Mr. Kendrick, one hand holding the receiver, the other gripping the back of the couch.

"Yes, I have a son named Declan, Officer." He listens.

Officer? He's *talking* to the police? Declan's face registers surprise, confusion. He mouths the word *why*.

His father's voice booms, like he can't hear what the person on the other end is saying, so he's talking louder. "I don't understand. Why do you want to speak with my son?"

Chapter Twenty-Six

WILLOW IS NOWHERE TO BE FOUND AT SCHOOL. SHE DIDN'T show up for Mrs. Navarro's math class and I looked for her in the halls and cafeteria. Today, her beat-up car is parked in the farthest end of the parking lot, so I know she's got to be here. I need to talk to her about the glove. Why did she take it, and more than that, why did she slip it in my pack? Now Declan is in trouble with the police because of her.

I'm crouched against Willow's car, waiting, when she walks up from the other side. She doesn't see me when I stand up.

"You avoiding me or what?" I ask.

Willow presses a hand to her chest. "God, you scared me."

"I need to talk to you."

She lifts a shoulder and cocks her head. "Sure." But her face is wary. "What about?"

"Want to sit in your car?"

She chews her lip. "Okay, but I've got to get to the barn. Eddie's assigned me more horses to ride, and she gets mad if I'm late."

I stomp my feet to stay warm. "C'mon, I'm freezing."

Willow gets in and reaches across to unlock the passenger side. I nudge some trash away with my foot and slide in while she starts the engine. "Declan got called to the police station." She stops fiddling with the heater. Her blue eyes latch onto mine.

"What for?"

"For a glove he found in his truck. The same one you planted on me." My breath comes in smoky clouds in the cold car. "What was with that, anyway?"

"How did the police find out?" A pink swirl unfolds like a slow-motion flower across her cheek and down her neck.

"What does it matter how they found out? The thing is the cops have the glove now, and it happens to match one they found in Trey's car. That makes Declan look bad. So now they're real interested in how the two gloves got separated. Get it? You've got to tell them you found it. And *where*."

She sits bolts upright. "Did Declan tell them I found it?"

Willow is only thinking of herself. I grip the edges of my seat until my fingernails sink into the fake leather. "You don't get it." My teeth ache from crushing them together. "Declan's in trouble. Maybe they think he's a suspect. You have to tell them you're the one who took the glove from Trey's locker. Now you say it wasn't in his locker. You have to quit lying and make sure the police understand Declan didn't have anything to do with it."

"I can't."

"Why not?" I fire back. She looks away. "Why *not*?"

She turns so fast, a wisp of hair sticks to her lips.

"Why can't you say you found it and before you could return it, you lost it in his truck? You could have found it in the barn."

"But I didn't."

She fingers the keychain dangling from the ignition. This whole thing makes no sense. I want to wrap my hands around her throat and shake the words out of her.

"Look, Willow, it's super weird that you found Trey's glove—just one glove—took it, and then shoved it in my backpack when I wouldn't take it. What's really going on?"

A sharp up and down of bony shoulders. She chews her bottom lip.

"C'mon, the truth. Where was it?"

Willow's eyes shift to a spot over my shoulder and I'm afraid she's cooking up another story. "Never mind. Drive to the barn. You can tell me on the way. I'll get Declan to pick me up there."

She shoots me a worried look before shifting into drive. When she speaks, her voice is low. The words are flat like she hates the taste of them.

"I can't go to the police because I have a record."

My mind flashes back to what Cory said about Willow. I shake the thought away.

"Not like a criminal or anything." She sighs and shoots me a beat dog kind of look. "And because I didn't find the glove in Trey's locker, either."

The heater's blasting so I unzip my coat. "So where did you find it?"

"The vet's car."

My heart slides up my throat. "Wade's car?"

She nods. "The day after the party. My car was parked next to his when I went to leave the barn. I saw it on the console and knew whose it was."

My stomach flips. I remember the blood on his shirt at the party. "But why'd you take it? Why didn't you just leave it there and tell someone?" My head is shaking no, no, no, and I can't make it stop.

"I needed someone to help me!" She grips the steering wheel.

"Help you what?" It feels like I've drunk three cups of espresso with waves of caffeine rushing through my veins, making my heart slam against my chest.

She takes a breath that sounds like it's catching on something all the way down her throat. "I'm on probation, so I can't have anything bad happen."

"*You* didn't do anything except take a glove." I can't resist adding, "And lie about it to me."

"I was going to tell you."

"When?"

"I can't have anything to do with the cops. I don't want them coming to the barn and asking me questions about stuff." Her words get faster. "They'd look up my record and that wouldn't be good because then they'd look into stuff, ask questions. If Eddie found out…"

I'm not sure what she's talking about. A nagging thought pulls at my brain. What did she do to get in trouble, and is she still doing it?

"Okay!" A little nudge against Willow's shoulder unsticks the broken record. "I get it, I guess. You wanted someone else to find the glove and give it to the police. Tell them where it was, just not you."

Her blue eyes are teary, like lights shining from under water. "I was going to tell you that day at school, then I got scared. And later. I thought you'd be the best person." She blows a strand of hair away from her face. "Because you were there," she whispers. "You saw."

She's right, I saw. And I didn't say anything, either. We're both liars. "You were there, too. Remember, you're the one who invited me to that party." I turn to the window. If I hadn't gone, I wouldn't be in this mess. Now she's trying to bow out and let everyone else deal with it.

"I had to go."

"No one *has* to go to a party." I turn to her, my eyes narrowed.

"Well, I did. It's a job. Sort of." She taps an index finger on the steering wheel.

The question *what kind of job* springs to my lips, but I slam my mouth shut. All comes clear suddenly. That night there were older guys at the party but lots of young girls. A lot more girls than men. And they didn't seem to go together, not like they were couples who knew each other. My mind flips through a slide show of memories—the guy on the couch with the shiny Rolex pulling a girl out of the crowd onto his lap, the bald one with big biceps calling down the stairs for a girl to bring him a beer when she comes up, the nurse in the short-short uniform hanging on Wade's arm. Willow in the little girl Wendy outfit, disappearing when I needed her.

"You're *paid* by those guys?"

Willow shoots me a sideways glance. "It's not like that. I don't have sex with them or anything."

"Did I say that?"

"No, but it's what you're thinking."

She turns in the driveway of the barn, and her car bottoms out on the first rut.

"So, what do you get paid for and why the hell did you drag me there with you?"

Willow pulls behind the barn and slams the car into park. "I thought I was helping you. To get a job."

I feel my mouth stretch into a grimace.

"Not that—a job at the barn. People were there who could help out. I was there because I was called and told to show up. It was a party for some big client, and he wanted a lot of young girls there."

"What client?"

"I don't know. We never know who orders the service."

"That's what you call it? A service?"

Willow blows out a long, slow breath. "Escort service. It's what *they* call it."

The car gets cold with the engine off. Willow gets out, but leans back in. "I've got something to show you. But not here. C'mon."

Chapter Twenty-Seven

WILLOW'S ROOM AT TWIN ELMS LOOKS LIKE A BUNKHOUSE I stayed in at summer camp when I was ten. She rummages in a dresser drawer, pulls out a necklace, and holds it up. It's a big, ugly locket with a cameo on a cheap-looking chain. The mattress on her bunk is hard. Willow sits on a trunk opposite, twisting the necklace chain around her finger.

"Hey, Willow, you don't have to tell me anything about your… job…if you don't want to."

The chain twists around two fingers until they turn white, then she releases it.

She sits straighter. "I do. Someone has to know." The locket drops in her lap. "I'm really scared."

A spidery-legged tingle runs up my back when Willow goes to the door, looks out, then closes it quietly. She leans against the frame.

"I need to get out of here." She sniffs and wipes her nose on her sleeve. "At first, I started doing the escort parties because I really needed the money. There was a girl here back then who told me about them. How to hook up with the contact and all. She said I could make enough money in a few months to go anywhere I wanted."

"How much money do you need?"

Her head drops and her hair covers her face.

"A lot. I owe too much. It just got worse instead of better."

"So just quit. You have the job here."

A snort. "Yeah, right."

"Did I say something dumb?"

Willow perches on the trunk. "I owe way more than I can make here. Each party pays between three to five hundred a night, depending. At first, it was so easy. Some guy contacts me on this game site, gives me the address in a code that's worked out, and they pay in cash." She flips open the locket and unfolds a small, worn slip of paper. "This is what that girl gave me. How to contact the guy who sets it all up."

I take the paper between two fingers, feeling like it's tainted or will suck me into the same nightmare. In faded blue ink it says:

#Siegfried
Do you play this game all nite?
No, only after midnite.

"What is it?" I ask.

"The guy. When you log on to the game, he's the player. He sees you're active, and if he's got a job, he asks you that question. If you want the job, you answer, but you have to answer exactly, then he sends a PM with the address, time, all the stuff in a sort of code."

She takes the slip of paper, folds it exactly as it was, and places it back in the locket. It snaps closed in her squeezed fist.

"Show me."

"I can't. He hasn't been online for a couple weeks." She hunches her shoulders, gets up, and replaces the locket.

All of a sudden, I get a feeling she's not telling me the whole story. "You asked me to the party for more than the barn job."

Willow stands at the dresser with her back to me. Her shoulders slump. "I wanted to be normal. I don't know. I wanted to go to a party with a friend, like it was a regular party." She looks over her shoulder. "Yeah, maybe I thought you'd want to make some money, too."

I turn away. I'd never be that desperate.

"You said you needed money, to get away from home, same as me. I thought maybe I could help you. If you went to the party and saw it wasn't, you know, like we had to do anything...big...then when I brought it up, you might say yes."

Her words tumble out. When she's done, she sits on the trunk, hugging her sides.

The clop of a horse walking past outside the window breaks the silence.

Willow lifts her head. "I'm sorry."

"It's okay." I should go sit next to her and maybe put my arm around her shoulders, but instead I keep my butt glued to her lumpy mattress. I wonder just how much money she owes. Must be a lot. And to who? I figure it must be the guy on the other end of those mysterious messages. "What're we going to do now?"

"Dunno."

"I'm sure the police are doing something. They've got Trey's glove matching the one found in his car. Doesn't take much to figure out he probably had both of them with him that night, so how one ended up in Declan's truck is a real problem."

Willow twirls a strand of hair. "Trey knew something. That's why he showed up at the party."

"Knew something about...?"

"The business. Both me and Janie are doing it here. Before that, the girl who told me about it, his girlfriend. Then she disappeared."

I scoot to the edge of the bed. My voice drops. "What do you mean disappeared?"

For about the hundredth time this week I wish I could talk to Brenda. Maybe she'd know what to do.

Willow jiggles her leg on the ball of one foot. "Her name's Rachael. Trey was dating her, sort of. I don't know how much she told him, but he started saying stuff to me and Janie about quitting. Then one day Rachael didn't come back to work. Her stuff was gone, so we figured she quit."

"But Trey didn't think so?"

The side of her mouth twists. "Nope. And, besides, he told me he thought what she was doing—what we were doing—was why she disappeared."

"So he went to the party looking for her?"

She shakes her head once, fast. "No way. Don't think so. She'd been gone a while before that party."

"Then he must have wanted to meet someone there. Wade, maybe? How did he know where it was? Did you tell him?"

"I don't think so. I never talked to him about it."

"Maybe Janie did." Then I remember what Declan showed me— the piece of paper he found in the truck. I wonder if it's still in my pocket. I dip a finger in and pull it out.

"Hey, does this mean anything to you?"

I've never seen color drain from a face like they describe it in books. Until now. Judging by Willow's expression, she has a very good idea what the message means.

Chapter Twenty-Eight

I T'S SATURDAY. I DON'T HAVE TO FACE SCHOOL, OR WORKING AT THE barn, or Willow. I keep turning over and over in my head the thought that she was getting paid to meet guys at parties and entertain them any way they wanted. It makes me wonder how badly she needs the money. And why.

Now I know the name of the other girl who went missing—a girl called Rachael. And Trey was looking for her. When I asked Willow, she said she never saw the slip of paper in the glove when she had it, if it really fell out of the glove at all. But what other explanation could there be for a piece of paper with Trey's handwriting on it ending up in Declan's truck? But Willow knew what it was—a code for the address of a client. Unfortunately, she didn't have that code. I hate all this. I only wanted to get a job to make money and get a place to live that would get me away from Angela. Now I'm running from a lot more.

But here, with Declan, I feel safe. At least safer than anywhere else. In the past month, I've even gotten used to Rosie and her mean stares. All the bad stuff melts away when I'm alone in the woods with Declan watching Rosie fly across the sky. He doesn't talk much when he's working the hawk, but that's okay. I don't always want to talk much, either.

Like now.

Declan opens the door to Rosie's mew, and she greets him with a squawk. "I told the police I found the glove in my truck and that someone at the barn gave it to my girlfriend. I didn't know who." He prompts her to hop on his arm.

I drop my head. Now I've got Declan lying for me. Not lying, but not telling the whole truth.

"Sorry," I say. "I'm sorry you had to go because of me."

"It's okay." Rosie hops off his arm onto the scales to be weighed. "But they want to talk to you, too."

I lean against the wall and tilt my head back until it hits with a thud. "Why? They know everything already." But they don't. They don't know half of it. Even worse, they don't know about Wade. And if I say anything, it will eventually get back to him and...what? I'll be the next to disappear. "Did you tell them about the note, too?"

He nods. "I wrote down the name and number. They want the actual note. I told them I'd have to find it."

I fish it out of my pocket and hand it to him.

He puts Rosie back on her perch and writes down her weight.

"Are we going to hunt her?" I ask.

He makes a small clicking noise with his tongue and shakes his head at the logbook. "Not today. Weight's too high." He flashes me a grin. "I've got a better idea."

Outside Rosie's mew, Roheryn runs along the fence line. She whinnies when she sees me now. The last bit of life in the grass shines like a green haze over the field.

"A perfect day for riding," Declan says.

A quick check to see if he's kidding. "What do you mean?" I've saddled Roheryn, flung a leg over her a few times, and jumped off. Then we moved to a pony ride with Declan reluctantly leading her in a circle. Last week I rode her around in her small paddock but never pushed it beyond a slow trot.

"You want to take her for training, and dad says it's okay. Maybe you should make sure..." The blue of his eyes matches the sky behind him.

Make sure of what, I want to ask. Rummaging in a pocket, I come up with a mummified carrot stub. Roheryn's prickly muzzle scoops it up before she rushes off.

"She'll be back," Mr. Kendrick calls, walking down the path toward us. "You've got her coming to you, now you won't be able to get rid of her." He props his elbows up on the fence next to me. "You ride her…" The rest of his words are whipped away by the light breeze.

Mr. Kendrick looks older outside in the sunshine. His skin is grayish. Under a plaid coat the rolled neck of his raglan sweater peeks out.

"I've been on her," I tell him, even though he knows. I've reported all the progress I've made with Roh, every training session, every step forward.

He nods to the field rolling uphill to the tree line. "Out there."

I'm wondering if he's getting impatient with my training method. Most owners want fast results.

Mr. Kendrick grips the fence with his gloved hands. "It's the anniversary."

He doesn't say our anniversary but *the* anniversary, so I think I know what he's talking about—the day his wife died. My lips are rough, dry, as my tongue sweeps over them. Roh stomps her left front—the sign she's impatient. I know her habits. I know so much about this horse, except how she feels to ride. A gust of wind pushes my back as my feet run to the barn.

When I go into her stall, she's waiting for me just outside the back door. We're both breathing hard. The saddle slides into place on her back, and I slip a sugar lump in the corner of her mouth with the bit. Bribery never hurts.

We form a little parade, leading her to the paddock, with Declan and his dad following behind. My fingers fumble with the girth's buckles, and I realize I'm scared. Roh bends her neck around to watch me adjust the girth. I go slowly, careful to avoid the dull pain of teeth sinking into my upper arm. I gather the reins and take two steps up on the mounting block. Roh stands, stretches her neck, relaxed. No pulling, bucks, or running backward like before.

Declan stamps his feet. His dad looks like a fuzzy bird, his head disappearing inside the collar of the coat. The sun is fading already—almost touching the tops of the trees—and there's a sudden dampness to the air that feels like snow. I praise Roh with a soft stroke down her neck and ask her to walk. Her gait is swinging and long. When we turn and start in the other direction, her head telescopes up in front of me, and her back goes rigid. Trouble. I take one rein and turn her head, hoping to get through to her brain and remind her I'm on board. She jigs and skitters into a short, choppy little trot.

"What's wrong?" Declan calls.

"Not sure. She saw something." I force my teeth to unclench.

I've ridden plenty of hot horses. Don't buy into their fears, they say. I give Roh a longer rein and encourage her to go forward into the trot. Move her feet if that's what she wants. Roh launches into an enormous trot. Instead of settling down she's spinning up. She changes direction, crow hops along the long side, and stretches her neck down for a buck.

"Oh, no you don't." I kick her forward. She runs along the fence line, her nose to the outside. Like she's looking for something.

"Don't get hurt!" Declan calls.

Good advice.

The ground is a long way down off of this mare. She runs to the gate, skids to a halt, then bolts off. I give Roh her head as much as I dare, and she spins back to the gate. Then it hits me. It's like I see things through her eyes, in her mind.

"Open the gate!" I yell.

Declan stands straight. "What? Are you crazy?"

"Open it!"

Declan glances at Mr. Kendrick, who nods. He swings open the gate and stands behind it. Roh's ears prick up at the sound of the clatter, and she shoots through the opening, kicking up clods of dirt. I catch Declan's contorted expression as we fly past. She stretches her neck and throttles into a higher speed. Perched up off her back in two-point, I loop a couple strands of her mane through my fingers and hang on. We're headed for the open field at a gallop.

At the top of the hill in a flat, grassy area, she slows.

I need to get it together. Taking up some rein and sitting—thank you, Eddie, for the dressage lessons! I ask her to collect. She does. Steering in a big circle, she bends around my inside leg like she's molded around a pole. I press that leg, and she moves out and away, side passing. It's like riding a stream of water, not a horse. She listens to each movement of my body and forms hers to match. It's magic. We turn and loop and ride circles, big and small. When I ask her to collect more, she almost trots in place. She knows all this stuff. And she's great at it! A bubble of lightness forms in my chest, floats up through my body, and explodes in laughter. I collapse, drape my arms around her neck, and suck in the smell of her damp hair. I love her.

I sit up and let her walk, my head tilted back, watching the clouds and not caring where we're going. The ground begins to climb upward, and she breaks into a jog. As I gather the slack in the reins, she picks up speed. I don't want to go too far or too fast because I don't know the area. Roh pulls on the reins and ignores my attempt to slow her with a head toss. At the top of the next hill, an open field spreads out before us, the ground rutted and littered with cornstalks. One side of the field is bordered by woods.

I turn her head, but she only bends her neck and keeps moving forward. "Roh, we'd better go back." Her head is up, sniffing the air. "Okay, girl, show me what you want, then we're going home." I touch her side, and she launches into a rolling canter.

She veers left and follows a track parallel to the woods. I glance to the side, but my peripheral vision is blurred from the speed. At the bottom of the field she starts to gallop, and I crouch forward, peering through her ears. That's when I see it.

I squeeze my eyes shut and open them again. It can't be. The ground is white—it's covered in snow. But it didn't snow. I hear hard earth under her hooves. I turn my head to look around, but my vision is blurred in any direction but forward. Ahead the sun is blurred behind a veil of falling snow. Beneath Roh's hooves it swirls and drifts. This is crazy. I shake my head, blink, but it's still there. Roh slows and stops at an entrance to the woods. A hawk's high-pitched call echoes through the cold air.

Under us, the snow turns red.

Blood.

Blood against the white snow. So much blood, like someone hurled a bucket of red paint. Drops of it splatter the edges, but in the middle its almost black. I look for a dead deer, but there's no carcass nearby, no source for the blood. It's not hunting season but there could be poachers... I run my hand over my eyes, and when I open them, the ground is a barren field. Brown with scattered leaves. No snow, no blood. Sailing on the currents, a hawk dips her wing and calls before disappearing in the woods. A gust of wind whips over the open field, picking up dried-out corn stalks and lifting leaves into the air. A chill creeps under my jacket and up my damp back. What did I see?

Roh has no interest in running anymore and walks down the other side of the hill toward home. My hands, gripping the reins, tremble. Salty tears stream down my face, into the corner of my mouth, and I lick them away. I'm going insane.

As we ride down the hill to the barn, everything seems normal. Declan and Mr. Kendrick are standing by the gate, waiting. They're smiling, waving. They didn't see anything. If there was anything at all.

I slide the saddle and pad off Roh as soon as we enter the paddock. A cloud of steam rises from her damp skin.

Declan hands me the halter. "She looked good out there."

I don't answer. My voice will crack. Roh walks calmly beside me back to her stall where I throw a cooler over her and toss a few flakes of hay into the rack. It all feels normal—things I've done a thousand times with hundreds of different horses. How can it be so normal here when a minute ago I was in some alternate universe? Seeing things that don't exist? Declan struggles to untangle the reins from the bridle. His face is full of calm concentration as he works on righting the noseband and getting the bit going in the correct direction.

"What did you see?" I ask, keeping all my words calm and slow.

A one-shoulder shrug. "Looked like an old pro. Real good. Great job, Reggie. She's as good as those show horses you take care of."

I slip out of the stall and close the door. Mr. Kendrick watches me as I fold and hang up her turnout blanket. The red splatter on a field of white is burned into my vision.

"Are there many hunters around here?" I ask.

Mr. Kendrick's voice is warm like caramel in the crazy cold of my thoughts. "It's not hunting season yet, not for deer, anyway. We could get poachers, but I haven't heard any gunshots." He steps into view, making me look up at him. "Why?"

"No reason. Just..." I stop. What can I say that won't sound like I'm a lunatic?

His bushy eyebrows inch up his forehead. Grabbing up the saddle and bridle, I brush by him, rushing to the tack room. I don't bother with the light. In fact, the small dark room smelling of leather oil comforts me. My back complains when I lift the saddle onto its peg. When I turn, Mr. Kendrick is standing in the open doorway, framed by the light.

"You saw something, didn't you? Roheryn showed you something."

A sharp shake of my head, no. "No." I didn't see *anything*.

Chapter Twenty-Nine

NO ONE PAYS ATTENTION IN CLASS DURING SHORT WEEKS BEFORE A holiday, not even the teachers. Except Mr. Curtis. Nicknamed Tweedy Bird because of his round, bulging forehead surrounded by a fringe of wispy hair that stands up like feathers. A little pursed mouth like a bill makes the picture complete. He also wears this raggedy yellow sweater a lot.

He's been beating us over the head with *Call of the Wild*, it seems, since school started. He likes to explore themes in the novel. We can't just read it for the story, apparently. Last week we had to hand in a paper analyzing a theme in the book—the Law of the Club and Fang. He harped on the idea of the dog's natural wild nature and tried to apply it to people, particularly high school students. Yeah, we're all one disastrous experience away from going feral and attacking each other. I snort, thinking about it and get some weird looks from the kids around me. The Law of the Club and Fang is easy to understand—get beaten up if you're on the bottom or attack first and scare them off. Mr. Curtis walks down the rows, placing a paper upside down on everyone's desk. He stands over mine, flips through his papers with his beak mouth pinched together, and slaps it down. His hand rests over the paper, fingers splayed—like a chicken foot, I think and smile.

"I'd like to discuss this with you." His voice is low.

When he continues down the aisle, I curl up the corner and see the grade—an A minus—next to a whole bunch of comments I don't read. I slide the paper into a notebook.

When the bell rings, I make sure I'm in a bunch of other kids as I glide to the door.

"Miss Hamilton, do you have a minute?"

My feet freeze on the spot. So close to my escape. I get my smile ready and turn to face him. "Sure." I have lunch next, which is only a half hour. So, by talking to you about this stupid paper, I get to miss it and starve the rest of the day. "I have a few minutes before my next class."

"Pull up a chair." He clears a spot on the edge of his desk. "Your analysis was quite unique, do you know that?"

Unique. That word can be good or bad.

"Most readers, especially modern readers these days, condemn the message of violence in the story. They would prefer Buck find a nice owner, go back to being a domestic dog, comfortable and cared for. But you, Miss Hamilton, you espouse a different ideal."

He sits, hands folded on his desk. I guess this is where I'm supposed to talk.

"Uh, I didn't have a chance to read your comments yet."

"No? Well, in a nutshell, it's this: Your paper raises some provocative ideas. I'd like you to consider expanding it. Taking some of the arguments you put forward and exploring them further. It might have some potential for online publication, in a blog forum or such."

"What ideas?" My insides are shot through with lead, getting heavy at the idea of having to do any more work.

"Take for instance your position on Buck's fate—that the dog was better off at the end of the story than at the beginning. Why?" He cocks his head, birdlike. "It ends with him totally on his own, wild, having to fight off other dogs and his survival in question."

His brows furrow. I sigh. I'm not getting out of here any time soon.

"He didn't have to trust anyone anymore. He was finally free."

Mr. Curtis opens his mouth then slams it shut like he changed his mind. He taps a finger on his chin.

Three guys burst through the classroom door at once, punching and shoving like the Three Stooges.

Mr. Curtis jumps to his feet. "Boys! Yearbook meeting's not for another ten minutes. Wait outside."

I use the interruption to pick up my backpack and head for the door. "That's okay. I got to go." A backward wave to Mr. Curtis and I keep walking, straight into Cory. She's standing just outside the doorway. I jump back like she's on fire. "Sorry."

Her notebook is on the floor. I stoop to get it, but she beats me to it.

"That's okay." The notebook is clutched to her chest like a shield. "How are you?"

It's an automatic *how are you*, not one when you really care what the answer is.

"Okay. Thanks." Pointing to the notebook, I ask, "You on yearbook?"

A nod.

"Thought so." *I'm really sorry I was such an ass* are words crawling up my throat, but they get stuck behind my teeth and don't get out. I want to say them and don't. I take a breath. I'm going to say *something*, but just then she ducks her head and walks by me into the classroom.

I head down the hall, digging in my backpack for a granola bar or something to eat when the bell rings for the next class. Survival. Me and Buck, we got it all figured out.

Right.

Chapter Thirty

THIS IS A HORRIBLE WEEK. IT'S BAD ENOUGH I HAVE TO SPEND Thanksgiving tomorrow in a prison, but today I also have to go to the police station. The detective in charge of Trey's case called. Aunt Sophia made the appointment, and she is actually taking me there, and hopefully back, for a change. Apparently, a minor—that's me—has to be accompanied by an adult when questioned. I had to tell Eddie I couldn't make it for my shift at the barn this afternoon. When she asked why, I told her the cops wanted to talk to me. I feel like calling to tell Detective Maggiano that he should call Willow—tell him I had nothing to do with it. But that wouldn't be entirely true.

What do you wear to be interrogated? I stand in front of my dresser, staring down at an open drawer. A pair of black jeans are clean, so I pull them out. I have a blouse in the closet that looks okay.

"Are you ready?" Aunt Sophia calls from the kitchen. I hear her keys rattling.

"Almost!" I pull on the jeans while I hit Brenda's number I programmed into Declan's phone. I text her, even though she never answers.

Police questioning me at 4. Come? Regina.

I know Angela had her pulled off my case, but maybe Brenda can still help. Somehow. The new social worker sent me an email questionnaire and a promise to be in touch. I cram Declan's oversized phone in a back pocket, run fingers through my hair, and walk out to the kitchen.

"I hope this doesn't take too long." Aunt Sophia holds the door for me. "The restaurant wants me there by six."

Inside the door to the station there's a big front desk with a cross-looking officer behind it. She's whacking a stapler down on stacks of papers like she's smooshing bugs. A few chairs line the wall in a waiting area. Aunt Soph announces to the killer stapler lady that we're here to see Detective Maggiano. While we're standing at the desk, waiting for instructions, I hear my name. Brenda is standing against the wall by the door.

I walk over to her. "Hey. You got my text."

She gives her phone a little shake and smiles. "Was on my way to the courthouse next door. Got to be there in an hour, but listen"— she drops her voice—"I'm not here officially. Your case has been transferred."

"Regina, c'mon." Aunt Sophia gestures. She's next to the desk officer who is holding a door open to another section of the station. I walk over with Brenda. The officer rushes us through the door and down a hallway.

"Mrs. Zaccaro, how are you?" Brenda adjusts her giant pocketbook higher on her shoulder. "I want to assure you I'm here at Regina's request—as a personal favor, not in an official capacity."

Aunt Sophia shoots her a worried look but doesn't respond. The officer leads us to a small room. Inside, a big guy stands up. My eye goes straight to a holster on his side. He thrusts out a beefy hand to Aunt Soph, Brenda, then me last. Introductions over, he realizes there are only two chairs. He grabs some guy in the hall and orders him to bring in another. Brenda takes the extra chair and places it farther back, behind us, and sits.

"Regina, you understand that this is an informal inquiry. You are not under oath or even required to answer any or all of my questions." He pushes some paper across his desk with a pen. "This form acknowledges that I advised you of this. If both you and your—" He looks up at Aunt Sophia.

"Aunt."

"Aunt can sign, we can begin. How are you doing, Brenda?"

I swivel in my seat to catch her give the detective a little wave. They know each other.

The detective flips open a small black case to display his badge and leaves it face up on the corner of the desk. "Okay. Let's cover the facts." He leans back in his chair. I lean forward.

Detective Maggiano seems nice, just like Declan said he was. He asks me to tell him in my own words—like whose else would I use?—how I came by the glove. While I'm going through all the weird conversation I had with Willow, he's nodding like he's heard it all before, and that's good. I don't mention where Willow got the glove. Just then, like he can read my mind, he asks, "When you and Willow were talking about the glove, did she mention where she found it?"

A zing goes through me, and I wonder if he can read anything on my face. I know some cops can tell whenever people are hiding something by watching body language. Crossing my legs to look casual, I replay Willow's words in my head and repeat them, so it's not a lie. Not my lie, at least. "She said she found it in Trey's locker at the barn."

He scribbles a note on a yellow legal pad.

My face feels hot.

"And she gave it to you because...?"

My focus shifts from his face to the corner of the room. "I didn't take it. She stuck it in my backpack." I look him in the eye and try not to look away again. "Willow's kind of strange. She said later she thought maybe someone could use it as scent for dogs to search for Trey. Then she thought she'd get in trouble for taking it, so she stuck it in my stuff." I shrug. "I dunno." I'm talking fast, and he's got the pen hovering over the paper not writing anything down.

"All right." He drops the pen. "Mr. Kendrick also found a note that he believes might have been in the glove."

When he says Mr. Kendrick I picture Declan's dad and am confused for a second until I realize he's talking about Declan. "I never saw the note until Declan found it later, in his truck."

"Do you have any idea what it means? Who wrote it?" He fishes in a side drawer and pulls out a little plastic bag with the note inside. He puts it on the desk next to his badge.

One sharp nod is all I can manage. I see the handwriting.

"You know what it means?"

"No." The word bursts out. "No, I mean, I know it's Trey's handwriting. I've seen his writing at the barn, on his stuff."

Aunt Sophia leans forward to examine the note. Her brow wrinkles and she sits back.

The detective's index finger taps the bag. "So Trey wrote this."

"I guess."

He picks up the phone, holding up one finger, and speaks into it. "Give me that whiz-bang new kid in computer forensics. Yeah, that's his name." He glances at all of us while I pretend not to be listening. "Yeah, Stan, I got a confirmation. Get that kid on it." He hangs up. Opening his palms, he says that's it. He stands up and somehow weaves his large body through the chairs crammed in that small room to open the door.

Outside his office, Aunt Sophia places a hand on my back. "That wasn't so bad, was it?"

If you think threading a needle around the truth is easy, no, it wasn't so bad. I tell her he was nice and she agrees. I look around for Brenda because I want to say thanks, but she's still in the office.

"How much of that was the whole story?" Aunt Sophia inclines her head toward the detective's office.

"What do you mean?"

She runs a hand down my arm. "I've had a lot of experience with people who can step around the truth."

When we get outside, she pushes a number on her phone and puts it to her ear. "Hi, Vickie, yeah, I can't come in this eve after all. Sick. Think it's the flu." She smiles at me with the phone pressed to her ear, nodding. "Okay, thanks, I'll let you know when I'm better." She drops the phone in her purse. "Let's go get some dinner. You can fill me in on what's really going on."

Chapter Thirty-One

WHEN WE GET BACK FROM DINNER, WADE'S CAR IS IN THE driveway. He gets out and meets us at the front door.

"I've been waiting forty minutes for you to get home. Where were you?" He doesn't ask if it's okay to come in, he just walks through the door first.

Even Aunt Sophia looks a little upset about him being here, and takes her time hanging up her Dallas Cowboys parka before she answers. "We went to dinner. We weren't expecting anyone to be waiting on us."

Wade sits on the arm of the couch. "Listen, we're all going tomorrow, and I wanted to make sure we have our story straight." He looks pointedly at me. "I don't want to upset Angela with this police business. More than that, I want to make sure you're going to behave and not do anything that would call attention to us."

Aunt Sophia remains standing in the middle of the room. "What do you imagine Regina would do, Wade?" Her nose scrunches like she's smelling the stink in this place for the first time. A hand goes to her hip. I don't know who this new Aunt Sophia is, but I'm glad she finally showed up.

Wade blows off her question with a wave of his hand. "I don't know what she'd do. She's a teenager. She's likely to pull anything for attention."

"Hey. I'm right here in the room."

Wade takes a step in my direction, towering over me. His voice is a low rumble. "Don't pull another scene like last time. Remember our talk."

As if I could forget the syringe. The thought of Tucker in danger takes the wind out of me. And that's exactly what Wade wants. He must see it in my face. He smirks.

"Good. Just so everything goes okay."

Aunt Sophia moves toward the kitchen. "Anyone want coffee?"

I'm praying he says no and leaves.

"No, I've got to get going." Wade walks to the entrance of the kitchen. "By the way, how did it go with the police?"

Wade's worried about the police questioning, but not for my sake. Aunt Sophia says we were only there about a half hour.

"They got any leads on this kid's disappearance?" He leans on the doorframe, crossing his arms. What's with *this kid*, like he doesn't know Trey's name?

Before Aunt Sophia can respond, I call across the room.

"We're not supposed to talk about it. The detective told us not to."

Wade turns to me. His face is twisted, then immediately clears like a quick thunderstorm. "Of course. That makes sense. I hope they find him." He picks his coat off the couch where he tossed it earlier. "I'll leave you gals." He struggles with the zipper for a moment, and with one hand on the front door, he points to us. "See you tomorrow."

The door slams, sealing off a wave of bitter cold. I think I hear Aunt Soph mutter *prick*, but I couldn't swear to it. Standing in the entrance to the kitchen, still wearing my coat, I watch her put a few dishes in the dishwasher and wipe down the counter.

"Is that offer for coffee still good?" I ask.

She looks surprised. "Sure."

It's been a long afternoon and evening. The kitchen window is black, reflecting back my own image sitting at the table. Aunt Soph sets the sugar bowl and spoons down, even though neither one of us takes sugar. She returns with two steaming mugs and places one in front of me. Black liquid scalds down the back of my throat with the first gulp, and it feels wonderful. Sophia sits down with a sigh like all her air is leaking out.

"Long night." She speaks my thoughts.

"Tomorrow's going to be worse."

She takes a tentative sip.

We've spent a lot of time today sitting across from each other like this while I told her what was going on. I wove together the bits and pieces I could tell her, leaving some gaps, like the fact that I didn't tell the police Wade had argued with Trey the night of the party and returned with blood on his shirt. I also don't know how far I can trust Aunt Soph. She's nice, but Angela knows how to make even nice people do what she wants.

I look up and Soph's eyes are on me. They droop on the outside corners, giving her a constant sad puppy look. Her skin is tanned, even in the winter here, with deep lines around her mouth and fanning out from her eyes. Her hand slides across the table and covers mine. Funny, I think of Mr. Kendrick when she does this, and it makes me sad.

"I'm really sorry, Regina."

"About what?"

She takes her hand away and wraps it around the coffee mug.

"I'm sorry things turned out like this for you."

To lighten things up, I give a dismissive wave. "Oh, that. Yeah, going off to live with two depraved criminals in a few months. Maybe I can get my own reality show out of it."

"Two?"

"Oh." I think quick. "I mean Angela along with Wade. I just threw him in the same category. You know."

Soph eyes me over the brim of her coffee cup while she takes a sip. Calculating everything I've said. I'm definitely going to shut up now.

"I'm sorry I couldn't help you, you know, keep you with me in Texas. I wanted to, but..."

I didn't know this.

She chews her lip and looks away. "Legally, Angela has custody. And I couldn't go against her."

"No one can go against her. I've tried. Got the scars to prove it."

Aunt Soph winces. I didn't mean to make her feel worse. Well, maybe I did. "So, why not? Angela knows where you buried the bodies or something?" I put on my best gangster accent.

She gives me a thin smile. A crimson flush blooms up her cheek. "Yeah, in a matter of speaking, she does."

I clamp my lips closed. Stupid. Words leak out before I've really thought about them. "I'm sorry."

"We're a pair, both apologizing to each other." She stands, dumps the dregs of her coffee in the sink, and leans against the counter.

"You were going to tell me what she was like. You know, growing up."

Aunt Sophia looks down at her boots.

"Forget it. You don't have to say."

"No." She slides back in her seat. "It's something we have in common." A tight smile. "Angela could be your best friend or your worst enemy all within the span of a few minutes. She was lots of fun and always had exciting plans, but if you went against her, watch out."

"Sounds like my experience, except for the fun part."

Her face tells me maybe she's had Angela beat her up some, too. Maybe not physically, but Angela's got something that keeps Aunt Sophia afraid, some kind of blackmail. "Aunt Soph," I begin, not sure what I can or can't say. Not sure what she'll tell Angela to protect her own secrets, whatever they are. "Wouldn't it be great if we could do something to keep her there? In prison, I mean."

She laughs, but it's not a happy laugh.

"Really. Like what if we did something to make sure she didn't get out. What if I told them I'm not going to go live with her because she's crazy and you backed me up. What if—"

"What if? I'll tell you. She'd find a way to work the system, and it would end up good for her and bad for us. If what you told me is true, you'd have a dead horse on your conscience, and I'd end up taking her place in prison."

Prison? Wow. She's right. I slump and rest my forehead against my folded arms. My voice comes out muffled. "Maybe we can just run away together."

There's no sound but the ticking of the kitchen clock. I'm too tired to get up, change into pajamas, and get into bed. The shrill ring of the landline phone on the wall sends a charge down my spine. Aunt Soph catches it on the second ring.

"Yes, I'll accept the call." She covers the receiver and mouths, "It's her."

I get up to leave, but she signals for me to wait. Aunt Soph goes through some chitchat about how we're doing well, we went out to dinner, yes, we're all coming tomorrow. Then she holds the phone out to me.

The receiver is still warm from where Soph was gripping it.

"Hi." My voice is flat.

"Hello, dear. Looking forward to seeing you tomorrow."

The silence echoes back in my ear.

"Are you there?"

"Yeah, I'm here."

Angela's peeved voice ordering someone in the background to "wait one minute" sounds muffled, like she has a hand over the mouthpiece. Then her voice roars into my ear again. "I don't have much time. They only give us fifteen minutes." No doubt she is giving some poor guard a dirty look now. "Wear something nice tomorrow, and for God's sake, do something with your hair. Do you hear me?"

"Yeah, I'll do something."

"Don't say 'yeah.' I spoke with Wade, and I've decided that boy you've been seeing is not a good influence."

"Declan?" I sit bolt up in the chair. "He hasn't done anything."

"No? Got you called in to the police station. I'd say that's something."

"It wasn't his fault. It has nothing to do with him. He just found—"

"I've got to go. You're not seeing him, do you understand?" Before she hangs up, her voice drops. The words are a poison dripping through the line. "And if you disobey me, I'll know."

I hang up and text Declan right away. I don't know what Angela's done, but I'm sure she's got some way to spy on me.

Meet me at 8am tmrw Lisbon Diner. Emergency.

"Angela's spying on me."

"From prison? She's got a lot of tricks, but—"

I hold up the phone. "Through my phone. Tracking, call monitoring, blocking numbers. Now she's forbidden me to see Declan. Says if I do, she'll know."

"She knows because Wade's tells her everything."

"No. Declan thinks he found spyware on my phone."

Aunt Sophia stares at hers as if it were a snake sitting on the table. She grabs it and powers it down.

Declan's phone chimes and a message pops up.

I'll B there.

A warm wave of relief.

Next, I call Willow. When she answers, I pray she'll be able to help me get Roheryn over to Twin Elms. If Angela's forbidding me to see Declan, that means I'll lose the mare, too. Until I can figure something out, I have to get Roheryn where I can still work with her, have her near me. If I have to lose Declan for a while, I can't lose Roheryn, too. She's more than just a nice horse to ride, I'm beginning to think she's my horse god.

"I need you to arrange with Eddie for me to bring a horse over… Yeah, for boarding…Yeah I know it's really expensive. I'll figure a way to work it off." I shake the image of the cowboy boots out of my head. I'm sinking in deeper. "How? I don't know. I just know I have to keep this horse close to me."

Chapter Thirty-Two

S O, TODAY'S THE DAY I'VE BEEN DREADING—THANKSGIVING. AUNT Sophia drops me at the curb outside the Lisbon Diner. I told her I was meeting a friend for breakfast, but she knows it's Declan. She brought me anyway.

Before pulling away, she leans out the window. "Don't even think of not showing up in time to see your mom this afternoon."

"I won't," I tell her, shutting the door. Only because I don't want her to get in trouble.

Declan is waiting just inside the door. The place smells like burnt coffee and grease. We slide into a booth in the back and look at the laminated menus. Mine is still sticky from someone else's fingers. A waitress slams two mugs down on the table. Coffee sloshes over the rim of one.

I don't even know how to start. Declan pulls off his hat, and his hair flies around his head like a rosy halo. The restaurant is dark and empty. I guess only losers go out for breakfast on Thanksgiving morning. The sound of dishes rattling in the kitchen leaks out to the seating area and brings my focus back.

"I'm getting the breakfast burrito," he announces. "I'm starving."

"Not saving room for turkey?"

"Nah. Dad's is dry. I end up feeding most of it to the dogs."

"I'll take dry over institutional prison turkey any day." I chew on the corner of a nail.

After the waitress takes our order, he gets up and moves to sit next to me. His fingers entwine in mine under the table. "What's up, Reggie?"

A gloppy lump the size of a bolder blocks my throat right at the point where the words are supposed to come out. He's so nice to me. My fingers squeeze his, hard. I can't look up at his face, so I direct my words to the surface of the table. "My mother's forbidden me to hang out with you. She called last night. Said you're a bad influence, but really it's because she wants to cut me off from everything or everyone I care about. It's how she works."

A little snort laugh shakes his side. I feel it on the bench seat. "I've never been a bad influence before."

"It's serious." I catch his eye. "She'll do stuff."

His smile melts.

"She's probably tapped my phone with that parental spyware. Said she'd know if I did anything."

Declan picks up my cell. "The good news is it's limited to your phone. You can use another one and not be tracked." He pushes his phone back in front of me. "We'll stick with the swap."

"But if she gets all the messages on my phone—"

"She'll get mine. It will confuse her and maybe she'll give up."

His knee bumps mine under the table. I reach around the back of his neck and pull his face closer. Leaning in, our lips touch lightly, then press harder. He shifts and arms slide around my waist, hands cup the back of my head, pressing me closer. His lips slide under mine, move, and fit together like a puzzle piece dropping into place.

He pulls back and the warmth fades.

"She won't win." His whispered words are as powerful as a kiss.

The waitress appears, holding two heavy plates. "Who had the burrito?"

I cock a thumb at Declan. She puts an omelet and toast in front of me. I nibble on one corner of the over-buttered triangle of bread. My stomach lurches at the site of the eggs.

"You know this means I can't come work with Roh anymore." I poke at my food.

He slides his fork under the burrito and peers beneath it. He lets it drop. "Didn't think about that."

"Yeah, well, I did last night. If it's okay, I asked if I could bring her to Twin Elms. At least for a while, until we figure something out."

"But that place is expensive, right?"

"I'll work it off," I rush to tell him before he thinks up more excuses. I grip his arm. "Maybe if your dad could pay what he does to keep her at home, that would help, and I can figure something out for the rest." Twisting in the seat, I remember what I told Willow about the parties. "Roh has a ton of talent. She should be at a place where she can get the right training. I can do some stuff, but this place has a Grand Prix trainer. If he sees how good she is…" The words tumble out faster and faster.

"Okay. I'll talk to Dad."

My hand drops from his arm. "Thanks. I just can't lose her, too."

The waitress fills our coffee and asks if we need anything more. Declan shakes his head. She slaps the check on the table and leaves. Behind us in the next booth, a man sits down with two little kids. I hear crayons roll across the table and onto the floor. A cry.

It makes me sad. I wonder if this family was sent out so the mother can get Thanksgiving dinner done in peace without two little kids. A normal mother with normal plans to have a normal holiday for her normal family. I look at Declan's face, his cheeks and tip of his nose flushed with the heat from his spicy burrito. I wonder what his mom was like, if she made Thanksgiving turkey dinner, even though she was Irish. A dinner of dry turkey with him and his dad would be all I'd want right now. A tear sneaks over my eyelid and streams down my face. I snatch up a napkin and wipe it.

Warm fingers touch my chin and turn my face. Declan's forehead lightly bumps mine and his arms go around my shoulders. Breath with a slight scent of coffee glides over my skin.

"It will be okay, Reg. You have to trust me."

Trust. I don't even know what it means. "What can you do?" I pull away from his hug and press my back against the wall. "No one can do anything." A coil of fear unwinds like a snake inside me. I'm afraid of this fear snake. It's mean, and when it shows up I say things, do things to people and hurt them. "What can you do, really?" His face shows surprise at my reaction. The snake uncoils, raising its head to strike.

"I'll go with you. If you want to talk to the social worker lady, the police, whoever."

My turn to snort. "Right, like I can trust them. I tell Brenda some stuff, and she blabs to Angela when I told her not to. Where does that get me? Brenda gets fired, and now Angela's working her revenge on me. I count on Aunt Soph to help me, and she's too afraid." The kids in the next booth cheer when their food arrives. I look at my plate, at food I've hardly touched. "Even Cory turned on me."

This isn't true. I know that. I turned on her. Because I didn't believe she was a real friend. One who would stick with me through everything. A friend who wouldn't judge. Before she rejected me, I pushed her away first.

Declan is rigid beside me, his hands on the table, framing his half-eaten burrito. I catch the waitress looking at us.

He talks down into his plate. "You have to start trusting someone, Reg. Let someone in."

"I do. Me." I take a gulp of lukewarm coffee and shoot him a confident grin.

"I'm serious. You know what I mean. Someone who can help you."

"Like who?" My eyebrow shoots up my forehead. "Trusting people hasn't worked out so great for me in the past. I can't even trust my mother to be a real mother." My nose is running, and I can feel that tightness building in my throat.

"It takes time. You have to build trust. Give people a little chance, maybe ask them for something small, then when they come through, ask for more."

"I don't know what you're talking about. People are either going to help me or they're not. Usually not."

"Sometimes you have to let them prove you can depend on them a little at a time. That's what I mean. Like training Rosie. I gave her a chance to trust me for little things—flying to my hand from her perch for a treat—long before I took her outside to fly off her line."

"Hawks and horses are easier to train than people. People let you down. They don't follow the same rules. You can't trust *people*, that's what I'm saying." A hangnail I'm picking at blooms red blood. I sit on my hand.

"Do you trust me?"

Declan's blue eyes are paler, grayer than usual this morning. Gray sky, gray tabletop, gray day. I look down. Do I trust him? Trust him not to leave? What if he decides I'm too much trouble, too many bad connections? Do I trust him to stick with me if I tell about Wade? Will he still like me when he finds out I'm really a coward? I don't even trust me.

"Reg? You didn't answer me. Do you trust *me* at least?"

His hands grip my forearms and shake.

"You could leave, too. You could decide you're better off—"

"I could. If I were an A-hole." His hands drop to his side. "I hope you know I'm not."

"You're not. I'd never think that. It's just that, well, I can never rely on what someone else will do. Or not do."

He pushes his plate away, rocks onto one hip to pull out his wallet, and drops some bills on the table. "To trust someone, you have to take a risk. Believe in them. But to do that, you've also got to believe there's good in the world. I don't know if you believe that anymore, Reg. Do you?"

His eyes shift back and forth, searching for something in my face. He sighs, stands, and grabs his coat. The air is heavy with bacon grease and unspoken words. Right now, I should stand up and hug him and tell him of course I trust him. He's the only one I've come close to trusting. The waitress is hovering with a pot of coffee. Declan waves her off. He's waiting for me to say it. To say of course I trust him, I believe in him, I love him. But I don't say those words. I say safe words, armored words, ones that protect me.

"You sound like a guy who should be on Oprah."

Declan heads to the door. With one hand on the handle, he turns to where I'm still sitting in the booth and calls, "Good luck today." It doesn't sound like he means it. He crams his hat down low over his ears and disappears into grayness. When the door closes, a waft of cold air, smelling of snow, washes over the room.

Chapter Thirty-Three

THE PRISON GUARD ESCORTS US TO A RECEPTION ROOM. IT'S decorated for Thanksgiving. That is, if you're celebrating it in a cross between a kindergarten and a dungeon. Tablecloths and matching napkins have happy Pilgrims dancing along their borders. There are cutouts of fat turkeys taped to the walls. But unlike a classroom, this place has locked doors and barred windows. I note the plastic forks and spoons at each place setting. No knives, not even plastic ones. The room is overheated and smells of a mixture of bleach and gravy.

There are other families in here. Two little kids wrap their arms around a woman's leg and hang on her. A guy with slicked back hair and a spider neck tattoo gives a small dark-haired woman a kiss on her cheek. Guards stand against the walls but don't interfere. I guess all this hugging and stuff is allowed today. Which makes me more nervous. I like it better when the lady guard keeps everyone in line.

Aunt Sophia strains her neck, looking over the crowd. "I don't see her."

"Good. Maybe she's not coming."

That earns me a warning look. "Just try. Okay?" Aunt Soph's lipstick is too bright with a pinkish tint in the harsh light. Makeup has crept into the deep lines in her face. I tug at the neckline of my blouse. The edge is rubbing on me, irritating my skin. But that's not all that's irritated.

A door opens. Angela enters, escorted by a thin woman in a baggy uniform. An official at the desk asks her name, holding up a clipboard. Angela walks by without answering, headed straight for us. My finger hooks the neck of the blouse for a savage tug.

"There you are!" she calls, arms stretched wide. In an instant, my vision is blocked when she envelops me, pushing my head down into her bony shoulder. Fingers run down the back of my head, pinching a bit of hair there. "It's growing at last."

The hand is removed, and I step away, sucking in a breath like I've just surfaced from a pool of dark water. Angela strains her neck, scanning the room on tip-toes.

"Where's Wade?"

A bubble of glee wells up in me when I recognize her disappointment.

"Maybe he forgot," I say.

She shoots me a hate beam. I'm delighted.

"He got hung up in security check-in," Aunt Sophia says, always the peacemaker. "Let's grab a seat."

We find a table we don't have to share with another family, and Soph drapes her blazer over the extra chair. When I sit down and scoot the chair in, it catches on the paper tablecloth and pulls everything to the edge.

"Regina." Angela sighs, sitting next to me. She straightens everything. "You act like a bull in a china shop. Pay attention to what you're doing." A perfectly manicured finger nudges the fork into line.

She turns to Aunt Soph, across the table. "Fill me in on what's going on." She lowers her voice. "What's this about a trip to the police station?"

No polite chitchat for Angela. She dives right in, taking charge.

Sophia wraps her fingers around the paper Pilgrim cup in front of her, no doubt wishing it had something more in it than fruit punch.

"Nothing much to tell, Angela. Really. There's a missing boy, and the police are talking to a number of kids who work with him. He probably got himself in some kind of trouble and took off. Nothing more."

Soph's eyes cut to mine. I hope mine are saying thanks. Before Angela can interrogate further, Wade appears with an escort. He's wearing a dark suit over a shirt so white it glows under the lights. His tie is perfect, his shoes are shined. He looks like a corporate lawyer or big-time banker. In a few strides, he appears at Angela's side and pulls her to her feet in a hug.

"Sorry to be late," he says.

Wade takes a seat next to Aunt Sophia, opposite me. I don't look at him. A server dressed in kitchen whites rolls a cart along the tables, setting down plates of turkey, potatoes, green bean casserole, and gravy. Another one comes behind, placing a knife only at places where a person is seated.

"Wonder if they'll collect the knives afterwards and count them." I hold mine up and wave it in the air. My hand is slapped down to the table.

Wade's eyes narrow. His hand presses mine. "What are you doing?"

My heart is pounding in my throat. "Nothing."

"That's right." He smiles, removes his hand. "You're doing nothing."

Sophia's voice breaks in like a light breeze. "Regina's been working at a farm after school. Why don't you tell your mother more about it?"

Soph gives an encouraging tilt of her head, as if to say, *go on*.

"It's at that dressage barn, Twin Elms. There's a Grand Prix trainer there, and I'm working with some horses." That's a lie, of course. I'm only working with Tucker.

"Dressage?" Angela's eyebrows crease.

"Galen Ekerd's place," Wade says.

They exchange a look. I'm not sure what it means.

The light brown gravy on my plate has a shimmering gelatinous quality to it. I slice through the turkey and take a bite. The food rolls around in my mouth without much taste. It's only lukewarm, but I'm hungry. I remember with a pang that I didn't eat breakfast and suddenly recall the image of Declan's dark figure walking away from the diner. I shovel the potatoes in my mouth.

"Take it easy on the potatoes, dear." A light touch on my shoveling elbow. "You don't want to pack on weight."

Angela, obsessed with weight gain, is stick thin. Her skin hangs on her like a shrunken elephant.

"After I get—" She stops. Probably she was going to say *when I get out of prison* but then goes in another direction. "When we are all together again, you'll have no time for an after-school job."

"Oh yeah? What will I be doing then?" I put down my fork and knife and stare at her.

"For one thing, real riding. Dressage is fine to give you good basics on the flat, but I don't want you to lose your edge for jumping. You'll need to sharpen your skills again."

"What do you know about my skills? You haven't seen me ride since you got put in prison." I say the word no one else dares say—*prison*. It's like we're all pretending we're not here. I pull the front of my blouse away from my skin where it's scratching me.

"Regina," Soph murmurs my name.

"When you get out of *prison*, what is it you see me doing for you? Because I don't think I owe you anything."

Everyone stops eating. Wade's fork hovers in midair.

I think about Tucker, but I can't stop.

"I'm not going to work for you, if that's what you think. Hell, I'm not going to live with you if I can help it."

Angela's green eyes take on a golden cast as if something started burning inside of her. But there's no expression on her face. When she talks, her voice is flat. Just words, like she's reading a sign.

"You are coming to live with me. That's non-negotiable. And you will be riding for our farm, and you will learn to obey what I tell you."

No one else notices our table. No one is looking. One guard stares into the empty air in the middle of the room. Another watches a family with a little kid climbing on his chair to reach the decoration in the middle of the table. Angela stares at me with her flaming eyes. Wade puts a hand on her shoulder, but she shrugs it off. I know the signs. I know her hand is itching to lash out like a serpent, ready to strike. But she can't here.

"No, Angela, I'm not. I don't care what I have to do. I'll live on the street, but I'm not living with you again."

Her head cocks, questioning. It is incomprehensible to her that anyone would tell her no. It's all I can do to keep myself from moving backward, away from her. But that would give her the advantage, to see me retreat. I can't yield. I started this. I didn't mean to, but now I have to finish it.

"Then where will you live, dear?" Her eyes cut to the guard by the door.

I remember what Brenda said, about emancipation of minors. It will kill her that I have a plan, that I've thought things out—even if I don't have a job that will pay me enough to live on.

"I'm filing for my independence. I talked to a lawyer. It's called emancipation of a minor."

Her face pales. She must sense she's losing this hand in her mind's poker game.

"I have cause. It's called 'unfit mother.'"

Angela spins to face Aunt Sophia. "What do you know about this?"

She raises both her hands like she's under arrest. "Nothing. First I've heard of it." Soph shoots me a scowl. I don't care.

Angela's fingernails dig into my forearm. "And where would you live? What would you live on?" The fingers are cold. "This is ridiculous. Who put this idea in your head?"

Her grip tightens on my arm, and I cry out, one sharp bark of pain. The staring guard's head snaps in the direction of our table, and Angela drops her hand.

"Shape up, Regina. Right now." Wade points the end of his plastic knife in my face. "Stop making things worse."

"Worse? How can they get worse?" I fire a burning glare at Sophia, knowing she could do something and she doesn't. "Locking me up here would be less of a prison than living with her." I don't look at

Angela. My voice lowers so only those at the table can hear. "At least the guards aren't allowed to beat up the prisoners."

Angela hisses through clenched teeth. "I've never beaten you."

Her face blooms red under her orangey makeup. Maybe she really believes that, I don't know. I point to my collarbone where a huge lump attests to the break there.

"You fell off a horse."

"You pulled me off a horse. Like you pushed me down stairs, shoved me out of the car once onto the side of the road, and slammed my hand with the lid of a tack trunk."

"You're the one who does it." Her voice rises above the noise in the room. "You're the one who can't behave, can't follow rules or do what you're told."

Wade reaches across the table and grasps Angela's wrist. "Calm down. We'll settle this later."

I know for a fact that telling Angela to calm down is like throwing a bucket of kerosene on a fire. She slaps the table with the flat of her hand. "I will not calm down."

A guard pushes off from the wall and approaches. Angela's face is focused on me. It's hard, her mouth tight and downturned.

"And at least in prison they have to feed you." My voice is mocking, light. "You used to lock me in my room without dinner. Or don't you remember that, *Mom?*"

Her hands reach across the table and lock around my upper arms like talons. The room starts to shake. I squeeze my eyes shut. The shaking stops, but I feel a sting against my cheek. A chair is knocked over, and when I open my eyes, Angela's seat is empty. Two guards clamp her on either side, pulling her backward.

Everyone jumps up. A little kid starts wailing. Angela demands to be let go, and the guards loosen their hold. The one in charge is at our table in about three strides.

"What's going on here?"

Wade steps in. "An accident, Officer." He points to the upset table settings and the overturned chair. His voice is level, reasonable, and calm. "She tipped in her chair and, trying to right herself, grabbed out at anything to keep from falling. She accidently struck her daughter in the process."

The officer looks at Angela. "What do you have to say?"

She straightens, shrugging off the guards. "I don't know what happened. All of a sudden the chair slipped, and my poor daughter tried to catch me, and my arms were flailing around... I'm so sorry, darling." She looks at me from under her lashes.

The officer turns to me. "That right?"

I rub my arms where her fingers dug into me. From the corner of my eye, I see Wade making a barely perceptible nod of his head, urging me to say yes. Aunt Soph stands with her hand over her mouth, her eyes round. They're afraid. They're afraid of what I'll say. The officer raises his brows, waiting for my answer. If I say no, if I tell him she struck me, maybe I'll get out of having to live with her. Maybe. But, also, I know Tucker is in danger, and maybe Roh. The air flees from my lungs, and I crumple like a wet tissue. I hear Declan's words this morning ringing in my head. I want to trust in someone besides myself, to believe something good will happen for me, but I can't. Not today.

"Yes." Sinking back down in the chair, I take my place at the table like a good daughter. "Yes, that's what happened." I glance at Wade. "Exactly."

Chapter Thirty-Four

AUNT SOPHIA TUGS THE SASH OF HER BATHROBE, CINCHING IT TIGHT around her middle. "I don't know what you were thinking today. Why did you have to antagonize Angela like that?"

The kitchen is freezing, like usual. A snake of cold air drifts in under the door and circles around my feet. A wind has kicked up. I pull the hood up on my sweatshirt and huddle over a cup of tea. Soph stands over me. She's probably glaring at the top of my head, but I'm not going to turn around and check.

"Well? What did you hope to achieve?"

She sounds pissed. Can't blame her. Angela will blame her for not controlling me. Angela will blame anyone but herself.

I clamp my bottom lip between my teeth. What can I say that anyone will understand?

Soph sighs and collapses in a rickety chair at the table opposite me. Her face is shiny and red, scrubbed of makeup.

"They say it might snow tomorrow." My eyes wander to the dark window.

"You're talking about the weather?" Soph's hand never leaves her red Solo Cup.

I stare at her hand. I can't look at anyone. "She's a monster."

Her foot taps on the floor. Another sigh. "I know."

It feels like the room gets colder, darker.

"I know, but you can't act out like that. Not until it's safe."

My head snaps up. "It will never be safe."

"Maybe if social services can do something. Maybe that case worker lady—"

"She's off my case, remember? Besides, now Wade is backing Angela up, and he's worse. You heard what he said to me when we left this afternoon?" I deepen my voice and strike a cocky pose. "*You made the right choice. Too bad you couldn't have learned that sooner.*' Whatever that means. I have no choice now. I have to keep Tucker and Roh safe."

"What do you mean *safe*? You think he'd harm the horses?"

"Yes!" Both palms slap onto the table. I can't believe no one else sees what's going on. "To keep me in line. Or else." A throat slitting motion makes Soph's eyes pop open wide. "He's the one who killed the horses for the insurance money. What's to stop him from doing it again? Too bad it was only Angela who went to prison for it."

Aunt Soph takes a big gulp from her cup. She eyes me over the rim and sets it down. "Have you told anyone about him?"

"Who's going to believe me? No proof." I reach over to take her cup and raise it to my lips. She doesn't stop me. The liquid has a nice burn rolling down my throat, turning all the words and feelings and useless hope to ash. It hits my stomach like a boulder in a small pond. One more sip, and I push the cup back to her. "Did you ever wonder why he sticks with her? Through jail and all? I figure it's because she knows stuff about him, and he has to make sure he can control her."

"About the insurance fraud and the horses?"

"Way worse than that." My face is glowing. A warmth radiates through my chest, down to my fingers.

"So Angela's blackmailing him?"

I shake my head. "No, I think she's afraid of him, too." I remember him with the girl at the party and decide that it was probably smart after all that I never mentioned it to Angela. Not yet.

An hour later I wash up and head to bed. My stomach is raw from not eating much prison turkey and the gulps from Soph's cup. The bedroom is cold and the window frame whistles from the wind seeping through it. I sleep in my sweats and socks, pulling a pile of thin blankets over my head. My phone—actually Declan's phone—glows like a camp light under the tent of covers. I hit the message icon and write:

I trust you.

There's a message from Willow. *Red mare delivery set.* I roll my head back and sigh with relief. Good. I can keep working with Roh and not risk having to go to the Kendrick's. I'll make sure Wade never finds out whose horse she really is. Eddie's ready to pick her up tomorrow. I check, but there's no reply from Declan. Maybe he's in bed already.

Or maybe he's really mad at me.

I sit up and tug a blanket around my shoulders. My stocking feet rest on the bed rail as I pull up Google search, looking for a good definition of *trust*. I find one right away that makes my lips curl in a cynical smile:

If you give your trust to a person who does not deserve it, you actually give him the power to destroy you.- Khaled Saad

True, but not the message I want to send Declan. What was it his dad told us about Celtic legends about trust? They called it *tairise*. I remember now. He said the ancient people thought loyalty, steadfastness, and taking action for another's benefit led to trust. Makes sense. By that definition, of course I should trust Declan. So why do I have so much trouble saying so? He's there when I need a ride or anything else, he invites me home to dinner, tells me embarrassing stuff about his family… Most of all, he let me into his private world with Rosie. He trusted *me*. I'm not sure I would have.

Google displays a bunch of quotes that are too religious or sound like a cheap Hallmark card. I can't find one that's exactly what I want to say. The toilet flushes and Aunt Sophia's bedroom door clicks shut. The phone remains stubbornly quiet. No reply from Declan. I stare at the screen as it fades and shuts down.

Chapter Thirty-Five

TWO DAYS SINCE THE THANKSGIVING INCIDENT. MENTALLY I GO OVER everything that's happened. I haven't seen Wade at the farm or at home, but I feel like I'm walking around, waiting for the boogieman to jump out any minute. Bad thing.

Roh arrived at Twin Elms and settled in better than I expected. Good thing. Eddie took off to visit her family, so that buys me extra time before she demands the board for Roh. Another good thing. No message from Declan. Very bad thing.

The barn is deserted. Most of the boarders are out of town. The rest are probably scared off by the predicted bad weather. It's a perfect time to get on Roh when no one is around. I don't know if she has ever been in an indoor arena. Guess I'll find out.

Roh bends her neck to look at me when I lift the saddle up onto her back. She still has to know who is brushing her, who is tacking her up, who is riding her. And if she doesn't approve, she lets you know.

I flick the switch and the arena lights warm to life, illuminating the darkest corners and shiny mirrors. Roh stands next to me and for the first time, I see the place through her eyes.

"Don't worry, girl. I wouldn't put you in a bad place." A walk around inside gives her a chance to see everything before I get on. Easing into the saddle, she's stiff when we walk off, with her head up, looking. I urge her on, but I can tell she's got one eye cocked on that phantom horse following her in the mirror. When I laugh, she loosens her back, drops her head, and softly meets my hands on the reins.

Lifting into trot, she floats around the arena. She responds to every aid, like she was in the field, so coming around the turn I try something Eddie taught me on Eleganz. A slight shift of weight in my hips and closing a leg on her side, and she glides laterally, dancing across the open expanse of the arena. We trot the short side, and when I point her nose down the diagonal line, she explodes forward. Stomach muscles tighten like pushing off on a swing, and I flow with the extended trot. We turn right. I square my shoulders and sit deep, closing my eyes to absorb the footfalls like a heartbeat....

"Hey!"

Roh spooks and takes a stutter step. Galen is standing at the in-gate.

"Which horse is that?" His gloved hand points at Roh. "No one told me another horse was coming in for training."

I wonder how long he's been watching. I drop the reins and walk closer. "She's my horse."

"And which one are you?"

All the working students look alike to him, I guess. I hop down and take off my helmet. "Regina Hamilton. I work with Tucker mostly. Eddie's training me on Eleganz."

Galen's not listening. He slips through the gate, runs a hand down Roh's forehead, and walks around her, pausing at her hindquarters. "Powerful mare. What are you doing with her?"

By that, I know he means what level of showing.

"Mostly trail riding."

A sound like a seal's bark echoes around the empty arena. "You're one of the smart ones, huh?" The corners of his mouth curve down like he's assessing some fancy piece of artwork. "The extended trot is developing, but not clean. Does she have changes?"

I've been at a dressage barn long enough to know tempi changes are the gold standard for judging whether a horse is worth the training or not. They want the horse to be able to swap their leads over and over on command like some girl jump-roping on amphetamines.

"Dunno. I'm just finding out what she can do. I haven't had her long."

"Want to find out?"

"I don't know how—"

He gives me a weird little smile. Deprecating. That's one of my English vocabulary words coming in handy.

"I meant me." He takes the reins out of my hand, kind of shoves me out of the way, and leads Roh to the mounting block. When he swings up into the saddle, the stirrups need some adjusting down about a million holes for his long legs. I check out Roh's expression. Her head comes up, and an ear flickers back as he gathers up the reins.

He turns her and walks away.

"She's not fit," I say. As he walks her around, I pull the phone out of my coat pocket. Still no messages.

Galen sits like a statue, yet the mare lifts into a trot. He takes her around both directions. I hear a satisfied grunt when she steps to canter. A circle, down the long side. He has her going in a wider circle then changes direction, and she flips to the other lead. Easy. He repeats the exercise, tighter, sooner. She changes. Then he rides across the long diagonal and asks. She lifts and changes. He asks again, and I'm amazed she flips to the other lead.

My heart is pounding, but I'm not sure if it is excitement over discovering Roh can do upper-level movements or worry that he might be pressuring her too much. He drops the reins, gives her a resounding slap on the neck, and slides off.

"Not clean behind. She's late with her right hind, but that's typical." He hands me the reins. "She has potential."

Coming from Galen, this is like saying she's a diamond dipped in chocolate.

"Thanks."

He stands, looking at her. I take a hesitant step toward the stalls.

"Needs a bit of educating. I can tell she has her own opinion about things." He winks at me. "Like most mares."

The wink gives me a little shiver as I lead Roh back to her stall. The mare is sweated up, despite the cold weather, so I remove the saddle and swing a heavy cooler onto her back to walk her up and down the aisles. When I return to her stall, Galen is leaning against her door.

"You own this mare?"

"Half," I lie. Mr. Kendrick entrusted her to me. He never said she was half mine.

Galen pushes himself off the wall. "What do they want to do with her? Show? Sell?"

I walk Roh into her stall and slip off the halter. "I'm not sure."

"I tell you what. She'll be worth a bit of change if we can get her going. Get her some exposure at the big shows."

Roh dives into her hay as I slide the door shut. The word *we* sticks in my ears. "You could help me with her?"

"I'd squeeze her in."

I have no idea how I'm going to pay her board, let alone training from a Grand Prix rider. "I don't know…"

Galen rests a hand on my shoulder. "Think about it. It could be an investment if you wanted to sell her. With the right training, she'd be worth a lot."

I know Mr. Kendrick would never sell Roh. "How much money?" A filthy film slides over my tongue when I ask. I think of the mare's registration papers in my backpack. A stream of words like a snake's tongue tickling my ear filter into my brain: if Roheryn were sold for a lot of money, it could mean my freedom from Angela…

Galen lifts his chin. His eyes cut to Roheryn, then back to me. "Depends. If I work with her, it goes up. In a few months, if she does well at some local shows, in the low six figures."

The digits swim before my eyes. I've never seen money like that. Money equals freedom. Roh knickers. She stands by her feed bucket, waiting for the treat that's still in my pocket. I drop it in her bowl without looking at her.

"I don't think the owners can afford a full-time trainer like you." I secretly hope he'll drop it, walk away, and that will be the end.

"She won't need full-time training. Besides, she's not fit enough for that yet. I can work her in on a time-available basis and give you some tips in the meantime. You and your partners can pay me out of the sale, plus commission."

I picture Roh doing those movements when Galen is riding her, and I imagine her winning shows. I see Eddie watching me ride her after a few lessons with Galen and telling me I've got the position as a resident student trainer...

"Come down to the office and look over the training and sales commission agreements. It's pretty much boilerplate." Galen heads off toward the office, and I follow in his wake, pulled by a tractor beam of fantasy ideas. I'd show Eddie! I'd get the job! I'd tell Angela I'm free from her crazy world! I'd see Roheryn winning at all the shows! I'd start to work with Galen directly because he'll see my potential, unlike Eddie, and I'll get horses to show and ones to sell. The only thing I can't see is me taking a check with all those zeroes and watching a stranger load Roh on a trailer to take her away forever. And how I'd explain it to Mr. Kendrick.

In the office, Galen hands me the training agreement papers to sign. I stuff them in my jacket and promise I'll show them to the other owners, but Galen can get started right away. Yes, I'm sure they'll sign. I try to tell myself that maybe Mr. Kendrick would want to sell her, especially for a lot of money. He probably needs the money, too, right? And he wasn't doing anything with Roh. Maybe, I keep telling myself, but I know it's a lie.

Chapter Thirty-Six

WILLOW'S CAR IS PARKED OUTSIDE THE BARN. IT LOOKS MORE rust covered than ever, if that's possible. The door creaks when I get in.

"Just drop me at Declan's," I tell her. "He'll bring me home."

More lies. I check my phone. Still no message. I've decided I'm going to just show up at his door. I'll say I needed some of Roheryn's tack. He'll have to talk to me then. He'll have to drive me home. At least I hope so.

"Galen's been working with Roh in the mornings when I come in to feed," Willow says, keeping her eyes on the road.

"Yeah? How does she look?"

Her mouth hitches up on one side. "Like all his horses."

I check out her face. "You mean, like a dressage horse that's going to win at the big shows."

"That's what people pay for. He gets results." Pause. "One way or another." Her fingers clench the wheel.

We pull up in front of Declan's house, and I forget all about what Willow just said. His truck's gone. My stomach suddenly feels like it's full of cold cement. I thank Willow for the ride like nothing's wrong, drag my stuff out of the backseat, and slam the door. I'm hardly aware of the car spewing gravel on the way back down the drive as I walk up to the front door. Before knocking, it swings open. Mr. Kendrick stands in the doorway.

"Regina, my queen! Why haven't you visited?"

He's wearing that same cardigan sweater. His arm wraps around my shoulder as he walks me inside. The room smells like herbs and roasting meat. Is this Thursday, chicken dinner night? The smell transports me to a safe place as my muscles unclench and my blood turns to hot fudge, gooey and warm.

"I've had to work extra hours at the barn." Lie.

He pulls out a chair at the big wooden table. "Coffee?"

Ducking into the kitchen, he returns with a steaming mug. I see his tea next to an open book, flipped over to save the place.

"I don't want to interrupt what you were doing, Mr. Kendrick. I'm just here to meet Declan, and…" And what? Hope he doesn't throw me out.

"Declan's gone with the dogs. Said he wanted to scope out some new hunting areas for the bird."

Mr. Kendrick never calls Rosie by her name. She's always *the bird* or *that creature* to him.

"I have to apologize for my son if he made arrangements to meet you and he isn't here. Probably lost track of the time." He lifts his mug and smiles over the rim at me.

"That's okay." I wrap my hands around my mug. The heat seeps into my cold fingers. "It wasn't exactly a firm date. I said I'd come by sometime in the afternoon." More lies. I think about Roh and the training and bite the corner of my bottom lip. How to start? "Roh is doing really great at the barn."

His eyebrows arch up and he nods.

"The head trainer there, a Grand Prix-level rider, says she has lots of talent."

He nods like this is no surprise.

His face is open, trusting, as I debate telling him people send horses to this trainer from all over the country to ride, and he's going to ride Roheryn. Then I have to get to the part where I tell him all we have to do is sell her in order to pay for it. Maybe Mr. Kendrick could use the money. "What do you want to do with Roh? Do you want her to go to some dressage competitions? You know, she'd be worth tons of money if she wins."

He holds up a hand and shuts off my words like a faucet. "Roh's value is in what she can teach you. I don't care what she's worth to someone else."

A prick stings behind my eyes. I have her papers. I've thought about selling her, not to help him, or the horse, but because it would help me. My vision swims behind tears and falls on the spine of his book. Something about Celtic mythology. Change of subject.

"Is Nuallan in that book?"

Mr. Kendrick's face brightens. "He is, indeed. The story of the hero's journey. I'm preparing a lecture on it." One eyebrow shoots up. "Do you want to hear it?"

I do. I want to hear about someone who is a hero, someone not like me. "Only if nothing really bad happens. Especially to his horse."

He barks out a laugh, drags the book toward him, and flips a few pages. "Let me check. Hmm. Yes, looks like both our hero and his horse survive."

I cross my arms and lean back in the chair. "I guess it's easy to be heroic when you have a horse god protecting you all the time."

Mr. Kendrick closes the book and holds it against his chest. "He was brave to *believe* that the horse god protected him—in order to have faith enough to act."

I poke a finger through the mug's handle and spin it around. "What if he didn't believe? Would the horse god let him die then?" I feel an eyebrow inch up, waiting for the answer.

He sets the book on the table. "I don't know, Regina." Leaning forward, he taps the book. "Let's find out."

After a little cough to clear his throat, his story telling voice takes over. "Nuallan and his silver horse were known throughout the land. He had bested the evil queen and saved his horse..."

"Hey, you never finished telling that part of the story."

He rubs a hand over his face. "This one's better."

"Promise?"

"Promise." He takes a sip of tea, which must be lukewarm by now.

"Nuallan was known for his bravery, and because of this, a lord called on him to save his son. You see, an evil magician had taken him and—"

"What was his name?"

"Who?" Mr. Kendrick's brows crease.

"The evil magician. I like to know their names."

"Elymas. The magician was called Elymas. The son was Cary, a young boy, the light of the lord's life."

I point to the book. "What did he look like? Any pictures?"

Mr. Kendrick sighs. "Is it important?"

I nod.

"He was red-haired and fair."

"Okay." He looks at me, probably expecting another outburst, but I press my lips together.

"Nuallan and the silver horse accept the quest with reluctance, knowing Elymas was a powerful magician and the rescue would be dangerous. Before they set out, however, the lord gives Nuallan a guide, a helper. He tells Nuallan the guide—his name was Bealach—is very powerful and wise, but Nuallan doubts this. He looks like a poor servant boy."

"Nuallan gets another helper? Besides the horse? Some hero."

Mr. Kendrick shifts in his chair. "I sense you want to see Nuallan prove himself, so I'll jump ahead to that part of the story. Nuallan has defeated many monsters in their path and is now faced with entering the innermost cave, the lair of the magician Elymas—the place where true darkness lives. Riding the silver horse, with Bealach at his side, Nuallan breaks down the door and rushes in. But instead of being met with evil creatures, they walk into a room lined with crystals and filled with light. A beautiful woman with long golden hair, wearing a shimmering gown appears. 'I am Aveen' her musical voice announces, 'sent to greet you.' For three days, Aveen shows Nuallan the beauty of the underground realm. He's treated to sumptuous feasts, musicians play day and night, and servants attend to every need. Nuallan's memory starts to fade, along with his promise to save the lord's son. Instead, he rests and eats and imagines a carefree life. When Aveen returns on the fourth day, she tells Nuallan that he can stay, live like a king, and never worry about anything ever again."

"But there's a catch," I say.

"There *is* a catch. He must surrender the silver horse."

My stomach gives a little lurch. I'm not liking where this story is going.

"By now, however, Nuallan has been enchanted by the temptress Aveen and convinces himself the horse will likewise enjoy a fine life. His promise to return the lord's son fades with each luxury set before him. But it is Bealach, the guide, who is not fooled. He whispers in Nuallan's ear to beware, but Nuallan turns away. One night, while Nuallan is sleeping on his satin bed, Bealach steals into the room and covers him with ashes. When he awakens in the morning, Nuallan's eyes are opened. The crystal palace is a dark cave, filled with rats and spiders. 'Aveen is the evil magician Elymas in disguise!' Bealach tells him. Nuallan runs to find his beloved silver horse chained in a filthy stall. With tears streaming down his face, he breaks the chains. Nuallan gathers his strength to fight the darkness closing around him, and together with his fierce mount gallops out in search of the lost child."

"About time he woke up." I rest my chin in my palm and stare at the fire.

"Don't be too hard on him, Regina." Something in Mr. Kendrick's voice makes me sit up. The words of the story hang in the air.

"With the help of his guide, Nuallan finds the evil magician Elymas, no longer disguised as the beautiful Aveen. The lord's son is dressed in rags, shivering in the corner. Nuallan draws his sword to strike the fatal blow..."

Mr. Kendrick stops.

"What? What happens?"

"Elymas, cunning as he is, realizes Bealach the guide opened Nuallan's eyes and showed him the way. He strikes Bealach with a serpent-headed scepter, releasing deadly venom into his body."

"No! He was the good guy in this. Why does someone always have to die in these stories?"

Mr. Kendick holds up a hand. "Nuallan runs Elymas through with his sword then, and kneeling by Bealach's side, he bows his head. 'Do you forgive me?' he asks. 'For doubting you?' Bealach smiles and says, 'You'll have another chance,' then breathes his last. After Nuallan releases the boy he looks around the cave. He has no guide and no idea how to escape the dark labyrinth of the underground caves that hold him prisoner. In despair, he collapses and throws himself on Bealach's body, which dissolves into dust beneath him. Nuallan, scooping up a handful, swears an oath of trust to his friend and out of the dust, a hawk arises."

"Declan likes this part, I bet."

"He does. Especially because it's the hawk that leads them out of the cave."

Mr. Kendrick takes a deep breath and eases back in his chair.

"Wait. That's the end? A hawk leads them out? Then what happens?"

"What do you mean?" He looks surprised.

"I mean, what happens when he brings the boy back? Does he get a big reward? What's it all supposed to mean?"

"It means whatever you think it means." He scoops the book off the table and cradles it in his arms. "As for the rest of the legend, it's lost to history."

"Ugh." I set my mug down hard. "That's great. So we never find out what happens to Nuallan in the end? Plus, you won't tell me what all the stuff with the ashes and hawk mean. Does it have something to do with not trusting Bealach?"

He opens his mouth, but the sound of barking catches my attention. The dogs are on the porch, howling up a storm.

Mr. Kendrick stands. "It sounds like Declan has returned. Just in time to spare me from your interrogation." He collects the mugs and heads to the kitchen. I swivel in my chair, face the front door, and rehearse in my head what I'm going to say when he walks through it. *Hi, I just thought I'd stop by…*

The dogs are on the porch. I can hear their nails scrabbling against the boards. The door remains shut. Should I go outside to meet Declan? It may be a chance to say something to him when his father isn't around. I get up, my legs stiff and shaky, and take a deep breath. I pull open the door. The dogs run past me. I look down to the end of the porch, which is empty. His truck isn't in the driveway. Inside, the dogs rush around, their tongues dripping and their thick tails beating against my leg. I reach down to pet Buck and pull my hand away. It's wet. Sticky. He got into something. My palm is stained dark red. His tail continues to beat my leg in a steady rhythm. Thornton's golden coat is smeared with something dark on one side.

"My God, are you hurt?" I stoop and gingerly probe along his ribs. No wound. I check Buck's head. No wound, but blood on them. The dogs aren't hurt. Declan's missing. He was with the dogs.

"Mr. Kendrick!"

He emerges from the kitchen, wiping a dish with a towel.

I hold up my blood-stained hands.

"It's Declan. He's hurt."

Chapter Thirty-Seven

MR. KENDRICK TOSSES THE DISH ON THE TABLE AND FALLS TO HIS knees beside me. His hands comb through Buck's matted fur and come away sticky with blood.

"The dogs might have gotten into something." His eyes lock onto mine and plea for me to agree.

I can't.

"Then where's Declan?"

He stands, wringing his hands in the dishtowel, and stares out the window.

"We have to go find him." I join him at the window. The dogs circle my legs and whine. "Where did he go exactly?"

He turns and looks at me as if he can't understand my words. "He took the truck. He said he was going to the Linden area of the park. To scope out the game."

"Linden? That's the one with the parking off of Thunder Cloud Road?" Buck's tail thumps against my leg. I look down at him. "That's a long way to come along a busy road and no one stopped them." I pull the phone out and punch in 9-1-1.

"Dogs might have come through the fields. The park backs up to our place."

Now I stare out the window. Across the field, into the woods. If the dogs came straight back, dead reckoning, it makes sense they would make it home. The border of the park would be about a mile away.

A woman's voice rings in my ear. "This is 911. What's the nature of your emergency, please?"

"We need help. My boyfriend's hurt."

"We'll get you help right away, but you'll have to answer some questions. Please give me your name and confirm your location."

I can't breathe. My voice is whispery when I give my name. "I don't even know the address here." I shoot a look at Declan's dad.

"Fifteen Hillcrest."

I repeat the address to the dispatcher. "But he's not here. Don't come here. My boyfriend's hurt in the woods. His dogs came home covered in blood."

The voice on the phone rumbles in my ear. More questions. She wants the phone number. I don't remember the phone number. I fumble with the screen, afraid of dropping the call.

"His truck is a burgundy Chevy half-ton. He probably parked at the Linden area of Patapsco Park." I check the driveway for the hundredth time, praying I'll see his truck pull in any second and I can tell them it's all a mistake. Everything is still outside, not even a bird in sight. "I'm going out looking for him."

Declan's dad starts shaking his head and waves his hands signaling *no!*

The lady on the phone cautions me to stay put and stand by the phone.

"I'll leave it on, but I'm going. The dogs know where he is." I push open the door, and the two dogs scramble across the porch and down the stairs. They take off across the yard, checking once to see if I'm following. They duck under the fence while I slip through the boards, and the three of us speed across the pasture at a full run. The blood pounds in my ears, but I think I hear a siren in the distance. I can't slow down, or I'll lose sight of Buck and Thornton. When they enter the woods, they hesitate, sniffing the ground.

"Which way?" I plead. "You remember."

They run to the right in tandem. Sucking in the cold air hurts my chest, and the stiff work boots bite my ankles when I run. The path is narrow and rocky, but we keep going. Buck turns to look back at me as the trail rises steeply, causing me to slow down. The gap between the dogs and me widens. I can't lose sight. Buck's chocolate coat blends with the dead leaves and bare trees. I catch a glimpse of Thornton's yellow tail flickering through the brush up ahead. My chest is burning and my thighs are on fire.

A bark rings through the empty woods. Another. I speed up.

Both dogs are barking like crazy. They're circling something ahead.

I come to the top of the rise, turn the corner, and see a dark form sprawled across the trail. My brain isn't making sense of what my eyes are seeing. A camo jacket, wool hat. The curve of his back faces me, his legs tucked up as if sleeping. It can't be. I call, but he doesn't move. Running, collapsing to my knees, a sound like a screaming seagull vibrates through the still air. My throat burns raw before I realize it's me. The front of his coat is black and wet like the ground in front of him. One hand is flung out, palm open. A phone in a sparkling case on the ground glints in the sun a foot away.

"My God, my God! Declan." I shake his shoulder. "You can't be dead. You can't be."

I rock back on my heels and look around. The dogs sniff at Declan's face. Buck drops to a crouch by his side, whimpering. The edges of my phone crush into my fingers and a voice calls my name. I hold it to my ear.

"Are you still there? Help. Please come quick."

"Miss Hamilton? Regina. Listen carefully. We've got your locational data and a team is on its way. Please remain calm."

"He's shot! He's bleeding to death! It's my fault."

"Is anyone else in the area with you?"

My God, whoever did this might be here still. Waiting. Watching. A shot of cold adrenaline races through my stomach, tingling down my arms and hands. I bolt to my feet.

The woods are still. I stand rigid, every cell listening for a crunch of a twig. Just the dogs panting, no other sounds.

"Please." Tears tip over the edge of my eyelids and run down my face. "Please."

No other words come. My throat closes on them. Nothing is making sense.

"The team is about ten minutes out, Regina." The voice is steady in my ear, like a warm, heavy blanket draped over my shoulders. "Don't move. Don't touch anything. The team will be arriving from the south."

Which way is south? I move along the trail a step so I can look up to the sky beyond the canopy of trees. Where is the sun? This late in the afternoon, it's setting. That will be west.

A flicker of scarlet catches my eye, and I spin to the left. The pounding in my chest creeps up to my throat. What was that? My eyes burn into the gray thickness of the woods, hoping to see it was a bird. It wasn't a bird. It was too big. Buck gets to his feet slowly and stares into the woods. A rumble sounds deep in his body. The team, maybe it's the team. But that's not south. The cracking of branches echo through the silence, moving away. I can't see anything.

"Help!" The word bounces off the trees and echoes back to my ears. The sound of branches snapping and feet marching through dead leaves comes toward me from the other direction. Louder. Rhythmic. Feet running. "Help!"

"Regina," a man shouts. "Emergency response, we're coming."

Orange flashes appear and disappear through the trees. Men running up the path toward me. The dogs leap to their feet, barking.

"Regina, it's Detective Maggiano."

I recognize the big man rushing to me and double over with a racking sob.

Chapter Thirty-Eight

THE HOSPITAL CORRIDOR HAS WALLS THE COLOR OF A CREAMSICLE. The longer I stare at them, the more the color swirls into peach and beige and maybe some yellow. I've been staring at them for a long time because the Nazi nurse at the desk won't let me in to see Declan, and I'm not leaving. She glares at me once in a while, maybe to let me know she's still watching. I glare back.

Two days, and Declan is still unconscious. Mr. Kendrick was sent home with some pills after he had a breakdown in the ER. He hasn't been back. I promised him I'd see Declan and tell him everything, but they won't let me in.

I'm thinking about making a dash for the ICU entrance when the nurse's back is turned, but just when I'm ready to make the move, a big hand clamps down on my shoulder.

"I thought I'd find you here."

Detective Maggiano squeezes into a plastic chair, leaving an empty one between us. I rest my elbows on my knees and stare at the floor.

"I wanted to talk to you," he says.

I tilt my head enough to peer at him out of the corner of one eye. "I thought we already talked about everything." Feels like I've spent about a million years answering questions lately.

"Do you want to go to the cafeteria and talk? I'll buy you a coffee."

The nurse gives me another glare.

"Sure." I stand and say really loud, "But I'm coming right back."

Detective M pushes through some swinging doors with me on his heels and walks down the hall to the elevator.

"You did a great job finding him in the woods. You probably saved his life." He pushes the down button.

"He's not awake yet. I'm not sure I saved anything."

The elevator pings, and together we step into the empty car. The door slides shut.

"There's one other thing I was wondering about, though," he says, watching the floor indicator light.

My stomach drops like we're on a roller coaster.

"You mentioned to the dispatcher that it was your fault."

I don't look up but feel him looking at me.

"What did you mean?"

My brain feels like a gerbil on fire, racing around the inside of my skull. What did I say? I don't remember.

"I don't know. I was just scared."

"I don't think so."

The doors open, and I burst out and walk to the cafeteria ahead of him. This was a bad idea. He veers off to get us some coffee, and I drop down in the first empty booth. I pull out my phone—Declan's phone—for any messages, and it all comes back to me. The image of a sparkling phone a few inches from his hand. My phone. The one that was bugged, tracked, and monitored by Wade.

Detective Maggiano slides in the booth and pushes a Styrofoam cup across the table to me. I open the lid, and the dark smell of roasted coffee floats up to kiss my face.

"Cream and sugar. I guessed. Hope it's okay."

I nod and take a sip. A mix of sweet, hot bitterness glides over my tongue. "Thanks."

The detective removes the lid on his and swallows a few gulps. Someone drops a tray, and the rattle of dishes makes me jump. I catch him looking at me.

Thick fingers grip his cup. "Do you know why I was there the day you found Declan?"

His face, red from the hike up the trail, flashes before my eyes.

"I was there when the call came in. I heard your voice. I heard you say Declan was shot, and it was your fault." He leans back and the bench squeaks. "Regina, this is off the record, but we can make it official if we have to. I wanted to talk to you alone because I have a feeling there is a lot you're not telling me. You and Declan."

"Declan doesn't know anything. Really."

An eyebrow arches up. "So you do."

Stupid. "Neither of us knows anything. You mean about Trey? That's what you're talking about?"

He takes the lid off his coffee and pours in more sugar. I keep my eyes on the cup in front of me and say nothing.

"Not necessarily. Not just Trey Morales. I think there's something bigger going on."

My head is shaking no, but my brain's running ahead. Of course there's something else. Willow's locket flashes through my brain. I will my face to stay blank.

"No?" He leans forward on his elbows and folds his hands. His forearms are big and muscular, like he lifts weights. A tattoo is visible on the inside of one, just beyond the rolled-back sleeve. I bet he was a Marine. I look up to show that I'm telling the truth.

He stares. I shake my head again, but he goes on staring.

"Declan just found the glove in his truck, like I told you before. It fell out of my backpack. He didn't know anything about it when he brought it to me."

"He thought it was yours? A man's glove?"

"Maybe." One casual hitch of my shoulder and a smile while I try to remember what Declan said he told Maggiano—and what I told him before.

"Lots of maybes." He slaps his palms on the table. "And none of them really make sense, Regina." He holds up one finger. "First of all, why would you pick up one glove—a man's glove at that—and not notice? And why would Trey leave one glove at the barn and the other one in his car? Gloves usually go together in order to be effective. Second"—he holds up another finger—"why did this glove have a note tucked inside, written in Trey's handwriting as you told me, that has some words on it no one understood? Until now."

Until now? My face flashes fire, and I know he can see the blush. I hate being a redhead. "What did it mean?" He's not buying the tight smile, I can tell.

"It was code for an address. Computer Forensics has been working with vice on a case involving underage prostitution. I can't divulge any details, but suffice it to say that little piece of paper tucked inside your friend's glove pointed to some bad stuff."

Bad stuff. I try to run it down, make sense of it all. Willow, telling me she found the glove in Wade's car. If Wade had the glove, he probably found it after he dragged Trey from the party. Was Trey in Wade's car? Maybe the note is what got Wade so mad that night. What did Trey tell him?

I tell Maggiano, "I don't know anything about that. Neither does Declan."

"But you know who does." The third finger goes up. He pivots his hand to point a finger at me. "*You* know who does."

"No." I clutch my lukewarm coffee and watch a group of doctors get up from their table.

"Why did you switch phones with Declan?"

My attention snaps back. "What?"

He grabs the cell phone off the table and waggles it in my face. "Caller ID on the 911. Declan's phone, this one. Why the switch?"

"I have to get back." I turn and check for the exit.

"Regina." He sighs. "I can order a search, confiscate your phones and have forensics go through them, and call you in officially for questioning. But my gut tells me it would be better this way. I've a feeling there might be some sensitive issues—things you might be able to tell me if they weren't official." One eyebrow goes up.

I take a quick check of the exit again, then sit up and go on the offensive. "So, I don't even have to be here, right? If it's not official?" I risk a bold stare into his eyes. Bingo. They shift away. "I bet you're not even supposed to be talking to me without a warrant or something."

He laughs. "You're not under arrest."

"And I bet you're breaking like a million police rules right now, right?"

"At least a half dozen, yeah."

A guy who doesn't follow rules. Good. "Can you get me in to see Declan?"

His bulk flings back in the seat like I hit him. "Are you trying to work a deal?"

I rub my fingers through my hair. They come away feeling gritty. "Yeah, maybe."

He gets up. "Wait here."

After about fifteen minutes he comes back. He leans on the table with both hands and looks me in the eye. "They said five minutes." I scoot out of the booth and follow him back to ICU.

The head nurse shoots me hate beams as I walk by the station. My hand twitches with the urge to give her the finger, but before I do, Detective Maggiano grabs my arm and ushers me in the unit. Inside the door, there are separate rooms with big windows. I spot Declan's name on the door of the first room. A nurse with what looks like a shower cap on her head gives me blue paper booties to slip over my shoes, then opens Declan's door.

"He's sedated," she says. "Just step around on this side of the bed and mind the cords."

Declan's face is the color of putty and is round, bloated. A tube snakes up his nose. Others are stuck to the inside of his elbow. A cord, attached to a machine with glowing green digits, is taped to the back of his hand. There's a sucking noise in the room, but nothing else. A whiteboard on the opposite wall says Kendrick. It lists mysterious numbers and times. It makes me angry. He's not just Kendrick—he's Declan. He's a guy. He has a name.

"Hey." I move closer to the bed and touch what I guess is his foot under the light blanket. He doesn't move. I didn't really expect him to.

"I told you you'd be okay." Even I can tell my voice is full of crap.

There's a chair on the other side, but I don't feel like sitting. What I feel like is crawling in the bed next to him, taking away all the hoses and monitors, and curling up to sleep together. Holding him. Smelling the wood smoke in his hair. Keeping him safe.

But I can't keep him safe. I can't keep myself safe.

What if the person shot him because of the glove? What if it was Wade, tracking him using my phone? What if it was supposed to be me?

The nurse's head appears in the doorway. "One minute." She pulls the door closed. Before it shuts, I see Detective Maggiano sitting outside, watching me. If I tell him *I* found the glove in Wade's car, can I trust him?

Declan makes a little noise in the back of his throat. A tiny moan. My chest is cracking open with the pain. I want to fall on my knees and beg him to forgive me. All my fault. If he had never met me—

"You'll have to leave now." Two nurses appear. One is pushing a cart full of medicine. I rush out the door.

Detective M blocks the exit and guides me to a chair. "Got to toss your booties." He nods to a special waste container. I sit, slide them off, crumble them into a ball, and toss it into the opening.

"Nice shot."

My look makes his smile vanish.

"How's he doing?" He nods to the room.

"I don't know. Why don't you ask a nurse?" If I scream it might keep me from crying.

He sinks down in a chair next to mine. "We're going to find who did this."

I can't hold back a sarcastic little laugh because it sounds like a cliché cop show line.

"Do you want to help us or not?" Now he sounds mad. His neck is red above the collar.

The ring around my throat tightens, and my vision blurs. I wipe my face with the back of my sleeve. I look through the glass window into Declan's room. His red hair, standing on end against the pillow, is the only spot of color in the sterile room. The nurses are hooking him up to another machine. It's my fault he's here. I have to make it right.

"Yeah. I'll help."

Chapter Thirty-Nine

FIRE ANTS ARE CRAWLING ALONG MY VEINS ALL THE TIME NOW THAT I told Detective Maggiano the truth about where the glove was found—in Wade's truck. He didn't write it down or anything. I told him who Wade is. I told him how he owns the house I live in and how my mother in prison depends on him to *keep an eye on me*. I used finger quotes for that last part. I gave him my phone—really Declan's phone—for the forensic team to look at. I had to tell Aunt Sophia I lost mine, and that didn't go over too well. The detective told me to go to school, go to work, and act like everything was exactly the same. Easy for him to say. That's when the tingly fire ants started, running up my back and down my arms like every nerve is electrified. And the bad dreams.

"Hey!" Galen appears outside the stall where I'm tacking up Roh. I jump and the ants start running like crazy. "I've got forty minutes, tops. You going to stand there all day or are you going to get on that horse?" He taps his shiny diamond watch. "I'll be back in five minutes. Have her ready."

I have to snap out of it—this spacing out. I lift the bridle to slide it over Roh's ears and she twists away, ears back. Strange. I step closer, and her head snakes toward me, ears flattened.

One shout, and she flies to the corner of the stall, head against the wall. The reins have slipped off her neck, and the bridle is a hopeless tangle in the bedding. I bend to get it when the door slides open.

"Get out." Galen pushes me out the door. "This mare has to be taught some manners." He shakes out the bridle, flings the reins over her head, and drags her from the stall. He's got a short jumping bat in his hand. Like swatting a fly, it whistles through the air and smacks Roh on the side of her mouth. She lurches backward, head turned away and eye rolling, but Galen has her by the reins and steps forward. He raises the bat near her eye and waves it. "You want to bite, do you? I'll show you what happens to horses that bite."

My feet are glued to the floor. I want to push him away, to take Roh and tell her it's okay, but my mouth won't open. He slips the bit in her mouth. She drops her head as he glides the headstall over her ears. Thank God.

"Come." He looks at me. "Now I only have thirty minutes."

I follow behind Roh, sending mental thought waves to her, telling her I'm sorry. Willow is with a horse a few stalls down, her fist full of wormer tubes. When Galen's back is to her, she sneers and raises the one-finger salute.

In the arena, he tosses me the reins. "Mares take over if you don't show them who's boss. Especially strong mares, like this one. Today, you are going to show her."

A pile of leather straps drape over his shoulder like leather snakes, looping, ominous. What do we need all that for?

I find out soon enough, and it makes me sick. Galen attaches draw reins and, from the ground, pulls her head into her chest. He hands me the reins.

"Keep her in this position."

Roh flips her nose, straining against the confining reins. Galen stomps over and buckles a strap into place. "Now she can't pull."

I'm terrified she'll freak out, rear and flip. The corner of her eye is white with terror.

Galen starts the lesson without any warm up. Roh is stiff in my hands, but after a while, something lets go. It's not like she's softened and submissive, but more like she's just broken and gives up. The thirty minutes of torture feels more like thirty hours. Roh is almost black from sweat. Veins stand out along the surface of her neck, her jaw, even one that runs down the side of her face. Her nostrils are flared, so open I can see pink and red inside. Steam rises off her, and I can almost see her soul floating away with it. Everything that was Roh—her sparkle and her tricks—seem to be fading away. I release the reins, and her head drops between her front legs. My knees buckle when I dismount, lurching into her sweaty side. Galen checks his watch and strides out of the arena without a second glance. I loosen the flash around her mouth and hold out a carrot stub, a peace offering, but Roh doesn't look at me. Even pressed under her nose, her mouth remains a closed line. Dark, flat eyes with no light behind them stare straight ahead.

"I guess you showed her." Willow leans on a broom outside the arena.

"What's that supposed to mean?" My words bite back.

She fumbles, opening the gate. "Do you think you taught her submission?"

Roh looms behind me, head lowered. "No. I think I taught her she can't trust me."

Willow's face relaxes. The flat line of her mouth tilts up. "Sorry. I didn't mean to get snarky on you."

"Galen said she needs to learn obedience." My heart hurts looking at the mare.

Willow's eyes narrow. "Obedient unto death."

I don't know why she's using weird words, but she's right. "What was I supposed to do? He's a Grand Prix trainer. What was I going to say?" My voice catches.

Willow props the broom against the wall and takes the reins. "C'mon, let's get her cooled out." Roh drags her back feet as she's led down the aisle to the wash stall. After she hooks the mare to the crossties, Willow juts her head out into the aisle and looks left and right. She turns on the water, hard, so it splashes against the cement floor and waves the warm spray over Roh's body. Willow pushes me into the corner, her voice a whisper, barely audible over the splashing water. "I wanted to warn you. He hits her."

"What?" I take the hose from Willow and let it run over Roheryn's shoulders and haunches. "What for?"

"Who knows what for. He's a psycho. He hates females, including horses. Especially strong ones." Willow backs away from the spray, so I turn it off and whisper.

"But he shows upper-level horses. He wins ribbons."

Willow nods. "Yup, but have you seen any of those horses for more than a season or two? He gets the results fast. He pushes them up the levels—that is, if they don't break down or go nuts first. Think about it. His customers want results, and he gives them what they want. When the horse breaks, they buy a new one." She makes a motion of wiping her hands. "Disposable."

I touch the place on Roh's mouth where he hit her. "He's hit her before." It's not a question. "No wonder she threatened me." The hose soaks my hands as I roll it up.

"Horses he thinks he can make a fast buck on"—she nods at Roh—"he'll drive harder."

Willow moves to slide past me, but I grab her arm. "What can I do?"

Roh lifts her tail and drops a pile of manure by the drain. Willow stares back at me, her expression like Rosie's when she spots her target. Fierce.

"Don't let him near her again."

"But I made a deal...I signed. A stupid deal." I put Roh in danger, betraying her to get what I wanted. I'm not better than Nuallan, I think, letting Galen fool me like the magician. I treated Roheryn like she was something I owned and controlled. Like she was *disposable*. Not like she was an amazing gift to me. A cold tear runs down my face and I dash it away before Willow can see it.

Willow gives a little shake of her head like I've said the stupidest thing she's ever heard. "You can't make any deals. You're a minor. Not a valid contract." She flattens against the wall to slide past me, but before exiting the wash stall, she runs a hand down Roh's face. "If she were my horse, I'd get her the hell out of here."

Chapter Forty

SITTING IN THE BACK IN TWEETY'S CLASSROOM DURING A STUDY PERIOD, I struggle to come up with anything more to say for the *Call of the Wild* essay he wants me to develop into an article. I scratch a few words out on some crap about the meaning of nature's brutality in a civilized world. Just my luck, it's the same time period the yearbook meets in here. Meaning Cory will be here. I keep looking up at the door, expecting to see her breeze in with all her new friends. Maybe I should call them her *real* friends. One line of my essay stares back at me: *Nature is brutal because it has to be in order to survive.* I cross it out.

Laughter in the hall and some lockers slam. A storm of students blows into the room, circling around a tall girl with auburn hair. I know it's Cory. Before I can force my eyes back down to the paper, she catches mine. Her expression is—*what?* Like she wants to smile but censors her face. It goes serious. Then a girl grabs her attention, and she turns away. That's when I see the other girl in the group—Amy— the one who started the fight with Willow.

I scratch out a few more lines on the essay, but my attention wanders back to Cory. The group pushes desks together in the middle of the room. Their heads bow over a spread of pictures. A girl squeals and stabs her finger at one, laughing. Cory catches me watching them. This time I smile, but I'm afraid it looks like a grimace. Her hand lifts in a wave. I think it's a wave. Warmth floods over me, and I struggle out of my hoodie.

Bits of their discussion float across the room. They talk about their yearbook assignments: covering the games, who will do the prom, running the best-in-school contests…dumb stuff like that.

A voice chirps above the buzz. "I think we need to cover gun violence." Amy sits up straighter and lifts her pointy chin. "It's a school issue we need to address. Especially now."

Some heads swivel in my direction and snap back. Tweety looks up from grading papers at his desk.

Amy pins each kid at the table with her stare. "We can't ignore the elephant in the room." She pauses. "A student was shot. Yeah, not here in *school*, but maybe the fact that he owned guns and went hunting had a lot to do with it."

She's talking about Declan. I want to shove an eraser down her throat.

A tall guy with impossibly neat hair puts down his pen. "I don't know, Amy. That's not yearbook material, really, and it had nothing to do with the school."

"No? Then how come we all have to go to an assembly on heightened awareness—see something, say something?"

"That has nothing to do with it," Cory says.

"If you ask me, that kid had all the signs of someone who would come in here and blow everyone away. What was with that camo jacket he always wore? Weird. And he didn't have any friends. Classic warning signs." She gives a look like she scored a winning goal.

My face is flaming hot.

"Amy, let's move on." It's Tweety. He gets up from his desk. "This is not the place for that."

"He goes to school here. I don't know who shot him, but maybe it was self-defense, we don't know." Amy juts out her chin.

I'm on my feet when an angry voice rings out.

"*You* don't know." It's Cory. She's pointing her pen at Amy. "You don't know anything about that kid except that he wore a camo jacket. That doesn't make him a terrorist."

Amy's face twists up into a smug grin. "You're the one who said he was weird. You said you were afraid of him, remember?"

Cory shoots a look in my direction. "I was wrong."

"Let's take up this discussion at another time, another place." The teacher leans on his desk.

"I don't agree." Amy tilts back in her chair. "It's a timely issue. A touchstone of our time." She looks especially pleased with her stupid expression. "What do you want to write instead? A sappy memorial after he dies? Put a picture of him in the back of the yearbook with a touching Hallmark quote?"

"Shut up." Cory's face blooms red. "Who said he's dying?"

"He's not going to die! He's not!" My scream rips through the room and leaves it shattered. Flushed faces stare, then heads quickly bow, afraid to look. Feet shuffle under the desks. A book drops to the floor.

A murmur floats to my ears just under the noise. "Maybe he deserves to."

Heads jerk up. Tweety pushes off the desk and heads toward the group. It all happens fast, but slow, like we're underwater. My feet move toward the huddled group, toward Amy's pale ponytail that I want to rip out by the roots. But my path is blocked.

Cory springs out of her seat and flies at Amy. "What did you say?"

Amy scuttles backward, away from Cory, and her chair leg catches. Cory grabs out for a fistful of Amy's sweater, and the two fall onto the grungy carpet, Cory on top.

"He doesn't deserve to die," Cory's voice croaks. She rolls off Amy and sits on the floor, her face in her hands. Amy jumps to her feet, rubbing her hip.

A soft whine starts in the back of my throat. I kneel beside Cory, and she wraps me in a hug, pulling me beside her.

Her breath is warm when it encircles my ear. "I'm so sorry, Regina. I was wrong. I'm so sorry."

Before I can pull away, the teacher grabs me by the elbow and drags us both to our feet. I'm expecting the march to the vice principal's office. Instead, he pulls out two chairs side by side and gestures for us to sit. Amy scoots her chair away. She points at Cory and opens her mouth to speak.

"I'd keep still if I were you." Tweety crosses his arms. "You're off yearbook." He backs it up with a jerk of his head toward the exit.

Amy shoots Cory a hateful look as she gathers her notebooks and rushes for the door. The guy with the perfect hair picks stuff up off the floor and hands it to Cory. He leans over us and says some really, really crude words about Amy I'd never expect to come out of his Ivy League-looking face. We both laugh.

God, it feels so good to hear Cory laugh.

After school, I hop in Cory's car. It's almost as bad as Willow's. She offered to drive me home, and I grab at the chance to talk to her. The chance to make sure we really are still friends again. Moving some bags and extra clothes from the passenger side, she tells me over and over how sorry she was about the things she said about Declan. And Willow, too. Before she turns the ignition key, she pulls me in a hug. My neck gets cramped, but I don't pull back.

She lets go. Mascara is smudged under her eyes, giving her the raccoon look. "I missed you so much."

"Me, too."

"Tell me what's going on. How's Declan?" She twists the key and the car whines to life. "What's really going on?"

I bite the edge of my lip. I'm having trouble remembering what I've told people. What Detective Maggiano knows, what Aunt Sophia knows, what Mr. Kendrick or Galen or Eddie or half a dozen other people know about all the bits and pieces and half-truths. About what I saw or didn't see. About who found Trey's glove and where. About Willow's secret contact and how she's making money, about the deal I made with Galen to train Roh. And how I feel about Declan—the truth I never had a chance to tell him. Because I can never trust anyone, not even myself.

Cory pulls out of the parking space and glances over when I don't answer her.

"It's a long story," I say.

"That's okay. You don't have to tell me if you don't want to."

"No, I do." I really do. I want to tell someone. But instead I stare out the window. Cory reaches for the radio dial, but draws back her hand instead.

"I'm pretty sure Wade killed someone." The words roll out of me.

"What the hell!"

I'm nodding. "Not the first time, either."

"Oh, my God, Regina! Do the police know?" Cory keeps turning to look at me, and I'm afraid we'll crash into something.

"Don't take me home, okay? Let's go somewhere."

Cory makes a hard right turn. "I know a place."

In a few minutes we pull up in front of a strip mall and enter a small restaurant. The air smells of coffee, grilled herbs, and fresh bread. The walls are painted in colorful murals.

Cory asks for a booth. The hostess leads us to a back corner and brings iced water. I suck mine down like a racehorse after a workout. When Cory orders an appetizer, my stomach growls, and I realize I haven't had a real meal in a while.

The food and steaming coffee help, but it's still hard to know where to start. Cory takes a bite, and a string of cheese stretches and breaks against her chin. I take a breath.

"There was a girl named Penny who used to work for us when I was a kid…"

The whole story winds out while Cory listens. She doesn't say anything, even when I come to the bad stuff—the things I did or should have done. The waitress takes away the appetizer plates and puts an enormous bowl of pasta in front of Cory. I poke at my sandwich and eat a few chips.

"So, I'm afraid Wade shot Declan. Maybe Wade thought he knew something about Trey. We switched phones, so Wade would have been able to find him." My voice fades. "Alone, in the woods. Where he told Wade he likes to go hunting."

Cory scowls. "It all points back to Wade, doesn't it?"

I nod. "I always thought Angela was my biggest problem. Surprise! There's someone worse."

The waitress refills our drinks.

"Wade killed the horses, right?" Cory spears a forkful of pasta and narrows her eyes.

I nod. "Most likely."

"Then why didn't Angela point the finger at him? Maybe save herself from prison."

"I don't think the insurance company cares who killed the horses. They don't care about horses, they care about fraud and getting their millions back. Like Wade always says, somebody's got to pay."

"Yeah, but you would think Angela could have worked a deal if she gave them an accomplice. You think she was protecting him out of love?"

Water almost squirts through my nose while I'm drinking. "Angela doesn't do anything for anybody or for any reason other than it helps Angela."

"So why'd she keep quiet?"

The waitress brings a to-go box for me, and we pass on dessert.

Cory has a point. It's weird Angela never said anything, and I don't have an answer why. "I never thought about it." I pick up the bill, but Cory snatches it out of my hands.

"My treat."

I fish some dollars out of my pocket and throw them on the table for the tip. She nods.

Why *did* Angela keep quiet? Cory pays the bill, and we open the door to a blast of cold air. The sky is dark and feels like it is pressing close to earth. We both turn our faces up and feel the first drops of freezing rain.

"Better get home before this gets worse," Cory says.

"Right." She has another couple miles in the other direction after she drops me off. We get in her car and crank up the heat.

"Speaking of getting worse," I begin.

Cory's profile is outlined with a bluish cast from the security lights as she fiddles with the wipers.

"I think it's going to get a whole lot worse."

She mistakes what I'm talking about and peers up under the windshield at the sky. "Maybe no school tomorrow."

"No. I mean about what we were talking about. Wade. Why Angela didn't tell."

She scrunches her face. "Because she has something on him. She can control him?"

"She can control him to leave me alone. Keep me safe. Think about it."

Her lips press together. "That's a good thing. Right?"

"Until he decides I'm more of a threat than Angela. Then what?"

Chapter Forty-One

CORY DROPS ME OFF AT THE KENDRICK'S HOUSE ON SATURDAY. I TELL her it's okay, she doesn't have to come in with me. I eye Declan's truck sitting under a tree. The police must have brought it back.

"Are you sure? Doesn't look like anyone's home." She cranes her neck to check out the house. Only one small lamp glows through the curtained window.

"His dad's home," I tell her.

"How do you know? He might be at the hospital."

I shake my head and reach for the door handle. "He never leaves the farm. He can't."

"Wait." Cory grips my upper arm. "What are you talking about? You mean he hasn't even gone to visit his son?"

"He's got some anxiety disorder. He has a meltdown if he goes farther than the house, the barn, and the yard. He almost lost it the night the EMTs brought him to the hospital. The night I found..." I push the door open and look up at the empty porch and the dark windows. "But you're right. He has to visit Declan. Declan has to know his dad is there."

"Oh, Regina. I'm so sorry." Cory lets go of my arm. "How is he?"

I sit back in the seat, suddenly exhausted. "Not good. He hasn't woken up yet."

Cory's face scrunches together—her brows, her lips. "What are you going to do?"

"I'm going to get Mr. Kendrick there." I nod to the house.

"Want me to wait? How you getting home?"

"Nah. But thanks. I can call someone later." Not exactly true, but I need Cory to leave. I step out and shut the door. Looking back, I give her a confident thumbs-up that doesn't match how I feel at all. Her car disappears down the gravel drive.

No one answers the knock, so I turn the knob and the door swings open.

"Mr. Kendrick? It's Regina." I step inside.

The table is covered with dirty dishes, books, and papers. There's a weird smell like the lid of the garbage can is open. Buck and Thornton rush from the back hallway and circle me. When I take one step toward the kitchen, the dogs rush ahead and stand over empty bowls. I pick up the water bowl and refill it at the sink, moving aside more dirty dishes.

"Where is everyone, guys?" I ask the dogs as I set the bowl down. They slurp it up, pushing each other out of the way.

I find the bag of kibble in the pantry and drop a few handfuls in the other two bowls. The noise of their crunching masks the sound of Mr. Kendrick walking in behind me. When I turn and spot him, I jump back. He's wearing his usual old cardigan, but the front of his shirt is stained, and his hair is sticking up on one side like he just got out of bed, even though it's late afternoon. He rubs his eyes. They're red and ringed in dark skin.

"Mr. Kendrick. Hi. The door was open—"

He waves me off from any further explanation. "Hello, Regina. How are you?"

He turns and shuffles to the living room before I can answer.

"Mr. Kendrick, I came over to see how you're doing. They let me in to see Declan."

He falls into his armchair like someone took a baseball bat to the back of his legs.

"How is he?"

His face is so hopeful I hate to tell him the truth. Declan is still unconscious in ICU, and he looks like a gray lump connected to tubes and machines. His chart lists a bunch of scary-sounding medicines, and nurses float in and out adjusting things every few minutes.

"I couldn't stay long, but he looked better." I push aside a half-empty pizza box and sit at the table.

"But not conscious." He looks down at his lap.

I shake my head. I know it's not good. It's been days. "What did the doctor tell you? They weren't going to let me in, let alone answer any questions, because I'm not family, they said."

His head snaps up. "Nonsense."

"I know, right? The head nurse is a Nazi."

This gets a small smile.

"But you got past her?"

I smile back. "With some help, but yeah."

He rakes fingers through his wild hair. "I'll call them. Tell them to let you see Declan whenever you want." His hand rests on the old phone, but he doesn't lift the receiver.

"Won't help. They won't listen." I suck in a deep breath and just say it. "You have to come with me."

"To the hospital?" He says it like he doesn't understand the words. His hand on the receiver shakes. He pulls it away and clasps them together in his lap. "No. No, I can't do that."

"Okay, but they won't let me in. Declan may wake up and think nobody cares about him if no one's there."

His face is gray and puffy. "The doctors said he may not regain consciousness."

The words are scientific and cold, but the meaning is clear. The doctors warned Mr. Kendrick that Declan might have suffered brain damage, or worse, he might die.

I forget all about trying to get him to go with me to the hospital as the thought washes through me. The smell of old food and wet dogs turns my stomach. I swallow hard and eye the door, picturing myself walking through it. Coming back some other time.

That's when I hear a screech. A screech or a scream or something piercing the walls of the house.

"Where's Rosie?" Panic rises in my voice.

Mr. Kendrick points to the door. "Out there, tied to her perch." His shoulders slump. "Tied or twisted up. I looked in on her but didn't want to go inside. Her food's gone, but no matter. She won't eat for anyone but Declan."

"Can we let her go? She can hunt—"

He looks down and shakes his head. "She's hungry. I hear her struggling, trying to fly, calling for him." He bites down on his bottom lip and looks away. "Don't get near her, Regina. She's dangerous. Especially now."

"Call someone. Some hawk guy that worked with Declan—"

"Tried that. No one around. Or no one willing to come." He pulls his cardigan tight around him.

No one willing to come? "But she'll die." The words are soft like scurrying mice in the stillness. "She'll starve."

Mr. Kendrick drops his head in his hands. The outline of his shoulders shakes. He told us hawks are messengers. They foretell death. Declan's death. I watch, helpless. Then a thought whispers in my head, *Maybe they prevent it, too.*

"We have to get Declan to wake up. To tell us what to do." I rush over to his chair and perch on the edge of the coffee table in front of him. "A hawk led Nuallan out of the cave. A hawk saved the king's son, remember?"

He looks up at me with a tight smile. "Those are just stories, Regina."

"But stories that are about truth. Real stuff in life. You said so. You said there's magic still in life if you look for it."

"They're metaphors." He grips his hands together so hard his fingers turn white. "They aren't a secret formula for life."

I stand up. "I just know that if Rosie dies, so will Declan. We have to save her. Save them both."

Mr. Kendrick struggles to the edge of the armchair and leans forward. His eyes show a glimmer of hope, looking up at me under his bushy dark eyebrows. "How do we do that?"

"We go to the hospital and see Declan. You talk to him. You let him know you're there." I reach down and grab one hand. It's cold. "Trust me."

Declan's dad doesn't say anything but lets me pull him to his feet. Finally, he gives one curt nod. He disappears into a back room and returns wearing a fresh shirt, and his hair is wet and slicked down. In his trembling hand, he holds a set of keys out to me. They jingle together like bells.

"I'd like you to drive."

The words *I don't have a license* almost blurt out, but I'm smart enough to bite them back. If we don't go now, he might change his mind. I take the keys. After all, I used to drive Aunt Sophia's truck around the ranch in Texas, so it's almost like having a driver's license.

"No problem." More lies.

Chapter Forty-Two

THERE IS NO PLACE AS DEPRESSING AS A HOSPITAL AT CHRISTMASTIME. Since my last visit, shiny silver garland has appeared, draped in the front of the reception desk, and cardboard elves dance across the glass partition. The receptionist sees Mr. Kendrick and me standing there but turns her back to get something off the printer. I knock on the Plexiglas, but the receptionist grabs the papers and disappears around the corner.

"Why don't you sit down," I tell Mr. Kendrick. "I'll get someone to help us."

The television in the waiting room is blaring the news, and a kid is bawling over something he can't have. Mr. Kendrick doesn't look too good. There's a waxy sheen on his forehead, and his color is gray except where bluish veins stand out along his neck.

A blond nurse, young, wearing scrubs with little kittens all over them slides open the partition. "Is anyone helping you?"

"You are." I smile. "We were told to check in here. To see Declan Kendrick?"

She pulls out a chair and sits down in front of a computer screen, typing in information. Her mouth turns down. "Declan Kendrick is an ICU patient. There's a visitor restriction." Her blues eyes snap up to meet mine. "Only two at a time, family only."

Declan's dad swivels in his chair and calls over to the nurse. "It's just the two of us, miss. His sister and me." He flashes a smile at me.

We follow the directions to the ICU suite. The troublemaker nurse must be off tonight. A different one hands us shoe covers and leads us to Declan's room. She walks in, pushes the curtain surrounding his bed back, and writes down some readings off the machines.

Mr. Kendrick stands in the doorway like he's stuck half in, half out. One hand grasps the doorframe.

"His vitals are much better today." The nurse's tone is rehearsed, like she dialed in the *chipper voice to encourage the family* option. She checks out Mr. Kendrick, and her eyebrows pinch together. He's starting to look like an opium addict crashing after a high. "Maybe you'd like to sit down. Can I get you some water?"

Mr. Kendrick lurches over to the chair without answering her.

"Water would be great. Thanks," I tell her, retreating.

A sound like a trapped moose comes out of Declan's dad. His head drops in his hands.

"He's better. The nurse said so." I stand by the chair and stare at the quiet, pale form under the thin blanket. Much too quiet. The machines beep and make sucking noises, and we barely breathe, waiting for something to happen.

"Talk to him," I whisper.

The nurse steps in long enough to leave a little paper cup of water on the rolling cart near the door.

"Tell him you're here."

He shakes his head and sniffs.

"C'mon." I nudge the arm of the chair, my voice impatient.

Mr. Kendrick leans forward and fishes under the blanket to draw out Declan's hand. He clasps it in both of his.

"Son." His eyes follow the tubes snaking along his arm, up to the stand holding a clear bladder of some kind of fluid. "I'm here. I came to see you."

I nod, willing him to go on.

"To see you get better and take you home."

Declan is still. There is a sound like a soft hiss of air.

Mr. Kendrick squeezes his hand and drops his forehead to touch it. I hold my breath. I don't know if he's crying. I don't know what to do if he is. He draws in a sharp breath.

I step closer to the bed, touch what I figure is Declan's calf, and give it a little shake. "C'mon, Declan, you've got to get home and take care of Rosie. You know she won't eat without you." A strangled laugh bursts past my lips. "You know you've got her so spoiled. Stupid bird." I wipe a tear before it rolls down my face.

Mr. Kendrick scoots the big armchair closer to the bed so it's touching the side. He kisses Declan's hand. I sit down on the very bottom of the bed away from any tubes or wires.

Mr. Kendrick releases his hand and sits back. "Well, if you won't answer us, I take it to mean you're just waiting to hear a story. What kind of story would you like? A quest? An epic battle?" His eyes search mine out for encouragement.

"A love story." I wiggle my eyebrows. "He'll leap out of bed to get away from that."

A hopeful look ghosts across his face. "A love story it is, then."

We look at each other, and I force a brave expression to settle over my face. Mr. Kendrick's bushy brows unclench, and his eyes get soft like a horse that's relaxed and trusting. I try to act like we're just sitting around the table at Declan's house while his dad goes off on some Celtic story rant. Mr. Kendrick clears his throat and shifts in the oversized chair, but we're both grasping at some bit of normal in this weird place.

"Well, let's see." He studies his hands. "A love story that's not tragic." He gives a huff of a laugh. "Not many of those in Celtic lore. Um, there's the one about—no, they both die in the end."

"How about a story from—"

He holds up a hand and raises one eyebrow. "Don't worry. I've got one."

I retrieve the water cup and set it on the bedside table.

"According to Celtic legend, when two people are born to cross paths and their hearts are entwined, something magical happens. A third entity comes into being as a spirit companion who watches over the two to help them love each other into fullness. If they choose to turn away from the path of their fated entwined lives, the spirit companion will fade away."

"Like Tinkerbell?"

Declan's dad lifts his head. "Tinkerbell?"

"She fades and is going to die because no one believes in fairies, remember? The third spirit is like Tinkerbell. It will die because the two people don't believe they belong together, there's no love anymore."

He sips some water. "Powerful emotions—belief, love..."

"Trust."

I feel his eyes on me, but I can't look up.

"Yes, trust. Very much, trust." He clears his throat. "This is one of the greatest love stories—the tale of Diarmuid and Grainne. Grainne was the most beautiful woman in Ireland and daughter of the high king. She was courted by all the most eligible princes and chieftains, including Fionn MacCool, who was significantly older than the maid. She agreed to marry him, but during an engagement party, she met and instantly fell in love with one of Fionn's best warriors, Diarmuid, and ran away. ..."

My mind drifts, lulled by the sound of Mr. Kendrick's voice and the overheated room. The story drones on with magic spells, the lovers running away, vows for revenge, and, of course, the hero becoming mortally wounded.

"As Fionn and his men came upon their long-sought quarry, he found Diarmuid dying in Grainne's arms. Despairing, Grainne knew she had one chance to save her lover. She implored Fionn to have mercy and save his former friend by curing him with a drink of water brought to him in Fionn's magic hands. Fionn, full of pride, refuses, but seeing that Grainne's love for Diarmuid is so strong she'll never agree to marry him, Fionn is eventually persuaded. A peace between the warring parties is negotiated, and Fionn settles for marrying Grainne's sister instead, leaving the couple to live happily ever after."

Mr. Kendrick tilts his head back, staring at the ceiling.

"What? That's not how it really ends."

He lifts his head. "You doubt me? The expert?"

"Let's just say I think you changed the ending."

He opens his mouth to protest, but a small movement in the bed catches his attention. He stands, leaning over Declan.

A dry whisper comes from deep in the back of Declan's throat.

"Should I call the nurse?" I ask.

We stare at each other. No one moves.

"Declan. Do you hear me?" Mr.Kendrick's voice is deep, calming. "Do you want anything?"

Dry lips move. Declan thrashes. A machine spikes a high tone.

"I'm getting the nurse." When I reach the door, the nurse and another woman rush in. The woman goes to the machine, takes a quick glance, and smiles. Smiles!

My feet are glued to the spot near the door.

She leans over the bed and encircles Declan's other wrist. She looks across the bed to his dad. "This is good. It looks like he's coming out of it."

Declan's eyes flutter. I see the white, then they close again.

He's waking up!

I want to push the woman away and be the first person he sees. I want to ask him what happened in the woods that day. I want to ask him to forgive me for being such a jerk and tell him I trust him. Of course I trust him.

Instead, I take only one step closer. The woman puts a hand to the small of her back and stretches. "It's been a long few days, Mr. Declan Kendrick." She gives some orders to the nurse, who rushes out of the room.

She looks up over Declan's chart. "I'm the attending, Dr. Ryan."

Mr. Kendrick sighs with relief. "I'm Declan's dad."

She spots me standing by the door. "You must be his sister."

"Regina." I leave off the last name.

Dr. Ryan scans through his chart and adjusts something on the IV. "Declan's sedation has been reduced. He may come around, or he may float in and out of consciousness for a while yet." She glances at the green line on the machine behind her. "Patients are often confused, sometimes frightened or anxious waking in ICU." She pins both of us in turn with sharp eyes. "I'm glad you're here if he wakes. Tell him something comforting. Assure him he's in good hands. Can you do that?"

Mr. Kendrick's head is nodding like a bobblehead.

"The nurse will be back in a minute to remove the respirator."

I want to ask how he's doing and when he can go home, but her back is to me.

"I'll be on the floor if you need me or have any questions."

She brushes past me and is gone.

Any questions? We have like a million questions because no one has told us anything.

Mr. Kendrick hovers over Declan, staring. A leg moves under the blanket, but his eyes remain closed. The nurse comes back with some helpers and asks us to step back. She slides the thing that looks like a shower curtain around his bed, and all we can do is stand there and listen to weird noises. There's a sucking sound and a burst of air. Then a click and the curtain slides open along its rings.

"We'll take his vitals and be out of your way," the nurse tells us.

Declan looks much better with the tube removed from his nose. Some adhesive residue lines his cheek, and I look around for something to wipe it off with. The nurses wheel one of the machines out with them when they go, leaving more space in the cramped room.

"Declan. Your dad's here. Me, too." I ease myself down on the side of the bed. His face is calm. I detect his eyes moving under the closed lids. Willing him to just open them, to say something, I lean over and whisper next to his ear.

"You were right."

His eyes roll open. He sucks in air. The nurse reappears in the doorway.

"He's awake!" Declan's dad lays a hand along Declan's pale cheek. "We're here. Don't worry."

A raspy voice like an old man who has spent a lifetime smoking ten packs a day comes out of Declan. "Dad?"

"You're in the hospital. Don't worry."

Mr. Kendrick's eyes shoot over to me. The message is clear.

"Declan, it's okay. Your dad and I came—"

"Dad?" Declan turns his face to his father. "How?"

I'm not sure if he's asking how his dad got here or how he got here. The nurse adjusts the drip bag and moves in to check his blood pressure. I inch down toward the end of the bed.

"Your family is here, honey," she tells him. "Try to relax. The doctor will be in later to check on you."

She smiles at us. We smile back. We're all smiling like crazy. I wonder if they feel like me, awash in relief. I scoot closer to Declan. His eyes search out mine, trying to focus.

"Reggie." He lifts a hand a few inches, but it drops. "Reg. I want to tell you—"

His face collapses, scrunches, like he's lost his thought. Brows slide together.

I grab his hand. "It's okay. Get better, then you can tell me."

His eyelids roll closed like a shade. I sit back.

We stare at Declan like he'll awaken again any moment, even though it's not likely.

The room is dark. The nurses turn on the lights in the hallway. Christmas music wafts in from an open door.

"I'd better call my aunt to come get me." I realize I'm not sure how Mr. Kendrick is going to get home. "I'm not really supposed to drive." I shoot him a sheepish grin.

"I know."

"You know? But you got in the truck with me."

"I had to see Declan. I needed your help." Declan's dad lumbers around the bed and folds me in a bear hug. "Regina, my queen. Thank you." He holds me at arm's length. "When you're a parent, you'll realize you'll do anything for your child."

I look aside. "I've heard that."

"Regina, trust me. A parent will do anything to protect their child."

I slide my arms around him to hug him back. His old sweater smells like pipe tobacco and garlic. "I'm not so sure."

Aunt Sophia doesn't say much when she meets me in the reception area. When we walk to the parking garage, snow flurries float through the air. She slams the door and inserts her seatbelt with a sharp click. Before she turns the key, a sigh escapes.

"What were you thinking? Driving without a license?"

"He had to see Declan. He wouldn't go if I didn't take him."

Our breaths mingle in the cold air. The engine whines and turns over. Aunt Sophia backs up and heads toward the exit signs.

In the dark, her words warm the small interior of the car. "You did a good thing."

The road is empty. The streetlights illuminate each flake and make them sparkle.

"If Angela was convinced I was in danger, do you think she'd help me?" I ask.

The dashboard lights cast an eerie glow on Sophia's profile. "What are you talking about?"

"I'm thinking of visiting her tomorrow. To tell her Wade is dangerous and ask her to do something."

"To do something? Like what?"

"A deal. To turn him in, then I'll come live with her."

Chapter Forty-Three

I ALMOST BACK OUT FROM GOING TO SEE ANGELA. WHEN WE PULLED IN last night, I saw a car parked at Wade's house. After we got inside, I looked out the window. The outdoor lighting was on, and Wade's front doorstep was lit up. Detective Maggiano walked out with another officer, and the front door shut behind them. It must have been around nine thirty. Detective Maggiano going to Wade's house could not be good. Mostly meaning, it would not be good for me. I had a choice to make. Go through with seeing Angela, or try to stay out of Wade's gunsights.

It's a little too late for the second option.

Aunt Sophia drives me to the prison the next morning. We pass through the security procedure that almost feels routine.

"Do you want me to go in with you?"

She means the little fish bowl visiting room.

"Nah, it's okay. You can hang out in the waiting room."

I straighten up my back and square my shoulders so I feel stronger, braver. It's not working. When the door sweeps open, Angela is already sitting at a small table. I slide out the other chair and sit down opposite her. The guard is behind me. Even though I can't see her, it makes me feel better knowing she's there.

I went over in my head what I was going to say last night. It all made sense then, and the words flowed. Now, I'm not so sure.

"How is school going?" Angela asks.

I'm relieved to talk about something safe like school, but I know I don't have much time and need to steer the conversation to Wade.

"It's good. I'm doing good, especially English." The incomplete *Call of the Wild* article springs to mind. "I'd like to stay there."

One side of Angela's mouth curls up. "Is that what this is about? An appeal to keep you at Glenwood High?" She shifts in her chair and leans on one elbow. "And here I was telling myself you just wanted to visit your mother."

"You brought up school. I'm just telling you what I feel." I sit on my hands. They're shaking.

She sits, staring at me. My face gets hotter. She doesn't say anything. My tongue feels like polar fleece is growing on it, and my throat is tight.

"That's not it, though. School, I mean. What is it you really came here for?" Her voice is low and even. Her eyes bore into mine.

I run my thick tongue over my lips. "It's about Wade."

Whatever she expected, this was not it. Her head twists to the right, and she looks at me out of the corner of her eye. "What about Wade?"

This is it. I suck in a ragged breath, lean in, and lower my voice so the guard might not hear every word. "I wanted to know why you didn't turn him in, for, you know."

Her mouth turns to a flat line. "Why does that matter to you?"

"Because he did it, but you went to prison. He's out free. Why are you protecting him?"

Her eyes close to slits, and she nods slowly like she's reading my mind. Sitting back, she crosses her arms over her chest. "What do you think, little girl? You've got it all figured out?"

My thoughts race back to what Cory said. Angela was either as afraid of Wade as I am, or she was using her protection against him— to control him for something.

"I don't think it's because you're afraid of him," I tell her.

Laughter erupts out of Angela and transforms her face into something unnatural. A face that laughs but the eyes stay hard and wary. "No, not afraid. Not for me." She looks out through the scratched

Plexiglas into the waiting room. I follow her glance to Aunt Sophia reading a magazine. The television in the corner is broadcasting a map covered in blue while a ticker tape on the bottom warns of a snow-storm. Angela juts her chin at Sophia. "She's been talking to you?"

"No," I'm quick to answer. I don't want Aunt Sophia pulled into this. "No. So, if you're not afraid, then you're protecting him for some reason. To get him to do something."

"Or not do something."

This is what I was afraid of, and now I'm hearing it.

"Not do something. Involving me?"

Angela's eyes cut to the guard and back. "Something like that."

"It's not working."

For the first time, her face registers something. Concern? "What are you talking about?" She leans in close to me.

"Wade's said things," I say.

Angela blinks. Her head moves an almost imperceptible amount, but I read it as a nod of acknowledgement. I don't have to explain. She blows air forcefully through her nose. "It started with Penny. You had to say something, didn't you?"

My mouth falls open. "You said you didn't believe me."

She's shaking her head. "You think you've got it all figured. You have no idea."

Penny. When I told her what I saw, she said I was imagining things. "He killed Penny, didn't he?"

"And you couldn't keep your mouth shut. You put us all at risk."

"You could have told the police!" My voice is shrill. I hear the guard shuffle behind me. Angela shoots me a cross look. I lower my voice. "Same as now. You could tell them what Wade did. And more stuff. Stuff he's doing now."

She doesn't ask me what stuff. Her face goes pale under the fake orangey tan. "I can't."

"Why not?" My words come out angry. She has the power and won't use it.

"Because of you," she spits back. "Because of you." Her words are slower, measured. "Because it keeps you safe, knowing what I know and not telling."

I collapse against the back of the hard chair. She had a "get out of jail" free card she could have used but didn't. Because she wanted to protect me. My mouth shapes the word *blackmail*, and she barks out a laugh.

"I prefer insurance policy."

"You could have told, maybe got out of prison or had a much shorter sentence, or—"

Her hand covers mine, and instead of snatching it away I let it rest underneath. My heart feels weird, like it's beating slower but knocking against my breastbone. I hear a rush of blood in my ears.

"Please." I force myself to look up, to catch her eyes. "Please tell them. I'll come home with you if you tell them and Wade's not there. Please." My vision blurs.

The guard steps over to our table. "You have one minute." She nods to the door and stands by it.

Angela taps my hand and withdraws hers. "He won't do anything, trust me. He's under control."

I swipe the cuff of my sweatshirt under my nose and sniff. She always has to be in control. But now I'm not so sure. "Maybe there's some things you *can't* control."

"Time!" the guard calls out.

We both stand. She walks ahead of me to the door. I clutch the back of her arm. She looks at my hand, then turns. Her eyes show surprise.

"Do something, Mom. Please."

"Mom?" One side of her mouth lifts in a smirk.

My hand drops.

"I told you. Trust me," Angela says.

The lock clicks and the outer door slides open. Angela, walking beside the guard, disappears down the hallway without a backward glance.

Chapter Forty-Four

EDDIE IS HOLLERING FROM THE TACK ROOM. I CAN HEAR HER FROM the other end of the barn. The big Dutch warmblood I'm bridling spooks and lands on my foot. The yelling continues, followed by banging, like a tack trunk lid slamming down.

"Who hung up these bridles like this? They're a tangled mess. And why are there dirty saddle pads in here? They belong in the laundry room."

Eddie's on a rant. I slip the headstall over Romantique's head without touching his ears. He flips out if you touch his ears. I lead the horse to the entrance of the arena where Galen is waiting. He bends to adjust the leg wraps and looks at me with narrowed eyes.

"Get your mare next. She's giving me trouble with her changes still."

Romantique makes the mistake of swishing his tail and catching Galen in the face. It earns him a jerk on the reins.

"Stand still, you moron."

My gut sends out a wave of something that feels like sulphuric acid washing halfway up my chest. Everyone's in a pissy mood. Eddie is stressed out over getting the horses ready to ship to Florida. Galen's mad about who knows what, and it's been days since I visited Angela, and I haven't heard anything. To make it all so much worse, every few minutes the radio updates the weather report about the coming snowstorm. Nothing panics people in Maryland more than a big blizzard.

On my way to Roh's stall, Eddie stomps up beside me.

"You've got to start getting the horses in and changing their blankets. The weather's moving in faster." Her nose and cheeks are red under a green wool cap, so if she weren't so mean-looking she might be mistaken for a Christmas elf. "And the board, Regina. Remember?"

"I have to get Roh ready for Galen, then I'll start getting everyone in." I don't say anything about the money I owe.

Eddie jogs beside me and stands outside Roh's stall. The mare swishes her tail and pins her ears. When I slide open the door, she swings her butt in my direction.

"Regina." Her tone makes me whip around.

"Yeah?" I brace for her saying something about the money again. Instead, she motions for me to come out of the stall. I slide the door shut. My stomach is really not happy, and I'm wondering if this will be a long conversation because I might have to run to the bathroom.

"I don't know what agreement you've made with Galen, but drop it. Don't let him ride your horse."

My heart thumps hard against my chest. "We made a deal, and I don't know how to tell him—"

"Blame it on the owners. Tell him they're switching trainers. Happens all the time with show people."

Eddie looks in at Roh and clicks her tongue. "Look at her."

We stand side by side and watch Roh snake her head at us, ears pinned.

"She's getting dangerous, Regina. She's fighting back. You can't let a sensitive mare like this one be bullied and treated unfairly. She's too nice a horse."

Roh had become sulky and fought me more. When I asked for a difficult movement, she questioned me, evaded, or outright refused with a buck or running off.

"All I know is he's ruining her. I've watched him ride her, and I want to vomit."

"What do I tell him? When he's done with Romantique, he wants her ready."

"Tell him she's lame. He won't check." Eddie pulls out her phone.

Her fingers scroll over the screen. "They're saying maybe up to two feet overnight." She shoves the phone back in a pocket and pulls on her glove. "Get the horses in. We're short staffed today."

Twenty horses brought inside, blankets changed. I slip my pocketknife under the twine of the hay bales, breaking open more to give extra hay tonight. My feet are two blocks of frozen ice. I can't feel anything. My pants, wet and muddy from the knees down, sag at my waist and slap against my calves when I walk. The sky is dirty gray and hangs down so low it's like being under a dark tent. A few flakes swirl through the air, but nothing big yet.

The regular workers have gone home to beat the storm. Some of the resident working students are going out with Galen to some fancy party today that I can't believe wasn't cancelled. Good luck getting back, I tell them when they get in his truck. They laugh.

Janie sticks her head out the window and waves. "We'll just stay over if we have to. Lots of booze to keep us going!"

When the truck rolls down the long driveway, fading into the grayish mist, I turn back to the barn. Snow swirls inside and down the aisle. The majority of the horses are in, munching hay, warm and dry in their blankets. My back muscles tighten as I slide the heavy doors shut, sealing off the sound of the wind.

In the other wing of the barn, I scoot out the half-open door and slog to the back pasture to get Tucker. He's always the last to come in because he likes being outside better than in his stall. But tonight he's coming in for sure.

Jogging down the gravel drive to his field, I call, but my words are carried off by the wind. Tucker is usually at the gate at dinnertime, but since it's early he's nowhere in sight. That means I have to go after him. Grabbing his halter off the post, I open the gate and notice that it wasn't latched completely. I'm glad I caught that mistake and not Eddie. My feet are so wet already, the damp seeping in through the seams doesn't matter anymore. Hands framing my mouth, I call in every direction and wait to hear hoof beats. Nothing is visible beyond a couple of feet, so I head in the general direction of where he likes to hang out, flexing my fingers to keep them from freezing.

I spot him at the bottom of the hill. It looks like he's standing in water or in a big area without any snow. Jogging downhill, my feet feel like they're going to shatter from cold.

"Tucker," I holler. "C'mon, you jerk. Don't make me come after you."

He doesn't move, standing, head low, butt to the wind.

I jog closer, yelling, but he doesn't move or lift his head.

"Tucker, what the heck is wrong with you?"

Then I see. It's not water. Not a bare patch. He's standing in blood. Black in the center, redder on outside edges. So much blood. Blood—on snow.

I don't know how I get to him so fast, but I'm suddenly by his side, standing in the dark pool surrounded by bright white snow. Dropping to one knee, I search his belly, his legs, his chest. Where is the cut? Where is it coming from? I run my hand down his face.

"It's okay, boy. I'm here. I'll help you now."

I whip out my phone and punch in Willow's number. My heavy breathing sends clouds into the air. I walk around the other side.

"Oh, my God!"

"Hello?" Willow's voice sounds in my ear. "What's up?"

"Willow. I'm in Tucker's field. His leg's cut open, and there's a ton of blood." I suck the stream of snot back up into my nose and run a sleeve across it. "Call a vet, quick! Then get down here. I'll try to get him inside, but I don't know."

"How bad is it? Is it broken?"

"I don't know!" I scream into the phone. "Just call someone. And help me."

I shove the phone in a pocket and shrug out of my jacket and slip the sweatshirt up over my head. The wind bites through the thin shirt.

The wound is flayed open, showing the muscle and maybe the

white is bone underneath. Kneeling in the snow, I wrap my sweatshirt around the cut, tying it up as tight as I can with the sleeves. I pull my coat on, shivering. My teeth knock together like a windup toy, and I can't stop them. I find the halter I dropped and slip it on Tucker's head. I have no idea if he can even walk.

Where is Willow? Who will she get to come out tonight in a storm?

I fish around in my coat pocket for something. I always have treats—why can't I find something? My finger probes again and something crinkles. When I unwrap the starlight mint, Tucker raises his head.

"C'mon boy." I hold my palm out with the mint. "One step."

He lurches forward, buckling on the hurt leg but moving. The sweatshirt is stained red already.

"Good boy. One more."

I scan the whole area for a sign of how he did this to himself. A bloody jagged fence board or a ragged edge of a water trough...something that would make sense.

Nothing. He's in the middle of a pasture with his leg torn open. In a pool of blood without a trail. Like what I saw before...

He takes a few more steps, and now that he's moved, it seems he's willing to keep it up. We get to the part of the field that slopes uphill. Willow runs toward us, slipping and skidding, with a black box banging against her leg.

She runs over, drops to her knees in front of the box, and snaps open the lid.

"I got ahold of Dr. Polks."

A brief moment of relief washes over me to hear a vet is coming. And double relief it's not Wade.

Willow twists the dose ring on a tube of Banamine and squirts it into Tucker's mouth. He lolls his tongue around, licking off the bits of painkiller stuck around his lips. She tosses the tube in the box and pulls out clean leg wraps and bandages.

"How bad is it?" She pulls at the sweatshirt, already stiff with blood. Gently, she unwraps the wound and gasps.

"It looks like someone gutted him like a fish."

The sweatshirt soaked up a lot of the blood, so now the flesh on his leg looks like pages of a book, peeled back and open, exposing the tendon beneath. Willow pulls off her other glove and drops it in the snow. She holds the flaps of the wound closed and winds the cotton bandage around his leg.

"The drugs should give him some relief. I gave him a load. Maybe we can get him up to the barn."

With her leaning against his shoulder to support the hurt leg and me pulling him forward, we manage to arrive at the entrance to the barn just as Dr. Polk drives in. She jumps out of her truck and runs to us.

"Get him inside," she orders. "Warm water if you got it and get a dry blanket on him."

Tucker's ears swivel when the horses call out, and he seems to muster his last ounce of energy as we lead him through the doors. Willow runs to get water while I throw my whole body weight against the doors to close them, shutting out the wind and sealing the barn like a cold tomb.

Dr. Polk squats beside Tucker's leg, unwinding the blood-soaked bandages. The last layer is stuck to his skin. Willow sets a bucket of steaming water beside her, which she uses to ease the material away from the loose tissue.

"These types of injuries bleed like crazy." She states the obvious as a small dark pool forms around his hoof. She glides the warm sponge down the leg with one hand and probes the lose skin with the other. Tucker hangs his head and snorts out a breath.

"It's not as bad as it looks." Dr. Polk glances up and our eyes meet. She turns back to the cut. "In fact, it's strange. A few millimeters in either direction and he would have severed the tendon." She shakes her head, sending the pom-pom on her hat bobbing. She stands, pulls a syringe out of her jacket pocket and a small bottle. She inserts the needle. "Do you have any idea what he caught it on?"

"No. There's nothing out there." I turn to the outside doors, as if I can see through them, down to Tucker's field. Blood on snow, nothing else in sight. "I'll look again tomorrow." But I'm sure I'll find nothing.

Dr. Polk slips the needle into his neck and checks her watch. "We'll let this take effect and then stitch it up. It may not heal too pretty, but I'm confident he'll be sound again. I'll give him a dose of antibiotics to ward off infection."

She sinks down to look at the wound, probing lightly with her fingers. "See, this is a ligament that runs right alongside the line of this cut. The tendon sits just behind it. It's almost like surgical precision the way the injury split open the leg without hitting anything major."

Surgical precision.

Her words conjure the memory of Wade in his truck, the syringe rolling on top of the console. Dr. Polk becomes a watery image as my eyes fill with tears. Tucker is so trusting. He would stand still, maybe even nicker when a stranger came up to him in the field. He'd never suspect a man, maybe with a treat for him, would then bend down and flay open his leg with a razor-sharp scalpel. And walk away. Leaving him to bleed out, leaving a message in blood. For me.

I start hiccupping and crying. My nose runs, and my lips are cracked open from the cold.

Dr. Polk wraps me in her arms. She's small but strong. "He'll be okay," she says, thinking I'm only worried about Tucker getting better. I wish that were all. When she stoops to check the bandaging, she stops halfway and puts a hand to her back. "Storm coming makes it feel worse," she explains.

Willow cleans up the discarded bloody gauze and leaves to dump the water.

The vet sits on a tack trunk and writes out instructions. "No hay until the tranq wears off, about a half hour." She hands me several tubes of Banamine and a bottle of antibiotic pills. I take the medicine and wonder who's going to pay for all this.

A cascade of snow slides off the roof, rumbling like a train, and darkens the windows. "Getting bad out there," she says but makes no move to leave.

I pull another blanket off the rack outside Tucker's stall and throw it over him.

"I'm sorry I have to ask," she says, "but have you had any other, err, such injuries? Or other strange incidents, like tails cut off, strange illnesses? I'd have to report anything that may be suspicious."

"No." I picture what else Wade could have done—or might do. "You think someone did this?"

She sits up straight and waves her hand. "No. I don't want to set off any alarms. It's just the cut was clean—no jagged edges, no torn flesh."

"Like a knife." A gust of wind rattles the gutters and the vet turns to look out the windows.

"Or a very sharp edge on something. Look around the field tomorrow, if you can. And, like I said, it's a miracle nothing vital was cut."

A miracle. More like a vet who knew exactly what he was doing.

Dr. Polk heaves herself to her feet and zips up her coat. Her phone beeps, and she frowns at the screen. "Better get back. Long night ahead of us."

Willow reappears and runs a hand down Tucker's face. "Galen just called. No one's coming back tonight."

Dr. Polk squeezes my arm. "Keep an eye on him. And here." She presses a business card into my hand. "If you need me."

She slips outside and her truck roars to life. Willow and I struggle to shut and latch the door.

"I guess you're staying here with me tonight." Willow nods to Tucker who finally has his head up and is looking around. "Let's put him away and get warmed up."

"Thanks for your help. I don't know what I would have done if you hadn't been here."

"Don't worry, you'll pay me back." She smiles as we walk toward the office. "Eddie's taken off, too, and probably won't be able to get in until late tomorrow. Everyone else is at that stupid party, so I'll be stuck doing everything until they can get back."

I open the door to the office, and a blast of warm air kisses my frozen face. I drop my wet coat on a chair and feel my shoulders unknot. Willow opens cabinets and drawers, looking for something.

A brown tabby, curled up in the in-box on the desk, stretches and yawns. "Hey, I don't think she's supposed to be in here." I point.

"Neither are we."

That's true. Galen doesn't allow workers in here, and Eddie only calls you in when you're in trouble. But for tonight it's close to Tucker's stall and it's warm.

Willow rattles a locked drawer. "What are you looking for? Booze?"

That earns me a pitying look. "Nah, got some of that in my room. I'm looking for the books."

"What books?" I ask, but I don't really care. I'm too tired to care. I drop onto the couch like an anchor.

"The ones that tell exactly what everybody makes around here."

I'm a little interested. I wonder how much the best rider makes. Whether it will be enough for me to convince a judge—or a social worker—that I can be free from Angela. If Angela doesn't come through on her promise to deal with Wade. The thought makes me even more tired.

A pair of bandaging scissors appears in Willow's hand, and the drawer rattles again. Breaking and entering. Who cares? My thoughts wander and shift. I'd better text Aunt Sophia that I'm staying over. I hope she's not out in this, coming home from work.

"That did it," Willow says. The drawer opens, squeaking along its tracks.

"Don't most people keep that stuff online these days?" I ask, leaning back and closing my eyes.

Willow doesn't answer. I hear a rustle of papers. The click of a pen. Scratches on paper.

"Why do you care so much?"

"Insurance."

I don't know what she's talking about. "So, how much does Janie make?" I ask, my eyes still closed.

Willow laughs. It doesn't sound happy. "More than me."

I sit up in time to see her stuffing everything back in the drawer and closing it. I dash off a text to Aunt Sophia, telling her where I am. "I'm hungry." All of a sudden a wave of empty stomach nausea washes over me, and I realize I haven't had any food since breakfast. "Did you find any food while you were snooping around?"

She stands and shoves some papers in her pocket. "I'll check the lounge. People are always leaving good stuff in the fridge there. You can check on Tucker."

I struggle to stand. The couch is pulling me back into its embrace like a magnet, but I know Willow is right. Time to check on Tucker. I shoot my arm through the sleeve of my coat and open the door. The cold slaps me in the face.

The only lights are the few lining the aisle. Outside is nearly dark from the snowfall, though it's not even four o'clock yet. Horses bang their buckets.

I pull out my phone to see if Aunt Sophia got my message and realize I'd shut off the ringer while the vet was here. There are a ton of messages.

I tap the first and put the phone to my ear. Mr. Kendrick's voice bellows into the quiet.

"They're taking Declan to Hopkins. It's bad." Labored breaths huff in my ear as if he is right beside me. He must be confused, thinking I had answered the phone and not the voicemail. "They called and said he's bleeding. I don't know—" The voicemail cuts off.

I stare at the screen. My heart's hammering against my chest. There are seven more messages. I tap the most recent one, hoping he'll tell me everything's okay.

His voice slurs. "It's Rosie's fault. She's trapped. Screaming to be free." He isn't making sense. I hear banging in the background, like a door slamming. "I'm freeing her."

"What are you talking about?" I yell into the phone, knowing he's not there.

Another noise like a lock clicked open. He curses softly at the sound of something dropping like a million coins hitting the hardwood floor. A dog barks, probably Buck. I'm trying to picture what's going on while I stare at Tucker. I need to call him back, but his voice rattles on. "Hawks are messengers of death, sent from the other world. The Celts knew it. Now I know. I'll free her, so she'll free Declan." The next sound sends a wave of bile from my empty stomach burning up my throat. The soft but unmistakable sound of a gun being cocked.

Chapter Forty-Five

I TOUCH THE REDIAL AND HOLD THE PHONE TO MY EAR. VOICEMAIL. I HIT the number again, running back to the lounge to find Willow. It's ringing.

"Regina." His voice sounds calm.

"Mr. Kendrick, where are you? I just got your message."

Willow looks up in surprise when I burst through the door. She asks if it's Tucker, and I wave her questions away.

No answer.

"Mr. Kendrick!" I yell into the phone. A squawk. It's Rosie. "Mr. Kendrick, don't shoot Rosie!"

"I'm freeing her. She's dying, Regina. She wants to bring Declan with her."

"No." None of this makes sense. Willow is mouthing the question *what* to me, but I turn my back. I have to think. "No, Mr. Kendrick, listen. I'll come over. I'll free Rosie, and she'll be okay. She'll live. You don't have to kill her."

"No?" He sounds like a small boy, suddenly full of hope.

"No, please, trust me."

The last two words echo down the phone and through time, to the last time I asked him to trust me. When I lied about being able to drive. I draw in a deep breath and hold it. Waiting.

The line crackles with static. I'm about to ask if he's still there when his answer rumbles in my ear.

"All right."

No more words.

"Okay, listen, I'll be right there." How? The windows are dark. Snow is piling up. I turn to Willow. "Can you drive me?"

Her pale eyebrows scrunch together in a V shape. "Where?"

"Declan's house."

Her eyes cut to the television running silently on the counter. The weather map shows a big blue blob all across the state. A woman in a form-fitting dress indicates an area marked *up to 18 inches*. Exactly where we are.

Willow's face wears a pained expression. "I don't know. What's going on?"

I hold my finger over the tiny speaker. "I think he's gone nuts. He's going to shoot Rosie."

"Declan's bird?" Willow grimaces. "What if he does?"

"What if he doesn't stop with just the hawk?"

Mr. Kendrick's voice comes on and snatches my attention back to the phone. "I'd better hang up. The hospital may be calling me."

"Right. Go back to the house. Stay by the phone and wait. Okay?" I need to hear him agree.

"Okay, Regina. Just come."

The line goes dead.

I let out a long sigh. "This is crazy."

Willow asks me again what's going on, and I fill her in. I zip the phone into the vest pocket of my coat so I'll hear it ring. We push open the door closest to the parking area and ice pellets blast my face. Willow's car is a tiny blob in the endless white.

"Looks bad," she says over my shoulder. "I don't think I could make it down Declan's long driveway through the woods and all."

I know she's right. I don't think she would make it out of the driveway here to the main road.

"I promised to come."

"Maybe if someone had a truck?"

My aunt has a compact. Cory only has a little Toyota. Brenda's car always looks like it's going to fall apart under the best of circumstances. No one. "It's so frustrating. It's not that far at all—it's just the roads are so bad."

I pull my phone out and stare at it. Maybe if I called him back, convinced him to wait until tomorrow. We duck back inside, and the door slides shut with a bang.

"Could you ride there?" Willow stomps her feet to stay warm. "If you cut across the fields, through the woods, you'd come in the back, right?"

My mouth falls open, and my head's shaking no even while I'm considering it. If I skirted the perimeter of the fence around the far field, I know where the trail into the woods is. I've taken Tucker back there trail riding. I'd have to find a way dead east and hope there isn't another fence or something we can't get around. If I could find the back of Roh's old field, I'd recognize it. Maybe *she'd* recognize it.

"I'll have to take Roh." I run down the aisle. Roh, who doesn't trust me anymore. Roh, who has been acting so aggressive to people that Eddie called her dangerous. Thoughts are squirreling through my mind as I gather her tack and a quarter sheet to cover her haunches. Roh, I'm going to ride you into a blizzard, into the woods where you've never been. Into woods, where Declan was shot. Please just trust me, it will be okay.

Right.

Willow hands me my helmet and I cram it on over a fleece headband. It presses against my forehead, igniting a pain building there. I tack up Roh and lead her out. Her metal shoes clop against the floor, sending echoes through the barn. At the back door, she pins her ears and turns her head to look at me with her dark eyes.

"Yeah, you hate me now. Just wait till you see what I've got in store for you."

Willow opens the door, and I flip the reins over Roh's head. The mare skitters sideways as Willow catches me under the knee to hoist me up into the saddle. She tightens the girth and looks up at me.

"Sure about this?"

"Nope." I pull on an extra pair of gloves. As long as I can hold onto the reins, it won't matter much about steering her. Roh lifts her head and sniffs the air as I urge her toward the opening. "Oh, wait." I pull off the gloves and loop the reins through my arm. "Call this guy, Detective Maggiano, and tell him where I went. What's happening."

Willow's face, burnt pink with the cold wind, pales.

"You don't even have to talk to him. Just leave a message." I pull on the gloves. "Just in case."

I nudge Roh, and she steps into the snow. It's only a few inches around the barn, but it's slick underneath. The freezing rain came first, then the snow. At least the wind died down. Roh dances underneath me, anxious to move.

"Are you sure you're okay?" Willow stands in the gap in the doorway.

I shrug. I can't answer. I'm afraid my voice will crack. I'm afraid I'll jump off and bring Roh back inside and forget my promise. I manage to croak out, "Just take care of Tucker," before I turn and point Roh toward the edge of the woods.

Chapter Forty-Six

ROH SLOWS, SINKING UP TO HER HOCKS IN THE DRIFTS, BUT PRESSES ON toward the woods. I'm surprised she hasn't whipped around and bolted back to the barn. It's weird, but it feels like she's taking over and leading *me* into the woods. Maybe she senses she's going home. We duck through a gap in the trees and follow the trail. Now that we're under tree cover, the going is easier. The snow isn't as high, and the trees cut the wind, but it's much darker. The sun is a barely visible milky blotch above the bare trees, but I'm heading to it because I know that's west. That's where the park should open up to the back of the Kendrick's property.

Should.

We make good time moving along the trail until we come to the place where it bends away to the south. I yank off a glove and pull out my phone to bring up the compass. I never was any good at reading these things. Holding it flat in the palm of my hand, I watch the numbers spin and the dial turn against its black background. We're at 330 degrees, whatever that means. Says northwest. When I slide my leg back, Roh turns on her forehand, and the dial spins like crazy.

"Wait! We went past west."

She moves until the needle is pointing exactly at 270 degrees, dead west, and I look up. A wall of trees over a tangle of brush. I have no choice but to go farther south down the trail to look for a path to tack back west. Roh is anxious to get moving again as I struggle to hold the reins. Before I pull my gloves back on, I send Willow a quick text message on my location, and that's when it happens. As if someone bumped my elbow, I fumble the phone. It arcs through the air as I reach, swiping at emptiness, and it sinks into the snow.

"Oh, my God!" I stare at the place I think it landed as if my eyes have X-ray vision. I don't see anything but white, some hoofprints, a dead branch. "It has to be here."

Roh shifts, stomps a foot.

"Stand still!" I bark at her. If she crushes my phone...

I slide out of the saddle and sink above my ankles in powdery whiteness. Looping the reins through one arm, I walk around the other side of Roh where the phone dropped. The snow is smooth, untouched. Bent over, my nose inches from the surface, I scan the place where it has to be. It has to. Roh stands behind me, snorting. Gently, I run my palm over the top of the snow. Nothing. Desperate, I scoop up chunks of it, hoping I don't drive the phone in deeper, farther out of sight.

My gloves are wet, and my fingers tingle. I dig and scoop farther and farther away from where we were standing. I listen for a dreaded crunch as Roh follows behind me. Where did it go? I glance over my shoulder at the sun sinking below the tree line. With my back turned, Roh head-butts me, sending me sprawling onto my knees. I throw out my hands to stop from doing a face-plant, and my fingers touch something hard.

Rolling over, sitting in the snow, I pull my hand up in front of my face and see the edge of the phone case. After I scramble to my feet, grab Roh's dangling reins, I brush off what I can of the wet snow clinging to it and turn on the screen. A box warning about low battery glows white. Ignoring it, I check the compass and haul myself back up into the saddle. I check my position in relation to the weak sun.

"We've got to hurry." My words echo back in the frozen air. A long-needled pine bough drops a load of snow, and Roh scuttles away. She pulls at the reins and takes off along the path until we come to a small cut through the woods. It's heading west.

She scans the path ahead, and I drop the reins. The way is clear.

She moves down the narrow deer trail, stepping over brush, heading into the waning sun. It feels right. We're on our way, but how much farther? After what feels like twenty minutes or more, I risk pulling out the phone. I hold it tight in my bare fingers and swipe to the compass and watch in horror as the screen turns black.

Dead.

I'm cut off.

Willow knows where I was headed, but who knows if I'm on the right trail. The woods are huge.

Darkness creeps up behind us and surrounds the trail. I can barely make out the sun at all through the clouds and snow. Dampness seeps through my coat and along my back.

I'm going to die out here.

I put the dead phone away and zip my coat up higher under my chin. The snow rides the wind currents and hurls icy drops in my face, up coat sleeves, and down my collar. Who knows what Mr. Kendrick thinks happened to me, what he's doing now. How long has it been? My eyelids droop, lulled by the rocking motion of Roh's walk. Strange. I just want to fall asleep. I lean over Roh's neck, the welcome warmth of her body radiating up into my chest. A great mare, I let her down, too.

One tear rolls out of the corner of my eye and falls into the snow. My cheeks burn with the cold.

No.

I sit up straight. I've got to think. We were heading west. "This trail has to go somewhere." The words are muffled by the woods, the snow. Roh stops.

I look around at the walls of white all around me, then down at the red mare. I'm not alone. I've never been truly alone, even now.

"Roh, you're the seventh mare of a seventh mare. You have special powers. I've seen them. I trust you. Show me the way."

I drop the reins and nudge her with my legs.

Roh snorts, stamps a hoof, and bolts forward. I grab two fistfuls of mane and lift up out of the saddle as she flies through the woods, over the snow, as if her feet never touch the ground. As if she's swimming through water. Branches whip past my face, inches from slashing me. I hunch closer to her neck and press my face into her mane. I can't see. I can only hear the pounding.

It goes on and on, Roh's running. My muscles scream with pain from stiffness and cold. I'm being ripped apart, but I don't care. Steam floats off her neck, enveloping my face. I breathe in the scent and feel transported to another time. I'm Nuallan, galloping across ancient Ireland. Galloping over the sea.

And then the fence is in front of us.

I clutch, grabbing at the reins. Roh is running straight at it. A fence, overgrown with brush and thorns, blocking the path. It's snow-covered so I can't tell how wide it is. There's no way around. Roheryn rips the reins from me, stretching her neck.

"Stop!" Sitting back, I pull one rein to turn her, but she shakes her head and picks up speed.

Instinct takes over. If she's taking the jump, I'm making darn sure I'm still on her on the other side. I close my hip angle, grab mane, and hang on.

As she lifts, the dressage saddle slams into my groin, and my right foot drops out of the irons. She arcs over the fence with inches to spare. When I sit back, stars spark in my vision. We're in an open field. An ocean of snow.

Roh stands, shakes her head, sending ice crystals flying off her frozen mane.

I have no idea where we are. No idea where to go. We're in a white cave, and I don't see the exit.

The mare lifts her head and sniffs. Even the air is white. Nothing to smell but cold, blank air. We stand still, snow slowly covering and muting her bright red color. Soon we'll be swallowed up, too, and made invisible.

I push her to move, but she locks her legs in place.

"What?" I ask. I can't imagine why she wants to stay here. I pull out my phone to check just in case. Still dead.

"Now what?" Slumped in the saddle, my feet numb, I imagine what the Donner party must have felt like. A strange calm washes over me, replacing the tingling nervous dread. Is this what it's like to give up? Or is this trusting everything is going to be okay even though I have no reason to think so? I take a deep breath and close my eyes. I'll be okay. I have to be, to save Rosie. When I open my eyes, I see her.

A red tail swoops low along the sheet of white sky framed between Roh's ears. She's watching it, too.

It's not Rosie. But it's alive and the only thing out here that's moving. Before I can nudge Roh on, she moves off on her own, tracking the hawk.

Declan told me they don't just fly around like other birds. He said they land in trees and move from perch to perch or dive after prey. Soaring, he called it, instead of active flight. This bird is flying. It's flying in loops back and forth in front of us, as if it's leading somewhere.

And Roh is following it. She picks up her pace as we follow after the red speck in the sky. When the hawk disappears, Roh lifts her head and calls out.

The hawk reappears, emerging from a cloud. It soars upward, loops, and dives back down, almost hovering over my right shoulder. Then, almost as if it were sucked up by a vacuum, it soars straight up and disappears. We wait, but it's gone.

A weight pulls my heart down. Roh stops. She's probably looking for it, too. The horizon is a blurred line between the drifting snow and the dull sky. I clench and clap my hands to keep my fingers alive. My coat is heavier from the wet, melted snow seeping into it. Ice forms on my eyelashes, blurring my vision. But there's something new, I feel it. The blank, frozen air has changed, and I think I smell wood smoke. Inch by inch I squint my eyes, straining to see anything along the gray line of the horizon. And there it is. Over my right shoulder, a thin dark line perpendicular to the edge of the hill appears. Smoke?

I turn Roh's head, and we make for it as fast as possible in the deep footing. Closer, a thicker dark square materializes. A roof line. I urge Roh on. The roof is covered with snow, but the chimney, clear and black, billows smoke from a wood fire.

Wood smoke. Declan.

I recognize the wooden house, the porch. Roh is heaving, cantering as fast as she can through the snow.

"Mr. Kendrick!" I scream over and over until my throat is raw. A figure appears on the porch. A hand lifts in greeting, then waves frantically as we plow through the heavy snow and along the lane between the pastures.

He runs down the steps to meet us, sinking in over his short boots. Jumping off Roh, I stagger. My knees buckle and I collapse. Strong arms lift and embrace me.

"I said I'd come." The words are muffled as I press my face against his scratchy woolen overcoat and breathe in the familiar scents lingering in the threads.

I pull off my helmet and look up at his face, his bushy eyebrows pinched together with worry. "Nuallan helped me." It doesn't make any sense what I'm saying, but I believe it. His stories helped me get here. "And Roheryn."

He encircles me into another hug, pressing my head against his chest, and I feel more than hear his words.

"You trusted the horse gods, Regina. They protected you."

Chapter Forty-Seven

WITH THE LAST BIT OF STRENGTH I HAVE, TOGETHER WE MANAGE to get Roh put away with some hay and water. Inside the doorway to the house, shotgun shells are strewn across the floor. Buck and Thornton greet me with happy dog smiles. A Christmas tree stands in the corner, unlit, but decorated with ornaments placed from the middle to the top. Mr. Kendrick goes to the kitchen while I struggle to get out of my wet boots and coat. When he returns, he's holding a steaming mug and a plate of cookies. I watch for how steady he is on his feet or any other signs. I also look around for the gun.

"Eat, warm up a while." He puts the plate on the table. "Then we'll go."

I know where he means—Rosie's mew. I wrap my hands around the mug to warm them but don't answer. My feet hurt. Padding over to the fire, I drape my wet socks over a chair and stand the boots nearby. A big gulp of hot tea burns the back of my throat, but I don't care and take another. Collapsing into the armchair, I can't imagine getting up and going out again. The wool blanket draped over my shoulders is heavy and scratchy. I pick up the plate, and the cookies slide around on it. They're stale, but I crunch into one after another, wondering if Mr. Kendrick has had any regular meals to eat. Declan always did the food shopping for both of them.

Buck's nose appears over the edge of the plate of cookies, nostrils pulsing in and out with each sniff. I slip him the last one, and he skulks off with it, avoiding Thornton. I set the plate down and spot the black phone on the end table. I should call Willow to let her know I made it.

When I put the receiver down, Mr. Kendrick is standing in front of me with an armload of clothes. "Here. They're dry. Then we'll go."

A spray of ice pellets hits the window. The shiver starts at the back of my neck and cascades down to my feet. I have to go out there again. To the mew.

The socks are too big, but they're the thick gray kind hunters wear. I toss my damp sweatshirt on the couch and pull the raglan sweater over my head. It smells like Declan, and my throat closes. I have to help his hawk. I grab the boots and pull them on and pick my wet coat up off the coat tree. Mr. Kendrick hands me a knife, sheathed in a leather case. I slide it out, gripping its bone handle. The blade is razor sharp. I catch his eye.

"What's this for?"

"Freeing the bird."

The zipper of my coat catches, and I have to tug to get it up to my chin. I jam the knife into a pocket and step out into the glow from the porch light. The snow has slowed down. Mr. Kendrick follows in my footsteps to the door but stays outside.

The mew is musty and reeks of decomposing flesh. Something moves in the shadows. A claw scratches against the perch. I pull the cord and the small room floods with light. Rosie blinks while I look around and scramble for a good idea. None come to mind. Mr. Kendrick, in his bulky dark overcoat, lurks in the doorway.

Rosie opens her beak and lifts a small pink tongue, like a worm resting in her mouth. No sound comes out. She hunches her wings, turns her head, and watches me out of one eye. A leather strap as wide as a pencil is wrapped around her feet and the perch. I can't really see the beginning or the end of it and am not sure how she is caught there. I take one step and bend to get a closer look. She lifts her wings and screams.

A bolt of electrical energy shoots through my body and sends me backward.

"Okay." I gulp in a deep breath. "Okay, we're here to help you." My hand slides into the pocket and fingers the point of the knife sheath.

I turn to the open doorway. "How am I supposed to cut her free before she tears my hand open? Or worse?"

Declan's father doesn't answer. His eyes drift to the corner where the shotgun is propped against the wall. The meaning is clear.

Rosie emits a long raspy screech, pulling my attention back to the dank interior of the mew. I feel Mr. Kendrick step outside and close the door behind him. Footsteps crunch around the mew. Rosie tracks the sound, moving her head to follow the footsteps along the outside wall to the small screened-in yard. Mr. Kendrick shoves at the door until he can yank it open. It's wide and inviting. Maybe if I can cut the thong that's tangled around her feet, she can fly through that door and be free.

Her eyes are dark amber in the dim light.

"I don't trust you."

The hawk blinks. A flash of the gold in her eye, like a wink. She shifts on her perch, stretching out one claw, gripping the perch again, then stretching the other. Long ringed claws with talons at the end of each. My flesh shrinks imaging what they could do to me.

One step closer. "I don't trust you." The word *trust* comes out in a warble. I'm so tired, I feel as though my legs, my shoulders have bricks strapped to them. Breath streams form a cloud, encircling the bird like a wreath.

Blink. Wink?

"Please, God, don't let her hurt me."

Rosie draws one leg up to her body until it stops, halted by the strap. She strains, moving the foot in a circle, the thong stretched tight around it. She drops the foot and lifts the other, testing the resistance— or maybe showing me. Maybe asking me.

Death floats on the frosted air. The hawk hasn't eaten, her food rejected. She has to hunt. To hunt, she has to be free. To be free, I have to cut her from that cord. I have to step near her. I have to trust her.

"Help." The word leaks out of my chest on a sob.

Rosie opens her mouth and her throat convulses with a series of chirps. I don't know what it means. A threat? A welcome?

One step closer. I pull the knife from the sheath and grip it as hard as I can through the thick glove. My breath is coming quicker, sending billows up in front of my face.

"You have to trust me."

Another step.

A chirp, softly.

Rosie lifts a leg and holds it in the air like a person who has chewing gum stuck to his shoe.

Closer. The knife tip touches the leather. I turn my face away, twist my shoulders, clenching them for an attack. Thrusting the blade out, I feel the leather resisting, and I draw it upward in a sharp stroke. A sawing motion, praying it doesn't slip. Back and forth, back and—

The tension breaks. Her leg is free. She lifts it and spreads her wings.

"No!" She falls, hanging from one leg as she tries to fly.

I pick up the other leather, inches from her claws and cut it in one fast hard stroke. When the leather gives, the knife flies out of my hand. I run to the door and wait, sweating in my coat, covering my face with the heavy gloves—only spreading fingers wide enough to watch.

Rosie bobs on her perch. Once, twice, then lifts into the air and glides out the opening and is gone.

Chapter Forty-Eight

THE DOOR IS HARD AGAINST MY BACK WHEN I FALL AGAINST IT. My knees can't hold me, and I slide down, squatting on the bare floor. My skin feels like an iron coat I'm too weak to carry, and my head is too heavy for my neck. It falls forward and my eyes shut. I'm so tired.

The crunch of tires on the deep snow, churning up the gravel, doesn't register until I hear my name. It floats to my ears in a dream, drifting on wind. The door pushes against my back.

"Regina. Are you okay?"

The door bumps me again, and I struggle to my feet.

"Regina, open the door!"

It's a woman's voice. The door swings open, and Aunt Sophia is standing there. She grabs me in a hug, smashing my nose against her shoulder, and almost pulls me off my feet. She's saying something I can't quite get. When she lets go, I see Detective Maggiano behind her. A big black Tahoe SUV, engine running, is billowing exhaust in the driveway.

Declan's dad turns the corner and stops when he spots the newcomers.

Detective Maggiano holds up his badge. "Mr. Kendrick. We got a report that assistance was needed here." His dark eyes land on me.

Declan's dad shakes his head. His eyebrows pinch together under the edge of his knit cap. "No, no help's needed. Not anymore."

The detective rubs his bare hands to warm them. "Let's go inside, then. We can talk. Maybe you can fix us up with a cup of coffee?"

Mr. Kendrick looks confused. "I'd be glad to, Officer." He turns to Aunt Sophia. "I don't believe we've been introduced."

"My aunt. Sophia." I take a step closer, and she drapes her arm over my shoulders. "This is Mr. Kendrick—Declan's dad."

"Nice to meet you. And I'm sorry about…" Her fingers clench my shoulder.

Mr. Kendrick gestures to the path leading to the house.

As we approach the porch, Buck and Thornton rush to the window, barking. Stepping inside, I see why. The Christmas tree is on the floor, surrounded by fallen ornaments mixed with the shotgun shells. Aunt Sophia stoops to retrieve a wooden reindeer and places it on the table.

"That's why no glass ornaments. They do it at least once every year." Mr. Kendrick ignores the tree, hangs up his coat, and checks his phone. "No word from the hospital." He mumbles as he disappears in the kitchen, and I'm surprised when Aunt Sophia follows him.

Detective Maggiano rights the tree and picks up a few of the fallen ornaments before he shrugs out of his coat. I know he sees the shells but doesn't say anything about them. He pins me with his eyes.

"That was a crazy thing you did." He drapes his coat over a dining room chair and leans on it. "I put some men on stand-by in case we had to search the woods tonight if we didn't find you here. Glad we didn't have to."

"Then you called my aunt?"

"After I got the message from your friend at the barn about your hair-brained scheme to ride across the county in a blizzard. Your aunt thought you were staying overnight at the farm." One caterpillar eyebrow shoots up.

"I was. Honest. Then I got the call from Declan's dad."

"And you couldn't wait." He stares me down.

I look away, picturing the shotgun leaned up against the wall in the mew. I heard the way his dad was talking—like maybe he took too much of that medicine they gave him the night Declan was shot. Biting my lip, I struggle over what to say. I don't want Mr. Kendrick to get in trouble.

"It was an emergency." A quick check of the kitchen doorway. I lower my voice. "He was going to shoot Declan's hawk. There's a gun in there. You might want to, I don't know, confiscate it?"

I expect Detective Maggiano to demand to know more about the gun. Instead, he laughs and pulls out a chair to sit down.

"Not sure I can arrest him for shooting a bird." He holds up his palm to stop the words coming out of my mouth. "But I'll talk to him. We can keep an eye on him, maybe have an officer come by and check while the boy is in the hospital."

I pull out a chair opposite him. That sounds good. "He doesn't drive. Maybe get someone to bring him groceries, too."

He looks like he's going to say something, but Aunt Sophia comes to the table with a pot of coffee, mugs, and some spoons on a tray. Detective Maggiano leaps out of his chair to help her set it on the table.

Aunt Sophia brushes back a strand of hair that just falls right back over her face. "After we warm up a bit, I think we should drive to the hospital." She glances back to the kitchen. "He told me his son was supposed to be transferred to Hopkins, but they cancelled because of the storm. The doctors are worried about internal bleeding. He didn't seem too clear on the details." She leans in and whispers, "I don't think he's been taking care of himself."

Detective Maggiano gets up and walks over to the window. He pushes the curtains aside. "Looks like it's stopped. The plows can get the main roads cleared."

Mr. Kendrick appears with the same stale cookies. Now I'm really worried about what he's been eating. After he sets them on the table, he pulls out his phone and frowns.

I doctor up the strong coffee with a lot of milk and dump in a few sugars. "Have you heard anything more about Declan?" I ask, guessing the answer.

Mr. Kendrick slumps into a chair. "Not a thing." He wraps his hands around the coffee cup and stares into it.

Sophia puts a hand on his arm.

"We should just go," I say. Faces look up at me.

Detective Maggiano empties his cup in two gulps and plucks his coat off the chair. "I'll get the vehicle cleared off and warmed up. Meet me out there when you're done, and I'll drive you all over to the hospital." A blast of cold air sweeps the room when he steps out.

The coffee cups are gathered up in record time and we all pile into the big black Tahoe. It plows down the driveway, sliding a few times, but blasts through the snowdrifts until we hit the main road.

The hospital reception area is dim and nearly empty after hours. Maggiano waves to the attendant at the desk who seems to know him. We pass by without question and take the elevators up to the intensive care suite. A cheery rendition of *A Holly, Jolly Christmas* is playing through the tinny speakers, making my eyes sting. The doors open and the first face I see is the Nazi head nurse. Turning around to see who it is, instead of the usual sour look, she actually smiles.

"Mr. Kendrick! It's wonderful." She grabs his hand and pulls him to Declan's room. "He's awake and eating."

We follow and the nurse doesn't give me, Aunt Sophia, or Detective M a second glance when we crowd into the room. Dr. Ryan is leaning over the bed. At first I can't see Declan, but I hear his voice.

"When can I go home?"

The doctor moves aside. His freckles look ten times darker against his pale face in the weird hospital light. His eyes catch mine.

"Reggie!" He shifts like he wants to sit up, and the nurse eases him back down. "Reg, I had the weirdest dream about you."

A laugh from the doctor. "You've been through a lot, young man." She dispenses a bunch of medical instructions to the head nurse. I hear *move from ICU* and a breath eases out of me. Declan's dad is in the chair by the bed. Maggiano lurks in the doorway.

The doctor clutches a manila folder to her chest. "We were going to do a transfer to Johns Hopkins today. The head of thoracic surgery there is a specialist in this type of injury and when the bleeding started..." She shakes her head. "It was impossible in the storm.

Turns out it was a miracle. The move may have, well, it was better we didn't move Declan, and then this evening everything suddenly turned around." Her mouth gives a little sideways hitch like she can't explain it and that's giving her problems. She gives her usual "I'm available for further questions" promise and glides out of the room. Detective Maggiano has to move sideways to let her pass.

It's then the head nurse seems to realize how many people are crammed into the room. She makes a shooing motion, trying to get some of us to leave.

Maggiano raises a hand. "I'll get us something to eat, and I've got to check on a few things." He touches the foot of the bed. "Maybe later, when I get back, we can talk."

Aunt Sophia calls to him. "Need a hand?" He gestures for her to come along.

I perch on the arm of Mr. Kendrick's chair. He asks Declan over and over how he's feeling. Then he puts a hand lightly on my back.

"Regina found you. She saved your life."

"Not really. I mean, the dogs led me to you. When they came back alone we were worried and went looking for you."

Declan's voice is raspy like an old man. "Good dogs."

"Not really." Declan's dad laughs. "I put up the Christmas tree—for when you come home. They've knocked it down already."

"Every year."

It feels normal. Except for the fact that I haven't eaten all day, and we're in an intensive care room, and there's about two feet of snow outside. Otherwise, it feels normal, finally.

Then Mr. Kendrick's asks the question on everyone's mind.

"Do you remember? Do you know what happened?"

Declan's smile leaves his face and is replaced with deep lines between his brows. "Yeah." He turns his head.

My empty stomach churns, and I'm suddenly not so hungry anymore. *It's your fault*, my brain whispers.

"I don't want him to get in trouble," Declan says into the pillow.

"Who?" His dad moves to the edge of the chair.

I wait to hear the name I dread.

"Chester Farlan." Declan takes a breath that sounds like his chest is going to crack open. "He was drunk. I came up on him hunting deer. He had baited the bottom of a tree stand with apples and was trying to climb back up the rungs of the ladder. When I started walking over to him, I saw he had his rifle loaded, and I thought the safety was off. Turns out, I was right." Declan tries a smile, but only half his face reacts. It looks like a grimace.

Declan's dad makes a very small noise. A noise like maybe he's holding back something much louder. Much more powerful.

"I called to him, but he didn't seem to hear me. He had one foot on the rung, then maybe he decided he forgot something because he swung back around and that's when it happened. He tripped, fell off the rung. The rifle fired. I don't remember a whole lot after, except that the ground was wet, and I couldn't talk, couldn't yell for help. I just remember watching Chester's dark blue jacket running down the trail."

A burst of laughter from the nurses' station outside the room punctuates the silence.

"That guy, Chester, was he alone?" I ask. I recall the noise in the woods, the flash of color before the emergency team arrived.

Declan nods.

"You know him?" I ask.

Mr. Kendrick rubs his face. "He's a neighbor. And he left you there."

I put a hand on his shoulder, more to keep him sitting than to comfort him. "I'm texting Aunt Sophia. She's with the policeman. She can tell him what Declan told us. He'll know what to do."

It was an accident, not Wade. I feel like I'm filled with helium and will float up to the ceiling soon. I slide onto the bed and lean close to Declan.

"Ah, better back off some, Reg. Don't know how long it's been since I brushed my teeth."

"Don't care," I whisper and look over my shoulder. Mr. Kendrick smiles and turns away to adjust something on the rolling table. Careful to avoid Declan's bandaged side, I brush his lips with mine. His are dry. His hair is stiff and spiky.

The phone pings.

"Saved by the bell." Declan laughs.

I sit back up and see the message is from Aunt Sophia.

Detective M wants us to meet downstairs in the cafeteria in ten minutes.

The cafeteria food line is closed, but the vending machines work. A few night shift workers sit at a far table. They look over when Detective M unloads a grease-stained shopping bag, and the room fills with the smell of fried rice, General Tao's chicken, and egg rolls. My stomach roars as soon as my nose lets it know what's going on. Aunt Sophia hands out paper plates like she's dealing cards and drops a fistful of plastic utensils in the middle of the table.

"Dig in." She turns to Mr. Kendrick sitting beside her. "You must be starved, Aldwin. And I'm sure you want to get back to Declan right away."

Aldwin? My aunt knows Mr. Kendrick's first name?

I don't give it another thought and pull a carton marked *lo mein* toward me.

Mr. Kendrick pinches a spring roll between chopsticks and holds it in the air. "This may become a new tradition for Saturday night dinners."

Detective Maggiano asks Mr. Kendrick some more questions about the neighbor, but eating has my full attention. Maggiano checks his messages throughout dinner, responding with a frown or occasional grunt. After a while, he places the phone face down on the table. Heads turn in his direction.

"Officers went to Mr. Farlan's home this evening," he says.

Declan's dad puts down the chopsticks.

"They found him at home. He was"—Maggiano hesitates for a

minute—"impaired, but he admitted to the shooting right away. The officers confiscated the rifle for further analysis, but we're confident it will be a match."

Mr. Kendrick stares down at his plate. "Poor Chester." He shakes his head.

I don't get how he can feel sorry at all for the guy.

"You'll have to come to the station tomorrow and file a report," Maggiano tells Mr. Kendrick. "You may want to speak with a lawyer about further action."

Aunt Sophia's hand disappears under the table but I catch her patting Mr. Kendrick's knee. "Don't worry about that now. We can give you a ride. Right now, why don't you go up and check on Declan. We'll clean up here."

Who is this woman, I wonder, and what has she done with my aunt?

She stands, folds down the tops of the containers, and grabs a wad of napkins to wipe the table. Mr. Kendrick wanders to the exit, and I worry whether he'll find his way back to the room okay. Aunt Sophia gives him a worried look. "Maybe I should go with him?"

"I'd prefer you stay," Maggiano says. It doesn't sound like there's an option. "I need to talk to both of you."

Aunt Sophia sinks into her chair.

Maggiano's lips curl in. He huffs out some air and leans his elbows on the table. "There's no way to preface this, so I'll just come out with it. Trey Morales' body was found."

Oh, God, I feel sick. "Where?" I think I know where.

"The investigation is ongoing so..." He flips over his phone to check it, then sets it down. "Near where his car was found. It's not conclusive, but it looks like this will scale up from missing person to a murder investigation. More computer forensics experts were assigned to the code on that slip of paper you found."

The cafeteria is too hot all of a sudden.

He looks at me. "You're linked with the glove and the note—that puts you in a dangerous position."

A sweaty film breaks out around my neck.

"What kind of danger?" Aunt Sophia's mouth has a crust of mustard in one corner. "What's going on?"

I told her some of the story. Now I can't remember exactly what.

"So is Declan," I say.

Detective Maggiano rubs his chin. "The code's been linked to a human trafficking ring. Vice has been working the case for more than a year now and this—"

"What does that have to do with us?" Aunt Sophia scrubs her mouth with a thick wad of napkins. "Trafficking? Like sweat shops and illegal aliens?"

"No, in this case, worse. Prostitution. A lot of it involving underage girls."

Oh, I really feel sick now. I shift in my chair and scope out the nearest bathroom. What is Willow into? I promised I wouldn't get her involved.

Aunt Sophia shakes her head as Maggiano explains. "The codes are used on gaming sites to direct the girls to where they meet the customers. We're not sure who's running it, but vice tells me they're getting close to tracking it down. I don't pretend to understand what those computer forensics guys do, but they're good."

"So why do you think Regina is involved?" A balled-up wad of napkins is clutched in Aunt Sophia's fist.

"I don't, but I think she's close to someone who is involved. And that someone may think Regina knows something that could be dangerous."

Maggiano doesn't mention Wade, but I can feel him weighing everything I've told him. I really want to ask what Wade told the police when they came to his house to question him, but I fold my lips shut, afraid what else might come out.

Aunt Sophia sits stunned, a wad of napkins pressed against her lips. Maggiano looks at each of us, expecting...what?

"Right." He raps the table with his knuckles and pushes back his chair. "We're looking into all leads. In the meantime, I'm posting an officer to do some drive-bys, check in with you occasionally. And I've been in touch with your case manager, Brenda Schwartz, to coordinate between agencies."

I'm about to tell him Brenda's not assigned to me anymore, but I'm starting to figure out that if I keep my mouth shut, I'm better off. But I make a mental note to talk to Willow. Tomorrow.

Maggiano stands and shrugs into his heavy coat. "I've got a car coming by in a few to get all of you home." He picks his phone up off the table. "I've got one other thing to check out tonight."

He heads for the exit and, before leaving, turns.

"And Regina." He points a finger at me. "Stay home for a while. Enjoy the snow." He gives a half-smile and disappears.

Chapter Forty-Nine

THERE'S NO SCHOOL, AND THE RESTAURANT WHERE AUNT SOPHIA works isn't opening. We try to enjoy a day off, but it isn't long before we both have cabin fever, get on each other's nerves, and need to get out. She decides to pick up some things for Declan's dad and bring them over. As I watch her little car slide down the driveway, I pray someone has plowed the long road to the Kendricks' house.

My phone's been pinging. Word gets around fast that Trey is dead. People who didn't know him at all say it was probably a gang revenge killing. Other people guessed he was into drugs and OD'ed. Idiots. In the past day or so I've left a ton of messages with Willow, but she hasn't called me back. Maybe she's busy as part of the crew getting ready to head out to Florida with the show horses for the winter.

I punch in Cory's number to see if she'll take me to Twin Elms. I want to get out of the house but also have an ulterior motive—to show her Tucker. I know a horse with show jumper potential, and he is it. His dressage training only made him better. Just wish Trey could see him.

But now Tucker's stuck on stall rest with his leg wrapped up, but I've been thinking about that a lot, too. I thought Declan was shot on purpose, and it turned out it was a drunk hunter, not someone out to get him. Maybe Tucker cut his leg on something I never found in his field. Another accident. *Just* an accident.

The phone pings.

Be there in 5.

Five minutes is an eternity while I stand at the window with my coat on, waiting for Cory to roll up to the house. It feels normal to hang out with her again. I want everything to just be normal.

Cory's car glides into sight. Without waiting for her to park, I take old lady steps along the icy walk and hop in. The car smells like sugar cookies baking.

"Want some beignets? They're still warm." She holds out a pastry bag.

"What the hell's a beignet?" I ask.

"Powdered sugar heaven. Try one." She rattles the bag.

There's a white dust over her lap, the console, maybe even under where I'm sitting. The round pastries spew powdered sugar as soon as you get them anywhere near your mouth, but it's so worth it for the creamy, achingly sweet inside.

"Oh, my God." The moan leaks out of the side of my full mouth.

"Right?" Cory puts the car in gear and turns toward the road. "Touché Touchet Bakery strikes again. I'm addicted."

"You mean you've been there already this morning?"

She gives me a look like I'm asking if she has a toilet in her house or something. "Had to take Jess to her appointment this morn, and that absolutely requires we swing by for beignets." She points to a take-away cup in the holder. "That's yours."

I check the bag and snag another, then take a swig of dark, hot coffee. "You know how to live."

She gives me a great big Cory smile, and all the time we spent apart shrinks down to a nanosecond.

When we turn through Twin Elm's gates at the head of the drive-way, Cory emits a low whistle.

"Wait until you see inside," I say.

The parking area is neatly plowed but nearly empty of cars. Cory has the same jaw-dropping reaction I did the first time I set foot inside this place—all polished wood, brass lanterns, and money.

"Almost everyone is gone to Florida already," I tell Cory. "The big-time competition horses shipped out last week, and another bunch of boarders' horses are set to go today or tomorrow. It's okay—gives us the place to ourselves."

We turn the corner to head to where Tucker is stalled, and I almost smash right into Galen.

"I've been looking for you." His voice echoes around the empty stalls. "Where's the mare?"

I'm pushed back by a force field of negative energy surrounding him. Now I know why horses move away from him. The various options for a reply run through my mind like a marble bouncing along a roulette wheel, but not one lands. Some non-committal noise comes out instead.

His finger is in my face. "It better be good because I'm owed a lot of money for training her."

I'm thinking, more like *torturing* her.

"The owners came and took her back." I deflect his response by grabbing Cory's arm. "This is my friend, Cory. This is Galen, the head trainer here."

Galen responds with a grunt. "I have a bill for them, and I want the money before we take off for Florida. You tell them that." He looks down at me. His voice curdles with threats. "Better yet, I'll talk to them. Give them a call."

"Right now?"

"They're in Europe." Cory's voice is steady, reasonable. "It's the middle of the night there."

Galen's focus drills into her. "And you know that, why? Who are you again?" His eyes narrow.

I swear Cory stands up straighter and lifts her chin. "I'm a representative of Vee Stewart. I'm looking at some horses for her. Roheryn's owners are friends of hers."

I bite my lip to keep from smiling. She sounds like some of the snooty clients we used to work for.

Galen consults his sparkly watch and storms off. After only a few steps, he turns. "Look, somebody's got to pay."

The click of his boot heels fades away, but his words stick in my head. That expression. That's what Wade always says.

"What a jerk." Cory stifles a laugh.

"A very pissed off jerk." Eddie materializes behind me. I spin to catch the look on her face—a combination of worry and anger. "He's not someone you want to mess with, Regina. What's the story on the horse?" She eyes Cory. "Are you part of this, too?"

Cory shakes her head.

"This is Cory," I say. "She works for a jumper trainer you might have heard of. Vee Stewart?"

Recognition softens Eddie's gaze. "Good trainer."

"I thought they might be interested in seeing Tucker. Now that…" My throat closes. I don't say, *now that we know Trey is dead.*

It's like all the bones in Eddie's body slump. Her shoulders droop, and she exhales a cloud of breath. "Sure. Good idea." Her words are clipped but quiet. She must be more upset than anyone about the news since she knew Trey the longest. They worked together every day.

Three of us walk to Tucker's stall in silence, haunted by thoughts of Trey. What happened to him in the woods that night? If I had said something… But then Wade would come looking for me.

Eddie slides open the stall door. "It's too bad you can't see him go. He's quite a jumper."

I check her face. She hitches a quick smile at me.

"Regina's done a great job with him. Seems despite his dressage training, he's telling us he really wants to jump."

Cory runs her hand down Tucker's long face and looks over his conformation. "Built for it. How long before he's sound again you suppose?"

Eddie frowns at the bandaged leg. "Hard to say. Luckily nothing critical injured, but it won't look pretty." She drapes an arm over Tucker's shoulder and rolls her face against the horse's skin. "He's such a sweetie. Just like his owner."

Is she crying?

I swallow hard. Cory looks away.

Eddie straightens and gives Tucker one firm pat with the flat of her hand. She looks at me, but her eyes skitter past. "I'll try to work out keeping him as long as I can, but…"

We all know what the *but* means. No board payment, no room at the inn. The wind catches the swags of fake Christmas greenery draped along the stall door.

We step out of the stall, and Eddie slides the door shut and sends the bolt home with extra force. "I'm here till the end of the year, then I'm leaving, too."

Her back is to me. Eddie is always here. Eddie lives here. She's the one who keeps everything going, keeps the horses happy…

"Why?"

"Because I can't stay here any longer and ignore what's going on." She tosses a treat in Tucker's feed tub. "You did the right thing, getting Roh out of here. Pissed his majesty off big time."

I don't know how much she knows about the deal I had with Galen. Not much goes on around here without her finding out about it.

She grabs my upper arm and leans closer. "You get out, too, okay? Before something happens."

Chapter Fifty

I'VE GOTTEN USED TO SLEEPING WITH THE PHONE RIGHT BY THE BED. When it pings, I don't check what time it is—I just see that it's Willow. Propped on an elbow, I blink about a million times to try to clear the sleep from my eyes and focus on her text.

Tucker's bad. Better come.

I snap on the light. *What's going on?* I try to type and pull on pants at the same time. Falling back on the bed, I read:

On my way to get you now.

I hurry to the bathroom and close the door before turning on the light to not wake Aunt Sophia. It's eleven thirty. She'd probably not let me go now, on a weeknight, even for a horse emergency. After dressing, I grab a bottle of water, get my coat, and slip out the front door, letting it click softly behind me. The air is so cold it burns the inside of my nostrils. I don't wait long before headlights arc around the bend. Willow's car pulls up in the darkness, and the passenger door cracks open.

I jump in and haven't even closed the door before she takes off.

"How is he? Did you call a vet?"

Willow's face is rigid, expressionless. Her eyes never stray from the road, "Tucker's spiked a fever and is acting colicky."

"Who's with him now?" Before she can say, I fire another question. "Where have you been? I've been texting you for days."

"Oh." She risks a quick glance at me, then back to the road. "My dad got real sick."

"Sorry." That doesn't mean you can't answer your phone, I think. I ask her what meds she's given Tucker, is someone walking him, and a dozen other things, but she just says the same thing—it must be colic.

"Okay, we made it." Her car slides a bit when we make the turn in to the barn's driveway. "I'll drop you off in front so you can run in. I've got to park around back because the shipper's coming in to get the rest of the horses headed for Florida tonight."

She stops the car. I have my hand on the door handle when she grabs my arm. Her eyes are ice blue and glassy. "Sorry."

"Right." I nod. "Thanks for getting me."

She lets go and turns away. I get out and run down the snowy path to the barn.

It's almost completely dark inside with only the few security night lights glowing. My fingers fumble for the switch, and the lights buzz and blink to life. I'm down the aisle, headed for Tucker's stall, before they all come on.

Why aren't the lights on? With a sick horse in here?

Horses blink at me in the harsh florescent light.

My voice echoes back to me when I call out. "I'm here! Hey, anyone here?" If Willow left a sick horse alone to come get me, I'm going to kill her. My steps fall hard along the brick aisle, anxious to see Tucker and afraid of what I'll find at the same time. I jog the last few feet and fling open the stall door.

Tucker shifts, a mouth full of hay.

"What the hell are you doing eating hay?" I reach out to snatch it out of his mouth and remove the hay bag when out of the corner of my eye I catch movement.

He steps forward into the light from the back corner of the stall. Wade.

My mind's racing. What's he doing here? "Willow called you?"

I look at Tucker. He doesn't look sick at all.

The side of Wade's mouth inches up. "I called Willow. Willow called you."

"Because he's colicking? But he's okay now?"

Wade walks around me, running his hand over Tucker's haunches, and pushes the stall door shut. He leans against it. "No, the horse was never colicking." He has both hands in his coat pockets. The light from the aisle only illuminates half his face.

A pounding starts against my chest and rises up my throat. Blood rushes in my ears. "You did something." It's a question, but not a question.

He pulls one hand out of his pocket. His fingers roll open to reveal a syringe. "The power to heal and the power to destroy. Interesting that the decision is completely in the hands of the person using it." He rolls the syringe back and forth across his palm. "But you know that, right Regina?"

He looks up under heavy eyebrows. His dark eyes are flat, expressionless.

"You know."

It's a pronouncement. It's a sentence. I see Penny slumped in the front seat. I see Trey being dragged out of the party. I squeeze my eyes shut, but just for a second. It doesn't feel real.

"You're going to kill me?"

He laughs. Tucker spooks away from us.

Wade slowly shakes his head. "No, we're waiting for the shipper to arrive, then you're going with them."

"Where's Willow?" My voice is breathless. Trying not to cry, my chest won't stop convulsing long enough to suck in air.

"Long gone."

Willow set me up. Why? "Eddie? Where is everyone?"

"They're all gone. Galen sent them home." He wraps the syringe in his fist and eases it back in a side pocket. "Just us."

The squeal of truck brakes and a release of pressurized air pierce the heavy, cold silence.

"You're going to load the last of the horses, then get in the truck. There's a big bowl game in Tampa this weekend that attracts a lot of guys looking for a party. You're going to help them have a good time. You're going to disappear."

"Mom?"

"Your mother?" He cups my chin and thrust his face close. "You can't trust your mother." He talks patiently like a parent to a little kid. His fingers tighten around my chin. "Apparently, neither can I."

My eyes shift away. The hand moves and lightly pats the side of my face.

"There's a lot of people who'll be glad to see you go. You paid for Willow's freedom. You'll pay Galen back for screwing him over on the horse and making a fool of him—not hard to do, I admit. And, I won't have to look over my shoulder anymore."

Wade turns, his back to me, to open the door. There's nothing in the stall heavy or sharp. I rummage through my pockets. Extra gloves. A mummified carrot. Then I remember the breast pocket. Where I keep the pocket knife for cutting open hay bales.

I'll have one chance to drive it into him.

Dropping my bulky gloves on the ground, I slam my body weight behind the knife into the broad expanse of his back and thrust upward. It stops halfway, slowed by the dense fabric coat. I thrust against it again to drive it home.

Wade bellows and turns, groping behind him for the knife, for me. He bangs the hilt on the doorway.

"Son of a..."

I scoot around Tucker and flatten myself against the back wall. Trapped. He slowly, methodically reaches around and inch by inch draws the knife out of his side. A small rosette of blood blooms on the outside of his coat.

He spots me.

Tossing the knife outside, he ducks his head like a charging bull and comes after me. Tucker skitters to the side, trying to sidestep an insane man in the small stall. Huge hands grasp a fistful of my coat, scraping my skin layers underneath. He swings me around like a tetherball on a rope and I stumble, sprawling into the aisle. My palms burn, scraping the bricks. The wind is knocked out of me, but before I can suck air into my lungs he's pulled me up by the hair. All I see is blood vessels in his eyes, large pores along his nose as he slams me against a wall. His voice is a low, rumbling growl.

"You can go on your feet or on your back, doesn't matter to me." He searches my pockets and takes the phone.

Pinpricks of light dance along the bottom of my field of vision. I have to swallow something that tastes coppery. Blood.

Wade picks up the knife and drops it in his pocket.

My knees wobble as bolts of electricity run through my legs. A truck door slams, and men's voices float in on the night air. I run a coat sleeve under my streaming nose and try to get my head to clear. Maybe the drivers will let me go once we pull out of here. Maybe Wade's paid them, and I can convince them to let me go. That hope fades when the door opens, and they walk in.

One is small and muscular. He's holding a roll of duct tape and a pair of handcuffs. The taller one, wearing a grimy Peterbilt ball cap, smiles at Wade.

"Ready to roll!" He walks along the stalls, peering in on the horses. "Which ones we taking?"

The short one nods at me. "Put her in first?"

Wade snatches a white leg wrap from a rack and shoves it up under his coat, over the wound. "After she loads the horses. Then you can do whatever you want with her."

He slumps on a tack box.

Peterbilt leers at me.

"Just hurry up," Wade orders.

The muscular one pulls a rolled-up sheaf of papers out of a back pocket and reads off horse's names. "Go on. Get 'em loaded."

Maybe Aunt Sophia has woken up and sees I'm gone. Why didn't I leave her a note?

The first horse is hard to load, pulling away from the trailer ramp. The lead rope burns my already scraped palms. But he buys me time. The second horse walks right on. I curse him, attaching the trailer tie to his halter. The ramp is getting slick from the snow, but I don't stop to brush it off, thinking that if a horse slips, it will be another delay.

Maybe a chance to run. But where?

The night is clear. The sky is bright with stars and an almost full moon. Maybe someone will see the light on, wonder what's going on. But then again, everyone knows the shipper is coming.

Peterbilt and the little guy keep an eye on every move. They lean against the doorway and watch me walk the horses into the van, then follow me down the barn aisle to retrieve the next one. Only two more. Then we go.

Every time through the barn I scan the area for a weapon, a place to hide, anything. Nothing. There's no stray shovel or forgotten tool or even a longe whip lying around where it doesn't belong. Thanks, Eddie, for being so neat.

Wade perches on the tack box, watching me pass back and forth. He keeps his arm clamped to his side, and I wonder how badly he's hurt. I hope a lot.

Even so, I couldn't fight him and the drivers. My feet are freezing from the wet snow and drag like lead weights for the last few trips. If only someone knew where I was. I look up to the sky and wonder where Willow is. I trusted her. I shake the thought from my head and set it pounding again. My guards are getting restless, watching me less but yelling at me to hurry up more. I walk the big dark gelding into the trailer and clip him next to a passive gray, munching hay. Something rubs against my ankle, and I snatch my foot away, hoping it's not a mouse. This time it tugs my pants cuff.

Eddie is crouched in the corner of the van, her back against the wall.

"Don't look down!" she whispers.

"How?"

"My car's up by the road. Can you get away?"

I slowly shake my head and mouth, "Call the police." I swipe a hand over my face, hoping to wipe it clean of any expression Wade or the others might read.

The last horse.

What if the police don't get here in time?

I head down the ramp, turning to catch the crouching figure of Eddie in the corner of my eye, then slowly make my way to the barn for the last horse. What can I do to delay? Not latch his halter and let the horse get loose? Barricade myself in the office? Too far. Dragging my feet, I pass Peterbilt headed in the other direction. Where's he going?

In two minutes I have the answer. He appears at the door with Eddie struggling in his grasp. I catch her eye and ask the question across the void. Did she get through to the police? She drops her head.

"Look what I found!" Peterbilt pushes her and she stumbles.

Wade stands. He looks at Eddie, bringing his hand to his chin. He nods. "What's one more?" He reaches in his pocket, pulls out the syringe, and looks at the measure. He doesn't raise his eyes. "Just hurry."

Eddie takes a few steps and is grabbed by the back of her coat. "Don't take two of you to get one horse."

Galen's stallion is spinning in his stall, upset at the horses leaving. A hoof smashes against the wall.

"Go on." Wade cocks his head.

"I don't know the last horse. Rettung. Which one is he?" I say.

"Hell if I know," Wade says. He points to Eddie. "Show her."

Eddie walks shoulder to shoulder with me, and I try to read her expression whether she has a plan. Are we going to run for it? Not a clue.

We turn the corner. Out of sight for two seconds.

"Hey!" the muscled guy hollers. Feet come running.

Eddie raises her arm and runs her hand along the top of a narrow shelf running above our heads, lifts a black metal rod about as long as her forearm, spins it, and shoves it up under the back of her coat like a majorette twirling a baton. One quick nod.

Muscles stands in front of us, feet spread. "Get the horse."

Eddie opens the stall, and I walk in to halter the giant warmblood. The throat snap swings loose, and I attach it to the same side, not under his chin. I clip the lead to the other side and walk the horse down the aisle, Eddie following, past Wade, past Peterbilt standing in the doorway. A little flutter of hope makes me lift my eyes to the driveway, praying a big black car with a spinning blue light will show up. The farm is empty. I could scream my head off, and no one would hear it. Eddie shoots me a grim look. Her hand disappears up under her coat.

I check—Peterbilt is lurking in the doorway. Muscles is walking around the trailer, probably making sure that we're ready to roll. I back up, let the horse keep walking. The big gelding feels a tug, tosses his head, and ducks free of the halter. I flap it at him, and he bolts off.

"Loose horse!" I scream.

Peterbilt pushes off the side of the barn and jogs toward us, cursing. In the dark, Eddie pulls the iron bar out of her coat, swings it, and a sound like a watermelon dropped on the sidewalk, followed by a grunt, is all the noise I hear. Peterbilt's knees fold, and he collapses by the ramp.

Eddie ducks inside the trailer.

Muscleman comes running, skids to a halt in front of the body, and looks down. "What the hell!" When he raises his head, he pulls a buck knife from a holder strapped to his side and comes at me.

I take a step back. He keeps coming, his back to the trailer. Eddie rises out of the shadows and heads down the ramp. My eyes lift, past his shoulder, and shift to look. Eddie swings, but his fist goes out to block the blow and wrenches the rod from her hands. With the rod in one hand, the knife in the other, he steps onto the ramp toward Eddie.

"Hey!" Wade is behind me.

Muscleman freezes.

"Get him into the truck." He jerks his head at Peterbilt. "Close it up and deal with her later."

Muscleman swipes the knife at Eddie, forcing her back into the trailer. He props the bar against the fender and lifts the ramp, trapping Eddie inside. He drags Peterbuilt toward the truck cab.

Wade pulls the syringe from his pocket. The needle glints in the overhead light. He faces me. Is it for me? Am I going to end up like Penny? Trey? He taps it with a flick of his finger and shakes his head. "Regina. When are you going to learn? Somebody's always got to pay."

Instead of coming after me, he turns and enters the barn.

He's going to kill Tucker!

Chapter Fifty-One

ONE GLANCE AT THE ROD TELLS ME IT'S TOO FAR AWAY. MUSCLEMAN is headed back. I leave Eddie and run in the barn.

"Stop!" I scream, my nose streaming. My vision blurs. "I'll do what you want!"

Wade opens Tucker's door.

I run down the aisle, not knowing what to do. Slam the door? Beg him?

The horses still in the barn are spinning in their stalls, stirred up by the yelling. Banging feed buckets, kicking walls.

A sound of splintering wood makes me whip around. Rettung charges through the gap in the doorway, catching his hip and ripping off the doorframe. I duck out of the way as he bolts down the aisle in a panic, hoofs skidding.

Wade steps into his path, his hands raised, but is clipped by the bolting horse and flies into the wall. The rest of the horses are going nuts as Rettung turns on his hind legs and trots back, confused, peering into stalls. Revanche throws himself against his door, rattling it in the tracks. That crazy stallion's going to break out of there.

Wade searches the floor. He must have dropped the syringe.

I clench my sweating hands, itching for something to use as a weapon against him. My heart pounds in my throat as I sweep the area. What will stop him? Muscles will be back in a second. Back to take me and Eddie. No time.

I grab the lead rope off the stallion's stall door. The brass chain swings heavy on the end of it. Revanche lunges at the bars, teeth bared.

That horse is crazy. Driven crazy. I hear Eddie's words in my head as I quietly slide the bolt latch on his stall door and pray.

Wade's hand is on the syringe. He turns, just as I slam the reinforced toe of my boot into his side near the knife wound. He collapses sideways, and I slip the brass chain end of the lead rope around his neck and pull. The syringe drops from his hand as he grabs at the chain. I kick it away. He's going to kill my horse. Maybe me and Eddie, too. I pull tighter, but he staggers to his feet. He's taller, stronger. I back up, pulling him with me like a dog. Pulling him to Revanche's stall as his fingers rake at the chain.

My hip hits the stall latch. I lean into it, dragging the stallion's door open. Pivoting on the spot, facing the opening, I release the chain long enough to drive my knee into Wade's side. He staggers into the opening, into Revanche's stall. I drop the chain and with all my strength, shove him again and slam the door closed, bolted. I turn my back and hold my hands over my ears, sliding down the wall.

That's where they find me.

I don't remember much.

In the barn's office, Maggiano drapes a scratchy blanket over my shoulders and hands me a cup of something hot before something just outside the door catches his eye and he runs out, yelling orders at someone. I can't stop shaking. Policemen walk in and out, putting yellow tags on things. Outside the open door, EMTs zip up a black bag on a wheeled gurney.

I turn away. "Did someone catch Rettung?" My voice is scratchy.

Eddie sits down next to me on the couch. Her face is dirty, and there's a dark cut over her right eye. She pulls the opening of the blanket closed around me. "He's fine."

"How did you know?"

Eddie slumps and lets out a deep sigh. "I didn't for sure, but maybe

I suspected and just didn't do anything for too long. I knew Galen was up to something but wasn't sure what. Tonight, things just didn't seem right when he sent everyone home. That's why I parked on the street and walked in. To check."

"And saved me."

A policeman wheels the gurney away.

"Wade?" The name croaks out. Eddie follows my gaze.

"Yup."

The tea in the cup sloshes over the rim. Eddie takes it and sets it on the desk.

Wade is dead. He can't hurt me.

"Your aunt is on her way." A policewoman sits down on the edge of the desk in front of me. "And there's someone else here to see you."

Brenda walks in wearing a Capitals hat crammed down low on her head and trailing a cloud of strawberry scent. I'm so happy to see her I laugh. Which draws some weird looks from everyone. She sits in a chair opposite, touches my knee. The shaking stops.

"Nick called me as soon as he got word. Told me I might want to meet him here."

"Nick?"

"Detective Maggiano. He's kept me in the loop."

The policewoman with her ID pinned to the collar of her coat gestures for Eddie to follow her. Eddie stands, leans down, and gives me a savage hug. She lets go and steps back just as quickly. "You saved Tucker. As far as I'm concerned, he should be yours."

Maggiano comes in and lowers himself into a chair. His face is gray, and dark shadows hover under each eye.

Brenda unzips her coat and pulls off the Caps hat, making her hair stand up. "The courts have been reviewing your case. Nothing final, but there's a better than even chance your mother will not be awarded custody. We're looking into alternate arrangements."

"That's great news." The words are flat. I'm still a case. Funny thing, it doesn't seem to matter much anymore.

Brenda shoots Maggiano a worried look. "We don't have to worry about that now." Another knee pat. "The detective will make sure you get home all right. He's sent someone by to get your aunt."

"I'm not going to jail?"

Maggiano tilts his head. "Jail?"

"I killed someone." The words are fierce. "Worse. Cuz I didn't say something, it's like I killed Trey, too."

I jump when two whoops of a siren blare. The ambulance pulls away.

Maggiano turns to me. "Listen to me. It was an accident. You pushed a man, twice your size who was trying to hurt you, in a stall. *You* didn't kill him. It was an accident." He slaps the report folder against his leg each time he says *accident*. "Are you ready to tell me about Trey?"

I shrug out of the blanket wrapped around me. It's time. It's time to tell and whatever happens, happens.

He leans forward. "Trust me."

Chapter Fifty-Two

I T'S BEEN A FEW DAYS SINCE—I DON'T KNOW WHAT TO CALL IT. THE attack. The police report says attempted abduction for the purposes of human trafficking. I know it was more than that. Wade needed me to be gone, or dead, he didn't care which.

School let out for the holidays, and Brenda has been over almost every day. So have the police, asking endless questions. Questions about the night of the party, about Wade and Galen. Detective Maggiano says vice is cracking the network and will be making additional arrests.

"Trey was trying to find Rachael, who disappeared, too." I tell him.

Maggiano holds up his empty coffee cup to Aunt Sophia. "This hit the spot." She jumps off the couch to refill it. He tracks her steps until she's out of sight, then faces me.

"We know about Rachael. But there's something else you haven't told me. You didn't find that glove with the code in it. Who did?"

My mouth opens but no words fall out. Why *haven't* I told him about Willow? After all, she sold me out. But I can't help thinking there's a reason, and I want to find out what it is. Instead of answering, I ask my own question. "Eddie told me she never got through to 911 that night. So who called the police?"

"Is this another deal? You answer my question if I can answer yours?"

"Maybe."

Later at home the ping of a text message wakes me, and adrenaline dumps into my body like I chugged five Red Bulls. When I see the sender, make that fifty.

Willow.

Meet me at Hell House tomorrow at 11:00. I'll explain everything.

I stare at the screen, waiting for words to appear there that make sense. It goes dark. The clock glows eleven fifteen. I write back.

Who's going to show up instead this time?

I wait in the dark. My heart's hammering against my chest. Maybe I should call Maggiano, or Brenda. I'm calling Maggiano, I decide. I'll tell him about Willow, about everything. I'll tell him what she did to me.

A soft ping.

I have something to give you. It will help.

Clamping my bottom lip between teeth, I hit the keys hard:

Why should I believe you? Everything she told me that night was a lie. Her excuse about her sick father should have tipped me off right away.

There's no reply. Figures. I get up and pad quietly to the bathroom. Aunt Sophia sleeps with one ear open all the time since I slipped out that night. I get a drink and sit down on the bed.

Ping.

I called the police that night.

A purple truck pulls up in front of the house a little after ten. I tell Aunt Sophia I'm going with Cory and her boyfriend, Kevyn, to hike along the Patapsco. It's true, sort of.

Cory slides over the bench seat, closer to Kevyn, in order to make room for me. Kevyn, home from college for the holiday, offered to drive. I think Cory asked him, to have a guy with us when we go. I didn't argue.

"Hell House, really?" Cory says before I can get the door shut. "It sounds like some place in a bad slasher movie. Why does she want to meet there? And why is it called Hell House?"

"It's what's left of St. Mary's college—a seminary. The ruins became a teen hangout decades ago, and some people thought satanic rituals were going on there." Kevyn gives an exaggerated eye roll. "That's how it got its name. There's nothing much left of it now."

"Except the altar," I say.

Cory gives me a sideways look. "And that's not creepy and strange?"

I agree. It is weird she wants to meet at some ruins in the middle of the woods. But Willow always has been different. I'm only going to hear what she'll say.

Kevyn rolls down the highway, talking about normal things— dorm parties and roommates and some of the things he's done while away in Boston. Meanwhile my mind is playing over and over the conversation I had with Willow the night she dropped me off as ransom for her freedom. What could she do or say to make that all better?

We park near some railroad tracks.

"Hope it doesn't get ticketed," Kevyn says, patting his purple truck and locking the door. He points almost straight up a hill. "There used to be stone steps here, but they're mostly gone, too."

Cory shields her eyes from the winter sun shining on what's left of the snow. It's mostly a slushy mess now. "How far up?" she asks.

"I haven't been there in years." Kevyn looks up the hill. "We used to go up there as part of an initiation in high school. But I'm pretty sure I can still find it."

Cory mumbles, "Pretty sure?"

The climb is hard, and the slick surface doesn't make it any easier. When we enter the woods, trees drop frozen clods of snow and water on our heads. Kevyn walks fast on his long legs, and I struggle to keep up. I'm too winded to talk, even if I had something to say.

The woods open to what might have been an old road. On the right, what's left of two stone pillars frame a staircase. My eye travels up the crumbling stairs, overgrown with moss and roots, to a dome supported by columns almost two stories tall. Every inch is covered in faded, multi-color graffiti.

"That's it. Hell House altar." Kevyn scans the gazebo-looking structure. "Used to have a big metal cross inside on that stone altar. Guess someone stole it."

"Looks more like a Greek temple or something." Cory falls into step behind Kevyn as we go single file up the crumbling stairs.

I scan the structure and surrounding woods. I don't see anyone here. Figures Willow didn't come, after all.

A bird calls, and with a lot of flapping a bunch of them fly out of a tree. I unzip my coat halfway, warm from the climb and the intense sun. When I look up again, she emerges from behind the huge block altar.

Her silver-blond hair is dyed black. Her eyes follow us as we climb the last few steps and enter under the canopy of the colonnade. Sun streams through holes in the roof.

"I had to be sure it was you guys," Willow says.

I wave an arm at Kevyn and Cory. "I brought my friends."

"I get that."

Cory and Kevyn hang back near the entrance while I walk forward and stand on the other side of the altar. Willow remains behind it, like a shield. It occurs to me, maybe she's afraid of what I'll do.

That idea gives me strength. "So, I'm here." I struggle to look casual, in control, but my heart is thudding so loud I can feel the vibrations and imagine everyone else can hear it, too. My throat is dry.

"Thanks." She runs her fingers through unnaturally black hair. It's as wispy as ever and in the light breeze flies back in her face.

"What's with that?" My eyes cut to the hair.

"New look. For insurance purposes." She tries on a forced smile, but it melts away. "I'm out of here, but I had to talk to you first."

"Why?"

Her eyes drop. She runs a finger along the rough surface of the altar. "I'm sorry. I was scared." She gives me a desperate look. "I had to tell you that in person."

"Yeah, imagine how scared I was when three slime balls tried to drag me to Florida in a horse trailer to...you know."

"I know." She looks off into the woods. "Yeah, I know."

I wait.

Willow leans on the stone altar. "Wade threatened to kill one of the horses if I didn't call you. I wasn't sure what he was going to do, but he promised I could leave the job if I called. He'd pay off my debt. I could get out, get done with the escort thing." She looks up and her eyes pin mine. "Did you know he was the guy?"

I search Willow's eyes. They're the same color as the sky behind her. Do I believe her? "The guy who set everything up?"

She nods. "As soon as I pulled around the barn, I dialed that number you gave me. Remember? The night you rode Roh to Declan's? I called that detective guy, and I told him."

"Maggiano."

"Yeah, him. I told him, you know, everything."

"That you were the one who found the glove?"

She gives one small nod. "And more." Her eyes skitter off to the woods again. "I'm really sorry. You have to believe me."

A bough drops a load of melting snow. There's no other sound but the dripping.

"I guess I believe you," I whisper.

Willow bends and reaches behind the altar. Kevyn sucks in a breath, and I turn in time to see them cross the gap between us in a few strides. When Willow straightens up, she looks at Cory and

Kevyn, her mouth round with surprise. "You thought I had a gun or something?"

Kevyn shrugs.

Willow drops her old notebook on the altar. "Something much more dangerous."

"Your story?" I ask.

One side of her mouth curls up in a sarcastic grin. "You might call it that." She flips open the cover and rotates the book for us to read. A finger with a ragged nail points to a line. "It's a code book. The cover names, addresses, clients, the whole deal for every job, every girl that they ran in the op—me, Janie, Rachael... I've been recording everything for a while now."

I stamp my feet, soaked from the hike. "Are you kidding?"

A quick shake of her head. "Take it." She pushes the book at me.

Kevyn scans the page. "Are these IPs? Access codes?"

Willow flips a page. "It's all in the back, here, where it explains who the characters are in the online game. Those are the contacts. Each one has a code—how they reach us and hand out jobs. You can figure it all out."

"You're giving it to me? Why?"

"Like I said, it was my insurance. I'll be free when those guys aren't. But now it's your get out of jail free card. Give it to your friend the detective, and I guarantee you won't be going home with your mom. Trust me." Her mouth slides up in a half-smile. "I know, you'll probably never really trust me again."

"Angela's involved?"

She doesn't answer but pushes the book another inch toward me. She bends once more to pick up her backpack and hikes it on a shoulder. "Gotta go."

Willow steps from behind the altar. I track her progress across the pavilion toward the stairs. She looks small under the weight of her pack.

"Wait."

She stops and looks over a shoulder.

I cross under the broken ceiling and wrap my arms around her thin shoulders.

"Thanks." My breath moves a strand of her hair. It floats like a raven's feather.

Willow never looks back as she runs down the stairs and is swallowed up by the woods.

Chapter Fifty-Three

SOME FAMOUS PERSON SAID SOMETHING LIKE, "CHRISTMAS IS NOT A time or a season, but a state of mind." I'm not sure who said it, but it's true. I'd also add, Christmas is not a place. It can be wherever that state of mind takes you. This year the holiday has been really screwed up if you only judge it by the things like being home, opening gifts, stuffing your face, and being surrounded by relatives.

I have no home, we didn't manage to get any real gifts, and my closest relative is in prison. Christmas day comes whether you're ready or not.

The best thing about this Christmas is I'll have a home, the only gift I cared about was Declan being released from the hospital, and when you get right down to it, you can decide who's your family.

"Dinner!" Declan's dad announces, holding a platter so big and heavy I don't know why he doesn't topple face-first into it. Aunt Sophia rushes to grab the outside edge and ease it to the table. "Christmas goose."

I've never had goose and it sounds kind of creepy, but like Declan tells me, it's his dad's tradition, and I know better than to try to change his menu plans. I've had too much eggnog already along with the candied nuts to feel much like eating. The tree is still standing, even though the dogs have beat it with their tails and almost taken it out again. And if they do, we'll just laugh.

Declan struggles out of the couch to make it on his own to the table. I want to help him to his chair and push it in, but he's not having any of that. Instead, I sit first. He leans on the back of my chair, and I scoot it in more. He takes the seat next to me, and his fingers entwine in mine under the table.

The table is gorgeous. It's everything that is Christmas—the glow from the candles sparkling on the silver and crystal. And there's so much of it! Holly leaves studded with red berries encircle the candles, the serving trays, and there's even a sprig at each place setting. So different from the paper plates and takeout Christmas dinner from Boston Market we usually have.

Almost too perfect, it makes me a little afraid. Afraid, every time the phone rings that it will be bad news. Afraid someone will have too much to drink and say something hurtful. Afraid that I don't deserve to be this happy, and it just doesn't happen this way in my life.

Declan's dad sits at the head of the table and bows his head. He reaches for Aunt Sophia's hand. On his other side, he grasps Declan's, and Declan takes mine until we all form a circle around the table. Aunt Sophia locks eyes with me, and I give a quick shrug.

"Heavenly Father…err…or Mother, or whatever you believe in," Mr. Kendrick looks up. "We've been through a trial, all of us, and you've brought us through it. Like the trials faced by all great heroes of old, like Nuallan"—he smiles at me—"we have to trust and believe. Trust in something larger than ourselves. But trust is hard. A smart man once said anything we trust in which can be taken away from us brings insecurity."

His words send a jolt up my back. Like he's been reading my mind.

Declan looks up sideways at me and squeezes my fingers.

"So how do we trust if we're afraid?" Mr. Kendrick continues. "By believing in what cannot be taken away. God's promises. Believing builds trust, trust to love, trust to live life, trust to try again. And again, if necessary."

"Dad?"

Mr. Kendrick blinks as if someone just woke him.

"Merry Christmas and let's eat, okay?" Declan says.

Declan's dad picks up the carving utensils, shrugs back his cuffs, and stands poised over the goose. "Last words. . . A wise poet once said, 'Where there is ruin, there is hope for treasure.' Our ruin has brought us great treasure."

His eyes lock on me, then Aunt Sophia.

"That's Rumi," Aunt Sophia speaks up.

Declan's dad makes a little bow to her. How did she know that, I wonder.

"And," she says, "one of my favorites of his, 'Don't be satisfied with stories, how things have gone with others. Unfold your own myth.'" She raises her wine glass.

He sits and spreads his napkin on his lap. "Sophia. You know, your name means wisdom."

After dinner, Declan's dad and Aunt Sophia are in the kitchen having too much fun washing dishes. Snifters of brandy are precariously perched on the counter and on the window ledge within easy reach. I help dry for a while, until I'm shooed back in the living room to keep Declan company. He still can't stand for very long. Aunt Sophia waves a dishtowel at me like a matador and tells me I'm not needed.

I sit so close on the sagging couch, Declan's body rolls into mine. He uses it to his advantage, snaking an arm around my shoulder and pulling me into him. His face is still pale. I can feel ribs along his back where it used to be thick, smooth muscle. But his eyes are exactly the same. He lifts a curl and coils it around one finger, pulls it free, letting the finger ghost along my cheek. A low sigh leaks out of me before I can stop it. The blue of his eyes blurs as he moves closer. For once, my eyelids drop and my lips wait for the press of his against them.

Instead, he moves away. The cool air seeps between us.

"What?" I ask. "You feel okay?"

"Yeah." Not very convincing. He sits with elbows on knees, hands clasped, head dropped down.

"But?"

"You're going back to Texas."

"You can come visit." I say in my best, chipper-sounding voice.

"Don't think so." He nods toward the kitchen. I get it. He can't leave his dad.

"I don't really have a choice right now." I'm leaving with Aunt Sophia until the courts can work something out.

Declan leans forward and scratches Buck's belly, wedged between the couch and the coffee table.

"Let's go outside," I say. I'm hot, I've eaten too much, and I'm sick of listening to my aunt laughing and having a better time than I am. "I need to take some pictures of the snow if I'm going to be stuck in Texas. To remember." I waggle my phone and stand up. *And I'm taking pictures of you. To remember.*

"It's dark out."

I grab his hands and pull him to his feet. Probably not a great idea, judging by the wince that flits across his face.

"I didn't mean to hurt you."

He barks out a laugh, like his dad. His face creases into a broad grin, and the air sparkles and the candles in the room glow brighter all of a sudden. He gives me that crooked smile and slips his arms under mine to pull me close. "Women always say that afterwards." Warm breath puffs against my hair. His lips finally press against mine. Warm, soft. Hot, a tongue explores deeper. I lean, press into him. His arms tighten. A hand slides to the back of my head, stroking my hair. He eases back this time, not pulling away.

He stretches a tendril to its full length and lets it go. "It's getting longer."

Reaching up, I muss his nest of wild hair. "So's yours."

Outside, without agreeing beforehand, we follow the path down to Rosie's mew. Inside, he pulls the light cord, revealing debris and droppings on the ground, toppled over boxes, the stink of decay, but most of all, emptiness. He bends to pick up a feather.

"I'm sorry I let her go in the storm. I didn't know what else to do. I was sure she was going to die."

"No." He holds up a hand. "You gave her a chance. You were brave." He flashes a quick smile. "I know you were terrified of her."

"I wonder where she is now."

He looks through the screened yard into the cold darkness. I remember him telling me so many young red tails don't make it through the winter. They starve. That's why trapping them and training them to hunt increases their chances for survival. Rosie probably didn't survive, but he won't tell me that.

He strokes the feather running through his fingers. "Oh, she's probably on her way to Texas by now."

A million smart answers leap to mind, but I bite them off before they leak past my lips. I take a deep breath.

"I. Have. No. Choice."

"I know. I'm sorry."

"Things are pretty messed up."

"I know, I'm sorry." The words less sharp. "When do you have to leave?"

"Three more days. Aunt Sophia needs to get back. She's got legal custody now, so... But she promised she'd try to find a way for me to come back, to finish the school year here."

Declan reaches for the light. "Let's get out of here."

Outside, the moon is shining on the unbroken snow in the paddock. We both turn to the empty barn and look out over the hill.

"Roh's doing great at Cory's farm. She's going to be a star."

"Good." He gently slips the feather into a pocket. "We'd better get back in."

He doesn't move. Standing close, we brush shoulders.

A shadow glides across the moon. A flock of small birds call to each other and take off at once. Then silence.

The air is dark and still and cold. Sounds of laughter float from the house on the winter frost.

Without turning to him I whisper into the night.

"I trust you."

I sense something near us before we hear the call. A screech. It's close.

Declan scans the trees. "God, that even sounds like Rosie."

"Don't all red tails sound alike?"

His face is backlit, but I see the mocking grin. "Do all horses sound alike to you?"

"Well, no—"

The screech echoes through the trees.

Declan takes two long strides toward the sound, drawn into the darkness by the call. He raises his forearm and whistles.

"Rosie!"

A shadow moving as fast as a freight train swoops at him. With two strong flaps from broad wings, it lands on his outstretched arm. Declan turns and steps into the light, his hair flaming red and the hawk by his side.

"I can't believe it. She came back!" he says.

"So will I."

Acknowledgments

If it were not for several supportive friends, fellow writers, and professional editors, this story would be languishing in some half-baked form in my head. First, I must thank Liam Straton, a consummate falconer, who invited me along to observe his amazing red tail hawk, Freya, work and train. That hawk was the spark for this story. Today, Freya has returned to the wild where she hopefully is thriving and raising new baby red tails. Any mistakes or misinformation about the training, handling, or habits of these birds is entirely the fault of the author. I also thank everyone who provided their unique input in order to make this a better, stronger story: my beta readers Kim and Missy, who slogged through an early draft; my critique group friends, Susan, Michelle, and Deliah, who all have a keen eye; and my editors, both Amy and Traci, who challenged every character's motivation and every plot twist. Lastly, but most importantly, I thank all the horses I have known. They have taught and continue to teach me what is truly important in life.

Turn the page for an exclusive excerpt from L. R. Trovillion's next novel in the Maryland Equestrian Novel series

Excerpt: Just Gods

The Eventer's Revenge

Coming Fall 2020

Chapter One

IT'S BEEN ALMOST A YEAR AND I GUESS KARMA, GOD, OR WHATEVER hasn't found me yet. I figure that's the case, because I haven't been punished. Some days, I can't help but wonder if maybe He's forgotten all about me.

Hope so.

Tires crunch on the gravel and someone hollers out my name.

"Willow!"

Outside the stall, the bright sunshine reflecting off the big horse trailer makes me squint. Molly pokes her head out of the driver's side window of the truck. Her round face is red, maybe from the heat. More likely from shouting. "We need some more help here!"

The pitchfork fits snugly in the holder just outside the stall and I jog over to the horse trailer. Heat radiates from the diesel and I can hardly hear what Molly is saying over the engine noise and the banging coming from the trailer.

"May need help with this one." Molly's sun burnt elbow rests on the open window. Bilby jumps out of the passenger side, crosses in front of the truck, and walks along the length of the trailer, patting the side with his palm as he walks. When Molly cuts the engine, a hush falls over the yard, but only for a minute. The other rescue horses thrust their heads out of stall windows, sensing a new arrival, and whinny.

Whatever's inside the trailer screams back and doesn't stop. He punctuates it with a slam against the side.

Molly opens the door and swings her short legs around, reaching for the wide running board to ease her to exit to the ground. I wait, in case her bad knee gives out, but she steps from the truck and we walk together to the back of the trailer. Bilby—nicknamed after some Australian creature who is small, quick, with big ears—looks up at the latch, both hands jammed into his back pockets, like he has not intension of opening it. The sun emphasizes the deep lines in his face and has turned the tips of his protruding ears red and scaly. Two more loud kicks in quick succession causes me to step back. Molly pushes up the sleeves on an oversized Ravens shirt and rubs the back of her neck.

"Gave us a heck of a time loading."

For Molly, that means the horse must be part demon from hell, part Houdini escape artist…One thing I've learned from the couple months I've been here, is that she has a magic way with horses, even these abused, scared, freaked out ones, and can load anything. Bilby is likewise able to deal with any horse, even the crazy ones, from years of jockeying at the tracks here and in Australia. For them to admit this one was trouble…

A slam and the side of the trailer shakes.

"We better get him off." Molly sucks in a deep breath and reaches for the latch.

"What do you want me to do?" I ask, taking another step backward.

Bilby spreads his arms and pushes me to the side. "Stand by, in case he breaks loose."

"What the hell's in there?" I look at the ramp, expecting something to break the clasps and explode out any minute.

He rubs his palms down the front of his jeans and pulls on leather gloves. "One mighty pissed off Thoroughbred. A *big* one."

Molly gives him a nod and he jogs to the front of the trailer, opens the access door, and disappears inside. A muffled "Ready!" is heard, as if from inside a tin can.

Molly's face is shiny with sweat, lips pressed together. Her thick fingers fly over the latches and grab hold of the top of the ramp. "Stand back, if he comes busting out of there. What we're going to do is walk on either side of him as Bilby leads him to his stall. Keep him between all of us." She calls to Bilby, still inside the trailer. "You sure you're ready?"

"He's not going wait much longer!" Bilby's voice hits a high pitch I've never heard before.

The ramp drops and Molly, despite her bulk, moves quickly to the side. On the opposite side, I move toward the shelter of the trailer's wall as thundering hooves pound along the length of the van, shaking its sides, and down the ramp. A horse, dark with sweat, stands in front of us, head up, and eyes white. He looks around, then his sides ripple with the scream he pushes out from deep inside. Bilby hangs on to the end of the rope like tiny doll, attached to this beast.

A step closer. Something about him…

The horse must be a chestnut, but it's hard to tell. His coat is almost a dappled pink from a combination of rain rot darkening his skin and the dull, dry hair that hasn't shed out. He would be a good anatomical model since you can make out every rib, hipbone, raw joint, and knobs along his spine. He's emaciated.

"Ugh," comes deep from the bottom of my heart and leaks out my lips. "Poor horse."

He spins around Bilby, kicking up gravel and dust, and screams out again.

"Let's get him inside." Bilby nods to the quarantine barn and snaps the horse's lead to keep him in check. "Not sure he's going to let me hang on to him much longer."

Molly walks briskly on the other side of the horse. As I fall into step on the opposite side.

I glance back inside the trailer. It looks like the horse's insides exploded. Manure runs down the walls.

Bilby quick marches the horse to his stall like a prisoner with his escorts on each side. As soon as Bilby unsnaps the lead, the pink monster paws the feed bucket and spins around. But Bilby slips out and hurries to shut the door.

Inside the stall under the bright lights, the big horse looks even bonier, if that's possible. He's wears a track in the bedding, circling his stall. When he passes the hay, he snags a bite and gives everyone lined up outside a savage glare.

"Not sure, but we might have made a mistake taking this one on," Molly says. She slowly shakes her head back and forth.

Bilby slaps me on the back, sending my feet skittering forward to stay balanced. "This little gals up to it, right Willow? You've ridden those big dressage horses." He always says dressage like it's two words—*dress-age*. His sticking-out elf ears lift a fraction when he smiles.

"Big, yeah." The memory of riding passage on a huge Hanoverian mare, a favorite, floods my brain, but I squeeze my eyes shut to dismiss the image. "Big I can handle. Big and crazy, I'm not so sure."

The tall Thoroughbred stops pacing and stares through the bars. Something… There's just something familiar I can't reach…like a finger tap against a frosted glass pane of memory, saying, *Let me in. Remember me?*

Molly loops the lead rope attached to his halter and hangs it on his stall door. "We won't let you get on until we know a little bit more about this fella."

"What *do* you know about him? What's his name even?" I point to the blank nameplate.

Bilby wrestles with some papers in his back pocket and unfolds a thick sheet with the familiar Jockey Club logo at the top. His forehead folds into three neat creases as he reads. "Says here, his name is Delta Dawn Doggie." A bark of a laugh explodes and startles the horse.

The smoky glass blurring my memory explodes. That name! Before Molly can stop me, I fling open the stall and rush inside. The horse steps back, but doesn't turn away from me. A dark eye follows every move as I ease my hand out, stroke his shoulder, and bend to run it down his front leg. The raised scar is there, under the rough hair and mud. Like reading Braille, my fingers follow it, knowing exactly where it is, exactly how long it is… and how it came to be there.

The damp bedding seeps through my jeans as my knees give out at the horse's feet. I feel his muzzle touch the back of my shirt.

"Tucker. My God, what's happened to you?"

Meet L. R. Trovillion

L. R. Trovillion is a native of Massachusetts where she attended college in Boston and earned a degree in Russian Language and Literature. Since then, she has worked as a translator, language teacher, editor, reporter, and even horse stall cleaner. These days, when she isn't writing, she spends time riding and taking care of her horses on a farm in Maryland she shares with her husband, daughter, a tuxedo cat, and several spoiled dogs.

L. R. Trovillion loves to hear from her readers! Of course, a review of this book would be great and it helps writers keep writing and selling books, but a review is also helpful for friends and strangers out there looking for their next good read. Consider writing a short review in Amazon or Goodreads, telling others what *you* think.

You can also connect with L. R. Trovillion through her website www.lrtrovillion.com, find her on Facebook, Pinterest, or Twitter, or email her directly at lrtrovillion@lrtrovillion.com. Stop by and say hi.

Made in the USA
Middletown, DE
15 October 2021

50395524R00194